DESOLATION OF THE DRAGON

MATT MEMEMARO

To everyone who has supported my books,
You remind me that dreams are worth chasing.
Thank you for keeping me inspired.

Also by Matt Mememaro

The Toldar Series

Voyages of the Kaliban's Cradle Series

The Four Worlds Series

The Kai Flint Series

The Pursuit Series

St. Nick

Shadows of the Dragon

Revenge of the Dragon

Ironrock
Windrise
Talon's Peak
Bloodstone
The Haven
Travion's Roost
Desacourt
Nestlewood
Ashenfort
Sinibad's Lair
Thornton Grove
The Tomb of Chilijo
The Obelisk
The Dragon's Gore
Kressin
Gatestone
Montemayor
The Commonwealth

ONE

The charred cinders and blackened bone fragments were all that remained of Anton Ashbourne as they rained down upon the spectator's upturned faces. They could only watch in horror as the macabre confetti that was once Anton's body began to settle in the arena. The Colosseum had been alive only moments ago, filled with cheers and jeers, now held only the ragged breathing of ten thousand souls, all frozen in collective horror.

Dalton Ashbourne's demands echoed off the ancient stone, each syllable striking like a hammer on an anvil. The crowd cowered as the golden dragon unfurled its massive, membrane-thin wings that caught the afternoon sun, casting rippling shadows across the arena floor as it launched skyward with a thunderous beat of air. Only Major Kaladin moved against the tide of terror.

Gundrag!

I am coming, Kaladin.

"Dragon Lords, Sinibad sends his regards! I wish you luck without your Overlord at the helm! Release my son and his companions, otherwise the rest of the Haven will burn, starting with you and your dragons! You have been warned! You have three days to decide your fate!"

We need to take that dragon out of the sky!

I know!

Hurry!

Perhaps if you humans stopped insisting on creating such annoying structures without dragons in mind, I could have been at your side by now.

There's no time!

As Dalton continued to flee on the back of his golden mount, Gundrag's purple wings came into view over the raised seating of the Colosseum. He was twice the size of the golden dragon and landed just behind Baindussa on the floor of the arena. Gundrag stretched his neck out towards the orator's box that Kaladin stood in, tapping his foot with impatience. He was not alone. The Dragon Lords accompanied him, each of them in a stunned silence of their own, and as useless as the next.

Alexandria stood still with her hands shaking in fear, yet it was only as Kaladin took action that she noticed anything else. "Major Kaladin! Where do you think you're going?"

"To end this!"

"Put him in the ground, Kaladin."

The Colosseum was filled with the earth-shattering roar of another dragon, and as Kaladin pulled himself over the railing of the box, he paused as the enormous shadow of Anton's dragon, Drementhol passed overhead. His shadow blocked out the sun, plunging the Colosseum into darkness for a moment. The gathered crowd gasped again as Drementhol continued to make his presence felt.

Kaladin was already stepping onto Gundrag's neck, and with a well-practiced flick of his wrist, he pulled his mask from his jacket pocket. He had no time to marvel at the unique falcon pattern he had magically crafted into it all those years ago when he had first made it. They needed every moment to catch up to Dalton.

Are you ready, rider?

Kaladin's backside had barely touched the saddle, and he had no time to strap himself into it before he could feel Gundrag coiling beneath him. Gundrag was ready to take flight.

Go!

Despite Gundrag's size and the power that he exhibited as one of the largest dragons within the Commonwealth, the decades of practice and familiarisation with each other meant that Kaladin could trust Gundrag not to throw him off. Their bond was strong, and Kaladin was by no means a weak rider. Gundrag kicked off from the ground, launching himself straight into the air, rising above the Colosseum with a single beat of his wings.

Kaladin was still adjusting himself in the saddle as they rose into the sky. The scene before them was scarce. The sky above the Haven, was usually full of dragons moving between destinations, but today everybody was inside the Colosseum. There was almost nobody patrolling the skies, giving Dalton's golden dragon a free flight over the city. From what Kaladin could see through Gundrag's eyes, it appeared as if they were almost free, but Drementhol was hot on their tail.

Another ear shattering bellow ripped across the sky; however, it was not Drementhol that unleashed it. Kaladin's eyes scanned the skies and then he saw it. He wanted to turn Gundrag around as fear shot down his spine. Coming towards them head on, was a dragon larger than Drementhol. It matched the golden sparkle of Dalton's dragon. Drementhol rose to the challenge of this new dragon, but just from first glances, Kaladin knew that he would be outmatched. This could only have been Dalton's elder dragon.

Drementhol and the elder dragon flew at each other, their roars a challenge that shook the sky. If the consequences had not been so dire, Kaladin wanted to see this fight. The smaller golden dragon was slipping away as Drementhol focused on the new arrival. But what was more important? If this elder dragon was in the service of Dalton, would stopping it be the key to his downfall? Kaladin ground his teeth in frustration as Gundrag tried to calm his mind. He had seen what Dalton had been able to do with no dragon. The Commonwealth had lost Anton, but could they afford to lose Drementhol too?

Kaladin directed Gundrag towards Drementhol and the other behemoth. What was to say even if they managed to catch him that they could kill Dalton? Protecting Drementhol was protecting the Commonwealth and if the elder dragon fell sooner rather than later, it would be one less tool at Dalton's disposal. Kaladin could only watch as the two dragons collided with a thunderous force.

Drementhol managed to strike first, his rage spilling to the forefront of his actions like lava. It had been many years since Kaladin had seen him look this mobile. He tossed and turned in the air, trying to get underneath the golden dragon, snapping at his belly. The larger dragon was trying to do the same to Drementhol, but they were evenly matched. Both dragons were riderless, but Drementhol had just lost his, grief and desperation evident in his attacks.

Kaladin pushed Gundrag forward who was weary of the hurricane of fang and claws, yet they both were not willing to standby whilst the others did the fighting. Gundrag dove, trying to get underneath them, being cautious of their tails. The larger dragons spun in the air again, and the golden dragon was now on the bottom, clawing up at Drementhol. Gundrag saw his opportunity.

He was like an arrow. Gundrag folded his wings and increased his speed, angling for a strike against their foe. Kaladin urged him on, thinking that their attack angle was perfect, but the larger dragon was faster than they had considered. It was flipping already, working itself into a position of dominance. As they flew nearer a torrent of flame ripped from its mouth, shooting towards Drementhol as they spun. Gundrag saw the flames and the trajectory that they were taking and pulled out of his dive, now aiming for its foot. It was all that he could do to assist Drementhol. This dragon was too large to deliver one single killing blow on.

The flames soared overhead. Kaladin imagined how Anton would have felt in the split second before the flesh was incinerated from his bones. At least it had been quick. Gundrag spun through the air, his hunger for ripping scales from the golden dragon growing. He opened his mouth and struck. The golden dragon did not notice him at first until Gundrag began to shake his head, his weight adding to that of Drementhol, trying to bring the dragon to the ground.

It let out another ear shattering roar and Kaladin stumbled, his ears feeling like they were about to bleed. The momentary distraction cost them. The golden dragon turned, breaking contact with Drementhol and flinging Gundrag away like he was a child's toy. Realising it now had two sizeable attackers instead of one, the golden dragon unleashed another torrent of flame, as it tried to make an escape. Deterred by the flames, Gundrag and Drementhol both did not give chase.

The dragon was wounded and only a glancing wound at that based off its size. If it had been a normal dragon, that blow would have been fatal. Gundrag had given it his best shot and still failed. Drementhol rested in the air, beating his wings as his thunderous voice boomed from deep within his chest.

"I will have my revenge, Dalton!"

Drementhol appeared to be struggling to hold himself in the air and as Kaladin looked over, he could see why. The larger dragon was hurt, cut from half a dozen wounds all along his side. The gashes were deep, blood already starting to seep out of the wounds. Gundrag noticed it too.

"You are hurt, Drementhol."

Drementhol threw his head back to glance at them. Kaladin always found that there was something unnatural about looking into the eyes of a dragon so much larger than Gundrag. Gundrag was what he thought was a normal sized dragon. Drementhol then looked at the open wounds and sighed.

"Such a fight will not slow me down."

"No, but you did not land any significant hits on him. The golden dragon has escaped unwounded. He will fight another day."

"And our battles will be legendary, Gundrag. Just like the old wars."

Gundrag was taken back by the words. "We do not want to return to those days."

Drementhol hissed down at him, his eyes still flushed with anger. "You might not, but I do. I will have vengeance on those that took Anton from me."

"You would commit suicide? Just to get revenge?"

"What would you do if your rider was lost? Mourn for him? Pray to Chilijo himself that he be returned to you?"

Gundrag bowed his head, admitting defeat and accepting that he was in the wrong in the argument. Through their bond, Kaladin knew what Gundrag would do should the worst happen. It radiated through every fibre in his body, his burning desire to live for and serve Kaladin. If Kaladin no longer existed, there would be nothing left for him to lose. Drementhol started to slip from the sky.

"You should return to the rest of them. I will rest here for a moment."

"You are hurt, Drementhol. We need to help you."

"You cannot help me, Gundrag. If my promised was here, she may be able too, but alas, she was lost in the war. Send for all the healers, I do not care."

He is a stubborn old fool.

They do find themselves to an early grave.

Yes, Kaladin. Drementhol is not a small dragon, but for him to die now would be premature. Let us pray that we are not the same in following his lead.

Then keep your head on a swivel, Gundrag.

I will.

Drementhol groaned, a loud sombre sound that echoed over the valleys and city below them. They were high above the entrance to the Haven, the buildings far beneath them nothing more than specks on the ground, forming an intricate map of tiny puzzle pieces splattered against each other, sprawling in every direction. Every time that they came here, Kaladin was still surprised by the size of the city, which was only compared to the size of Drementhol, however even he paled in comparison.

Gundrag kept his eyes on the horizon, still tracking the retreating forms of the two golden dragons as they started to slip over the horizon. If they came back, Kaladin was ready for another fight, unlike Drementhol. The behemoth was lowering himself to the ground, his wingbeats now more uneven than they already were. Whilst Kaladin could do nothing if he fell and hurt himself even more, he kept a close watch on Drementhol, praying that he reached the ground. The wyrmguard would soon arrive to guard him. Even without his rider, Drementhol would still be the Commonwealth's crown jewel.

As Gundrag turned his head and started to head back towards the heart of the Haven, Kaladin spotted four dragons approaching. Each of them was as large as Gundrag, and each would prove to be a threat. From here, he could spot their saddles and the small black armoured riders in them. Kaladin nudged Gundrag down towards them and he followed the commands. Once Gundrag drew level with the wyrmguard, he levelled out, waiting for them to join them.

Apart from their leaders like Barrett who wore the white helmets, the wyrmguard were indistinguishable from each other whilst in their armoured uniforms. Kaladin knew that each man was among the sturdiest and most experienced of riders, but where had they been for Anton? Now was not the time to berate them. Kaladin also did not have the authority to. Instead, he greeted them with a wave.

"Ho! Wyrmguard! The Overlord's dragon is resting here for a time. The fight with the elder dragon has hurt him."

The first wyrmguard in line atop a green dragon spoke. "The Overlord is dead, Major Kaladin. We seek to avenge him."

Kaladin sat back in his saddle and laughed. "Do you four seriously think that you are prepared to take on an elder dragon by yourselves?"

"Sir, it is our duty."

Kaladin shook his head. "Unless you want to end up like the Overlord, I would suggest you wait here and protect his dragon."

"But sir! We have orders?"

"Orders from whom?"

"The Dragon Lords, sir. They told us to avenge Anton."

Kaladin rubbed the side of his face with his palm and let out a deep breath. "You know what. Your orders have changed. You will not seek vengeance for the death of Anton Ashbourne. Instead, you will protect his dragon like he is your own."

"On who's orders, sir?"

Kaladin sat upright in his saddle, drawing himself to his full height with his arms folded. "Mine. I will be your new Overlord."

He could not make out the wyrmguard's face underneath his mask, but he could hear the confusion in the man's voice. "Yes, sir?"

TWO

As the roaring raged on to the south, Ayr was curious just to see what was going on. Unfortunately for him he very much still had a larger problem much closer. Ayr squeezed Elanor's hand one more time and let it go. He did not feel anymore comforted than he had before. Baindussa was a wicked serpent, hundreds, if not thousands of times larger than he was. Azura's absence was also still noticeable. Even with her by his side, he would not have felt confident in their victory.

For a moment, Baindussa circled the pillar of rock that he had been wrapped around. His dead, empty eyes showed no emotion, his tongue flicking in and out of his head repeatedly. Was it the blindness, or something else? Baindussa raised his head towards the source of the noise as those higher up in the grandstands of the Colosseum gasped as they watched on. Something was happening. Had Drementhol caught Onoss and was ripping him to shreds?

Baindussa sampled the air once again with his tongue and a low rumbling came from his chest. He tightened around the rock pillar and Ayr flicked his hand, ensuring that his blade had not dropped from it. Knowing Baindussa could simply reach out and kill him was a terrifying prospect, but as Ayr readied himself, Baindussa spoke.

"I have made a mistake. I did not think it was possible. You were not the Ashbourne that killed Crassus. It was Dalton. I could taste your scent."

Ayr gripped his sword tighter. This dragon had accused him of being Crassus' killer, but now it was denying the claim. Dalton had been right all along. The Commonwealth were full of lies, all of them used to suit their agenda. If there was any fleeting sympathy Ayr had for them, it was gone. First, they had not believed him until Dalton had shown his face, and yet they were still adamant of his punishment. Nobody had called off the attack.

"So what? Are you still going to kill us?"

Another loud rumble exuded from Baindussa's chest as the green dragon shook his magnificent head. "No, there is a much greater threat here. One that I will need to see contained if I wish to ensure our survival as a species."

Ayr could feel Elanor tense beside him. "And what is that threat?"

Baindussa raised his head towards the sky. "The elder dragon. I will hunt."

Ayr tensed as well, not knowing what to expect. Was Baindussa's fiery breath ready to spill out and engulf the Colosseum in flames? Instead, as Baindussa drew in another breath, rather than unleashing a torrent of fire, he spread his wings as he stared around at the Colosseum. Each dragon and rider in the stands held their breath, waiting to see what the green titan would do. Even though he was blind, his stare filled Ayr with a sense of foreboding and worry. Baindussa leapt into the air, kicking up from the ground, leaving a swirl of dust and dirt in his wake.

Whilst not quite as large as Drementhol, Baindussa's bulk covered most of the Colosseum in a shadow as he rose above it. Whilst not as smooth and as graceful as Drementhol, it was easy to see that Baindussa would catch most dragons, even on their fastest days. As he reached his peak, Baindussa roared again and headed towards the south, chasing the sounds of violence.

Elanor leaned in close to him and whispered. "Well, that was unexpected."

"It appears we have Dalton to thank for that. What happens now?"

"I don't know."

Ayr stared at the figures of the Dragon Lords who were surveying the chaos from the safety of their observatory box. Without their voices amplified, it was impossible to hear what they were saying. The roaring above was dying, as if the chase from Drementhol had ceased. Not knowing what was going on was eating at the back of Ayr's mind. Had Dalton somehow felled Drementhol? Had this been his plan all along?

After a few more moments passed and Alexandria stood tall before the Dragon Lords raising her hands out in front of her, calling the crowd to silence. Once she had their attention, she pointed her finger at her throat and began to speak.

"There will be no executions today. Ayr Ashbourne and Elanor Sunfire have been cleared of any wrongdoing by Crassus' dragon, Baindussa. As a result, we will redouble our efforts to bring Dalton Ashbourne to his knees. You are all dismissed."

For the first time since entering the Colosseum, Ayr lowered his sword. There was a stern buzz like low hum that hung over the arena, as the spectators began to depart. Within moments the stands were only half as full as they had been, with dragons now beginning to take flight in every direction. Ayr wondered if any of them felt the need to fly down and commence an execution of their own. Ayr looked at the place where the first of Anton's ashes had been spread by Onoss, with there now no trace of them left behind.

Ayr indulged in the odd silence for a moment, before he heard the gate that he had walked through only moments ago opening behind him. As the gate clunked to its full height, Ayr waited for whatever wyrmguard that was behind him to crack him over the head with the butt of his sword or spear. The blow never came, instead he was greeted by the harsh voice of Barrett coming from behind him.

"Sword, Ashbourne!"

Knowing that Barrett would not be alone, Ayr raised the sword and presented it so that Barrett could take it from him without incident. He could almost feel a spear pressing into the small of his back, an extra encouragement that demanded his compliance. The sword fell from his hand as he felt Barrett tighten his grip around it. Out of the corner of his eye, he saw Elanor giving up her blade in a similar fashion.

"Come with us. Turn around."

Again, with no choice but to comply, Ayr turned and found himself face to face with the white helmeted wyrmguard. Against the muted colours of the Colosseum, the white helmet was a rare contrast, almost blinding Ayr. There was indeed a spear pointed at him, and Ayr wanted to push it out of his face with every fibre in his being. Something told him that even if he pushed past one, there would be half a dozen more jabbing into him before anyone would call off the attack. It was not worth the risk without Azura nearby.

Ayr turned, but it was not fast enough. As a reward for his slowness, he received a spear cracking across his shoulder blades. Ayr groaned and lurched forward, the wyrmguard seemingly not done with dishing out punishment. The men in front of him started to move, making their way out of the Colosseum. Ayr was glad to be free from the insides of the structure, but being surrounded by the wyrmguard did not entirely cull his sense of entrapment. Elanor cast him a glance as they made their way out of the cage that they had been held in.

Dalton's sudden appearance and murder of Anton had the population of the Haven on edge, with whispers on their tongues wondering what would come next for them. If his situation was not so dire, Ayr would have smirked, leaning into the hype and hysteria. Anton's death was only one part of the plan. There were still far too many people that had vexed Dalton during his rebellion that needed to pay the ultimate price. He already had a good start.

Ayr followed Elanor and the wyrmguard through the winding passages that made up the Colosseum. Judging from the direction they were travelling, Ayr figured that they were heading towards where the Dragon Lords waited. After a few minutes of walking, he was not proven wrong. The wyrmguard had led them to a grand staircase that ascended towards the sky in the exact direction of where their viewing box was. As Ayr took the first step up the stairs, the wyrmguard in front of him stopped.

Another vicious roar broke overhead, making Ayr clasp his hands to his ears. The dark shadow came over the Colosseum and enshrouded everything in view. Ayr froze, praying that it was not Sinibad, making another appearance at last. But as the dragon soared overhead, he was relieved to see the brown scales, rather than the brilliant gold of the elder dragon. At the same time, the Dragon Lords were now coming into view, led by Alexandria. Her stern expression still had not changed from how it had been in the council chambers.

A flash of purple shot by behind them, and Gundrag was making his presence felt as well. Gundrag landed with a loud thud where Baindussa had just been, revealing Kaladin standing on his head. Gundrag's fast moving head came in beside the gap and Kaladin stepped off him, removing his mask, revealing his face as it twisted and contorted out of anger.

"Where were you! Where were any of you?"

Alexandria raised her hands to calm the situation. "Major Kaladin! Please. Now is not the time. If you would, please bring Ashbourne and Sunfire back to the hall so that we may examine them further. I would like to find out if this was part of the Dalton Ashbourne master plan."

Kaladin exploded like a keg of dynamite. "You cannot be serious!"

Alexandria did her best to remain composed and stoic. "Kaladin, you know we are taking this matter seriously. Please cooperate or I will have you stripped of your rank."

"You would not."

"Nobody is above reprimand here. Have your dragon escort them, or I will find someone else more willing to move up in station."

Kaladin's eyes narrowed. "You threaten me, Alexandria?"

"In trying times like these, we must have order. We will see you at the hall, Major."

Kaladin nodded before flicking his mask back over itself so it was the correct way. He pulled it over his head and gestured towards Ayr and Elanor. Ayr could envision his scowl through the mask. He stepped back onto Gundrag's head who had not moved. The purple dragon grunted as he moved back to a more comfortable position, his enormous yellow eyes still watching the staircase with intent. He turned his body but could still see them.

"Right this way, you two."

Ayr pre-emptively winced as he could sense another blow from the spear coming at his shoulders. He shifted forwards, avoiding the blow, grabbing Elanor by the hand so that she avoided it as well. Whilst he did not want to be returning to the lair of the Dragon Lords, it was an infinitely better place to be than preparing for certain death by a vengeful dragon. Gundrag's open claw was almost a welcome sight. For what Ayr hoped would be the final time, he stepped inside it, alongside Elanor. As the claw closed around them, Alexandria spoke again.

"Kaladin, I hope you know that we appreciate your efforts."

Somewhere high above them, Kaladin chortled. "Yeah, we'll see about that. Don't I have somewhere to be?"

"You do. May your dragon always breathe fire."

"And may his wings carry you on his back."

With the final word spoken, Ayr felt weightless as Gundrag lifted himself into the sky. The roaring of the wind and of Gundrag's wing-beats filled his ears as the dragon started to move towards their new destination. There was still no communication from Azura as they flew, her silence Ayr's only concern. If they were letting him and Elanor go, why had they not yet released the dragons? Still feeling sore and defeated, and thankful that he had not fought Baindussa, Ayr sunk back into the grip of Gundrag, defeated.

THREE

After a short ride, Gundrag began to slow down. Their destination must have been nearby. Whilst the Haven was as large a city as Ayr had ever seen, it still had its boundaries. Ayr was ready to be freed from the purple dragon's grasp, and he prayed that he would be returned to Azura's side. Gundrag's wingbeats came to a stop, and Ayr waited for the inevitable drop that was to follow.

However, instead of falling from a great height, Gundrag's claw opened, revealing the ground only a few inches below his feet. Ayr stepped out of the claw with a sigh of relief. The Praetorium of the Dragon Lords awaited them, and one by one, the Dragon Lords were returning to their roost. As Gundrag moved over him, Ayr watched as Alexandria, followed by Roderick then Adonis made their way inside. The unknown lady who had not spoken landed and brought up the rear.

It seemed odd seeing them so out of place, without a wall close to their backs, making them seem larger than life. Adonis appeared even more frail than he had done when standing in front of his chair and it was if the only thing keeping him alive was his dragon's will. Ayr shook his head. Somehow, these men and women were among the most powerful that the Commonwealth had to offer. It was no wonder that Dalton had come so close to toppling them.

Once the Dragon Lords had shuffled inside, their dragons made their way onto the roof one by one. Each of them crawled like a giant lizard, not requiring the use of their wings to make their way up the structure. Once each dragon had roosted, Gundrag turned back towards them, despite his head being inside the hall.

"Are you coming, riders? We will not wait for you."

Not wanting to draw the ire of Gundrag anymore, Ayr took off, eager to catch up. Gundrag took one step for several hundred of his and Ayr half expected him to reach down and pluck him from the ground. Even Elanor's presence could not calm his mind. He needed Azura. The hairs on the back of his neck stood up, feeling the breath from Gundrag across his entire body. There would be nothing that could be done if he chose to use Ayr as a toothpick.

The Dragon Lords had left the door to their chambers open. There was no requirement to wait and as they were beginning to take their chairs, Gundrag lowered his head, allowing Kaladin to slide down. Kaladin landed in front of Ayr and Elanor with a thud as his boots echoed off the tiles. From the scowl he wore on his face he was not pleased and still had not spoken a word. Regardless, he puffed his chest out and strutted into the council room, not waiting for anyone.

"Before we begin, can I ask what has happened to Baindussa? Crassus' dragon would be a useful asset in the fight against Dalton Ashbourne."

Alexandria bowed her head. "Gone. He is now lost to us."

"If we had much use for a blind cripple, I may be saddened by the loss." Gundrag echoed his sediments with a sinister grumble of his own just outside the door.

"He will hunt Sinibad. That blind cripple may still be of use to us. This elder dragon is a threat that I have now seen with my own eyes."

"And yet nobody decided to help us. If it was not for Drementhol, Gundrag and I would be dead. With such a threat at our doorstep, we need action and men that will be willing to take it, Alexandria. What did you do?"

"We watched and we observed. It is now very clear to us that Dalton Ashbourne needs to be brought to justice."

Kaladin was not finished and turned his aggression towards Ayr as he raised his hand, pointing at him with a knife's edge. "And what about his spawn? You're just going to let him go?"

"I was hoping that you would be able to watch him. If Ayr Ashbourne does step out of line again, I am sure you will know what to do."

Kaladin folded his arms and grunted, a smirk coming to his lips. "Could have done it already, yet for some reason, you've just wanted to stop me. He deserves to die like his father."

"Then we would see the Commonwealth burn. He proved as much when he slew Anton. If a man would do that to his own brother, what do you think he would do to protect his son? We cannot let anything happen to him. Ayr Ashbourne is as much a pawn piece in this game as the rest of us are. We are better off seeing what Dalton wants from him in this game."

Kaladin snorted. "You're going to be the death of us."

Alexandria sat up firmly in her chair, her back straightening along with her facial expression. "We will not. Since Anton has left us in the most unfortunate of circumstances, we should discuss his successor as Overlord."

Kaladin bowed his head and went to depart the room. "Yes. I will return to the Obelisk and ensure its smooth operation."

"The Obelisk? Major Kaladin, you've made your opinion very clear before us here today. And it is clear to me that the man that is at the head of the Commonwealth needs to be a man of action, much like Anton Ashbourne was."

Kaladin turned back, pausing mid stride. He raised an eyebrow as he approached the Dragon Lords. "What are you saying?"

Alexandria leaned back in her chair and glanced at each of the other Dragon Lords. In turn each member of the council gave a firm nod, with the last coming from Adonis who turned to scowl at Kaladin, his nose over the edge of his hands like a hawk's beak. Ayr had not taken his eyes off Kaladin, who's own eyes were darting back and forth between the Dragon Lords. Silence filled the room until Alexandria spoke again.

"Considering the state of affairs that we find ourselves in, it is the opinion of this council, that the next Overlord of the Commonwealth is to be you, Major Kaladin Dawnscar."

For the first time since Ayr had known him, Kaladin stuttered, yet something about it seemed disingenuous. "I... I... Me? The Overlord?"

A sly smirk came to Alexandria's lips as the rest of the Dragon Lords nodded their heads with approval. Kaladin remained fixed in the middle of the room, a tear filling each of his eyes for a moment before he steeled himself. The illusion was gone, and he returned to the hardened figure that Ayr knew. With a sharp nod of his own, he turned back to the council.

"I should assume that word will be spread about my ascension, then?"

"It will. You will have the full privileges that Anton Ashbourne had before you. We trust that your priority will be bringing his murderer to justice."

Kaladin bowed again. He was milking this for everything that it was worth. "Of course, Alexandria."

Alexandria raised her head and continued. "As you'd expect, this arrangement is only temporary, Kaladin. The moment that Dalton Ashbourne is brought to justice will be the end of your reign. At which time we will hold a re-election for the new Overlord."

Kaladin winced like he had been stabbed. "A re-election? My lords, you have appointed me as Overlord! That position is for life."

The council shook their heads. "Not now. The only reason you were considered for the position was because of your heroics during the Ashbourne rebellion. We understand you have worked hard, Kaladin, but there are some things better left to the politicians."

Kaladin snorted. "The politicians? You mean just like Anton Ashbourne?"

"Anton Ashbourne was skilled at the art of war and waging it, as well as the diplomacy of how to avoid it. As a permanent Overlord, you would have us fight enemy after enemy, exhausting our riders and their resources."

"And what makes you think that won't happen quelling this second Ashbourne rebellion?"

"Killing the Lord Chairman of the Obelisk as well as the Overlord of the Commonwealth tells us what Dalton Ashbourne has planned. Your skillset is what is required. Now we will hear no more of this. Stand down before we strip your new title from you, Kaladin."

Kaladin chewed on his lip for a moment, before his eyes narrowed. He took a step away from the podium in what could only be described as rage. His fists curled and brushed against the hilt of his sword, but he did not draw it. Was this all Kaladin's doing, or was it partly Gundrag? The dragon remained silent, but that did not deny that he may well have been pushing his will onto his rider. A softness washed over Kaladin's gaze, and he bowed his head once again.

"So, what are your plans with Ashbourne and Sunfire?"

At last, Adonis stood up from his seat and spoke. His soft tone wavered as he beckoned towards them. "Step forward you two."

Ayr cast a side eye at Elanor. Kaladin retreated from the Dragon Lords, taking several paces backwards, allowing them to step forward and centre stage. It felt like they were being interrogated once again underneath the harsh light that made its way down through the hall. However, in the matter of hours it had been since Ayr had last stood here, the entire dynamic of the room had changed, despite the only missing person being Anton. Ayr stared at his chair, half expecting a spectre of the once giant man to come charging through it, laying his claim to his dominion.

Adonis glared down his long nose at the two of them. "All I can say is that the two of you are very fortunate that Dalton Ashbourne decided to attack when he did. Without his interference, Baindussa may not have been quite so easily restrained."

"I told you that we were innocent in the death of Chairman Crassus."

For his trouble, Ayr received a crack in his ribs from Elanor who hissed at him. "Not the time."

"You will be placed under arrest. We will return your dragons to you, but you are to reside here in the Haven until we deem it necessary that the two of you can leave. Not only as a punishment, but also for your safety. Dalton Ashbourne has a target on your backs, one that we would not imagine you can remove. We will call upon you when the time comes."

Alexandria cut across them. "I would like to iterate that Elanor Sunfire will also be pardoned for her crimes committed against the wyrmguard. If it was not for Dalton Ashbourne, you would be hung. Are we understood?"

This time Elanor took control before Ayr could interrupt. "Yes, lords. Where are we to be housed?"

Adonis held his arm in the air and pointed towards the main entrance which they had just come in from. "You will be housed in the Tower of Echoes. You will be able to reconnect with your dragons there, once we let them out of their cages. Major Kaladin!"

"Major?"

Adonis stuttered over his words. "Yes, apologies. The Overlord will take you. You are all dismissed. Kaladin, please return to us once these two are secured in their lodgings."

Kaladin bowed. "I find myself in a new position, and yet it is still your will and my hands. It will be done, my lords." He then flicked his mask out from underneath his arm and gestured towards Ayr and Elanor. "Come."

With no choice but to obey as Gundrag still loomed overhead, Ayr fell into line beside Kaladin. His presence loomed as large as ever as they turned their backs on the Dragon Lords. With the shadow of Gundrag above them, Ayr still felt insignificant in a dangerous game that was only just beginning.

FOUR

Now that she was outside Elanor could breathe again. Her breath had not quite settled properly since Dalton's appearance, however, there was now an end in sight. Kaladin had led them out of the hall, and into what was the upper echelon of the Haven. From here as they walked along the cliff walls, Elanor could see where they had emerged only hours ago from the prison. How the world had changed.

With each new elevation, they were greeted with a new building, that was as monotone in colour as the others in the city. Despite the option for them to use Gundrag to fly over the Haven, Kaladin had opted for the more painful approach. It was clear from his stature, power in his legs and the proximity to his dragon that he was not feeling the effects of the walk anywhere near as much as either Ayr or Elanor.

How the regular townspeople that worked and lived in this stretching and winding city was beyond her. The hills were cavernous, each new dip housing a new dragon within it some of whom were almost as large as Evor. Whilst the Obelisk and the adjoining city were considered one of the crown jewels of the Commonwealth, the Haven was it's larger and more esteemed cousin. The Haven was where Chilijo had first settled thousands of years ago, and the city was built up around him.

Exhaustion was setting over Elanor as they crested another winding hilltop path. Gundrag opted to fly up to the summit. As the purple dragon landed with vigour above them, the entirety of the surrounding hilltop shook. Gundrag was just showing off at this point, emboldened by Kaladin's appointment as the new Overlord. Elanor allowed herself a small smirk as she wondered what the Dragon Lords had in store for him. Whilst Anton Ashbourne was powerful and had commanded the respect of the entire Commonwealth due to his efforts in the war, the new Overlord would not be so fortunate.

Yes, she had heard the stories of his feats, but Kaladin was by no means the calibre of the man that the Ashbourne's were. As much as she despised Dalton, she had to admit that he was powerful. Any other man would have been ripped from the sky over the Haven if they were as wanted as he was. Yet Dalton had soared in on his golden wings of fire, commanded for the fucking Overlord of the Commonwealth to be executed, and it was done. She shuddered at the thought. Elanor prayed that Evor did not need more elixir.

She continued trying to reach him, wondering where he was. The eerie silence bounced back through the void at her. If their connection was as good as she thought it was, then Evor should have been able to reach her across the entirety of the Haven. Whilst the city was the largest within the Commonwealth it was not large enough to stop their bond, but Evor was seemingly still locked away inside a void cell.

They were passing underneath Gundrag's purple hue once again and a pit of jealously found its way into Elanor's belly. Kaladin paused, allowing Elanor and Ayr to pass him. He used the time to pet Gundrag's foot, scratching at his scales. Gundrag's massive head lurched around his body as to keep an eye on them as they walked underneath him. Elanor could feel the glare of the dragon pressing down upon her back. When would she be free of him and Kaladin?

Her answer was not far away. Kaladin stormed past them once again, taking the lead. He led them towards a monolithic structure that pierced the skyline ahead, its obsidian surface reflecting the sunlight in oily rainbows. The building reminded Elanor of the Obelisk, though this tower rose from the earth with more menace. It was jagged at its edges like a blade thrust through soil. Carved runes spiralled up its exterior, an ancient script that seemed to writhe as Elanor ran her eyes over it. Though smaller than the Obelisk, it still dwarfed the surrounding architecture. Kaladin's boots scraped against the stone path as he halted before the door that was made of hammered bronze.

"You'll reside here for now."

"Are we allowed to leave? This does not seem very dragon friendly. It looks like a fancier prison cell."

Kaladin pushed open on the low door that only would have allowed the smallest of dragons and their riders through it. Inside was a well-lit room, one that did not look dissimilar to the mess hall of the Obelisk. Two long tables were in the centre, running wall to wall. Kaladin held his arm gesturing towards the expanse that awaited them.

"You can leave whenever your dragons are returned to you."

"And when is that likely to be?"

"When we see fit. Now enter."

"What awaits us in here, Kaladin? This better not be another death trap you've failed to tell us about."

Kaladin let out a loud huff and folded his hands into his vest. "If only. No, I unfortunately could not create something so quickly in that time. This is our rehabilitation facility. You'll learn to rejoin polite society and remember what it is to be a rider."

"And we're going to learn to do that here are we?"

"Yes. If you don't, then unfortunately we cannot return Azura and Evor to your sides."

"We've done nothing wrong."

A dark twinkle ran through Kaladin's eyes. "I don't care!"

Gundrag snarled overhead, reinforcing Kaladin's message. As much as she wanted to fight against Kaladin, the fact that he had his dragon and that she did not, made it impossible. If she arced up, she'd be swatted like a fly. With a groan Elanor moved past Kaladin and into the structure. Ayr was a step behind her. Elanor turned back towards Kaladin who's figure now was the only thing they could see outside the door.

"Good luck. You'll need it."

With the final word, Kaladin pushed the door shut, leaving the outside world obscured to them. With a frustrated shout, Ayr stormed towards the door, attempting to push it open. Elanor sighed as they realised where they were. After several unsuccessful tries, Ayr shouted again and finally backed away from the door.

"It won't move."

"Yeah. There's a reason for that." Elanor averted her eyes away from the door and Ayr, as she took in the rest of her surroundings. "We're in the Tower of Echoes."

Ayr turned from the door. "The what?"

"The Tower of Echoes. This place was originally built to hold Dalton Ashbourne. At the start of the war, the Commonwealth thought in their infinite wisdom that a place somewhere between the void cell level of punishment and death was required. Whilst this place numbs the effect of magic, it does not completely inhibit it."

"Then why do you say this place was built for my father, Elanor?"

"The original idea was for it to house Dalton so that he could be rehabilitated, playing games with puzzles that would help him refocus his power for the good of the Commonwealth rather than against. When it became clear that he would not see reason, other fallen riders were brought here to see the error of their ways."

Ayr narrowed his eyes. "And how did they do that?"

"By taking their dragons and subjecting them to the horrors of this place. Visions of the past, torturing their soul."

"And that's why we've been put here?"

Elanor nodded. "Yep, now come on. We can't be stuck here forever."

"Well, how do we get out then?"

"Hopefully they release our dragons soon. Unless you know a phenomenal levitation spell, I can't see us surviving a fall from the top of the tower, can you?"

Ayr glanced up at the ceiling, trying to figure out what he'd need to do to survive a fall. As short as the door had been, the roof inside the tower could easily accommodate Evor, which surprised Elanor, even though the tower had been built just for Dalton. She needed to distract Ayr.

"Don't you want to explore?"

Ayr shrugged, unable to think of anything better to do. "Maybe we can find another way out."

Elanor took a deep breath, steeling herself against what she expected would come. The Tower of Echoes was made of just that. Echoes. Nothing could affect her now. It would play on their fears and aspirations, but if they had each other, Elanor had something to focus on. She just needed to ensure that Ayr was on the same page and could focus on her in return. She took his hand, wrapping her fingers around his, feeling a warmth in his embrace.

There was only one way out of the room that they were in, however unlike the first door, this was much more accommodating. Most dragons would be able to fit through here. As they walked down past the tables, Elanor heard a whisper to her right. Ayr was to her left and it certainly had not come from him. The tower was already playing tricks on her mind. This was how it started.

The whisper grew louder, a wordless chant that slithered through the air like smoke, vibrating at the base of Elanor's skull. She cast a glance over her shoulder and sure enough, there was nobody there. Ayr had sensed it as well and was looking with her.

"What is it?"

"Nothing."

"I can hear them too, you know."

"Are they saying anything to you?"

Ayr shook his head as he glanced around. "Not yet. Will they?"

Elanor nodded a response as they neared the large door that barred their entry to the rest of the tower. She leaned forward and pushed the door ajar, just enough so that they could slip between the crack. Once she was through, Elanor paused, her hand slipping from Ayr's. They couldn't be here already, could they? What stood before her was Crassus' chambers. What stood out to her more, was her father, sitting at his desk working away.

Elanor opened her mouth, gasping at Ayr. He nodded in response. "Go to him. I am here with you."

It was not possible. Her father was dead, wasn't he? Elanor shook her head, trying to clear her thoughts. She was in the Tower of Echoes, not the Obelisk. Yet her father sat before her at the end of the hallway, fussing about over papers. With a renewed purpose, knowing that Ayr was by her side, Elanor stormed forward, determined to dispel whatever illusion was in her way.

"Father!" At first Crassus did not look up from his work. Frustrated, Elanor called out to him again. "Father!"

The second call worked. Crassus looked up from his papers, his eyes narrowing as he realised who was coming towards him. With a deft touch, Crassus hid the papers that he had been working on, before sliding them neatly to the side with the edges aligned. He placed his hands on the desk before him and stared at Elanor as she approached. If it wasn't for his sneer, she might have thought that he had been happy to see her.

"Hello, Elanor. Why have you come here? Don't you have more important things to be doing?"

"No, father. We are in the Tower of Echoes. You died, didn't you?"

Crassus' glare only intensified. "I did. And I know the Ashbourne boy poisoned me, Elanor."

"It wasn't him, father. You were stabbed."

Crassus' eyes flared up. "I know who did it, Elanor. Do not try to convince me otherwise. Why are you laying with our enemy? He, like his father before him will bring the Commonwealth to its knees. Everyone else can see it, why can't you?"

"Ayr Ashbourne is not his father. Just like I am not you."

Crassus turned; his nose held aloft in the air. He snorted and then stared down his nose at her. "Perhaps you should have been. If only you were born as my son, Elanor. Then we would not be having this conversation."

"Father. I have done everything I can to help you to the best of my ability. If that is not enough…"

"No! It was not enough. Your hubris and your willingness to help another dragon that is not your responsibility will be yours and Evor's downfall. I could have told you this from the moment you took an interest in the boy."

"Azura chose him father. How am I not to have a vested interest in my dragon's promised?"

Crassus licked his lips in annoyance. "Do you not remember what happened to me and your mother? To Baindussa? I could have been the Overlord of the Commonwealth if not for them."

Elanor snorted and leaned back folding her arms across her chest. "Really, father? You're going to blame mother and Draxion for your shortcomings? The only reason you did not become the Overlord was because of your own ego."

Crassus rose to his feet. "My shortcomings? Elanor, I will not be spoken to like that. Baindussa made me into a better man."

"Then perhaps you need to look in the mirror!"

"Elanor! Elanor!"

She heard her name but did not know where it was coming from. Elanor turned and saw Ayr running towards her like he was appearing from a dream. There was a fog around him but with each step, he was becoming clearer.

"Elanor!"

Her head snapped around to face Crassus, except he was in front of the desk now, his face mere inches from hers, close enough that she could smell the acrid tang of smoke clinging to his skin. She stared into his dead angry eyes that were once the colour of burnished copper. Now the pupils were dilated to little more than black pits, consuming what little warmth remained in his gaze. The veins at his temples pulsed beneath skin stretched taut over sharp cheekbones, and his jaw clenched with such force she could hear the faint grinding of his teeth.

"Kill the Ashbourne boy and be done with this saga. End their line once and for all!"

"I can't!"

"Do what must be done, daughter! Avenge me!"

"Elanor!"

"Ahh!"

The room exploded into a flash of blinding light and Elanor covered her eyes, trying to escape from it. She felt body contact, something above her shielding her from the light. Tears were forming in her eyes. Her airways constricted involuntarily, and she began heaving on the floor at her feet. She was comforted by the weight above her, yet there was still a burning sensation of guilt inside her.

"Elanor! Elanor! Hey!"

She recognised the voice, but it sounded like it was from a far-off land, hidden behind a veil. As quickly as they had begun, her tears and her retching were slowing as she tried desperately to regain her composure. There was no reason why she should not have been in control, especially with Crassus. Nothing he had said was untrue, but it still cut her to the core.

"Elanor! Hey, are you still with us?"

It was Ayr. His calloused fingers splayed across the small of her back, warm through her vest. For a heartbeat, she tensed, muscles coiling to pull away, but then the gentle pressure of his palm steadied her like an anchor in a storm. The heat of his skin radiated into hers, and suddenly she couldn't bear the thought of that warmth vanishing. She drew air deep into her lungs, feeling the rise of her chest and the slow unwinding of the knot between her shoulder blades as his thumb traced a small, soothing circle against her spine.

"I'm here, Ayr."

"I saw it. It's okay. It's not real."

"I know it's not real, yet he felt so real."

"You said it yourself. This is the Tower of Echoes. It's going to play mind games on us. I've got you. You'll be okay."

Exhaling, Elanor finally raised her eyes towards him. His face was stern but concerned. In this moment, she realised that he truly cared for her. With a weak smile, she nodded.

"We've got each other. We can get through this."

At last Ayr removed his hand from her back, but all she wanted to do was go with him and remained snuggled into his chest. However, now was not the time. She needed to focus.

"You're right. We need to get out of here."

"Alright, well we'd best get looking for another way."

FIVE

"Have you got any ideas, Ayr?"

"We can always try the first room. I might be able to unlock the door. We can't go through that again. Come on."

Elanor was still shaking, and he did the only thing he could do. She needed to move away from this space. He took her by the hand, locking her fingers so that she could not get dragged away again if another hallucination appeared. The first room was still open to them, and Ayr pushed through the door making his way inside. For some reason, he was surprised that it had not changed, the furniture still in its initial arrangement. Ayr crossed the room to the door and inspected it.

There was no handle on the door and no way for him to get outside. Ayr began to beat upon it, wondering if there was any way that he would be able to use his magic to open it. There was no sound from the door as he hit it, making him wonder if it was an entirely magical entity. He had never seen anything like it before in his life.

Ayr ran his hands along the door, trying to examine it to see if there was any weakness or fault to it. He was unsuccessful on his first attempt, so he decided that a second run over would be beneficial. There was nothing that he could sense out of the ordinary. For all intents and purposes, this door was a normal wooden door, just with no substance for him to cling onto. It was like a void cell.

"Kaladin! Let us out!"

A deep, guttural rumble vibrated through the stone floor beneath his feet, rattling the iron sconces along the corridor. The sound rolled like distant thunder trapped within the tower's walls, each reverberation sending tiny pebbles skittering across the flagstones. Though the words remained indecipherable, the distinctive timbre could only belong to a dragon, somewhere in the shadowed chambers beyond his sight.

"You'll have to do better than that, Ashbourne. Even if you break the door down, you will not escape from the Tower of Echoes. Tell the Lady Sunfire that your dragons will be released soon."

"Soon? How soon? I want to see Azura!"

"Beggars cannot be choosers, Ashbourne. This is part of your latest test. When you have improved to a sufficient standard, we will release your dragons."

Elanor swore from behind him. "Fuck! I should have known."

"Known what?"

"That's what they're waiting for. We must wait this out."

"Are you going to be okay? I saw what you went through in there."

"Yeah, I'll be fine. I know that this place is meant to break us. We should see if we can find a safe room that we can relax in."

"Okay, so we've only got one way out."

Elanor nodded at him. "We do. Come on."

Her hand found his again and their fingers intertwined once again. This time it was Ayr that led the way back through the larger door that led into the tower. As he crossed the threshold, he felt something cut across his vision. It was like someone had slashed a blade in front of him, and he blinked, only to realise that he had made a mistake.

"Oh no."

He let go of Elanor's hand as the voices overtook him and his vision shifted again. He stood in the mess hall of the Obelisk, alone. There was no Elanor and no Azura. However, the mess hall was full of dragons and their riders, the latter of which sat across the tables that ran wall to wall. If there had only been a handful of them, he would have felt better about the situation, but their numbers rivalled a small army. Each rider was cloaked, most with their masks on, making their faces indistinguishable from the next. He had to walk forward between them to reach the exit. Taking a deep breath, Ayr took a step forward.

"Welcome to the Obelisk. You'll die here, Ashbourne."

Ayr shook his head. "No, I won't."

The whispers started to eat away at his mind. "You'll die here."

"You'll die here."

"You will pay for what your father did to us."

"You will never be a rider."

Ayr wanted to reach for his sword, but as he did, he realised it was no longer attached to his hip. Azura was deaf to his cries for help as well. The riders encircled him, each of them pushing the others closer. Their dragons loomed overhead, their shadows being cast over him, as he tried to push back against the riders. Where he pushed one, another surged forward taking his place. They drew no weapons, but their relentless verbal assault was weighing him down, each word becoming more pronounced.

"You will die here. You will die here."

"Enough!"

As the next rider approached him, Ayr struck with a closed fist. The rider that he struck all but vanished from sight, only to return in a flicker of a shadow in the darkness. They weren't real. Of course they weren't real. Ayr fell forward onto the ground, covering his head with his arms. He had no idea where Elanor was, and with his covered eyes, he tried to push the relentless chants out of his mind.

They kept coming, and he felt a weight pressing against him. The riders weren't real, they couldn't be. It was only him and Elanor in this tower alone. Elanor! Ayr pushed against the weight he could feel beside him, and it pushed back. Something reached down from above him and he tried to swat it away, finding that it was a firm hand. It gripped him, and Ayr resisted, but unlike the riders, the hand did not relent.

"Ayr! Ayr!" It was Elanor's voice, but she sounded so far away. "Ayr!"

Whatever cloud was hanging over his vision started to clear, and the shadows of the riders and their dragons was beginning to fade from existence. What was left before him was nothing more than the empty room that they had stumbled into. Sweat was pooling on his face as he tried to piece together what happened.

"The tower got you as well, did it?"

"Yeah." Ayr gripped his forehead, still trying to shake the thoughts out of his mind. "Did you see it?"

"No, Ayr. I couldn't. What happened?"

"I was at the Obelisk, surrounded and alone. They attacked me."

Elanor frowned as she helped him to his feet. "So why could you see mine, but I couldn't see yours."

"I'm not sure. One thing is clear; we need to get out of here."

"We do. The echoes will keep coming."

"Okay, what about up there?" Ayr pointed to a staircase that vanished from sight.

Elanor clicked her tongue and started forward. "Well, it's as good as any lead, I guess."

They ventured forward, and a paranoid slither of fear snuck its way up Ayr's spine. Having already experienced one echo, he was not so keen to experience another. If this was just the beginning, just how much more real and terrifying would they get? Without Azura by his side, he was vulnerable, and he knew it. Even though Dalton had trained him, preparing him for this eventuality, experiencing the unrelenting fear of the echoes was not something that he could take lightly.

Ayr followed Elanor and his paranoia still had him on edge as they walked up the staircase. The air was growing thick with magic the higher they rose. It lingered on the edge of Ayr's nostrils, like the warm smell of a bakery as it started its cooking first thing in the morning. He wanted to taste it, but he was afraid if he indulged that it would set off another echo.

They reached the first level of the tower and Elanor paused. Running off the stairwell was a walkway that extended in either direction. The hallways here once again lower than what could accommodate most dragons. A long glass window stretched across the top of the hallway from end to end, letting a limited amount of light filter in from outside. Elanor shot Ayr a look and started along the walkway to the right. Their footsteps created echoes of their own as they walked along it.

Neither of them seemed to have any idea what they were looking for, and the expansive tower was growing ever confusing, just like the Obelisk. If Ayr needed to find his way back to where they had come from, he'd have a hard task of it. The walls were bland and unremarkable, each of them the same as the next. Elanor continued to lead him and turned towards another door. She pried it open and shook her head, only to close it again. Elanor continued down the hallway and stopped at the next door. As she opened it a smile came across her face.

"That's more like it."

"What's more like it?"

Elanor pushed the door further open and stepped inside. Ayr followed her in, curious of what she had seen. There was no echo, even though as he crossed the threshold, he fully expected one to appear. Elanor did not appear in distress either, in fact, she was delighted. Ayr assessed the room before him and started to smile.

One bed stood in the centre of the room, not all that far away from a straw filled opening in the ground that would have perfectly suited either Evor or Azura if they were to stretch out and enjoy the space to the fullest. It was just like their accommodation at the Obelisk, and for a moment Ayr thought he was being pulled into another echo. Yet the room was quiet, and no further apparitions appeared.

"You know, Ayr. If they feed and water us, I don't see how this is punishment." Elanor started to laugh, even if there was a nervous undertone to it. "Good thing the only person here who knows about us being together is Kaladin."

"I'm sure everyone else has figured it out considered our dragons are promised to each other."

Elanor shrugged. "It could be worse. At least we've got one bed!"

"How is one bed a good thing?"

Elanor rolled her eyes and smirked at him. "I don't remember you complaining the last time we shared a bed. At least this one has room for activities."

A reciprocal smirk came to Ayr's lips. "You're right, I suppose that is a positive. What better way to pass the time?"

"We could train in hand-to-hand combat."

Ayr licked his lips, trying to keep his smile from spreading. "That's an interesting way to pass the time."

Elanor sighed. "Honestly, I just want to rest. Do you feel drained as well without Azura nearby?"

Ayr nodded and he tried to cast his mind around, probing for of Azura. After a few moments he stopped. If he could not reach her by now, there was no chance that she was out of the void cell. "They haven't released them yet."

Elanor hissed at him. "They said they would!"

"This isn't fair, Elanor! We did nothing wrong."

Elanor raised her forefinger towards his mouth and placed it over his lips. Ayr immediately ceased his protest. "Shh. For how long have we had silence for? We should take advantage of the moment."

"A moment for what? To rest, I agree."

Elanor sighed again, appalled at his inability to pick up on the hint that she had dropped. Elanor slid her finger from his mouth down his chin and towards his neck. Her finger joined her others as she clasped it around his shoulder. She spun Ayr, cluing him into what she was seeing.

"Oh."

Before him was an open shower, with no walls on any side of it, apart from where the valve and shower head stuck out from the wall. There was a small metal drain underneath the showerhead, and it did look inviting. Considering that they had not bathed for days, almost an entire week, Ayr was realising it was exactly what he needed given the events of the past days. Elanor pushed him forward, whispering in his ear. The hairs on the back of his neck stood up, like she was running her fingers down his spine.

"Come on."

It would have been stupid to resist her. With her hands on his back, Ayr stepped towards the shower, and it was only now that he was realising just how dirty he was as he started peeling his clothing from his skin. He half expected there to be a thick layer of dirt, sweat and grime. As his uniform fell to the ground, he was relieved that it was finally off him.

Whilst Ayr was accustomed to constantly being on the move without a fresh change of clothing on hand, it was nice to be able to have the freedom at last to strip down into nothing and bathe in something that would be sanitary. He heard Elanor stripping behind him as well, and as he stepped underneath the shower head, Ayr pulled on the valve. The hot water spurted out of the holes and Ayr gasped as the initially cold water hit his skin.

It was refreshing, almost like he had dived into a river or stream, and he raised his hands to his face to begin scrubbing his skin. The water warmed to a temperature that did not feel dissimilar to the fire that was in Azura's belly. Ayr felt Elanor's presence behind him as she too stepped underneath the water, almost pushing him towards the wall. He turned to face her, glad that he was not alone and could share the shower with her. Her auburn hair became soaked and tangled, but he smiled, enjoying the fact that for the time being they were safe.

Ayr could still not feel Azura's presence, but in this moment, he did not need her. With time to themselves, Elanor could be his only focus. As the dirt and grime was washed from their bodies, Ayr leaned forward, pulling Elanor tighter to him. The warmth of the water and her skin was embracing Ayr like a cloak and Elanor wrapped her arm around his neck. Her eyes darted between his and his lips and Ayr pulled her tighter. She leaned in and closed her eyes, their lips connecting.

He had not kissed her since facing down Baindussa, since he was assured of their mutual destruction at the hands of the giant green dragon. There was no hesitation in the kiss. Elanor explored his lips, pressing against them before she applied more pressure. Ayr gave as good as he got, his mouth opening so that his tongue could interlock with hers.

Everything else around them ceased to exist, Ayr half expecting the already warm water to start boiling and turn to steam. Elanor's hands tugged at the back of his hair, and then her mouth pulled away from his. Ayr went to grab her to pull her back to his lips but was pleasantly surprised as the first of many hot kisses pressed against his neck. Shivers ran down his spine, and he went with her motions, now fully out from underneath the running water with his back pressed against the wall.

An involuntary groan escaped his lips as her hand explored his body, snaking its way down towards his groin. Ayr stiffened at her touch, her fingers knowing what they were doing. Combined with her mouth on his body, he stood no chance of putting up any resistance.

Not that he wanted to. Ayr was at Elanor's mercy, the only thing missing was the warm water rushing over his body. Not that he cared. She was stoking the fire that burned within him. He was more than ready as Elanor pulled away from him and gazed up into his eyes.

"Ayr, I need you inside me."

There was no hesitation or lack of fluidity in his motions. Ayr placed his hands on her and turned her, so that she was where he had just been. Instead of her back being against the wall, Ayr guided her towards it, his hand snaking from her shoulder up towards the back of her neck. Elanor groaned as he pushed her, but she spread her legs all the same.

"Yes!"

Ayr positioned himself, noticing the arc in Elanor's back as she started to spread her hands up against the wall. He took in everything from her wet hair all the way down to the subtle curve in her back. She was perfect in every way; her body toned to perfection and a testament as to why she made for such a good fighter. Elanor's body twitched, urging him on. Ayr made sure he was hard enough and then rose up on his toes, placing his tip against her.

Elanor did the rest of the work, pushing herself back onto him. As she took each inch, Ayr's eyes started to roll, a long groan escaping his lips. With Elanor's help, Ayr started to thrust, working himself into her, in a way that he had not yet had a chance to. He could enjoy himself, there was no danger here, or the threat of being discovered. He pressed up against her, his hands moving to cover hers on the wall as he braced himself.

His fingers curled over hers, locking their hands and as she bounced backwards, Elanor groaned in response. He leaned forward, embracing her presence, pushing her hair to one side. She shuddered underneath him as he breathed into her ear, pushing forward with all his weight behind each thrust. Each thrust hit almost at a different angle, with each one eliciting a new response from Elanor's lips. Each moan that she uttered urged him on.

"Yes, Ayr! Yes!"

The water continued to spray them, Ayr half expecting it to turn to steam upon contact with their bodies. Elanor's nails continued to scrape against the tiled walls, but with nothing to properly grip onto, they kept slipping away. She continued to tighten as Ayr thrust into her, her breaths beginning to shorten, her moans increasing in volume. She had surrendered to him entirely. As he went to lay a kiss on her shoulder, Elanor turned her head to glance back at him, her green eyes locking onto his.

"I need your seed inside me, Ayr."

"Are you sure?"

Elanor gasped again as she nodded her head. "Yes, do it. We are promised to each other after all."

He went to hesitate, but the choice was removed from Ayr as Elanor rose onto her toes and tightened around him. He'd laid with many ladies before, but this was different. He was at Elanor's disposal. She continued to tighten her grip around his shaft, and within moments, Ayr could feel his climax coming. There was nothing he could do to stop it. His heartrate rose with her and seconds later, he let himself go inside her.

His groans filled the room; the only other sound was Elanor's, equally as loud. Ayr's calves tightened to the point that he thought they would explode, before he came back down to a grounded base. Elanor let go of him, and with another soft groan, Ayr pulled out from her, looking at what he had just done. Elanor was flat against the wall, her body convulsing, but there was still a broad smile across her face. Elanor was breathing heavily, like she had just run a marathon.

"By Chilijo, Ayr. Are you sure that Azura didn't help you with that."

Ayr shook his head. "Can you feel Evor yet?"

"No, but I can only imagine what that would have been like if their presence was nearby."

She turned, pressing her back against the wall. Elanor looked ready to drop to the floor, her legs continuing to shake. She sunk to the floor, beckoning for him to join her. Ayr lowered himself to her level, scrambling on the floor beside her before finally putting his back to the wall. The water continued to wash over them as they embraced, enjoying the solidarity of each other's presence.

SIX

Unable to tell the time and with no purpose to drive them forward, Ayr and Elanor continued to use the free time with each other. Hunger and thirst did not enter Ayr's mind as the time dragged on, and he was sure that days had passed. Ayr yawned as he stretched out beside Elanor on that bed that had more than adequate space for them. They both lay entwined in the maroon silk sheets that were strewn across the bed from their hours of relentless activity.

They both breathed in, Ayr feeling Elanor's heart racing against his chest. His left arm was wrapped around her, even though there was no need to be close to her for warmth. She was holding onto him, flipped onto her belly, her head titled so that she could gaze up into his eyes. She was searching for his soul, and all Ayr wanted to do was stare back.

The absence of Azura was weighing on his mind, feeling like one of his arms was missing. Surely, Azura would return to him soon. As much as Elanor was becoming entwined in his life, there was no replacing the connection that he had with Azura. The white dragon was the other half of his personality. Elanor was doing her best to fill the void, and he had no doubt in his mind that he was doing the same for her. She raised her hand to his right nipple and started tracing small circles around it.

"I miss them, you know."

"I know. It's all I can think about. What's the longest time that Evor has been absent from your side, Elanor?"

Elanor frowned, considering the question. "Honestly, he never truly has in all our years. The longest time I have been without him was when he was poisoned by the scalebane."

"I know how hard this must be for you."

A weak smile came to Elanor's lips. "Honestly, the peace is enjoyable. For all his power and his wisdom, Evor can be overbearing at times. I would not change him for the world, though. Without him I have no life and no purpose."

Ayr continued to move his hand across her back, teasing her hair as well. "I know exactly how you feel. Have you been bothered by any echoes lately? I haven't had one since we first arrived here."

"I had something come to me in my dream when we slept last, but otherwise they have been quiet."

"What did you see?"

Elanor still had not looked away. "You."

"Me? What did you see, Elanor?"

"You and Azura. But it was not Azura. She was... different. It was not the Azura that I know today. You both sat on a throne of stone and bone, shrouded in blood."

"You're not a watcher though. How can you see the future? What does it mean? It was just a dream, Elanor."

Elanor shook her head. "Upon reflection, it was different. It was vivid. I can see everything clearly. I knelt before you, looking up at you. You were my ruler."

"I do not want a throne."

Elanor removed her hand from his chest and shrugged as she sat up. "It was just a dream, Ayr. It doesn't mean anything."

"Where are you going?"

"To shower. I don't know how long we will be here, so we might as well enjoy it whilst we can, right? Do you want to join me?"

"I'll go after you. I want to see if I can call Azura."

"You know there's no point if she's still locked in a void cell, right?"

Ayr shrugged as Elanor rose to her full height. He could not take his eyes off her. Every part of her body was toned to perfection with nothing, but her flawless sun kissed skin filling his eyes. She was the picture of a goddess ripped straight from the tales of old. With an effortless grace, Elanor walked towards the shower and within moments had the water running again. Ayr followed her the entire way and then sat up on the bed as well.

Ayr sucked in several deep breaths as he aligned himself properly. He kept meditating, trying to call to her, hoping that she would hear him. It was like exercising a muscle. With any hope without Azura nearby, he could grow stronger. With Crassus and Anton both dead, there were surely not many within the Commonwealth that could best him in a magical feat of strength. However, Dalton had instilled in him from a young age that he needed to keep working his magic. The discipline that he had was what kept driving him forward and had been the reason why no more echoes had entered his mind.

With the water running in the background, he used it as a focal point, honing his attention on it. Straightening his back, Ayr reached out, searching for Azura. At first there was nothing but silence that reached him. It was like reaching out with his hand into an empty cavern, hoping to find something to grab onto. His first probe brought nothing as he stretched his mind as far as he could. The breath was short, his presence racing away from him like a pulse.

He had to keep trying. He had to know that she was safe. The days of no contact were beginning to get at him, eating away at his mind like a virus. The sickness was becoming all consuming. Ayr breathed in again and unleashed another surge of energy. This time, he got something back. It was faint, but there was something he could cling onto. Ayr breathed in again and flung his mind towards it, hoping to catch whatever it was. The faintness exploded in his mind like a wave crashing against a shoreline.

Rider!

Ayr almost tumbled backwards off the bed. He had not expected her to be able to hear him. He'd found the anchor point. It was her.

Azura!

Rider... I am still within a void cell. How is this possible?

Azura...

The connection faded out of existence. Ayr jolted out of the meditation, almost like he was coming out of a deep sleep. He fell forward on the bed, his head smashing into the mattress.

"Fuck!"

"Ayr? What was it?"

Ayr threw his head over his shoulder and saw Elanor racing towards him. "I had her! I had Azura!"

Elanor's jaw dropped. "Are they on their way?"

Ayr shook his head in disappointment. "No, they are still within the void cells."

Elanor paused, confused. She was clambering onto the bed despite still dripping wet from the shower. "I'm sorry. What did you just say?"

"I just spoke to Azura."

"No, the other thing."

"Azura is still within a void cell."

"And you're sure that you spoke to her? This wasn't an echo?"

Ayr nodded. He'd never been surer of anything in his life. "It was her. The connection was brief before I lost it, but she was there."

"What did she say?"

"Nothing, just that she was still in the void cell. I can try and get her back again."

Elanor shook her head in disbelief. Her face was close to his, her eyes darting between his, trying to assess if he was lying or not. He gave nothing to her except a steely stare in return.

"I'm not lying, Elanor."

"What the fuck is wrong with you, Ashbourne?"

"My father's lessons taught me discipline. There is nothing more important than using your magic as often as possible to strengthen it."

Elanor took in a deep breath of realisation. "But to reach her through not only this tower, but a void cell? Your family is fucking insane. Just how powerful are you, Ayr?"

Ayr could see the realisation finally hitting her. "Strong enough, but I need to be stronger."

"Anton was the same when he came to the Obelisk to give teachings to the more experienced riders."

Ayr wriggled his eyebrows at her. "It's almost like we know what we're talking about."

"First you kill a dragon on your own, now you're doing this?"

"Azura helped me to no end with Bersos. She helps me focus and gives me any extra magic that I ask her for. Killing Bersos would not have been possible without her."

"So, we would have died against Baindussa."

Ayr nodded. "Most likely. I still have limitations."

"Unlike Dalton."

"He still has his limits."

Elanor frowned. "So, then we need to help him exceed them."

"Indeed. I don't know what Sinibad brings to the equation."

"We need to find out. Can you reach Azura again?"

Ayr nodded and took another deep breath. Elanor clambered onto the bed properly. "Use me if you need to, Ayr."

Elanor held her hands out in front of him and he took them. The shower was still running in the distance. He used both things to steady himself before he ventured into the endless void once again. His first attempt this time was better, finding Azura, but not sealing the connection. Ayr tried again, and once more on the second attempt, he found her.

Azura. I am here.

I am alone, rider.

I am alone too, Azura.

They need to release me.

Soon, Azura.. We will be reunited.

Where are you, Ayr?

The Tower of Echoes. Have you heard of it?

Azura squealed, the sound whilst a thought, still pierced his mind. *Ayr! You need to leave that place immediately. They will destroy your mind.*

Azura, we can survive this place.

No, no you cannot. How long have you been there?

I am not sure of the time.

Have either you or Elanor experienced visions of the future?

Ayr almost lost the connection. Yes, why.

Then you are not safe! Pray that I am released soon!

Azura!

The connection snapped like a twig. Whether it was Ayr's fault or Azura's he wasn't sure. He stumbled forward again, almost crashing into Elanor, who kept him stable, pushing against his shoulders. She looked him in the eyes as he recovered.

"Did you find her?"

"She says we're not safe. You seeing the future is dangerous."

"I can't help what I saw, Ayr. This is a dangerous world that we are living in."

Ayr was insistent. "As great as this has been. We can't stay here."

"Then what are we doing?"

"Do you think that we can magic our way out of here?"

Elanor clicked her tongue and glanced to the windows that were their only look at the outside world. Would they open and reveal Azura and Evor flying to their aid? Or would they remain locked forever as the hallucinations and echoes continue to barrage their minds?

"What are you going to do?"

"If we open a hole, perhaps we can escape."

"We don't know how high up we are."

"If you give me time, perhaps I can craft a solid levitation spell."

Elanor raised an eyebrow at him. "You're putting a lot of hope into your abilities, Ayr. You don't seem confident."

"I've never crafted one before."

"Then you'd better get started."

"Let me get dressed."

The room that they had been staying in had a fully stocked wardrobe, not that they had needed it. Instead, Ayr and Elanor had opted to remain naked their whole time in this room. Whilst they had explored some more of the Tower of Echoes, leaving the one room in this place that was free from the echoes was a daunting task. Were the windows really a pathway to the outside, or were they another tool deployed by the Commonwealth to play with their minds?

Ayr crossed to the wardrobe and plucked what was a replica of his old uniform from it. The one that he had removed before the first shower they shared together was discarded in the furthest corner of the room, collated in a pile along with Elanor's. With his new breeches, vest and boots on, Ayr was once again feeling complete except for the one thing that he needed the most. Azura. Would she be able to feel his magic if he'd reached her in the void cell.

Elanor dressed along with him, and Ayr breathed in. He could just have easily taken her out of her uniform and had her on her back in the bed again. It would have just been wasting time. They'd done it enough. Now was the time to act. If they had been in here too long and Evor had not received his next dosage of the scalebane elixir, would the effects of the poison be irreversible? Dalton and Sinibad also weighed on Ayr's mind. What was his plan now that Anton had been removed as the Overlord?

"Ready?" Elanor patted her vest and glanced at Ayr.

Ayr nodded in response. "Yep. Let's do it."

"What do you need from me?"

"I need to see if we can get out of here first. Is that window just an illusion?"

Elanor's fist curled by her side. "I can find out. I don't know how much magic I have without Evor's reserve to tap into."

Ayr gestured to the window. "Go on then."

Elanor's brow furrowed, as she focused on the stained glass above their head. She pulled back her fist and sent a small energy ball surging towards it. It was slow at first, shifting the air as its transparent round shape then sped up before colliding with the window. Ayr was ready. He helped the energy ball along, giving it a much-needed push. The window buckled under the blow but did not break.

Ayr reached out and grabbed at the buckle. He tightened his grip around it, much like he would the hilt of his sword. At his command, the window gave way, shattering into a million pieces. The glass shards shot towards the floor, but Ayr already had them in mind. The glass shards slowed and clattered on the floor, causing no more harm than a soft breeze blowing through his hair. When the last of the glass touched the floor, he breathed out.

"I thought Azura helped you with the control of your magic, Ayr."

"She does, but I'm not completely incompetent."

Elanor frowned. "You're a lot stronger than you let on aren't you? Dalton taught you his ways."

Ayr ignored her, instead spending his valuable resources on the task at hand. He frowned with frustration. There was nothing behind the glass except for a black wall as blank as the canvas that was the Tower of Echoes. Ayr wanted to scream, he wanted to kick the black wall with frustration, but none of that would help him. Whilst this was his only attempt to escape thus far, the lack of a result was still frustration. His next step was to blow a hole in the wall, but that would be something he likely needed Azura for.

"I need your help, Elanor."

"What with?"

"Magic."

Rider...

Azura!

I am coming.

Have they let you out?

Yes, rider. Where are you?

I am coming to you now. Stay where you are.

I wouldn't dream of being anywhere else, Azura.

Ayr turned to Elanor who appeared ecstatic. "Did you hear her?"

Ayr smiled back at her. It was infectious. The connection was faint, but it was more stable than it had been previously. Anything was an improvement at this stage. "I did."

"Then we need to wait. They are on the way."

"How are they going to get in?"

The corners of Elanor's lips curved. "I think I know."

Ayr gestured towards the bed again. "Should we pass the time?"

Elanor for the first time since they had been in her declined his offer. Ayr went to ask why, but instead, was cut off by a tapping that seemingly came from outside. Ayr paused, thinking that this was the beginning of another echo, but the tapping started again. It was rhythmic and too precise to be a coincidence.

"Ayr, get away from the wall."

Without requiring further instructions, Ayr stepped away. The tapping grew louder, turning into a knocking, that sounded like an egg was going to crack. Then like a parting of the seas, the very wall in front of Ayr started to split open. For a moment, sunlight filtered in, only for it to be shrouded in darkness once again. Ayr saw a flash of his scales and realised that it was Evor, standing in the way. As the door continued to open, a wave smashed into Ayr's mind.

Rider!

Azura squealed with excitement, as she raced towards him. The white dragon zipped into the room; her wings tucked beside her like a falcon diving through the air. Whilst she was smaller than Evor, the room was not set up to accommodate her. Her excitement radiated through the air as she came into land. She zoomed over Ayr's head; however, the bed was not so lucky. It did not survive a direct hit from her enormous body. As she hit the ground, the bed shattered much like the glass. Azura recovered, coming to a stop as she slid across the tiles before the opposite wall hit her. She was just excited to see Ayr. He turned and ran towards her and out of the corner of his eye, he saw Elanor run for Evor.

Azura! By Chilijo I missed you.

And I missed you too, rider!

Due to her size Ayr was unable to wrap his arms around her neck. He instead settled for her legs, but that was like trying to hug a dragonblood's tree. She nestled over him as much as she could, both equally enjoying each other's presence as much as possible. Just with this simple interaction, despite what he had gone through, despite the desperate attempts to reach her, everything was now right in the world.

"Ayr Ashbourne. I see that you have been keeping well despite your father's actions." Evor's voice sent shivers down his spine.

"Yes, I have. You are still looking well despite the scalebane eating away at you."

Evor grumbled in agreement. "Time moves slower within the Tower of Echoes it seems. By my best estimation, Elanor, you were inside the tower for a month. I also cannot be certain due to our extended stay within the void cell."

"A month! Evor, you're still suffering from the scalebane."

"And yet, my time in the void cell has nullified its effects, Elanor. Now that I am free, it may begin to affect me again."

"Then we need to get you cured."

"That is not the only thing of concern. It appears that Overlord Kaladin has been busy. I have never seen the Haven in such a state. I am not sure if the Dragon Lords still control the city."

"Where would they have gone?"

Evor shook his mighty head as he pushed through the gap. "I am not sure. He may have very well have shipped them somewhere they cannot interfere in his plans. The Haven is ready to go to war."

Elanor frowned. "Yet we are going to war against one man."

Evor shook his head again. "Dalton Ashbourne is amassing an army, Elanor. Perhaps it is best if I show you what is going on in the city."

"Have you received any instructions for us, Evor?"

"Yes, we are to take you to your new lodgings. Overlord Kaladin awaits."

SEVEN

There was no better feeling. Whilst it was only a short and un-saddled flight, Elanor felt at home on Evor's back. The flight over the Haven was only low altitude and slow, as it should have been without the proper riding equipment given to her. Evor's head scales protected her from the elements as the wind rushed over his body. Elanor sat back and enjoyed the ride as much as she could, eager to reach their destination. The Haven was an almost endless expanse, but thanks to Evor, it passed quickly underneath.

Elanor had felt out of place, but now everything was right in the world. Even if there was uncertainty ahead, she could at least confide in her lifelong companion. Evor started to slow down and made his descent towards the city. The other dragons that rested upon the rooftops or in-between the buildings looked up at them. Elanor ran her hand along Evor's scales.

Do you know where we are going?

Of course, Elanor. Lord Kaladin has prepared a room for us. He says it is safe.

I would not trust him as far as I can throw him.

He has been a busy man.

I bet he has.

Take a look Elanor, when was the last time that the Haven was weaponised?

He was right, like always. Elanor smiled to herself, more than happy that he was with her. His calming and powerful presence was all encompassing even though he was not focused on her for the time being. Elanor leaned back and took notice of the surroundings. The Haven was indeed more mobile and active than it had been the day that Dalton Ashbourne had made his presence known. Whilst the dragons were much the same, relaxing in the sun, Elanor could make out people working around tall wooden contraptions that towered over their heads almost as tall as a medium sized dragon. In the distance, she could see a dragon flying towards the north of the city, with a carry tray hanging underneath its belly.

Is that what I think it is?

Yes, Elanor. There is ballista being installed all over the city. Kaladin is taking the threat of Dalton seriously.

As he should. You and I both know firsthand what awaits us.

How is the scalebane?

I can feel it exiting my body with each passing day, but I am concerned that I have not had the final dosage yet. Dalton Ashbourne is not a man that is beholden to his word. I only survived as long as I did because I was within the void cell.

He's delivered so far.

Yet I wonder what further tasks he has instore for you, Elanor. It is clear to me that he has spies everywhere. He seems to know everything that goes on here.

The less I must do for that man, the better.

I'm glad you feel that way, Elanor.

I only do it so that you can live on.

Evor rumbled, satisfied with her answer. He continued onwards, before steering himself down into the shadow of another tower that seemed much the same as the Tower of Echoes. This however seemed less foreboding. The front door was also much taller and wider, with enough room so that Evor could slip inside unencumbered. As they landed, Elanor did not bother to dismount from Evor, her head barely passing underneath the structure's tall door. She checked over her shoulder and saw both Ayr and Azura behind them. Without any question, they followed Elanor and Evor inside.

As Evor walked into the giant structure, Elanor was busy taking in their surroundings. Evor sniffed the air for her, and through him, Elanor felt at ease. There was no sign of magic here, much unlike the Tower of Echoes. Evor would not willingly lead her into a trap or to her demise.

Where are we going, Evor?

We have chambers that have been made available to us, Elanor.

Is Kaladin sick?

No.

Elanor frowned to herself and Evor sensed her frustration, a rumble escaping his chest in unison with hers. Evor took Elanor through the tower, climbing the extremely wide staircase with ease. There was no questioning him and as to where she was taking him, but as they moved up the stairs, it became clear to Elanor this, unlike the previous tower was a trap. She heard heavy footsteps that almost matched Evor's above them. It was not until they reached the top of the stairs that Gundrag came into sight.

"Evor. It is good to see you on your feet again."

Evor echoed Elanor's thoughts, speaking for her. "I wish that I could say the same for you, Gundrag."

A grin came to Gundrag's lips. "Perhaps you need more time in the void cell, Evor. I will make the recommendation to Kaladin."

"We don't have time for this, Gundrag. Where is he?"

"This way."

Gundrag turned, slinking like a cat that was only a fraction of his size. His tail swished above Evor's head and around it, feeling like a whip in the air, despite being so thick. Elanor wondered where in the tower that Gundrag was taking them. They stayed on the same floor, and it was not long until Gundrag had led them into a smaller chamber that he could barely fit into. Evor had to stoop to make it under the archways, Elanor also lowering her head to ensure it did not get taken off.

"Go forth. The Overlord awaits you."

Evor stepped past Gundrag with a snarl and into the smaller room. It was still spacious, but from what Elanor could see, this was what would be their quarters. The room stretched towards a wide-open window that would have been enough for Evor to fly between. This felt like the Obelisk and what she expected at home. Perhaps in their time in the Tower of Echoes, Kaladin had turned a new leaf, or he perhaps just wanted something from them.

As Evor strode into the room, Elanor could see a cloaked figure stood in the centre of the room with his back to him. His short, cropped dark hair and massive frame, marked him as only one man. Kaladin. Kaladin turned, a look of distain upon his face. Even though the man had been expecting them he still was not pleasant.

"Elanor. You have taken your time in getting here. Evor, I thought you would be faster. We do not have time to waste."

"My apologies, Overlord. But if our progress was not halted by your dragon we would have been here sooner."

"Don't try and blame your tardiness on my dragon. Gundrag was not complicit in preventing you from getting here."

Elanor removed herself from Evor's scales and climbed down him, wanting to slide to the ground. Evor knelt for her, making the journey to the ground much shorter than what it would have been normally.

"Why have they got you doing such medial tasks, Kaladin?"

"I chose to do it. With all the noise that has been going on due to my new position, I needed a moment of peace. Thank you for bringing them, Gundrag."

Gundrag bowed his head. "It was my pleasure, Overlord."

"You like hearing that, don't you, Kaladin?"

Kaladin smiled down at her. "Of course, Elanor. This position has been something that I have wanted for quite some time now. Thanks to the untimely death of Anton Ashbourne, the role needed filling sooner rather than later. I consider it fitting that the role now comes to me. I was as instrumental in the defeat of the Ashbourne rebellion as Anton was."

"How? By slaughtering innocents?"

Kaladin's eyes flicked over Elanor's shoulder towards Ayr, Gundrag rumbling not content with what he had just heard. "If you consider those that followed your father as innocent, Ashbourne, then yes." His lips curled ever so slightly, showing the faintest sign of amusement at Ayr's comment. "I would do it again if I had the choice. Choose your next words with care. I can throw you back into the Tower of Echoes."

Despite only having experienced few of the echoes and nightmares, the words sent a chill of fear shooting down Elanor's spine like ice water trickling between her vertebrae. Her skin prickled with goosebumps, and her breath caught in her throat as memories of twisted visions and distorted whispers clawed at the edges of her mind. It was not something she wanted to experience again anytime soon.

"We don't have time for games, Kaladin. Why have you brought us here?"

Kaladin put his hands inside his cloak and retrieved them a moment later. In his hands, he held two small black objects that were folded over each other. He opened his fists for them to see what he was holding. Elanor raised an eyebrow as she saw her mask unfolding before her eyes. The all too familiar blue plume stood out against the blackness of the mask, and she wanted to hurl at the thought that Kaladin was the one holding it. She would need to disinfect it after having been in his hands.

"Considering that you two are being brought back into the fold, I thought that it would be appropriate to return these to you."

"Is that why we're here? You're a piece of shit, Kaladin."

Kaladin raised her mask and shook it in his hand. "For returning your masks? I could have burned these, but Gundrag convinced me otherwise."

"Why the fuck did you keep us locked up in the Tower of Echoes for a month then?"

"Dalton did not attack us. We were supposed to release you within three days, yet we thought it best to test his mettle. Your father is weak, Ashbourne. I did not want either of you interfering in my plans."

"He'll have been preparing just as much as you have been, Kaladin. The Tower of Echoes was also not going to kill me. I must say, it's impressive with what you've managed to achieve in the past month. Travesty and tragedy can truly cause people to come together."

Kaladin snorted. "If only the Ashbourne conspirators were few and far between. It seems to me that their numbers are growing by the day with the more people that I investigate."

Now it was Elanor's turn to snort. "You'd be working them to the bone night and day. Is it any wonder? These people also respect strength. That is why they followed Anton for so long. Dalton Ashbourne executed his brother in cold blood in front of the entire city. What do you think that tale has done to those that did not see it?"

"I'm aware. That is why I have a new task. I will reawaken a Keeper."

"A Keeper? You cannot be serious. They were not even called upon in the Ashbourne rebellion. You need to reconsider this course of action, Kaladin."

"I sent the Dragon Lords away for questioning me, Lady Sunfire. What do you think I will to do you if I get the chance?"

"Kaladin. It's madness."

"We are running out of options. I will not let a madman burn the Commonwealth down to the ground. He has already murdered two of the men that stopped him last time. Do you know what he is capable of now that his ascension to glory is all but imminent? We cannot stop him without help."

"Surely you can stop him with your newfound position and power."

Kaladin shook his head and a tinge of regret spread across his features. "The moment that I saw the golden serpent that he now calls an ally; I knew that it would not be possible. If Anton were still alive and in charge of Drementhol, we may stand a chance, but Dalton knew that."

Ayr took a step closer to Kaladin. "That's not why he killed Crassus and Anton first, you fool."

"Show some respect, boy. I won't hesitate to put you in the ground."

"Kill me, I don't care. But I can tell you why my father killed those two men first. It wasn't just because they were the most powerful men in the Commonwealth. It's because they were instrumental in stopping him the first time. Dalton is a vengeful soul. I'd dare say that the next man on his list is you."

"I only played a hand in his defeat at Ashenfort and Thornton Grove."

"And yet those were two battles that Dalton considers to be his biggest failures. If he had won those, he would have won. He considers you to blame, Overlord, and you've just put a bigger target on your back than ever before."

Kaladin surged forward, his face twisting into an angry rage. "I'll kill you, first!"

Elanor darted between the two of them, raising her hands. "You'll do no such thing, Kaladin! As Overlord, I'd have thought that you'd have learned some restraint, rather than jumping at the first shadow you saw."

Gundrag snarled overhead and Evor responded in kind. The two dragons were within striking distance, and all that they needed was a word from either rider before exploding. "He's not a shadow! He's right there in front of me. You are blinded, Elanor."

"Ayr Ashbourne is under my protection. Don't make your time as Overlord the shortest in Commonwealth history."

A moment passed between them, Elanor not removing her eyes from Kaladin. She could see through his eyes, that Evor likewise did not remove his from Gundrag. The room was like a powder keg, ready to erupt in violence. Adding Ayr and Azura to the mix would have meant that Kaladin would not have escaped but now was not the time to be fighting. Kaladin knew it as well and withdrew.

"I know where your loyalties lie, Elanor, and I have to say that I am disappointed. Take your fucking masks. You will join me on my expedition to reawaken the Keeper, however, will remain here until I call for you. Your dragons will be permitted to leave to hunt for food and to ensure that they are exercised enough. You will not."

Elanor rolled her eyes; just glad the conversation was ending. "If it gets you to leave us alone in peace, I gladly accept your terms, Over-lord."

EIGHT

Their new lodgings in the Haven reminded Ayr of the home that they had at the Obelisk. Everything here was comfortable, and considering the amenities, Ayr and Elanor were both kept well-watered and fed. Azura and Evor came and went as they pleased, always returning with full bellies and or nutrients for their riders. The world around them outside passed by with each day seeming to bleed into the next. Ayr was enjoying this quiet time, unharrowed by the horrors of the Tower of Echoes or Kaladin. There was little that had required his sole focus to rid his mind of it, but the tower had been relentless. He was grateful of their current situation, with no more torturing bad memories coming to light.

With Azura by his side to assist him, Ayr's mental fortitude was greater than ever. Anytime one of the bad visions filled his mind, Azura was able to swoop in and either comfort him, wrapping her giant white wings around him, or remove it entirely. Clarity and gratitude were in abundance now that she was back with him, and as the days went on, their bond grew again.

I missed your presence, rider. I never want to be in another void cell again.

I know. I felt it too, Azura. When you were gone from my embrace, I felt like my arms had been cut off. I cannot live without you.

Everywhere he turned in their new quarters, Ayr was met with love and affection. The one bed, whilst cramped for their size, allowed Ayr and Elanor to lay together each night as the days dragged on. There was no greater comfort. As Ayr and Elanor lay on the bed, stroking each other's hair, they could hear the cooing of both Azura and Evor who were also snuggled up next to each other. There was peace, but at any point, the peace could be shattered.

Several days passed in silence until one morning as both riders and dragons laid with each other there was an enormous booming on the door. Ayr jolted upright in the bed, but Elanor grabbed his shoulder and pulled him back down to the bed, covering his naked body with one of the sheets.

"If he wants us, he can come and get us. We don't owe anything to this new Overlord."

"What if it's not him?"

"It will be. It's either Kaladin or the wyrmguard."

I can sense Gundrag on the other side of that door, rider. It will be Overlord Kaladin that wants to speak to us.

Great. But why now?

Did you damage something in the Tower of Echoes perhaps?

Now is not the time for jokes, Azura.

No rider, it is not.

Ayr stretched out like a cat, groaning as his body clicked in multiple places. The thudding continued, only for the door to burst open a moment later. Ayr turned his head and saw the muscular figure of Kaladin storming towards them. Behind him, looming just beyond the door was Gundrag, his tongue flicking in and out of his head in anticipation. Beneath him over a dozen wyrmguard had all gathered, their hands on the hilts of their swords. Elanor was the first to greet Kaladin whose face was like a storm cloud.

"Good morning, Kaladin. What brings you here so early?"

"Both of you need to get the fuck out of bed, now!"

"Why? We haven't done anything wrong for you to grace us with your presence like this. We were just getting comfortable."

Elanor slinked around Ayr, stretching her body out so that she covered him. As her leg brushed against him, Ayr felt himself growing hard at her touch. He was of half a mind to flip her over right in front of Kaladin and begin what was otherwise very much now a part of their morning routine. There would have been nothing stopping him apart from the wrath of Kaladin.

"I don't give a fuck if you were comfortable. You are coming with me to wake the Keeper."

Elanor yawned and rubbed her eyes. "Kaladin, this is the last thing you want to be doing, I promise you. If you unleash a Keeper, Sinibad will be just another problem you have. What if the Keeper does not want to go back to sleep?"

"Then we will defeat it!" He stood at the edge of their bed, looking ready to reef the covers off them. Considering their state, Ayr doubted that he wanted to, but he saw Kaladin's face twitch. "I will deal with that problem when the time comes. I am the Overlord. The Keeper will obey me."

Elanor was still sceptical. "And what makes you think that the Keeper will wake up for you? You've been Overlord a month out of nothing more than necessity. Do you think that will make it want to obey you?"

Kaladin broke. "What other choice do we have?"

"What have you done to the Commonwealth? You sent the Dragon Lords away."

"For their own protection. I have it on good authority, as well as you do, that Dalton Ashbourne is out for blood."

Elanor shrugged removing her arms from Ayr and sitting up. "I'd help you, I really would, but you've proven to me time and time again, that you cannot be trusted."

Kaladin cast a glance to the side as if eyeing off the wyrmguard before he lowered his voice. "I am asking you for your help, Elanor. Gundrag and Evor are among two of the strongest bonded dragons that we have left."

The sheet fell from Elanor's body and exposed her supple breasts. She seemed unbothered by the reveal, especially considering who she was in front of. Elanor made no effort to cover herself, but instead continued to stare Kaladin in the eyes, not backing down. Ayr saw the wyrmguard shift outside the room, each of them homing in on her nakedness. Ayr wanted to cover her, but something told him she would have bat his hands away if he tried. The wyrmguard were made of blood and bone, the same as him, and he in part could not blame them for looking.

Despite the evident staring of the wyrmguard, Elanor was unphased, her sole focus on none other than Kaladin. "Oh, so it's just my dragon you want. Just like when I loved you, all you wanted was what was between my legs."

"Elanor. I did not mean it like that."

Elanor's eyes narrowed. "The fact that you've meant worse to me says a lot, Kaladin. We'll come help you, but only because I want to be able to laugh in your face when you fail to summon a Keeper to your side."

Kaladin grit his teeth. "I will not fail."

"You keep telling yourself that. Look give us time to get ready, and we will join you. There was no need for the awakening party. You could have sent a messenger."

"I wanted to see you and him for myself." If looks could kill, Kaladin's glare would have thrust through Ayr's heart like a dagger. "You know, I find it fascinating just how bizarre some dragons make their bonds with their promised. You'd think that they'd consider the rider before making their choice."

"Do you have anything else constructive to say, Kaladin? Or would you not so kindly mind getting the fuck out of our room. It's been years since you and I were together. Clearly you still have not moved on."

Kaladin's lips curled into a smile. He knew he'd hit a nerve. "Until Ashbourne made his presence known at the Seminary of Fire, you were still warming my bed, Elanor. I was not the only one that had not moved on."

"Get the fuck out!" Elanor flicked her finger towards the door. "I don't want you coming back in here again without prior notice!"

With a huff, Kaladin turned on his heel and went to exit the room. There was no escaping Elanor's hard stare, one that was backed by the fierceness and intensity of Evor. She would not be denied, even by the Overlord. A sense of calm was returning to the room as Kaladin left them, closing the door behind him and obscuring any view of the wyrmguard beyond the threshold. It was only then that normality returned to Elanor, but she didn't stop scowling.

"He's a piece of shit."

Ayr was curious and pried. "Then why were you even with him in the first place?"

"How could I not have been? You've seen him. For all his flaws, Kaladin is the rider that we all aspire to be. Couple that with his feats that helped turn the war in our favour, and he was the most eligible bachelor within the entirety of the Commonwealth."

"If he was so decorated, how did he end up as head of security at the Obelisk?"

Elanor shook her head in disgust. "It was my fault. He was set to be elected as a Dragon Lord, but I begged my father to make them change their minds. We broke up not long after, but by then it was too late. Kaladin has been passed over multiple times until now."

Ayr nodded his understanding with a frown. "So that's the reason why he's angry all the time."

"Probably, but it's not my place to care anymore."

"What did Evor think?"

"I didn't listen to him. I should have sooner. The friction between us strained the relationship. Gundrag does not have a promised, therefore his heart was not set upon another. But with Azura always in the background, it made it harder for Evor to let another man touch me, considering that we were waiting on her rider to make themselves known."

"You were young and foolish, Elanor. I am here to guide and teach you, but I know you will not make the same mistake again."

Elanor smiled up at the enormous black dragon that was now starting to stand up in the bed, stretching out, making his presence known. "And I am forever grateful for your guidance, Evor. There is nothing that I would change about our past together."

"Nor I, Elanor."

"So, what's the plan now?"

Elanor nodded and threw what little remained of the sheets off her body. She then leapt out of bed in a single motion, not dissimilar to the motion of mounting a horse, throwing her legs over the side and standing in a heartbeat. She stretched out like a cat, extending to her full height, rising onto her tip toes, her body reminiscent of a serpent, but as her hair cascaded over her shoulders, Ayr was reminded of just how much more beautiful she was and just as deadly.

"You heard our great Overlord. We're off to find a Keeper, Ashbourne."

Ayr winced at the return of his last name. "Ashbourne? What happened to Ayr."

Elanor stuck her tongue out. "Oh, come on, a little bit of harmless fun never hurt anybody."

Ayr raised an eyebrow. "Alright, Sunfire."

Elanor dropped back to the flats of her feet with a scowl. In another moment he had been reminded of just how serious she could be if called upon. "Alright, there's no need for that. Nobody likes a wise arse, Ayr. Come on, are you getting out of bed?"

Ayr was still seated in the sheets and had no desire to go anywhere. If it was not for Kaladin, he'd still have her in his arms right now. Elanor had not moved away from the bed. It was almost as if she was teasing him with her body as she stretched out. Ayr let out a groan as he stretched out in response, and he started to shift towards her.

"Look, I have thought about it."

Elanor took half a step closer to the bed. Her knees brushed against the mattress. She was within arm's reach, and all Ayr had to do was reach out and grab her. If she did not resist, he could have her on her back in seconds. "Hmm. And what comes to your mind in all of your great wisdom?"

Ayr smiled before he continued. "I think that you and I have unfinished business to attend to."

"Oh, do we now?"

She was only inches from him and Ayr rose onto his knees to draw level with her. He lost himself in her eyes, her face unwavering, not willing to pull away. She knew exactly what was going on. Ayr's hands found their way to her waist, and he pulled her tight against him.

"We're not going anywhere, just yet."

"Is that so?"

"Yep!"

With a grunt, Ayr pulled Elanor back onto the bed, back where she belonged. She offered no resistance, and the only sound that escaped her lips was a small yelp as she was picked up. Despite her power and intensity, Elanor was of a petite stature, ready for Ayr to manipulate however he wanted. In another blink of an eye, Elanor was on her back, staring up at him, her hands gently placed against his chest and the back of his neck.

"Well, what a predicament we find ourselves in, Ashbourne."

"Don't call me that."

Elanor smiled up at him, poking her tongue out at him. "Sorry, old habit."

Ayr shook his head and lowered it to her skin, his lips beginning to trace the curve of her neck. "Old habit? Let us then see if I can help you remember some other habits."

I do not think it is wise to keep the Overlord waiting, rider.

Don't worry, he can wait. We won't be long.

He heard Azura sigh. *Not from what I've seen. Please do not take too long. We cannot afford to anger him anymore than we already have.*

Yes, Azura.

NINE

Ayr was more passionate as time went on, only resting to give her the breaks that they needed. He matched her for stamina, and in some cases, surpassed her. Even Kaladin had not been able to keep up with her for as long as Ayr could. Was it the magic that burned within his soul that kept him going, or was it the bond that he shared with Azura and through her, Evor?

There had not been enough studies done on the phenomenon that was promised dragons. All that they knew was the bond between promised riders and their dragons was one that was unbreakable, regardless of the consequences or what happened in the world around them. If the world burned and was reduced to cinders, and only two riders and their dragons remained, they would find solace in comfort from each other, able to rebuild the world from the ground up.

Whilst there had not been that level of connection between the two of them yet, Elanor could feel the slow burn bubbling under the surface. Every interaction that they had every day, she could feel herself being more drawn to him, as Evor was fostering his relationship with Azura. As she and Ayr finished again, Elanor let herself breathe as Ayr rolled off her, satisfied with what they had just achieved.

As she laid there beside him, she could feel him still inside her, and her body yearned for more, but now was not the right time. Her hand ran down his chest. There was no rhythm or rhyme as to where she was touching. She just wanted to be touching him in this moment. Elanor traced her finger down the thin layer of hair that ran along Ayr's chest.

Elanor...

Yes, Evor. I know. I'm present.

Are you?

Elanor smiled to herself; her eyes locked on the ceiling above her head. There was no reason to lie to Evor, not that she ever could. He was too engrained in her mind, every part of his personality and his soul touching every part of hers. They were two parts of the same soul, just inside two different bodies, forever intertwined. The years had been kind to him, and she could not have asked for a better life partner. Every emotion that flowed through her also flowed through him, and with the exceptions of the hellscapes that they had been through in terms of the void cells and the Tower of Echoes, they were inseparable.

No, Evor.

Do you want to keep the Overlord waiting longer, Elanor?

I don't give a fuck about Kaladin.

You want to make him jealous. I understand, but you knew this would always happen when Azura found her rider. Stop playing games, Elanor.

Alright.

With a heavy grunt, Elanor shuffled out of the bed. It seemed that Ayr was having a similar conversation with Azura beside him. The white dragon bore a hole into him with her gaze as he lay staring at the ceiling. As Elanor started to move about the room, she could feel Ayr's seed just inside her. With all the magic between them and their dragons, there was no doubt in Elanor's mind that they would be able to conceive, but with the pressing circumstances around the outside world, now was not the time. Evor had sworn to rid her of any such inconveniences should they appear in her womb, his power able to rip them from her body without a second thought from her.

Before she had even reached the dresser, Ayr had also caught her, coming up behind her, his naked flesh pressing against her back. She felt warmth in the comfort of his embrace, second only to Evor's. She could feel that there was a similar fire that raged within both of them, both males, her sole reason for living. Elanor melted to his touch, but she knew they had a job at hand.

"Come on, Ayr. Kaladin won't wait much longer for us."

"Just one final embrace before we leave this place."

His lips pressed against the back of her neck, and in that singular moment, everything felt right with the world. Elanor shuddered at his glowing touch and pushed back into him. Ayr groaned softly in her ear and Elanor closed her arms, wrapping her arm around his that had wrapped around her chest. Ayr planted another kiss on her neck and with one final shudder, Elanor pushed him off her.

"There will be more time for that when we return."

At last, there was true separation between them. "Yes, there will be."

Elanor dove into the dresser, searching through the dozens of identical items, for something that was in her size. She found it moments later, only rows from the top, pulling out a wooden coloured riding vest and a matching pair of black breeches. There had been no need for clothing since they had been here, particularly that of the formal kind that would allow them to ride at high speeds. With herself sorted, Elanor now searched for Ayr.

Ayr had truly come into his own in the short time frame that he had been with Azura. Already, he had grown, causing his smaller clothing to pull tight on his skin. He was two sizes larger than Elanor and that was enough to make her feel small in his presence. The changes had been subtle and would continue to be so if he and Azura continued to strengthen their bond. What he had achieved in a short amount of time was nothing but incredible. She retrieved a similar pair of breeches, however his vest was black with a white undershirt. The saddles would do most of the work, but if they were headed towards where a Keeper awaited them, they'd need their full range of motion.

The bottom of the dresser was full of black and brown boots, each of them seemingly left there by their previous owners, forgotten due to time. As Elanor retrieved the first pair that seemed to be about the right size, she was greeted by a thick cloud of dust. Elanor sneezed, sending the sound echoing into the dresser before she flung the boots away. She then grabbed another pair that once again looked to be two sizes bigger. They dressed within moments, Ayr having no complaints, the clothes seeming to fit him appropriately.

There was only one more item for each of them that remained in the dresser. An item that Elanor had put there the moment they had arrived and it was the only item that did not have a layer of dust on it. Elanor retrieved her mask, before throwing Ayr's to him. She stared down at the mask, the result of a weave that she had placed on the fabric so many years ago. So much had changed since that initial period with Evor, but perhaps it was soon time for a change. She stowed the mask into her vest pocket, not needing it for now.

"This feels weird."

Elanor raised her eyebrow. "How so?"

"I feel naked. Did they decide that we didn't need a belt and sword?"

"I feel like that will be given to us all in due time. We should go if you are ready."

"And breakfast?"

"We'll eat when we're fed. If Kaladin is in this much of a mood, I don't like our chances until sundown."

"Great." Ayr paused for a moment, only to perk up like he had a shot of energy. "When do we leave?"

It would be wise for us to get a saddle, Elanor.

I was just thinking that.

I know. Come.

"Will you need a saddle to ride on Azura?"

Ayr frowned and glanced over his shoulder at his white dragon that still had not taken her eyes off him. She was so cerebral. What was she thinking? If only Elanor could see into her mind as well as Evor's.

"If we're going to be doing anything dangerous, I think it's a good idea."

"Hmm, then we should get outfitted. No doubt Kaladin has the wyrmguard doing the same. We should get out of here."

"Where are we going?"

"To the armoury."

We take flight once more, Elanor.

I've missed flying with you.

I do not trust Overlord Kaladin with our lives. He does not have our best interests in heart. Particularly with this endeavour relating to the Keeper.

You and I both know that. There's nothing I can do to convince him to change his mind. I don't hold that power over him anymore.

Perhaps you could do something that would help get that back?

Like what, Evor? Even if I was so inclined, your bond with Azura all but prevents me from doing anything willingly. I despise the man with every fibre of my being.

Hmm. We have time to think Elanor. Come.

Do you know where the armoury is?

Something tells me I need to locate the wyrmguard. They will be our heading.

Elanor reached her arms up, grabbing at Evor's exposed scales. The countless times she had climbed onto his back over the years, meant she had a set path to follow, considering Evor was so big. Within moments she had climbed up his leg and onto his shoulder before taking her place near his head. They would not be flying fast until they had retrieved a saddle from the armoury.

"Ayr, are you set?"

Ayr was already on top of Azura, having less distance to climb. He looked well situated; the top of his head visible against the stark whiteness of Azura's scales. Ayr nodded deftly and retrieved his mask from his pocket.

"Ready when you are!"

Evor lurched upwards underneath her, standing up to his full height before turning and heading out of the large window. Elanor felt a sense of calm wash over her, just like the warm morning sun's rays did as they stepped into the light. She had been held up in the room for days, with nobody other than Ayr and the two dragons to keep her company. Now that they were taking to the skies again, Elanor felt alive once more. It was all up to Evor now.

Already, his black scales were beginning to absorb the sun's warmth, warming Elanor's soul. As he took the first step and extended his wings out to their full potential, Elanor's heart skipped a beat. Evor surged up into the air, leaving the ground behind. They were soon above the city, the landscape that Elanor had only seen days ago had already undergone more significant changes.

Kaladin had been working the city to the bone. More ballista lined the rooftops, each of their deadly weapons pointed towards the sky in case of a threat from Dalton and Sinibad. And now instead of men working to put the instillations in place, there were now small crews, mulling near each one, just waiting for something to happen. Beside some ballistae were dragons, each of them different from the last. It was clear that Kaladin had enlisted riders to guard the city as well, their dragons on alert should the worst happen.

The sheer magnitude of changes was evident, with the streets less populated than what they had once been. No longer was there a chaotic frantic movement as people rushed from one place to the other. Instead, it was replaced by a sense of calm and abandonment, as if the city was waiting for a storm to roll in from the north and engulf it in flames. The men and dragons guarding the ballista all turned their heads to see the new dragons rising from the ground.

Due to their lack of movement, they clearly were not a threat. Evor could shrug off several ballista hits, his armoured hide among the strongest in the Commonwealth. But with the sheer volume of firepower at Kaladin's disposal, if he wanted them dead, Evor's death would come in a volley of spears. Sinibad would not be immune either, and that was what Kaladin was banking on. The other dragons in the sky, though few and far between also seemed unbothered by the ballista, going about their business, their riders on their backs.

There he is.

Elanor turned her head to follow Evor's in order to see what he was seeing. There in the distance was none other than Gundrag, slinking around what Elanor could only assume was one of the Haven's many armouries. He made it easy to spot from a distance with his radiant purple scales glowing in the sunlight.

As they drew nearer, Elanor squinted, spotting something foreign on Gundrag's head. Silver plating lined Gundrag's skull, a thinly cast helm that had been made to fit him down to the scale. Judging from the slight charring around the edges of the steel, this was a helmet that he had worn in the war when he had battled Dalton's legions of winged monstrosities. It would be one of the few surviving relics. Gundrag's saddle was also fitted and in place, the beastly purple dragon ready to take flight at Kaladin's word. Gundrag spotted them and let loose with a mighty roar that shook the air around Elanor. With the challenge issued, Evor made his way towards the leviathan that plagued their existence.

Upon closer inspection, it was not just Gundrag's head that was coated in metal. Full plated armour across the entirety of a dragon's body was far too much and would weigh them down significantly, especially on a long flight. The compromise was to opt for smaller metal plates in this instance that could help reinforce a dragon's most vulnerable points. This included just behind the wing joint, bracers around the dragon's legs and along his tail.

"Evor. It is about time you showed up. The rest of the wyrmguard are almost prepared for our journey to the Frozen Wastelands."

"Forgive me if I did not want to be the first there. My rider was otherwise occupied."

Gundrag sneered at them. "Allowing your rider to partake in the process of creating new traitors is not something that Kaladin endorses. Perhaps you should keep her under control."

"My rider is not one to be tamed, Evor. Something that your rider would take care to remember."

They were drawing level with Gundrag on their descent and now the purple dragon was towering over them as the armoury grew taller as well. There was plenty of room for dragons of all sizes, even ones as large as Drementhol to feel comfortable within. It was built especially catering towards larger dragons. The door was wide open, so as Evor touched down to the ground, Elanor could see straight through the structure. Most of the armoury was taken up by a long walkway that split it down the middle.

There were raised platforms that overlooked the walkway and between each platform stood a different dragon of the wyrmguard. Each dragon was getting a similar treatment to the next one. Each of them had a small crew of workers on either side of them, bringing new pieces of armour plating to bear upon the dragons. The dragons knew the drill, with each of them moving and helping the humans appropriately.

In the days of the first war, Elanor had heard the stories. They spoke of horrors inflicted upon the dragons, which included the armour plating being drilled into their scales and hide. The procedure was far too evasive and time consuming but also made the armour a permanent fixture upon the dragons, causing them great pain. Now, it was a much simpler process. A simple weave was all it took for the armour to be attached to the dragon's hide.

It was the responsibility of the riders and the dragons to keep the armour attached, using some of their magical reserve to keep it in place. In Elanor's mind, it was worth the trade off, yet others had reservations about the process.

You know I do not like armour, Elanor.

Yet they measured you for it anyway. If you have a set, we would be unwise to refuse it.

It is uncomfortable, Elanor. There is only one dragon I perceive as a threat in these skies.

And what happens if he latches onto you? Think Evor. Do not let your need for comfort get to your head. What of the Keeper?

If the Keeper proves to be untamed, then there is nothing any of us can do about it, Elanor.

Elanor grunted. In the end, Evor was right. He always was and she could not bring herself to go against him. She had the utmost faith in the dragon and likewise, he to her. The Keeper was practically an unknown in this situation and if it was indeed untamed, could be more dangerous than Dalton and Sinibad combined. Yet, if Evor refused the armour, it would only draw ire from Kaladin and Gundrag, which was something else that she did not want.

You know what he will think, Evor. Please, for me.

You know that I do not agree with it, Elanor.

No, but once we complete this expedition, I will do whatever I can to see us free from Kaladin's grasp.

He will still chase you to the ends of the Commonwealth.

I pray to Chilijo that his new position means he will be more occupied than ever before.

For a woman that is not religious, you pray a lot, Elanor.

Figure of speech.

I will never understand you humans sometimes. Your metaphors and endless riddles sometime befuddle me.

At her direction, Evor continued to walk towards one of the now spare armouring platforms. Evor had ceased complaining and fell in line alongside it. He rested his head against the metal railing which allowed Elanor to climb from him with as little hassle as taking a step out of her front door. As she stepped down onto the platform, she turned her head and spotted Azura rising alongside them. She was moving to a smaller platform above that was suitable for the smaller dragons. Already, men were moving on the platforms towards the new arrivals with armour pieces in hand.

Kaladin made his presence known, striding along the walkway towards them. Ayr had dismounted from Azura in a similar fashion to Elanor, however there was already a saddle waiting there for them. He took it from the hands of the armourer as a wicked smile came over Kaladin's lips.

"You're late."

"I had business to attend to."

Kaladin snorted and rolled his eyes. "I didn't realise that Ashbourne constituted as business."

"What I do is none of your concern, Kaladin."

"Whatever. I'm glad you're finally about to make something of yourself. Do you want a sword, Lady Sunfire?"

"Yes, of course. Why would I say no to a weapon?"

"Well, I'm not about to give those who were my prisoners a weapon. At least not one that I am willing to give you directly. If you want one, might I suggest you inspect the blacksmith?"

Ayr rolled his eyes as he kept adjusting Azura's saddle. She had grown, and still at this early stage, any growth was significant enough to warrant major changes. Thankfully, Evor had stopped growing years ago. "Anything will do, Elanor, as long as it has a sharp edge."

"I know. You're not who I'm worried about."

With a shake of her head, Elanor turned away from the riders and their dragons, heading down the path towards the blacksmith. The way that the Dragon Lords had chosen to prepare the staging area was impressive. Everything that the dragon riders could need was here in one location. As Elanor turned down her ramp away from Evor, the blacksmith was just to the right, following the raised platform. The blacksmith was a small structure, one that would not allow any juvenile dragon or older to venture inside, despite it being open on all four sides, which allowed the hot air inside to flow out.

The forge stood at the centre of the blacksmith, with four enormous stone pillars that held the roof up, marking its boundaries. Despite the forge's angry appearance, the surging redness of an inferno lighting up the hut with its existence, nobody stood by manning it. Not that Elanor required any help from the smiths. They were also busy tending to the dragons that were scattered across the multiple platforms behind her, readying them for war.

As Elanor made her way through the blacksmith towards the weapons racks, she saw over a dozen workbenches all of them each with different projects laid on them. They ranged from small blades through to armour plating that was fit for a rider. Kaladin had employed the smiths to their full talents, ensuring that the Commonwealth would be ready when Dalton Ashbourne reared his head once again.

Elanor ran her hand along the first weapons rack that she approached, examining each of the weapons that were available to her. Dozens of sharpened axes and swords lined the rack, each of them being a suitable replacement for the sword that had been taken from her. There were plenty of straight blades, with no frills, which made them the perfect weapon for her. As Elanor saw a blade she liked, she reached out as something rustled on the rack above her head. She darted back, drawing the sword in response to the threat, and as she looked up, she saw a small dark shadow, no larger than a hand shield.

"Do not cry out, Lady Sunfire. I am not here to harm you."

The shadow shifted, and Chorru came into sight, crawling down the weapons rack until he drew level with Elanor's face. The dragon's breath was warm against her face as he swindled his neck down towards her.

"What do you want, Chorru?"

"I came to give you a gift."

"A gift? What in Chilijo's name could you possibly give me?"

"This is the final part of the scalebane elixir that you have been waiting for. You are only allowed to give it to Evor once you have accepted one more task that Dalton commands you undertake."

Elanor's heart sank. She thought she was through with it. She had done everything he had asked so far. With a cocked eyebrow, Elanor tried not to let her feelings be visible, but Evor, upon hearing the news, bore down on her, his heart also conflicted. "And what is that, Chorru?"

"You must kill the Dragon Lords."

"Or what?"

"Evor will be poisoned again. And this time, Dalton Ashbourne will not be so merciful. Vex him again and the consequences will be dire."

"How long do I have? I don't even know where the Dragon Lords are. Kaladin sent them away."

"Then I'd suggest you speak to Kaladin himself. You have two months to rid them from the face of the Commonwealth."

"And what of their replacements?"

Chorru's eyes flickered. "Dalton recommends that you put yourself forward as one replacement. He is most interested to see if you succeed in your mission or not. Whilst the new Overlord and others remain a threat, he must be cautious."

"You've got to be joking me."

"Dalton Ashbourne is not the kind of human that takes these things lightly, Lady Sunfire. Do you accept your task?"

Elanor wanted to resist, she wanted to tell Dalton no, that he could not have any more from her, but there was something in the back of her mind that told her she needed to. Dalton had strolled into the capital of the Commonwealth and cut the head off the snake with a single breath. What chance would Evor stand against him if he had access to more scalebane. She looked into Chorru's eyes, the small dragon something that she could kill with her sword. It would make her feel better in the short run, but it would not be worth it in the long. Not to Evor. Not to Azura. Not to Ayr.

I will help you, Elanor. You know I will. Accept the task. You know as well as I do that I may not survive another poisoning, even with the cure.

Elanor sighed. She had no connection to the Dragon Lords, but the being that was her world was telling her to act against them. He was the only thing that mattered to her now, the only thing that she had any influence over. Kaladin, Crassus, Anton and Dalton had seen to that. All four of them, powerful men that had control over her at one point or another. Why wasn't Ayr the one receiving the task? Would he be the fifth man? The closer they were getting the more she trusted him, but Elanor suspected an ulterior motive. She'd been the victim before.

Elanor!

The noise from Evor was enough to break her, all his power that he pressed into her mind feeling like that it was going to splinter her spine. She was used to the pressure from him, but this was a cry for help. He had no desire to be poisoned once again and at the mercy of a periodic cure.

"Fine! We accept the task."

Chorru's eyes opened wider. "We? I did not hear Evor speak through you."

"We are one."

A low grumble that sounded as much of a laugh as Evor's escaped Chorru. "Of course you are. I forget what funny creatures dragons that are bonded to riders are. They have no sense of worth, and everything is done to protect the rider."

"Are Dalton and Sinibad not bonded?"

"You'd best thank Chilijo that they are not. Regardless, I must be off. Dalton awaits, Lady Sunfire. I will inform him of the good news."

"Good news?"

"You will have this task completed before the moon sets in the south, Lady Sunfire. Without it, the great black dragon will begin to deteriorate as life fades from his eyes. Good luck with your mission."

Chorru went to turn as he stretched his small wings that were no longer than Elanor's torso. With another wingbeat, Chorru had launched himself into the air and vanished from view, rising into the smoky ceiling of the forge.

Fuck.

You can say that again, Elanor.

TEN

The smiths were efficient at their work. Despite the over a dozen dragons that were all waiting within the walls to be outfitted with their protective armour plating. Being the smallest of the assembled dragons meant that Azura had been the fastest to have her armour prepared and installed on her body. Whilst she did not agree with the concept, it was for her own good.

How does it feel, Azura?

It is lightweight; however, I cannot wait for this abomination to be removed from my body. Whilst it is unnatural, I know that is only to protect me.

Do you think we'll need it?

Better to be safe than sorry. With the armour on me, I will be able to fell many wyvern should we get attacked again.

And dragons?

We will see, rider. We should ready ourselves. Here comes Elanor.

Ayr looked back over his shoulder and saw Elanor marching towards them. She had a new sword in a sheath strapped to her waist and carried another one in her hands. As she reached Ayr, she held it out towards him, sheath first.

"Here, try this one on for size."

Ayr took the sheathed blade and held it in his left hand before drawing it with his right. It felt good to have steel back in his hands again. Ayr took in a deep breath and closed his eyes, feeling the weight and balance of the blade in his grip. With a satisfied nod, he opened his eyes again and sheathed it. It was as close to the weapon that had been taken from him, yet this one seemed to be of a finer quality. The hilt was slightly thinner and the blade ever so sharper. From his memory, his previous sword was a touch smaller than the last, making this a true hand and a half sword.

Ayr smiled at Elanor with warmth. He could have gotten his own sword, and could have made the same choice, but she had made it easy for him. "Thank you, Elanor."

"Anything to help you."

Around them Ayr could see that the last of the dragons were now being fitted with the final pieces of armour that they would wear into the Frozen Wastelands. How would they fare against a Keeper? He'd never heard of them before and from the sounds of it, a Keeper would be able to stop Sinibad and Dalton. Yet how could they stop it? As the final piece of armour went on the final wyrmguard dragon, Kaladin gave the word for the riders to mount up as Gundrag came crashing down to the ground.

Kaladin took his rightful place, climbing up Gundrag's body, pulling his mask over his face. He glared down at the rest of them, waiting for them to catch up. It was clear that if he did not need the support in approaching the Keeper, he would have left them all behind. Gundrag left the building, turning on his tail in the next moment, and now that all the dragons were free from the hands of the smiths, they followed the Overlord and his dragon.

Ayr climbed onto Azura's back who cooed at his touch, shaking her head, still getting used to the armour that was implanted throughout her hide. Ayr could feel where the smiths had stuck each bolt with its weave to ensure that it remained on her. He likened it to how he imagined a piercing on his body would feel, despite the lack of comfort that Azura displayed. He did what he could to soothe her, but he doubted his magic had the same effect on her that she had on him in times of distress.

Once Ayr was secure and he had pulled his mask over his face, Azura heeded his touch and took flight, stepping off from the raised platform. Her wings erupted from her side as they stretched out to their full size, beating down as the ground rushed up to greet them. She zipped past Evor who was taking his time in making his way out of his fitting area. Azura barked with a playful excitement as she passed him, causing Evor to echo in kind.

They burst outside into the sun once again, both Ayr and Azura feeling better as they followed Gundrag and the rest of the wyrmguard higher into the sky. The mid-morning sun reflected off their scales, and Ayr felt a sense of freedom despite knowing what lay before them. Azura had to work hard to gain altitude, the armour no longer a concern. All that worried Ayr was the fact that the larger dragons would be able to leave them behind. Yet with Evor and the last few remaining wyrmguard behind them, they were safely in the middle of the pack. If anything wanted to attack them, they'd have to face the wyrmguard first.

Just how long do you think this journey will take, Azura?

Azura hummed a slow tune, thinking the question over. *I have never been this far north, Ayr. Evor believes this journey will take us days.*

Days? And to think Kaladin did not provide us with any supplies.

Stay in the saddle. You know I will provide you with whatever you need. There will be plenty of opportunities for us to take in water.

I'm thirsty now.

There is a river not far from here. If we stop, the rest should slow down and wait for us.

Are you sure about that? Kaladin seems like he is in a hurry.

He does not trust us. He will follow.

Ayr frowned, not believing Azura. That was at least until they had travelled for some time and Azura started to descend from their altitude. It was slow at first but then became more apparent. The walls of the Haven had been left far behind, and they were now truly in the wilderness. Here the vegetation was different to the south. Where the south had been covered in more temperate suited trees, this area was covered in thick pines that were more suited to the cold.

He spotted a break in the trees which was what Azura was descending towards. A thin river cut through the gap and it was evident that this is what Azura had spoken about. As she descended, Ayr looked up at the sky above them. Sure enough, Azura was right. Gundrag who had been leagues in front of them, with a seemingly one-track mind was now heading back towards them, his altitude also lowering. The other wyrmguard dragons had also turned their heads and were coming back. For once, Ayr did not like the attention they were receiving. The dragons were descending upon them like vultures on a carcass. Azura touched down to the ground and dipped her neck making it easier for Ayr to dismount.

Go!

Ayr needed no further instruction. He clambered down Azura and leapt onto the grass. Giving himself no time to recover, Ayr dashed to the water's edge and began to drink in earnest. The water was clear and running fast enough for it to be drinkable. The only thing that would pose any danger to him was a creature rising from the depths, but with Azura looming over him, like a pale sentry casting her enormous shadow into the river, that event seemed unlikely. There was an eerie calmness, but as Azura looked to the sky, Ayr could feel her anxiety growing.

We can't be long!

I'm drinking as fast as I can.

No, you want to draw Kaladin's wrath.

Stay strong, Azura.

Within moments, shadows twice the size of Azura were now circling overhead. Ayr glanced up at them, seeing Gundrag looming closer to the river. He could sense Azura growing more anxious as Gundrag continued to circle, before he finally touched down in the river. The waves that he sent out in every direction from his body towered over Ayr as they raced towards the shore.

Get back!

Ayr did as he was told and watched as Gundrag swooped down towards them turning his head. The waves were dying out quickly, and realising he was safe to continue drinking retraced his steps. Gundrag's head swung around, and he lowered himself to the water's edge. Kaladin was already out of his saddle and standing upright, his face unreadable underneath his mask as Gundrag growled.

"Ashbourne! Why have you come here? We're supposed to be flying to the wastelands."

Ayr bent to the river with his hands cupped. "You provided us with nothing, Overlord. How do you expect me to stay in the saddle when my basic needs are not being met? I won't have Azura killing herself to sustain me when it's unnecessary."

Gundrag's growling ceased as Kaladin grumbled and fumbled with something on his saddle. A moment later something flew towards Ayr's head. He reached out, catching it before it struck him on the nose. Ayr scoffed, realising what the object was. A simple grey waterskin. It was not much, but it was better than nothing.

"There. Fill it. We will not stop again until nightfall. I hope this meets your needs, Ashbourne. Don't say I don't do anything for you."

A moment later and an earth-shattering landing sounded from behind Ayr. He turned and saw none other than Evor landing over the top of Azura. He grumbled, baring his teeth, flashing them at Gundrag who withdrew.

"Gundrag, what is the meaning of this. Why are you and the Overlord harassing my promised and her rider?"

"This is not your fight, Evor. They are holding us up."

"Azura will fly just as fast as any dragon here."

Kaladin was speaking through Gundrag. "Not when her rider is taking his time to fill his belly with water."

"Why did you not give them saddles with supplies? You are lucky that Elanor is better equipped to handle these conditions than Ashbourne."

"Our soldiers and other riders needed the provisions."

Evor's eyes narrowed. "We have sworn an oath to the Commonwealth, just as much as you have."

Gundrag snorted, flaring his nostrils as his tongue flicked out of his mouth. "We will see about that. Keep your promised in check, Evor. We will not stop again until nightfall."

Evor bowed his head. "As you command, Overlord."

With another huff, Gundrag turned his head to the sky and shook his neck as he kicked off out of the river. Residual water fell from his scales as he surged up, back towards the rest of the wyrmguard dragons that were still casting their long shadows over the surrounding landscape. As he rose into the sky, Ayr breathed a sigh of relief. They'd escaped again thanks to Elanor and Evor coming to their rescue. A glance over at Evor told him that Elanor was not done. She was out of her saddle and standing above Evor's eyes.

"I need to speak with you."

Ayr glanced up at her, a frown forming over his face. "Okay, what about?"

Elanor waited until Gundrag was high above them and out of earshot. She sighed and rubbed her face with both hands. "I have a job to do."

"Don't we all?"

Elanor shook her head. "Now isn't the time, Ashbourne! This task is time sensitive."

"Did Dalton put you up to this? Why didn't you tell me, Elanor?"

"I'm telling you now. We need to push onto the Keeper at Kaladin's pace. I didn't think you'd stop so soon. Use every part of Azura that you can to get there. She will endure."

"What if we can't keep up?"

"You will. Evor's life and power is at stake here."

She speaks the truth, Ayr. Evor can verify it. Look.

An image flooded Ayr's mind. There was no doubt that it was indeed Chorru in the armoury. The small devious dragon had evaded the Haven's security once again to make his presence known. Ayr grit his teeth. They could not stop again, even if his head was ready to fall off his shoulders. If Evor was dependent on getting the scalebane elixir, they needed to be done with this sooner rather than later.

"What's the task?"

"I can't tell you yet."

Ayr narrowed his eyes at her. If she was not willing to tell him there had to be a good reason for it."

"You know we are with you in whatever you do, Elanor. I swore a commitment to you."

"One that I am most grateful for."

"Just promise me that you will tell me when you can."

Elanor nodded a response and went to turn away. Azura lowered herself to the ground for him, as Evor did the same for Elanor. When he was secure in the saddle, Azura did not waste any time. She roared to Evor before she pushed off from the ground and headed skyward.

ELEVEN

The cold was inescapable. It crept in everywhere and despite Ayr being tucked up in his vest and even with Azura to help keep him warm, it still was not enough. They had travelled to the northeast for days, unable to stop unless Kaladin decreed it. Ayr took what he could out of these small breaks, only using them to eat, drink and confide with Elanor. As the days had slipped by, Elanor was growing more anxious about her task.

"I don't know if I can do it. The Dragon Lords are extremely powerful. More to the point, I don't even know where Kaladin has hidden them."

"Hmm. I don't think he will have sent them out of the Haven. That is the Commonwealth's most impenetrable city."

"Yet Dalton slipped inside it like it was an open door."

Ayr frowned, kicking at the ground under his feet. It was frosted over, because of how cold it was becoming the further north they went. "If we knew who had helped move them, perhaps I could break into their mind to reveal the location."

Elanor's eyes darted over Ayr's shoulder. "Lower your tone. We don't know who's listening."

Ayr shrugged and checked as well. The wyrmguard were all standing in a circle alongside Kaladin, discussing their next move and more of what they could expect when they came across the Keeper. "I think they're otherwise preoccupied. I also think that we should target the people in that circle."

"You can't use the spell on Kaladin. It will be too obvious."

Ayr shrugged again. "He would be the person that knows the most. I don't know what else you want me to do. I'm just trying to help you and Evor."

Elanor clicked her tongue and hissed. "I know, but this is a delicate situation. We can't just interrogate the Overlord."

"Then we need to pick on one of the wyrmguard."

"Ayr. There's too many of them. One wrong move could see the whole plan come undone and then there would be no saving Evor."

Ayr exhaled and shook his head. "I don't know what you want, Elanor."

She placed her hand on his shoulder and grimaced. "It's fine. We will get through this together. I'll think of something for when we return to the Haven."

"Oi!" A sharp whistle rang overhead, and Ayr snapped his neck around to see who had made the piercing sound. Kaladin waved at them. "We're getting a move on. I suspect we're approaching the Keeper's tomb soon. Prepare yourselves."

"What should we expect, Kaladin?"

"That's none of your concern. You'll know when we get there. Now move out."

Since the landing at the river, Ayr had not had an empty belly or thirsty throat, even with Kaladin insisting that they increase their pace. The last few days had been gruelling in the saddle, but now their journey was almost at an end. Ayr bid farewell to Elanor and turned his back on her, making his way to Azura. Azura was ready, the new armour still shining in the weakened daylight. She had grown accustomed to the modifications, but Ayr still thought it was strange

seeing such crude pieces of human ingenuity against her otherwise
flawless presentation.

Come, rider. I hope you are ready to face a Keeper.

I don't think I am.

I will protect you.

Azura placed herself on the ground and Ayr climbed onto her back
within moments, settling back down into the saddle. Whilst this saddle
was not the most comfortable the two of them had shared, now that
he had worn it in, it was becoming more agreeable with his body. They
waited for Kaladin and the rest of the wyrmguard to begin taking off
before they rose into the air. Evor and Elanor were right behind them,
with the last of the wyrmguard bringing up the rear.

If Azura had so chosen to slip away here, it would have been
easy for her to do so. The ice and snow-covered barren landscape was
littered with valleys and ravines that would have been otherwise near
impassable if not for the dragons. As they rose higher, Ayr kept his
head turning, peering in every direction just searching for any sign
of civilisation. The cold that rattled his teeth and the vastness of the
empty space meant that it would be near impossible for any creature
to live here, even with the sun glaring down from above them.

The dragons also did not fly as high as they usually did, given the
temperature. Ayr was grateful that Azura acted as a partial wind shield.
If he was getting hit with the full brunt of the elements like she was,
he would not have been able to cope. His teeth were already gnashing
against each other involuntarily, despite Azura's best efforts to keep
him warm. Perhaps it would be warmer when they found the Keeper.

Gundrag led the way, continuing on their northeastern trajectory,
chasing the sun. With the speed that Gundrag was moving, it was like
he was possessed and judging from their tired wingbeats, Ayr could tell
she was not the only one that was fatiguing. He placed a gloved hand
on Azura's hide, sending a trickle of energy towards her, praying that

it would be enough to keep her surging forwards. Giving her strength served a dual purpose. In return, Azura kept him warm, their direct body contacting making the journey more bearable.

They continued forwards for what seemed like more hours, evident as the sun started to dip towards the horizon. Their journey could have taken them anywhere, but they all followed the Overlord. The vastness of the frozen wastelands was seemingly endless, until a strange new figure rose out of the ground on the horizon. At first, Ayr thought it was just another mountain peak with more structure, but as they neared it, he could see that it was an enormous figure that had been carved out of a mountain.

It was still white and snow covered against the grey and bleak skyline, but Ayr was in awe of the structure. There was no possible explanation if it was indeed natural but judging by the smooth edges and the likeness to a dragon resting on its hind legs and roaring to the sky it was not. Gundrag had spotted it and was headed towards it. As they kept getting closer, the structure continued to grow, dwarfing even the size of the Obelisk. It stuck out of the ground and the mountains surrounding it, pointing to the sky.

Soon they were close enough and details on the structure started to become apparent. Whilst snow collected and sat in places on top of the structure, underneath it, Ayr was beginning to piece it together. It was a beacon of sorts, golden against the otherwise pure white and blue backdrop. The gold parts Ayr could see were representative of scales, and the figure overall represented a dragon rising out of the ground. He'd had enough bad experiences with gold plated dragons in recent times and did not need another one. Ayr sunk back in his saddle as they neared closer to it. Gundrag and the other wyrmguard dragons seemed set on their path. If he turned back now, he and Azura would get hunted again.

We will see this through, rider.

Gundrag started his descent as he neared the structure. As one, the rest of the wyrmguard followed his movements as they angled towards the ground for the first time in hours. Ayr urged for Azura to follow them, and she obliged, streamlining her body to help her pick up speed to keep pace with the larger dragons. Ayr tensed his body, leaning forward properly into the saddle as the wind picked up. The first of the wyrmguard dragons touched down and Azura began to slow her descent, pulling out of the dive. This close to the ground it was warmer, but that was only a marginal term. Ayr had gotten used to the creature comforts of the Haven and the Obelisk, and he cursed himself for it.

With his teeth chattering behind his mask, as Azura landed beside a calm blue dragon, Ayr surveyed their surroundings. The base underneath their feet seemed solid despite Azura sinking into the snow, coming well over her feet. Azura made her all too familiar cooing sound as she too tried to figure out just what they were standing on. She was not the only dragon. Gundrag opened his mouth and from deep within his belly came a rumble.

"Clear the snow!"

As Gundrag spoke, he kept his mouth open and a torrent of fire spilled from it, incinerating all the snow within a stone's throw of him. Following Gundrag's command, the rest of the dragons all began breathing fire in their own right, taking care to ensure that the other dragons were not engulfed by their flames. The snow around them was cleansed from sight, leaving nothing except for what had been underneath their feet remaining.

Much to Ayr's surprise, he was not greeted by a layer of golden scales, much like what graced the part of the structure that shot towards the sky. Instead, what was underneath Azura's claws was a flat surface, much akin to the floors of the Obelisk. There were no blemishes or other texturing to suggest that it was anything other than man-made. He frowned at the strangeness of it all, wondering where Kaladin had brought them. Ayr was not the only being in the area with a feeling of confusion. He glanced around at the other riders and their dragons.

Barrett was the first to speak. "Where have you brought us, Kaladin? We are supposed to be searching for a Keeper are we not?"

"That is why we are here. I'm glad that you have been keeping up with your scripture reading, wyrmguard."

Elanor ripped her mask off and shouted over both men. "Stop your squabbling! We've got a job to do here, don't we? Kaladin how do we get into where the Keeper is? If I was you, I'd sort your shit out. I did not come here to be led on a wild goose chase."

"The Keeper is nearby. Follow me."

Gundrag turned and then headed back towards where snow was piling up behind him. With another turn of his head, Gundrag filled the air with fire, scorching whatever snow remained in his way. More of the structure was revealed to them as Gundrag cleared the way. With the snow being eroded from everything in sight, the rest of the wyrmguard began to follow Gundrag down a steep valley. The purple giant continued to spray fire in every direction, and they were soon standing in front of a tall steel wall that housed a small entrance, not much taller than Azura.

Kaladin was once again giving instructions through Gundrag. "Wyrmguard dragons, take up positions here and search for another way in. It appears that Azura is the only dragon that can make it inside from here. As for the riders. You're all with me."

It seems like we're in luck.

I'm not sure if I would call this luck.

You're by my side when all the other riders will not have that luxury. That's all that matters, Azura.

One by one, Ayr watched as the riders all dismounted from their dragons. There was a disconnect as it was clear that each of the riders did not want to leave their dragons behind, but with no possible way to fit inside what was a small opening, they had no other choice. Each rider dismounted from their dragon and one by one the dragons rose into the air, clambering onto the structure at all different heights, searching for another entry point. Gundrag and Evor were the last to rise, their communication, if any with their riders internal.

Ayr remained on Azura as Kaladin strode towards the doorframe. He looked small against it, even with the wyrmguard at his back and from Ayr's evaluated position on Azura, watched the proceedings with great interest. As Kaladin approached the door and pressed against it with no response. Kaladin scowled and gestured back to the wyrmguard who stepped forward.

Two of them, including Barrett drew their swords and proceeded to begin to wedge the door open. Elanor stood back with her arms folded over her chest, her face hidden behind her mask. Regardless, she did not look impressed, based solely off her body language. The two wyrmguard struggled with the door, their swords no match for the heavy steel. Kaladin was growing more frustrated by the second until he turned back, scowling over his shoulder.

"Ashbourne! Get down here!"

Perplexed, Ayr patted Azura's neck next to the saddle before he unbound himself and dismounted from her. He touched down on the dark ground and strode towards the door where Kaladin was waiting for him with his arms folded.

What does he want?

Your magical ability, Ayr. The door holds strong.

I can't move that myself.

You have me by your side, Ayr. Anything is possible. Do as he asks. We need to find the Keeper. It is our best hope against Sinibad.

Ayr drew in a deep breath as he approached Kaladin. "Yes, Over-lord? How can I help you?"

"Did you think I'd bring you here to not utilise your talents? If strength and steel won't open this door, perhaps you will."

"What if I don't want to help you?"

Kaladin took a step forward, raising a closed fist. "Just remember where you are right now. You might have all the talent in the world, but how quickly can you cut down me and the rest of the wyrmguard? Can you do it before one of our dragons bites through Azura's neck?"

Ayr glanced around at the wyrmguard, all of whom were now focused on him. Even though their dragons were moving back up the mountain, he'd need time if he was going to pull a stunt off like that. He had no reason not to help. Elanor remained stationary with her arms still hugging against her chest. She had not taken her eyes off him.

"I don't know if I can do it."

"You can and you will. I know that you're hiding more power than you let on. Now open the door and see us inside."

It appears we have no choice.

Do not be concerned. I will guide your hand, Ayr. Let us look at this door.

Now that he was no longer physically touching Azura, Ayr started to shiver. The cold was bitter, biting through his clothing and seeping into his skin. Ayr stepped towards the door, and as he drew closer, he could see no discernible marks or weak points on it. The surface was flat, much like the flooring beneath his feet. There was only one point of entry, which was where the wyrmguard had stuck their swords trying to open it.

He took a step back and sighed. With nothing else to go by, he'd need to brute force this door open. Why could there not have just been a lock in the centre, giving him somewhere to focus his power. He exhaled and straightened his back, staring at the door in front of him.

Ayr pushed his hands out in front of his chest, and closed his fists, like he was wrapping them around the edge of the door. He focused on the entry point and envisioned it opening. Magic started to flow through his veins as he summoned it, the power feeling like a chilly drop of water than ran down his spine. Ayr shuddered as he gripped onto the door and started to inch it open.

The door was unforgiving. A momentary lapse would cause him to fail. Ayr's sole focus was on the door, until he felt a familiar presence washing over him. Azura was encouraging, her presence a light in the darkness of a tunnel. With her reassurance like a calming hand on his shoulder, Ayr continued to pull at the door, urging it to open. Even with Azura's help, the door was resistant to change, not wanting to open, but as Ayr sunk more energy into the spell, it started to move.

The door inched open, and it was enough for Kaladin to leap into action. "Get your blades in there! Force it open!"

Ayr opened his eyes and saw the wyrmguard surging forward as a unit, plunging their swords into the gap in the door that he had created. Knowing the true strength of the door, Ayr just shook his head, wondering what good they would do, if any. He doubted they were having any effect, but if they felt helpful, who was he to judge. The door was nearly only halfway open, and suddenly, Ayr felt his magic either doing more or facing less resistance.

We have it now. Just a little bit more.

Sweat was beginning to pool across his brow, with the more magic he pumped towards the door. Ayr could feel his back tightening, even with Azura's help, it was a sustained and demanding cast. With one final effort, Ayr groaned as the door slid the rest of the way open, like a phantom gliding across the ground. It locked into place and Ayr let go of the spell, keeling over out of exhaustion. Whilst it had been easy to cast, the duration and power required had drained him. Ayr placed his hands on his knees and took in deep breaths of the near freezing oxygen.

Kaladin was more than pleased. "Excellent. Now we must find whatever is in there."

"The Keeper, Overlord?"

Kaladin nodded in response to the wyrmguard. "We will stop Dalton Ashbourne once and for all. Let's see it done, gentlemen. Draw your weapons and be ready."

Beside him, Ayr saw Elanor draw her sword from out of the corner of his eye. She scoffed under her breath. "I don't think he knows what he's getting himself into."

"Are we going to make it out?"

Elanor shrugged. "Probably not. This was a bad idea, but we didn't have a choice in the matter."

"Does Evor see anything?"

"Not yet. He will let me know the moment they find anything. I don't like leaving him out here whilst we go inside. This reminds me of the tomb of Chilijo."

Ayr's stomach felt like it had fallen into freefall. He'd been so focused on the door, he'd forgotten about the possibility of what could be inside. Elanor moved closer to him and wrapped her arm over his shoulders.

"Are you okay, Ayr?"

Ayr jerked away, the sensation almost too much for him to handle along with Azura's all-encompassing presence. "I'm fine." The words came out, more ragged than his last few sentences. Why was he feeling the effects of the magic now more than a few moments ago? "Just a lot, you know."

There was a warmth in Elanor's voice. "You did well, Ayr. Come on, we don't want to be left out here, do we?"

"Food." The word came out in a low croak.

"What?"

"Food. I need food."

Elanor sheathed her blade and turned on her heel, sprinting back towards Azura. Ayr keeled over again as Azura reached out to him. She threw herself around him, Ayr feeling her wings wrapped around him in his mind. He wanted to collapse to the floor, but against the heated weight of her wings, he could only remain standing. The rest of the world was being blocked out, a droning sound filling his ears. Azura tightened her grip on his mind, saying nothing, as Ayr felt a presence bump into him. He turned to find Elanor wrapping her arms around him again. The sensation was overwhelming, the world starting to spin around him.

"Ayr! Here!"

Ayr followed her movements, and reached out, grabbing her by the arm. He blinked twice, trying to clear his vision. He recoiled as Elanor's hand flew up towards his face, with a small amount of a dark red-brown object in it. Ayr's mouth opened as Elanor fed him, stuffing more of what she carried into his mouth. Ayr barely felt like he was chewing what he was being fed, the food being inhaled faster than Elanor could provide it.

Ayr was ravenous and the more he ate, the more he started to feel balanced and like he was returning to normal. His strength was returning and along with assistance from Azura, he was beginning to feel better. He finished the last of the food in Elanor's hand and relaxed, taking another deep breath. His eyes met Elanor's as she took her hand away from him.

"By Chilijo. I've never felt anything like that before."

"Sustained magic will do that to you. I've never cast anything for a long period of time like that. Kaladin asks too much of you."

"I'll be fine."

"Are you sure?"

Ayr groaned and stood up to his full height. The food had been just what he needed. "Yes, Elanor. Trust me."

I need to get stronger, Azura.

Yes, rider. We do.

TWELVE

With the door now open thanks to Ashbourne's efforts, the wyrmguard all drew their swords and waited for their next orders. With a deft nod of his head, Kaladin gave the order for them to advance into the strange structure. As the first of the men ventured under the cover of the open door, Kaladin turned his head skyward. Gundrag sat roosted on the next outcrop and was glowering down at them.

This is dangerous, Kaladin. I cannot protect you should the Keeper prove to be hostile.

The Keeper will bend to our will, Gundrag. We have discussed this.

I am concerned, Kaladin. There must be an entryway. Keepers were not known to be small.

Your concern is not warranted, my old friend. Just find your way into the structure so you can support me when I need you.

Yes, Kaladin.

Gundrag reared his head and let loose a roar that reverberated around the surrounding mountains. Each echo made it sound like there was another copy of him, laying in rest on a different peak. There was nothing that Kaladin wanted more than to climb on his back and ride him into this mysterious cavern. This had to be the right location. Even though the knowledge on the Keepers was lacking, this strange structure had been mentioned as their resting place. The next challenge would be awakening one. With the threat of Dalton Ashbourne and the elder dragon looming over their heads, the Commonwealth was desperate.

As the shadows of the overhanging mountain grew more imposing the closer that he got to the open door, Kaladin grit his teeth. At least if Anton was still alive, he could have held his brother at bay, even if for a short period of time. Now that Drementhol was also now no longer going to be of proper use to them, their fight would be harder. Over the years, Drementhol had been one of their best defences against rogue elder dragons, and Anton was one of the few men that could go toe to toe with Dalton. The Keeper would be their salvation. He was sure of it. Behind the door was no light, their way forward obscured by nothing but darkness. Annoyed, Kaladin turned back to the only two riders behind him.

"Ashbourne. If you're still too weak to do it, get your dragon to light the way." He expected resistance from the insolent pup, but much to his surprise, Ashbourne responded with no complaints.

"Azura, please."

"Wyrmguard, be at the ready. If we see anything we can use to light our path, the better off we will be rather than having to rely on our magic."

The sparkling white dragon stood tall in the doorframe as she tried to squeeze through it. Why had the Keepers made the entrance to this structure so small? Surely, as this was the only one that they had found, there would be other entrances. Despite Gundrag and the other dragons swarming the outside, traversing all over the structure, Kaladin could not make any sounds out from above.

Azura raised her head once she was fully inside, her white scales only visible due to the sunlight still filtering in from outside. With her head up high above them, Azura sent a small jet of fire into the sky. Kaladin followed its arc high into the cavern as it illuminated the surrounding area. He half expected to see wyvern clinging from the cavern ceiling, but much to his surprise he saw nothing but darkness. There was more to the cavern. A moment later one of the wyrmguard, Tobias called out from beside him.

"Overlord! Look!"

In the last of the dying flames, Kaladin turned and saw the faintest outline of a stone dragon head almost level with them, only a stone's throw away. Kaladin started to wave Azura's attention towards it. He hoped that they had not missed something obvious.

"Azura, aim your fire there."

Azura aimed lower into the air this time, having some idea of what was in front of them. She sent another burst into the dark abyss and almost instantly, Kaladin spotted the dragon's head. It was almost as large as hers, laying on the floor, facing towards the middle of the room. A faint blue glow came from inside the dragon's head, a silent vigil overlooking what they could not see.

"That's magic." Ashbourne's voice came from beside him, curious and uncertain. "Perhaps you can ignite that, Azura?"

Azura nodded and adjusted her aim again, this time opening fire on the stone statue. Sure enough, the blue glow around the figure was engulfed in Azura's flames and they took to it like they would to the remains of a deer carcass. Rather than remaining blue, the glow mixed with Azura's flames and started to glow red until they were overpowered. Even despite their situation, Kaladin could not help but admire the change of lighting. As the flames continued to mix, more of the cavern became illuminated, revealing another statue much closer to them. Barrett wiped his eyes with his free hand as if he was seeing sunlight again for the first time in days.

"I never thought I'd see the day. That's made of bloodstone rock. Only someone incredibly talented with magic would be able to make it do that."

"But why here?" The question lingered on Kaladin's lips. "Azura, light the next statue."

"Yes, Overlord."

As Azura illuminated the next statue, their immediate surroundings in the cavern were beginning to take shape. Kaladin was glad he had not ventured much further forward. The solid ground that he was standing on gave way to open space within the next half a dozen steps, just in front of the first wyrmguard. The man stepped backwards, bumping the rest of his colleagues.

There was one path that led them out towards what appeared to be a floating platform which carried the statues. The path would not be wide enough to carry any dragons as they walked, barely being wide enough for one human to confidently walk down it without falling off. Kaladin shook his head. This reminded him of the catalyst, except there was more mystery about what lurked outside of their vision.

Now that the path had been lit, Kaladin stepped forward, leading the wyrmguard towards the growing pit of darkness. Another jet of flame shot overhead, as Azura tilted her head back. This time the blast was aimed underneath the platform. With the firelight, it was easy to see the rocky mound that the platform had been built on, and now where it led.

Kaladin followed the path as Azura found another dragon statue and ignited it. The cavern they found themselves in being revealed one piece at a time. He crossed the platform and started following the path down the descending steps. They wrapped around underneath the platform, leading into the darkness. Azura shot another jet of flame that just passed underneath his feet, and the next piece of the puzzle was revealed.

The path was wider here. Kaladin stopped and dropped to a knee to examine it. The path was not completely smooth. Had the narrow path been wider and more accommodating? What had befallen this place so much so that it had fallen into this state of disrepair. Kaladin rose and continued down the steps, as Azura took flight.

He snapped back around. "Ashbourne! Where is she going!"

"She's seen the floor, Kaladin. There are more statues down there. She lights the way."

"Could she perhaps see us there first?"

"There are no more statues."

If Kaladin could have stepped back to grab him, he would have done so. Between the path being so narrow and the wyrmguard standing between him and Ashbourne, it made it impossible to do so.

"If Azura is unavailable, then you light the way."

"But my magic is still recovering."

"I don't care. Light the way."

He could see Ashbourne's face change under the dim light that came down from above. It was a dangerous look, one of defiance, one that he had seen on the face of Dalton Ashbourne all those years ago. Kaladin wanted nothing more than to wipe it from his face and send him tumbling into the depths below. Yet without Ashbourne, the only dragon assistance they had would be gone.

Ashbourne sighed and raised his hand over his head, and a small triangle of light came from it. The light was dim, but it was enough to highlight the outline of the steps as they tracked around the rocky mountain beside them. The wyrmguard cast long shadows in the light, but if he could see the edge of the steps, Kaladin did not care.

Kaladin, can you hear me?

Yes, I can hear you, Gundrag.

We believe we have found another entrance into the structure.

Good, can you get inside?

No, Kaladin. This door is stronger than the one that you faced. It is sealed shut.

If Ashbourne can get inside, you will be able to. Keep trying, please.

Of course, Kaladin. I will not fail you.

Kaladin looked up from the steps as he heard wingbeats overhead. He breathed a sigh of relief, seeing that it was only the ethereal white form of Azura, making her way down with them. She shot another fireball from her mouth, the flames splashing below his feet and at last, Kaladin saw the ground as another statue was lit up. The flames danced, changing from red to blue and back again, providing them with their first glance of what awaited them beneath.

He was not sure what he had expected. Their destination was still as flat and featureless as the rest of the cavern had been. Except as he made his descent, something new came into view. There was a larger, much more prominent blue glow from some distance away. Azura continued to find new statues to ignite, each one she torched painting more of a picture beneath them. What Kaladin was more interested in however, was the blue glow that was becoming more pronounced.

The staircase was coming to an end and still there had been no further sign of life. The blue glow was the only thing that was evident in the cavern. Azura touched down onto the ground as the last of the steps passed underneath Kaladin's feet and with a sigh, he could see that there were still more levels of the cavern. The path that led towards the blue glow was much wider, allowing for more access and even the largest of dragons to walk across it.

Ashbourne approached Azura as she waited for them and rubbed her chin. "You did well. Thank you for lighting the way."

Kaladin ignored them, whistling to the wyrmguard, pointing them towards the blue glow. They surged forward, their swords held in by their side, waiting for the first sign of trouble. Not wanting to be left behind, he heard Azura's footsteps behind him, the only real sound of any life in this enormous cavern. There was another overpass in front of them that dimmed some of the blue light, but it was clear to Kaladin that this was their destination.

Kaladin kept his head on a swivel, half expecting something to charge at them from the shadows, declaring this strange place to be its home. At the same time, Kaladin welcomed the challenge, even if he felt uneasy about Gundrag not being by his side. If only they had found the larger entrance first. They were in far too deep now to go back.

The wyrmguard were increasing their pace as they passed under the overpass and towards the source of the blue light. Kaladin's height was tightening in his chest. Was this the final resting place of the Keepers?

A platform rose up another sloped path, and on it were five tall black pillars that ran from the floor to the ceiling. Each pillar had a clear, almost see through pane that appeared to be frosted over, whatever was inside hidden from view. In the centre of the platform in front of the pillars, stood an ice-coloured podium that rose up from the floor like a hand. As they neared it, Kaladin could make out pointed tips on the podium. It was a dragon's claw.

Behind the podium and the pillar, however, was where the blue light was coming from. It was unclear at first, a haze lingering over the enormous figure that loomed in the distance. They got closer and the haze began to dissipate, at last showing Kaladin the source of his curiosity. He paused in place.

It was a dragon, larger than either Gundrag or Evor, frozen in the wall. The blue light was coming from its hollow eyes. They burned like a wild blue fire as it stretched out with an open jaw. The dragon was unmoving, as only its head and claw were visible, the rest of it trapped inside the wall. Rather than having scales, the dragon was primarily bone, bleached white to match the icy wall that it was trapped in. It towered over them, the burning blue eyes engulfing the room in their allure. There was a magical presence around the dragon, and it sent chills down Kaladin's spine.

The wyrmguard were whispering among themselves. "Thank Chilijo that's not a real dragon."

Kaladin was quick to cut any chatter from the men. "Focus. We're here for the Keeper."

Elanor scoffed beside him. "Do you even know what the Keeper is, Kaladin? For all we know, it could be that dragon. Look at it."

He grunted, not wanting to admit that Elanor might be right. This dragon would be a threat on a similar scale to what Dalton's elder dragon presented. If it got free of the wall, there would be no stopping it.

"What do you want to do, Overlord?" Barrett's question came from the front of the formation. "Should we proceed?"

Kaladin grit his teeth. They'd come too far to go back without answers. "Yes. Proceed. Surround the podium."

Calm your mind, Kaladin. I will be with you soon.

It was cold and growing colder than it had been outside. Kaladin's breath floated up in front of him, like smoke that poured from Gundrag's, but everything about this situation was out of the ordinary. The wyrmguard followed their instructions, surrounding the podium and waited for Kaladin to join them. As he stepped up to the podium flanked by Elanor and Ashbourne, Kaladin looked back over his shoulder and saw Azura standing there, terrified. He smirked. At least he was not the only one that this new dragon's presence offput. There was a low growling, as if it was being emitted from the dragon's jaw. Kaladin locked his eyes onto the beast. It still had not moved.

The podium was as tall as he was, but with his height, he could at least see in between the claws of it. The pillars stood behind it, looming tall, only comparable to the dragon behind them. Curiosity got the better of Kaladin. He stepped up to the nearest pillar, curious to see if there was anything inside. The frosting obscured his view, and he raised his gloved fist to wipe at it. At first nothing moved, the frosting layered onto the pillar, thick. He scrubbed some more and in the next motion of his wrist, a piece of it came free, giving him the view that he sought.

It was a view that he immediately regretted. Kaladin threw his head back as the misshapen head of a humanoid figure splayed against the window as if it was alive. A mangled hand that had one too many fingers followed the head, smacking against the viewing pane.

"That better not be the Keeper."

"Overlord! There's a body in here!"

Kaladin turned his head and saw Barrett standing like he was, with a similarly clear part of the viewing pane on his pillar as well.

"Check the others. Are they all the same?"

Without waiting for an answer from the wyrmguard, Kaladin shot back towards the podium, retracing his steps. It should have been the first thing that he inspected. It was too late now. Now they knew what was inside the pillars, was there a way to get them out? Kaladin started to examine the podium once again, the glowing blue light from above, starting to put him off. Kaladin wiped his brow as he stood up to his full height so that he could see everything the podium offered.

It was nothing more than a round blue bubble on the top of it that the claws rose out of with no discernible instructions or noticeable features. Kaladin frowned wondering what he had to do to activate the podium. What did it activate? Would it open the pillars so that the bodies inside could be freed, even if they were still alive. Kaladin continued to frown at the podium as Barrett came up beside him.

"Sir. Should you be doing that? We will happily take your place. You don't know what is required."

Kaladin waved Barrett away. "Can you feel that, Barrett? There is magic drawing us to it. Let me explore."

"If you die now, sir, that means Gundrag will be another powerful dragon without a rider for when we face Dalton. Allow me."

"No!"

Without thinking any further, Kaladin reached into the podium, sending his hand plunging into the blue mass that was atop it. He had no idea what to expect, but as his hand entered the podium, he was surprised; was it liquid? Something gripped him in the next moment, pulling him by the fingers. Kaladin raised his arm, pressing against one of the claws to stop himself from falling into the strange ice-cold liquid. As he pressed against the claw, a grinding sound came from somewhere in the cavern.

"Kaladin! Look!"

Elanor raced into view as Kaladin glanced in the direction of her voice. She ran towards the nearest pillar that was turning against the ground. Kaladin reefed his hand out of the liquid and immediately felt warmth flood back to his fingers. Had he lost blood or had the strange otherworldly liquid simply frozen his hand instead.

Gundrag!

You need to flee! It is not safe, Kaladin!

We've come too far to back out now!

Kaladin!

I won't hear it! Either get here now or let me deal with this Gundrag!

You will not be able to without me!

The pillar continued to turn until it had completed a whole one-hundred-and-eighty-degree turn. The viewing panel was no longer in place, and rather in its place was a much taller and wider version. As the pillar came to a stop, it hissed, exuding a mist from underneath it that billowed up and encompassed the panels. Before Kaladin and the wyrmguard could take a step towards the door opened and a corpse fell from inside. Kaladin wrinkled his nose in disgust, but there was nothing else that he could do. The wyrmguard close to the pillar were all poised, waiting for something else to happen.

"We will awaken the Keepers by any means necessary! Check on him! Check on him!"

Kaladin! Stop!

Barrett crouched beside him, examining the body with a practiced caution. Part of Kaladin expected the body to wake, but as the seconds ticked by it seemed less likely. The growling overhead was more prevalent than before, a gradual increase in its volume, noticeable. Kaladin eyed the dragon, but it had still not moved.

"Nothing, sir."

Kaladin glanced back at the podium. There were still four other claws protruding from the blue liquid. One for each of the remaining pillars that had not yet turned around. Kaladin stretched out, his fingers searching for the middle one. Perhaps that would provide some answers instead. As he pressed down on the claw, Elanor turned away from the body, her expression wide with fear.

"Ayr! What is he doing! Stop him!"

As he continued to press down on the claw, Kaladin felt his body convulse as something struck him in the back. His hand let go of the claw, but it continued to sink beneath the surface of the blue liquid. He turned to see Ashbourne standing behind him with his fists raised. Had the boy just struck him with magic? The grinding continued behind him and Kaladin went to step down from the podium. If Ashbourne had wanted to strike him, he should have done it properly.

"Ashbourne!"

"Kaladin! Leave him alone!" Elanor's voice carried from the other side of the podium.

"Or what? I will crush him!"

"Avert your eyes, Kaladin! Look at the dragon!"

With an angry snarl, Kaladin backed away from Ashbourne and found his eyes turning towards the enormous dragon that loomed overhead. It was evident why the growling had grown louder. Even though it was not by much, the dragon in the ice wall had shifted, its blue eyes glowing with an intense hatred.

THIRTEEN

Kaladin had never been the most reasonable of men, even when they had been together, but he was passing the point of delusion. They had bigger issues to solve, and Ayr was not one of them. Elanor raised her own fist, ready to strike at Kaladin, even if just to turn him off Ayr, but her words had done enough. He turned and saw the dragon moving above their heads.

"Why is it doing that? How do we stop it!"

"I think what has been done cannot be undone, Kaladin!"

Kaladin realised his mistake. He flung himself onto the podium, desperate to grab the claw that was now sinking beneath the blue liquid. It was almost completely submerged, and he missed it on the first grab. Kaladin slipped, almost falling headfirst into the liquid, but his hand caught the side of the podium, keeping him from falling in.

It was just close enough to the liquid and Elanor heard a sizzling that elicited a violent response from Kaladin. He jerked back from the podium, almost falling to the floor, clutching his hand.

"Ah! Fuck!"

The sizzling continued to echo through the room, even once Kaladin had fallen away from the podium. Still screaming as the wyrmguard ran to his aid, Kaladin ripped the glove from his hand and flung it away from him like it was possessed. Elanor caught a glimpse of his flesh before his other gloved hand hid it from sight. The tips of his fingers and his knuckles were bloodied red, like all of the skin had been ripped from the bones.

"Overlord! Are you alright!"

"No, what the fuck does it look like?" Kaladin could barely sputter out the words as his face started to turn a similar red colour to his hand, but not from an ailment. This was out of anger. "Stop the claw from going under!"

The wyrmguard were already ahead of her, and Elanor could only watch as Barrett leapt into action, jumping onto the podium like he would a wild beast to wrangle it. Barrett by no means was a weak man, and as he pulled at the claw, it continued to sink into the liquid below. He was helped by his comrades who all surrounded the podium, their hands gripping onto the claw, desperate to pull it back up. Kaladin continued to breathe heavily beside them, clutching at his mangled hand.

Behind her, Elanor could hear another pillar turning. As the claw dipped fully below the surface, she turned, waiting to see what horror would emerge from within. The centre pillar came to a grinding halt, and much like the first, a thin veil of smoke obscured it for a moment. Then, as the chamber door opened, Elanor saw a tall silhouette emerge from within.

This was different to the first figure to emerge from within the pillars, however. The first one had fallen straight away, collapsing under its own weight, however this one was different. It stood tall, proud and strong, head and shoulders above her. Elanor gripped her sword tighter, as the rumbling overhead only grew louder. Kaladin had started a chain of events that he could not undo.

The smoke started to dissipate and the figure behind it took a step forward, coming into the light, allowing Elanor her first proper look at what stood before her. The figure was pale, covered in a dishevelled black cloak, that looked like it had been torn to shreds by baby dragons.

Elanor squinted trying to get a clearer picture of who stood before her. Their eyes were slender, angled like a dragon's, with no pupils, yet despite this they were feminine. The tall, slender body wrapped underneath the cloak was thin particularly for their height.

The strange figure spoke with a soft voice that trickled over the platform like a gentle stream of water rushing over the edge of a cliff. "Overlord Kaladin Dawnscar."

Elanor turned her head and despite Kaladin still nursing his hand, his back stiffened. Kaladin stood up straight, flinching as he shook his hand. He continued to grip hold of it but approached the new entity in the room. He had to, what were his other choices? The Keeper knew him by name.

Kaladin's response was slow, measured and deliberate. "Yes?"

"Why have you come here? I have not had any dragon riders here in my home for centuries. The doors are barred. How did you get inside?"

Kaladin took another step forward, his face hardened as he fought against the pain that must have been shooting through his body. "We forced them open."

The Keeper's already narrow eyes narrowed even further, placing her full attention onto Kaladin. "Overlord Kaladin. You brought men with you. You brought others with you and your dragons. This is a small army. You chose to invade my home under what circumstances?"

"It was only the direst of situations, Keeper. May I ask you for your name, so that I know whom I address."

The keeper paused and tasted the air like a snake or a dragon and much to Elanor's surprise, a forked tongue shot out from her parted lips. There was more to this strange creature than met the eye. Elanor could sense the magic flowing from her, but that appeared to only be what was on the surface. As the keeper glanced around at each one of the wyrmguard, they all seemed to shrink under her gaze.

"I am Otheria."

Grimacing, Kaladin lowered himself in a bow. "It is an honour, my lady. How do you know my name?"

"You are the one that placed your hand into the fire. It speaks to me, to inform me of who my liberator was and how I should address them."

"I am sorry, did you not want to go free?"

"No, I did. For that I am internally grateful and for that I will spare you. For now."

"Spare me? Why? What are your intentions now that you have gone free?"

Otheria's eyes lit up like a fire hand been ignited behind them. "I will feed."

"Feed? Feed on what. How can I help you."

Otheria gestured towards the pillars at her back, her long and spindly arm rising from underneath the cloak. For the first time Elanor made out her hand. Her fingers were abnormally long, the middle finger appearing to have three knuckles. Whatever this creature was, she was not human. "I fed when I slept."

There was confusion on Kaladin's face as he processed what Otheria was saying. He glanced at the pillars behind her and followed their long tendrils that led up to the ceiling. Elanor followed his gaze and realised what he was seeing. Each of the pillars was linked together in a network like a spider's web that ran across the ceiling. If they were all linked and Otheria had fed whilst she had been sleeping. Kaladin came to the same realisation.

"It's vampirism."

"It is the only way that I stay alive. Without my brothers and sisters, I would be dead, and the world would be out of balance."

"Your brothers and sisters have a right to life as well, do they not?"

Otheria's lips curled into a wicked smile. Rather than seeing straight, pearly white human teeth, Elanor was met with a vision of jagged edges, much like a dragon. Was the keeper human or some wild mix of two different species? Or was she something else entirely.

"As the Keeper, they exist to serve me. I feed on them, and their life source provides for me. My brothers and sisters know this, and should I choose to end their existence, they will die knowing they served me well."

"You're twisted!" Barrett's voice rose above the rest.

Otheria's head snapped around with a supernatural speed, her eyes locking onto him. "You would have made a fine addition to my brothers. You're a strong spirit." Otheria took a step forward, her eyes now darting between Kaladin and Barrett. "Who do I want? The Overlord or his loyal guard?"

Kaladin and the wyrmguard took a collective step back. "What do you want from us?"

"I seek balance. When you opened the first chamber, ejecting my sister, you destroyed that."

"So, you care not about a dragon seeking to destroy the world?"

"Is it after the world, or is it merely after your precious institution?"

"In my view, it is the world."

"You were ill informed to come here if you wished to keep the balance of the world in check, Overlord. Dalton Ashbourne has already awoken us and informed us of the Commonwealth's intentions to enslave the dragons. It is in my view that he is the true Overlord."

"Dalton Ashbourne is a madman and a liar! We have a mutually beneficial bond with our dragons. Chilijo himself saw to it!"

"And why do you think we fought against Chilijo? Just like you, he is incorrect in this matter. Dragons must be free to roam the skies like any other creature! Enslavement to humans only destroys their purpose!"

"You lie! You fought with Chilijo."

Otheria's teeth flashed again. "There are two sides to every story."

Even Elanor froze. She had heard the stories passed down for centuries. Every report had stated that the Keepers had fought with Chilijo rather than against him. Chilijo had been the hero of the first war. Now Otheria was twisting the narrative that every rider had been told since they had joined the Seminary. How had Kaladin gotten it so wrong and why had he been part of spreading the lie that her parents did?

Otheria laughed and raised her hand, stretching out towards Kaladin. In response he keeled over, still clutching at his hand. Then as if he was being pulled by an external wind that had somehow found its way down into the cavern, Kaladin was being dragged forward. Elanor's eyes darted between the two. It was Otheria's magic. Her eyes were solely locked onto Kaladin. There was no need to hesitate. As Kaladin was dragged closer to Otheria, Elanor darted forward with her sword in hand. With a startling cry, she arched her sword down onto the offending arm. Otheria never saw the blow coming until it was too late.

She let out a vicious scream as the blade cut through her pale skin, cutting down to the bone. Elanor heard a crack, but it was not enough to sever the limb in its entirety. Otheria reared her head back as she continued to scream with a banshee like shriek. No sooner than she had struck, Elanor darted away, running back towards where the wyrmguard stood along with Ayr and Kaladin.

"We can't do anything else here!"

Kaladin despite the magic that he had just been subjected to was steadfast. "We can kill her!"

"With the power of Ragoon, I am immortal! His power is only rivalled by Chilijo himself."

"That's not possible."

An even louder rumble echoed around the chamber, except this time, the floor also shook. Elanor stumbled, her footing uneven underneath her despite being on the level platform. Behind her Otheria was laughing.

"You should not have awoken me, riders. Now you have awoken Ragoon!"

The floor rattled again as another rumble tore through the area. This one made the floor vibrate as well and Elanor turned to look over her shoulder. Otheria now stood to her full height, with her wound still prevalent, her left hand hanging off the rest of her arm like dead weight. Her right hand, however, was raised straight towards the ceiling of the chamber, as well as the dragon that remained in the wall.

The dragon looked like it was on the way out. Whilst there were no extra limbs that it had released from its icy prison, it was clear to Elanor that it had moved more. There were only inches in the distance that it had moved, but every inch closer to the giant dragon was another inch closer to death. There was no Evor to protect her. The blue fire in its eyes had also been reignited, burning deeper than ever before.

I am coming, Elanor! Run!

"Ayr! Azura! Run!"

"Ragoon. Incinerate them!"

Elanor doubled her efforts, the hairs on the back of her neck rising as Otheria screamed into the chamber. She was the closest to the ice dragon and its slow extraction from the wall. The dragon being stuck in the wall did not mean that it could not breathe fire. The rumble grew louder, and even as they ran, Elanor knew that they would not get out of the chamber in time. A dragon of that size would ensure that the entire chamber was engulfed in flames.

The chamber entrance was only a stone's throw away, when the dragon's rumble turned into a roar. As it sucked in an enormous lung of air, Elanor screamed. A black shadow dropped the sky, soaring overhead, with enough force that she was pushed to the ground. as soon as the shockwave passed over her, Elanor turned her head as she heard two dragons roar, one significantly more recognisable than the other.

As she picked herself up, flames jettisoned from Ragoon towards Evor. He hit them head on, with a violent eruption of his own, meeting Ragoon with fury. Yet Evor was less than half of his size. Otheria still stood on the platform, her hand still raised towards Ragoon. As Evor skimmed overhead, he averted his stream for a moment, trying to catch Otheria. As he lowered his stream of fire, Ragoon's flames caught him in the side.

"Evor!"

Evor let out a mighty roar as he tumbled towards the platform. Ragoon kept his stream for a few more seconds until he relented. The smoke cloud billowed outwards, filling the entirety of the chamber in its darkness. Behind the initial layer, the bright flames of the dragon fire still burned. Elanor could sense Evor, but it was as if the smoke clouded their connection. She strained her eyes, trying to catch a glimpse of him in a substance that was perfect camouflage for him. With another bellow that shook the chamber around them, Evor emerged from the smoke cloud.

Flee, Elanor!

Ragoon had retreated, and another rumble ripped through the chamber. At last Elanor was passing underneath the overpass that barred entry into the chamber and was once again out in the more open cavern. All around her, the wyrmguard dragons were dropping into view, each one of them desperate to reclaim their rider. Ayr had already mounted Azura, his head over his shoulder as he watched the proceedings. If she needed to be Azura would be in the air in a moment.

Ragoon let out another ear shattering roar behind them which echoed around the cave. Evor was now over her, and Elanor heard the larger dragon draw in another breath. She did not look back to see what it was doing. Instead, she kept running, desperate to reach the outside world. The flames at her back were hot, but thankfully she was out of reach. Their brightness lit up the cavern in its entirety, bringing more colours within it to life. For the first time, she could make out more of the flooring, much of it littered with moss that was making its way up through the cracks.

Elanor, slow down. I will carry you out of here.

Should I not just ride you.

Not if there is more danger. Stop running.

Elanor obeyed his instructions and slowed down, which allowed her to get picked up into his claw. As Evor scooped her from the ground, Elanor was grateful to be surrounded by his safety and warmth once again. She leaned into his claw as he closed it around her, pressing hard against the scales of his paw. Evor reciprocated the feeling, their mutual love for each other amplified by the short time they had been apart and the danger that she had just been in.

We should have found the other way before entering the cavern.

I agree. I grow increasingly concerned for Kaladin. He will lead the Commonwealth to its ruin.

He is trying to do what is right, given the circumstances. Just like we all are.

With a grunt, Evor kicked off from the ground. His mind was elsewhere as he focused on getting them out of the cavern. Although she could not see with her own eyes, Elanor could see through Evor's. The wyrmguard dragons and Azura flew around them in a tight formation, only spreading as far wide as the tunnel would allow them to. As they moved away from the statues that Azura had lit, each dragon dropped in and out of sight. Whilst Evor's night vision was far better than Elanor's in the pitch blackness of this cavern, even it had its limitations.

Elanor relaxed with a heavy sigh, not wanting to leave Evor again anytime soon. She cast her mind back to Otheria. How in such a short period of time had Dalton managed to infiltrate everything from the highest reaches of the Commonwealth to the Keepers themselves. What role did the others that remained in the pillars play in this game? Were they just food to Otheria?

Elanor mulled over in her thoughts, trying to find answers to the questions that this venture had exposed. Moments later, sunlight began to creep into her vision, and they were drawing nearer to the entrance of the cavern. As more light filtered into the cavern, she could make out Azura and Gundrag just ahead of them. They flew up the tunnel and fully into the light. Gundrag immediately made a sharp left-hand turn and began to slow down, coming in for a landing. Azura copied his movements, leaving Evor with no choice but to follow.

Evor touched down onto the ground, landing on three feet to ensure that Elanor was protected. He stumbled and as he adjusted his stance, he lowered the paw that Elanor was into the ground. She stepped out of his paw, sinking feet first into the snow. Kaladin was in his saddle, staring up at the entrance to the tunnel as more of the wyrmguard surged through it.

"Why the fuck did you think that was a good idea? We could have dealt with Dalton on our own! Now you've just thrown another cog into the mix."

Gundrag's head snaked around, turning to her, drawing his full ire. Kaladin ripped his mask from his face with his one good hand, a sneer evident on it.

"What would you have me do, Elanor? Everything in our literature said that in the event of a world ending event the Keepers should be awoken. More to the point, how the fuck has Dalton Ashbourne been everywhere in this world before us?"

"This is what he does, Kaladin. You should know this. He distracts and deludes, giving himself more time to act. I did not fight him in the war, but my father told me as much. Dalton is playing you like a fiddle. If you want to beat him, you need to be on the front foot. We spent too much time preparing the Haven for an attack that has not come yet."

Kaladin ran his hand through his hair in frustration. "And now we have this to deal with."

Elanor shook her head. "That was your own mistake."

Kaladin grit his teeth and turned to the wyrmguard that surrounded them. "We haven't lost anyone. Good. We need to ensure that dragon does not get free."

The young wyrmguard was the first to snap to attention. "Sir! Some of us can stay here and attempt to collapse the tunnel."

Barrett snapped his head to the younger wyrmguard. "I don't remember volunteering. But yes, you can stay behind here, Massimo. Some of us should escort the Overlord back to the Haven to ensure his safety. Who knows if this was a trap designed by Dalton to skewer us on the flight back."

Kaladin leaned forward in his saddle. "How many will it take to ensure that the tunnel is sealed."

Barrett turned back and stared up at the mountain that housed the statue that rose above them. "Hard to say. If we split our forces evenly, that will provide adequate protection for you but also be enough of a force to fight back against that monster."

"Can I trust you to take control then?"

Barrett nodded with confidence. "Of course, sir. Will you take Lady Sunfire and Ashbourne back with you?"

For the first time in a long time, Kaladin paid her attention. His eyes flicked over her, yet they held no warmth or emotion behind them. "Yes. Someone needs to keep a close watch on these two."

FOURTEEN

Ayr was just glad to be back in the relative safety of the sky. He had a feeling of dread as they began to fly towards the Haven with only half the number of dragons that had been in the sky. The fact that they were all still alive was a miracle, but would Ragoon and Otheria rise from the depths before the remaining wyrmguard could close the cavern?

It seemed like too important of a task to just leave without it being seen to completion. Ayr understood that they needed to alert the Commonwealth of this newfound, threat. If it was true that they had fought against Chilijo in the first war, why had everyone, including Kaladin been under the impression that that was not the case? The question sat on Ayr's mind, and considering that they were in flight, only Azura could answer him.

These are stories that have been passed down for generations, Ayr. Even my great grandparents would not have been alive to see the first war. We have seen firsthand how even relative information about an elder dragon can be misconstrued in such a short period of time.

Yes, we have. And you know my father's views on the Commonwealth as a whole.

He does not trust them.

And for good reason. If neither of the two sides can tell us the truth regarding what happened during the Ashbourne rebellion, what makes you believe that we can trust ancient texts that our Overlord read?

You cannot suggest that Kaladin is working against the Common-wealth.

No, but he is not working for them either.

What are you saying, Ayr?

He was a little too eager when Anton was killed. He knew that the Overlord position was up for grabs. That man comes across as always wanting more.

So, he wants the Commonwealth for himself?

Even though she could not see it, underneath his mask, Ayr could not contain a grin. The sly dog.

He has already sent the Dragon Lords away. They are the true power of the Commonwealth. If he wishes to reshape the Commonwealth in his image, he is off to a strong start.

Using a crisis to gain advantage.

We need to stop him, Ayr.

Ayr sat back in the saddle and sighed. There was nothing that they could do right now. Even if Azura charged at Gundrag, before she could communicate to Evor and Elanor what they were trying to do, they would be torn from the sky. Gundrag still remained more than twice her size, and even with her armour, Azura would not be able to penetrate Gundrag's without assistance. Ayr could summon as much magic as he had left, but he was still feeling drained from the movement of the door to get into Otheria's chamber.

We need to become stronger. I am sick of playing second fiddle. It seems no matter where we turn there is always a higher power at play.

We will train harder then, Ayr.

Whilst he enjoyed his conversations with Azura, now was not the time. He was exhausted and needed rest. Azura supported him as best she could, but what Ayr needed was sleep, along with more food and water. His water skin that Kaladin had given him was still attached to the saddle. As he cracked it open, Ayr was disappointed with the contents that remained inside. Regardless, he was grateful for what he had. Would he be able to afford a stop or would Kaladin have them riding until their dragon's wings fell off.

The answer was the latter, as they did not stop. The day soon turned into night as they headed west, the cold sun beating down on their backs as they crossed the otherwise impassable terrain. They passed over countless icecaps and snowy ridges, but as time passed, the snow was becoming less prevalent, and greenery soon made a prominent feature on the horizon.

Whilst Ayr enjoyed the cold, the freezing temperatures, even though he was warmer on Azura's back were eating away at his skin. The further west they went the warmer and more secure he felt. He was curious if Otheria and Ragoon had managed to escape their icy tomb, or if the wyrmguard had managed to seal the door. Just as the thoughts consumed him, Gundrag started to turn, making a descent towards the ground. For a moment, Ayr wondered why, and then on the horizon, he saw a thin body of water cutting through the landscape.

Azura adjusted her angle and soon followed Gundrag down to the river. She, just like Ayr was feeling the effects of their long journey and now that Gundrag was heading towards it without any prompting meant that he and Kaladin must have been feeling the same way. As they neared the ground, Gundrag let out a roar that shook the sky and the trees. All around them birds rose up from the tree line, scattering in every direction, terrified of the behemoths that were coming towards their homes.

Gundrag touched down onto the ground first just beside the river, the water's edge lapping at his feet. Azura soon followed as did Evor and the rest of the wyrmguard. The wyrmguard it seemed were the ones most eager to relax for a moment. Kaladin rose up over the top of his saddle and scanned the wyrmguard.

"Rest a moment. We don't have far to go."

Confused by the sudden change of heart from Kaladin, Ayr questioned him. "Why did we stop then? You were so eager to return to the Haven sooner rather than later."

Kaladin's masked face turned to him. From his raised position that overlooked everything except for Evor, he looked menacing. "I'd rather not die in the saddle. We've made ground the past few days. The dragons do not deserve to be pushed beyond their limit."

"Why here?"

"Don't question me, Ashbourne."

Kaladin rose from his saddle and made his way across Gundrag, before sliding down the purple dragon as he lowered himself to the ground. Kaladin hit the ground with a thud and once his footing was solid, he leaned back stretching his back.

You should do the same. I can feel how tight you are. Days in the saddle will do you no good without resting for a few moments.

I don't trust him.

Has he ever given you reason to?

But why here out of all places? We could have stopped at any of the other rivers along the way back. The journey is almost over.

Perhaps Gundrag is not feeling well. Who are you to question the whims of the Overlord.

Ayr rose from the saddle and stretched upwards, stretching his back as he reached for the sky. It was nice to be free from the constraints of the saddle and Azura lowered herself so that Ayr could make his way to the ground. He picked up the water skin that hung off the saddle and slung it over his shoulder. As he slid off Azura, he met the ground harder than he expected to and his knee buckled.

Careful, Ayr. Don't rush these things.

Ayr groaned and massaged his leg. His descent had been too fast for the situation, nor had he been ready for his landing. Shaking his head, Ayr stood up to his full height and made his way towards the water. As he approached it the wyrmguard were doing the same, each of the half dozen men who had come with them filling their waterskins by the water's edge. Ayr glanced over his shoulder and saw Kaladin now going through an aerobic routine just in front of Gundrag some distance away.

Ayr removed his mask, glad to be breathing unfiltered clean air once again. Here beside the river, leagues from any of the Commonwealth cities, he truly felt at peace, despite the events that had occurred what seemed like only hours ago. With the cap of his waterskin off, Ayr knelt beside the water and plunged it into the cool green-blue stream as it rushed past.

"You did well."

Ayr's head snapped to the side, unfamiliar with the voice that had just spoken to him. "Huh?"

It was a younger wyrmguard beside him, a tall blonde man with wispy hair. He wore a thin moustache, the hair on his upper lip barely visible in the light. The wyrmguard was crouched beside Ayr and despite his armour, had come in beside him quietly.

"To open the door, you did well. I don't think I have ever seen such a powerful display of magic, outside of Crassus demonstrating his abilities to Anton."

Hearing it the second time did not make it any easier to digest. The wyrmguard was speaking next to him as clear as day. Ayr turned his head, not wanting to engage, suspicious that this was a setup by Kaladin. He could see him out of the corner of his eye, still indulging Gundrag. Assuming it was safe, Ayr spoke softly.

"Thank you?"

The wyrmguard smiled at him, a loose grin that revealed him to be missing three teeth to the left of his mouth. "There's no need to be coy. If the Overlord wants to berate me for speaking to you, I personally believe that he needs to go place his head in a chimney. The name's Marcello."

"Why are you speaking to me?"

Marcello rocked on his heels. "I just wanted to say that it was impressive magic. It's something that only someone like Dalton would have been able to pull off without killing themselves."

A cold slither of ice ran down Ayr's spine. "What are you talking about?"

Marcello shuffled in closer to Ayr, now no more than an arm's length away. He dunked his waterskin deeper under the surface of the water, staring at Ayr. "Not all of us agree with Kaladin being Overlord. Some of us think that the Overlord title belongs to an Ashbourne. Not Dalton, obviously."

Ayr's eyes narrowed. "You're speaking traitorous thoughts, Marcello. I'd be careful if I were you. What if the Overlord hears you?"

The easy smile spread over Marcello's face once again. "I know. I just thought I'd tell you, so you know where we stand. We don't approve what Kaladin did to the Dragon Lords. They are supposed to be the pinnacle of the Commonwealth."

"What did he do?"

"Those men and women are among the most powerful in the Commonwealth and he treated them like toys. I'm surprised that he did not send them after Dalton on their own like lambs to the slaughter."

"And where are they now, Marcello?"

Ayr turned his head more, hearing the new speaker standing over the top of them. Elanor had not removed her mask, the bright plum on the top of her head, striking against the blue sky overhead.

For the first time since the conversation had started, Marcello finally had something other than a smile on his face. "I'm not sure I should be telling you that, Lady Sunfire."

Elanor folded her arms over her chest. Ayr imagined that underneath her mask she looked anything but impressed. "Do I need to involve Kaladin and tell him what you're up to?"

Marcello's eyes darted back and forth between them. His expression darkened and he licked his lips. "No, of course not, but I still do not think I should tell you."

"Yet you were going to tell my dragon's promised rider. You realise that word would have gotten back to me, don't you?"

Marcello's head twitched and the smirk came back over his face. "I suppose you're right. What harm can it do? Kaladin fortified the Dragon Lords inside Ashenfort. Why you'd move them from the Haven is beyond me."

"Ashenfort? That's very interesting. What has he put in place there?"

Marcello removed his waterskin from the river and fastened the cap back onto it. With a grunt he rose from his crouched position and glanced over at Kaladin once more. "I've already said too much. The Overlord is playing games with the lives of the Dragon Lords to try and force Dalton into making an error. Perhaps he will listen to you, Lady Sunfire."

Elanor snorted. "Fat chance. He is obsessed with ending Dalton."

"Then I fear he leads us down a path that will only result in our destruction." Marcello winked at Ayr before he turned away. "Just think about what I said, Ashbourne."

Elanor turned, watching Marcello as he walked away, returning to the rest of the wyrmguard like nothing had happened. "What was that all about? I thought he might have been harassing you."

Ayr licked his lips and withdrew his own waterskin from the river. "The opposite. I don't know how I feel about it."

"Do you want to talk about it?"

Ayr shook his head. "Something tells me there's more at play here than just my father."

Elanor unfolded her arms and turned to cast a glance at Kaladin. "Well, you've only got a short window. If you ever figure it out, let me know, yeah?"

"You know I will. We don't keep secrets from each other."

"So, what did he tell you?"

"That Kaladin moved the Dragon Lords to Ashenfort and that many of the wyrmguard are not happy with him as Overlord."

Elanor's eyes lit up. "That is very interesting."

"Why's that interesting?"

In an instant, the fire that had been behind Elanor's eyes vanished, only to be replaced by cold, hard fury. "Never you worry. I have a lot to consider between now and the time we get back to the Haven."

FIFTEEN

She should not have let her emotions get the better of her down by the river. Ayr had only known her for a short period of time, and he was already beginning to read her. Or was she too obvious? Elanor pushed the questions out of her mind, allowing herself to stew on happier thoughts. Evor continued to hum to her, the sound filling her mind as they flew, allowing her to relax. It had not taken long for her to close her eyes and fall back in the saddle.

Elanor. We have arrived.

Evor spoke into her mind a softness that if anyone else had heard it, they would have assumed that Evor was nothing more than a harmless giant. Awoken from her sleep in the best way possible, Elanor opened her eyes underneath her mask and found the sun staring her in the face. If it was not for the added protection of her mask, she would have been blinded by the early morning light.

Giving herself a few more moments to wake, Elanor turned around and saw that Azura and the rest of the wyrmguard dragons were still in the sky around them. In front of her on the ground was the sprawling expanse of the Haven. The city appeared untouched, with its new and formidable defences still in place. The ballista and their colourful dragon guards stood out against the bleakness of the otherwise stone and wooden buildings that comprised the Haven's girth.

As they approached, the first of the ballista turned in their direction. A moment later, it was turned away as the onyx dragon beside them reared its head to inspect the newcomers to the Haven. It let out a puff of smoke as its head barely rose above its shoulders. The other dragons and ballista nearby saw this as well. They all averted their eyes towards the rest of the sky, now aware that the approaching party was no threat.

Thank you for waking me, Evor. Perhaps we should follow Gundrag. I doubt the Overlord is done with us.

That was also my thinking, Elanor. I am glad that we are back.

It's not home though.

No, it is not.

I'm beyond eager to get out of this saddle.

I am also looking forward to having this armour removed from my flesh.

Is that wise? We may need it sooner rather than later. I do not want to cause you pain, Evor, but it is for your own protection.

Evor's grumble was loud enough to shake her to her core. *I will endure.*

Then take us into the city behind Gundrag.

One by one, the wyrmguard followed Gundrag into a steep descent. Evor followed them, with Azura just in front of him. Elanor felt the delight shoot through his body at the thought of being so close to his promised and she could not help but cast her mind towards Ayr that was somewhere on top of Azura's back, hidden just by the ridgeline that her shoulder blades caused. She was beginning to feel something towards him, but would it ever be as instant and as overbearing as Evor's pull towards Azura?

She could see his face clearly, even though there was a barrier between them. He'd been prepared to fight and die for her like no other man had. Not even Kaladin. There was no doubt in her mind that part of it was because of Azura, yet underneath all that there was still something there. The ballista continued to pass under them, as Evor angled towards the ground more and at last Gundrag touched down in an opening that was near the hall of the Dragon Lords.

Already, Elanor could see more wyrmguard making their way towards Gundrag and Kaladin, the latter barking orders at those on the ground. From her view on Evor's back, with the dozens, if not hundreds of ballista and dragon guards along with it, Elanor did not know how much more they could defend the Haven. What was to say that Otheria and Nargoon would attack here if at all? The Commonwealth was an open target, the Haven only the crown jewel of her might. Kaladin had to start somewhere with his defence.

Azura touched down moments later, Evor shadowing her. As she came into view of Azura's neck, Ayr turned and waved at her. She raised her hand, waving back, smiling underneath her mask. It was good to be back on solid ground and protected. Kaladin was making his way into the Hall of the Dragon Lords, his broad stature retreating with the wyrmguard at his back at a rate of knots. If the Dragon Lords weren't here, why was he going in there?

Where does he think he's going?

I am not sure, Elanor.

Elanor paused for a moment and took a deep breath. *The library. Of course. He is going to see where he went wrong.*

What do you want to do?

He's leaving us alone. I have a more pressing matter to contend with.

The Dragon Lord's whereabouts?

Yes. Where is that wyrmguard?

Elanor's eyes scanned the wyrmguard at Kaladin's back. It appeared that they were all abandoning their dragons, leaving them to their own devices and following him inside. One by one as they were about to enter the hall, they removed their helmets, and Elanor spotted the light-haired Marcello. Clenching her jaw, she clambered down from Evor's back and hit the ground moments later. She started off in a jog, fast enough to begin to catch up to them, but not fast enough to arouse suspicion.

"Elanor! Elanor!" She was too homed in on her target to even register that she was being spoken to. "Elanor!"

On the third call, she turned to find Ayr running after her. "What?"

"Where are you going?"

"Kaladin has not dismissed us, and I need to speak with that wyrmguard you spoke to."

"Marcello? Why? You haven't been yourself since we left for the wastelands."

Elanor swallowed. If she wasn't going to tell him now, when was she? "Dalton set me another task."

She caught Ayr's face out of the side of her eye. He stiffened as he took his next step, taking a deep breath. "Alright. What was it this time?"

They were almost inside the hall, out of earshot of the wyrmguard and their dragons that were now climbing onto the roof of the enormous structure. "He threatened Evor, again. I am to kill the Dragon Lords."

Ayr released his breath and sighed. His reaction was not what she had expected. Rather than being explosive, Ayr was calm and collected, almost like he had expected it to be her task. Did he know what Dalton wanted?

"Alright. And when were you going to tell me this? I think I deserved to know."

"Now. I wanted to tell you before we left because Chorru ambushed me in the forge."

"We don't keep secrets from each other, Elanor. You should have told me. This also effects Azura."

"I know. That's why I'm telling you now." Her chest fluttered as a sense of relief washed over her.

The shadow from the doorway started to wash over them like a wave as they entered it. Kaladin turned a corner into one of the side hallways and for a moment, Elanor lost sight of the wyrmguard. She quickened her pace, as did Ayr beside her, still able to hear the wyrmguard boots smashing down onto the floor as they walked. Ayr remained silent for a moment before continuing. There was no doubt in her mind that he wasn't sharing the new information with Azura.

"And that's why you want to talk to Marcello."

Elanor nodded. "You're as sharp as a tack. He made mention of it by the river, but I need to know exactly where the Dragon Lords are."

"Ashenfort isn't exactly a big place if we can search it whilst on our dragons. They should not be that hard to find."

"Do you think Kaladin would have sent them there without extra protection? That's why I need to know exactly what we'll be up against."

"I think you're worrying too much, Elanor."

"Evor's life is on the line, again. I do not think that I am worrying enough!"

Ayr reached down and grabbed for her hand. Elanor tried to bring it back, moving out of his way, but Ayr found his target. He wrapped his fingers over hers and stopped walking, pulling her arm, forcing her to stop with him.

"So is Azura's."

"Let me go, Ashbourne!"

Ayr pulled her closer to him. He stood over her, close enough that she could see the hairs that were beginning to grow on his face. It had been a week or so since he last had the opportunity to shave, but now there was a noticeable difference in his structure with a light shadowing of darker hair. Today his eyes were a lighter blue than usual, glowing with an unusual intensity. Elanor wanted to reach up, caress his jaw and pull him into her. The only thing that mattered when he was nearby was Evor, and even then, Evor became an afterthought if he was not present in her mind.

"A threat against Evor is a threat against Azura and it is a threat against you. You tell me what you need from me, and I will help you accomplish your goal. You should have told me."

"Ayr... We were busy, we had other things to worry about."

"To Chilijo's tomb with Otheria and Kaladin's quest. Nothing is more important to Azura and I than you and Evor. I made you a promise. Have you figured out how you're going to corner Marcello?"

"Yeah. I've got a rough idea."

"Then lead on, Lady Sunfire."

At last, Ayr finally let her go. Elanor spun away from him, taking her time so that he would not think that she was hesitant about their contact. She resumed back on the path she had been walking before he had grabbed her. Why was Evor allowing her to be disarmed like that in a time like this? She needed to create some separation from him so that she could clear her head.

I can see what he is doing to you.

You need to rest.

I will rest when we are back at our quarters. Just get the information you need so that we can proceed with our plan. I will wait until we are done.

Ahead of them, the wyrmguard footsteps were fading from ear shot. Elanor quickened her pace, with Ayr matching her movements, almost stepping in time with her. As they turned the next corner, Elanor's suspicions were confirmed. Kaladin was indeed taking them to the library that resided within the hall of the Dragon Lords. The books were stacked high to the ceiling, dozens upon dozens of shelves all lining each wall in every direction.

"Bring me any information you can find about the Keepers. I need to understand what went wrong!"

Kaladin's voice broke the silence with a loud boom. He strode into the room, his hands on his hips. For all his flaws, Kaladin's presence was unmistakable. He folded down his mask and thrust it with a fury into his vest pocket. Elanor wanted to approach him, but she only had eyes for Marcello. Kaladin marched straight into the middle row of books, his back remaining facing Elanor and Ayr as they entered. Marcello split right from the rest of the wyrmguard and was alone as he started down the aisle of shelves.

Elanor once again quickened her pace, doing everything in her power to remain light footed to ensure that she was not heard. Marcello on the other hand, had no idea that he was being pursued. He held his hand on the hilt of his sword, with his left holding his helmet loosely by his side. The wyrmguard was oblivious to anything going on around him, his heels scraping the floor as he browsed the catalogue of books. Elanor was like a phantom as she approached him.

"Marcello!" Her voice cut through the still library like a whip, but faint enough to not be heard from behind the other bookshelves.

He spun on his heel, his face stoic, until he realised who was coming towards him. "Lady Sunfire! How can I help you?"

Elanor almost slammed into him, but Marcello took a step to the side, ensuring that he was out of harm's way. "You're going to tell me exactly what you told Ashbourne and more. Where the fuck are the Dragon Lords?"

"I'm not telling you anything. That is privileged information only."

"Yet you told him."

Ayr's hand found its way to her shoulder. The slight pressure that Ayr placed on her was enough to stop her from going further forward. "You can tell her. We're in this together."

Marcello's eyes darted between the two of them with increasing suspicion, almost as narrow as a sheet of parchment. He sighed and glanced over his shoulder before leaning in towards them.

"I already told him. The Dragon Lords were taken by the Overlord to Ashenfort."

"You've got more than that."

"Why do you want to know? What are you going to speak to them about."

Elanor bit her lip. "The Overlord. He's not himself. He needs to be replaced."

A smirk spread across Marcello's face. "You better not let him hear you. You speak of treasonous things, Lady Sunfire."

"I'm led to believe that you are not innocent of such accusations."

Marcello's back stiffened as he stood taller. "I have no comment."

Elanor pressed further. "The Dragon Lords, wyrmguard. Where are they?"

"Ashenfort, like I told you. After the Ashbourne rebellion, Anton thought it wise to leave it in its ruined state. There is a place there for them, carved into the mountains above the city. Unless the elder dragon wishes to dig them out from the mountain, the area is impregnable."

Elanor smiled at him with as much sincerity as she could in the moment as Evor entered her mind once more. She reached out to him, feeling his presence take over her entire being.

We've seen Ashenfort since the war. It's not what it once was.

Yes, Elanor. That is where we need to go. I don't see how we will be able to rat out the Dragon Lords. I also do not know how we are going to get free from Kaladin's grasp.

I could request that we return to the Obelisk to ensure that it is adequately prepared in the event of a Dalton Ashbourne attack.

Do you think that he is likely to buy it?

No, but it's worth a shot.

"Elanor!" As she came out of the conversation with Evor, she heard a voice that was not Ayr. She ignored it, gesturing for Ayr to follow her. "Elanor!"

"Ayr, go. I'll handle him."

"Are you sure?"

"Yes." Elanor turned with aggression on her heel. "For Chilijo's sake, Kaladin! What do you want?"

As she turned, she saw that Kaladin was upon her, only half a dozen steps away, his face was unreadable, except for the chewing of his lip as Marcello walked past him. Marcello avoided eye contact, preferring to stay looking at the bookshelves, pretending that he was searching for any tomes on the Keepers. Kaladin surged towards Elanor, and she took a step back towards the wall. This situation was not unfamiliar to her.

"What information are you trying to pry from my wyrmguard, Elanor? You have been free from prison for a matter of days, and it now appears you are plotting against us. It's considered impolite to follow the Overlord without letting one of his guards know."

"Maybe you should train the wyrmguard to be more observant."

"What do you want, Elanor?"

"Never you mind, Kaladin. It is not of importance."

"Anything you do is of importance to me. Especially when it relates to one of my wyrmguard. What were you speaking to Marcello about?"

Elanor recoiled, not wanting to be touched by him. "Kaladin, you need to let go. It has been months. My dragon has a promised now. You need to move on."

He moved closer. There was a time not that long ago she would have given anything for him to be this close to her, but now all she wanted was for him to be as far away as possible. "You know that is impossible for me to do."

"Then I am asking the impossible of you, Kaladin. If you don't need me for anything, I was just leaving."

Kaladin's eyes narrowed as he glared down at her. "I'd be careful if I was you."

SIXTEEN

As the candlelight flickered in the night, Kaladin looked up from his desk. The hour grew late, and he was growing tired, not because of the time, but due to the amount of paperwork that he had in front of him. This was part of the job that nobody had told him about. Yet logistics were a key part of preparing for any war. Was he going overboard? Possibly, but this was a war that the Commonwealth could not afford to lose. If Dalton Ashbourne was to emerge from his hovel with an army at his back, they would need one to counter it and raising an army was not an inexpensive task.

Yes, there were quartermasters and provisioners under him that could have signed off on this documentation, but within the span of a month, the Commonwealth was already feeling the strain of the war effort. How they had survived the first Ashbourne rebellion was almost beyond him. Judging from these financial reports, they had still not recovered. Kaladin frowned at the latest of the reports. How had the price of grain gone up almost fifty percent?

Frustrated, Kaladin sighed and leaned back in his chair, placing the report on the desk in front of him. He rubbed his eyes with the palm of his hands, yawning and then smiled out at the rest of his new office. There had been no need to change much of it since he had taken over the space, Anton Ashbourne being quite the minimalist. He had been a military man, and the only thing that Kaladin wished to change in the room were the portraits of the Dragon Lords, each of which hung over the fireplace behind him.

He could feel their disapproving gaze with every stroke of his quill and every move that he made around the room. The only time that he was not concerned with their presence on the wall behind him is when Gundrag was mobile. For now, the great purple dragon lay curled up beside the fire, breathing peacefully as he rested. Kaladin gazed with a soft fondness at his behemoth, wondering what was going on in his mind. He probed at Gundrag, reaching out through the space between them. Gundrag raised his head, a deep rumbling coming from within his chest.

"Yes, Kaladin?"

"It must be nice having your life."

"It is, Kaladin. I am fed whenever I want food, I am looked after by a strong and powerful rider, and unless there is someone for me to fight, I can sleep whenever I want."

Kaladin grinned at him. "You don't have much to worry about do you?"

"Only what troubles my rider, but my concerns are not to your level, Kaladin. Why do you let the paperwork bother you so much?"

"You can see into my head, Gundrag. You tell me."

Gundrag let out a prolonged yawn before placing his head back down on his tail. His yellow eyes blinked, and Kaladin could make himself out in their reflection. It was the only time he truly felt small, yet seeing through Gundrag's eyes made him feel like the most powerful man alive.

"I can, but I prefer to ask you what is on your mind. We have been together for decades, Kaladin, but I find that speaking with you like this is one way to deepen our bond."

Feeling a sense of reassurance from Gundrag, Kaladin wrapped himself up in his presence. It was like the warmth of a fire that coiled around him, and he felt Gundrag's within his mind once more.

"This is more than just paperwork. There's something else that bothers you, is there not?"

Kaladin nodded. "It's the same thing that has bothered me for months."

Gundrag yawned again. "We will never see eye to eye on her."

"I know, you were not approving of our union."

"You need to let her go, Kaladin. She is toxic and would only serve to bring you undone. The only reason it was worth seeing her before was because of her father's position. Now you are the Overlord, you answer to nobody."

"I did not answer to her."

Gundrag scoffed and a puff of smoke escaped from his nostrils. "Kaladin, to use one of your expressions; she had you by the balls. You would have done anything for her. Do not lie to me."

"That's what you do when you love someone, Gundrag."

Gundrag sighed and retreated more into his tail. "If only I had a promised that I could feel that way with. You are bold, Kaladin. She was just a human girl."

"Yet now she runs around with him, no different than we were when we first started."

"The bond between promised dragons is a strange one. Again, return to your work and occupy your mind with things more worth your time. Or perhaps, if you are so concerned with finding a human partner, might I suggest the local establishments offering such services?"

"Whores will age just like any other dragonless human. I have no interest in them."

"Then might I suggest finding a rider with a dragon that has no promised. You are overthinking the problem."

"I prefer problems that I can just plunge a sword into or ones that require the stroke of a pen."

"There is a desk full of problems right in front of you. Perhaps start there."

He could tell that Gundrag was beginning to get over the conversation. Offering solutions was what he did when he did not want to listen, and at times, it made it hard to relate to him. Yet deep down, Kaladin knew that he was right. He rubbed his eyes and glared at the stack of papers in front of him. When would it slow down? The sooner that Dalton Ashbourne had been dealt with the better. Sighing, Kaladin picked up his quill again and grabbed at the next sheet.

He began reading, more provisions for grain and water that had come from the finest springs, just outside Travion's Roost. How was spring water worth more than river water? What kind of magical properties did it possess? Shaking his head, Kaladin signed off on the bill. Just more money given away, but at least this was not going outside the Commonwealth. Anything to keep the economy going.

Time continued to slip away from him, and the candlelight started to grow dim as the candle burnt. He was at least making progress, at least until a loud knock on the door interrupted him. Gundrag turned his head towards the door and sniffed the air. Two wyrmguard were positioned outside the door, and they would have been the ones who had knocked. Kaladin nodded, giving Gundrag permission.

"Enter!"

The wide doors to the chambers opened and were pushed back to reveal none other than Barrett in the walkway, with his stark white helmet resting on his hip. His expression was stern, and over his shoulder stood his own dragon, the blue speckled Arrax. Whilst Arrax was not as tall as Gundrag, he matched Gundrag for mass, power and speed.

If they fought, Kaladin was not sure who would have come out on top. He backed his and Gundrag's abilities more than Barrett's, but in truth that may not have been the outcome of a struggle between the two forces. Barrett marched forward, his cloak swinging behind him. He nodded to Gundrag as he approached Kaladin's desk.

"Yes, Commander Barrett? The hour grows late."

"Sir, we managed to seal the tunnel as you requested, but we fear it may not be enough."

"May not be enough? What do you mean? If it's sealed, it's sealed."

"Sir, you know firsthand the result of the Keeper's magic."

Kaladin's eyes flicked to his hand that he had kept gloved since their adventure into the cavern. He checked on it throughout the day, yet it was almost as if it had been damaged beyond repair. Even Gundrag's tears were unable to cure this aliment, and the hand was now numb to the point where he could not write with it. For now, he could still grip his sword with it, but Kaladin wondered how long that it would be before that privilege was lost to him.

"Then we need to station a unit there in case of her escape from that cavern. I'll let you see to that, Commander."

Barrett stiffened. "Sir, do you really think that is wise?"

"Of course, I think it is wise. A unit of wyrmguard will ensure that we are not caught unawares by her treachery."

"Sir, that dragon should it rise from the snow is likely a bigger threat than even Dalton Ashbourne and the elder dragon that he has under his control."

Kaladin waved his hand, attempting to dismiss Barrett's fears. "Nonsense. Dalton Ashbourne is most existential crisis that we face as a society. If he gets his claws into our side, he may tear us apart never to be the same again."

"Dalton Ashbourne is a man, sir. He can be defeated. He is flesh and bone, no different than you and I. Whereas that thing in the cave may not even be human."

"I am unsure of what you want, Commander. We cannot afford to split our forces to take on both threats at once."

"We need to deal with one sooner rather than later. And considering the Keeper isn't likely to be going anywhere soon, we should seek her out and destroy her."

Kaladin pushed back from the desk, wincing as he applied pressure to his hand. "Dalton has spies everywhere in the Commonwealth. This is common knowledge. If we send dozens of our best riders and their dragons, rest assured, he will know about it and attack us with Chilijo knows what. Do you want him to attack, Commander?"

Barrett retreated, wincing as if he had been struck. "No, sir. I am merely offering a suggestion as to what course of action we should take, given the circumstances as is my duty as commander of the wyrm-guard."

Hearing the fight had gone out of his voice, Kaladin leaned back towards the desk, picking up the first sheet of parchment that his fingers laid on. He held it out to read it, and then titled it towards Barrett.

"Do you know what this is?"

"A piece of parchment, sir."

Kaladin rolled his eyes. What else had he expected? "No, this is a requisition request. I have hundreds of these here and all of these need to be completed so that we may crush Dalton Ashbourne before he can strike at us anymore than he already has. Nowhere on there does it say that they are to help contain a Keeper. Am I understood?"

"Perfectly sir."

"Good. Send a unit if you wish, but I will hear no more about the Keeper unless our circumstances are dire and she strikes out at us."

Barrett bowed his head and went to turn when another knock came from the door. Kaladin raised his eyes to see who was interrupting this time. Much to his surprise, it was one of the young wyrmguard that had accompanied them to Otheria's lair whose head poked around the corner of the door. Kaladin raised his hand and beckoned the wyrmguard forward.

"You may enter."

His stark blond hair marked him as Marcello. Barrett tucked his hands behind his back as they waited for him to draw near. Barrett raised an eyebrow, Marcello standing before them out of breath.

"Sirs! The great bronze dragon has returned to roost near the Haven."

Barrett perked up hearing the words. "Drementhol has been sighted?"

Marcello nodded his head with an enthusiastic excitement. "He has."

Kaladin scowled at the young wyrmguard. Whilst he had seen Marcello come up through the Seminary of Fire and the Obelisk with as sharp a sword as any, Kaladin wondered if he had been dropped on his head as a baby.

"If the great dragon wanted to speak to us by now, he would have made his presence known within the city."

"With all due respect sirs, this is the closest that Drementhol has been to the Haven since the death of Anton Ashbourne. Surely this is worth investigating. His services will be most valuable, given the situation with Dalton Ashbourne and his elder dragon. Without Drementhol what hope do we have against that monstrosity?"

Kaladin tightened his jaw. There were half a dozen dragons that could match Drementhol for size, but against the elder dragon none of the others would compare. Gundrag was already in his mind, pushing him to go.

This would be a missed opportunity if Drementhol was to leave again without a purpose to lend his power to. You are the Overlord now, Kaladin. You need to do what is best for the entirety of the Common-wealth, not just your personal glory.

He is Anton Ashbourne's dragon. If Dalton had not rebelled, we'd be dealing with Anton to this day.

I know your feelings for the previous Overlord. You'd be stupid to pass up the chance to use such an asset in the upcoming war.

He is riderless. How much assistance will he be?

Dalton Ashbourne does not have another dragon that he has bonded with. This will be a battle of power. If we can use Drementhol to kill the elder dragon, then Dalton will fall easier. I am ready to ride, even at this late hour.

"Fine. Take me to him. I would speak to the great dragon myself."

Gundrag rose, puffing out his chest with pride. Whilst their riders had never seen eye to eye, both Gundrag and Drementhol had treated each other like hatchlings. Kaladin was not sure if he was being pushed to the decision, but without pushing back against Gundrag, he would not find out. Not wanting to fight with Gundrag, he rose from his desk and crossed the room.

Barrett was already mounting Arrax, climbing up the blue drag-on's side. "Do you need an escort, sir?"

Kaladin pointed to Marcello. "I already have one."

"You know that you are not to leave the Haven with at least an escort of two wyrmguard."

Kaladin rolled his eyes as Gundrag's head came down to lay on the ground beside him. "You wyrmguard need to stop making the rules."

"You're the one that wants to point out we're at war, Kaladin. Perhaps we should reevaluate these measures that you have taken to ensure our safety."

Gundrag snarled beside him, echoing Kaladin's thoughts. "Did you fight in the Ashbourne rebellion, Barrett?"

Barrett shook his head in response. "No, sir. I was outside the Commonwealth training when the rebellion broke out. I wanted to come back, but my master forbade it."

Kaladin frowned at him. "So, you don't know war. Then how did you get appointed to your high station."

"Sir I don't think now is the right time to be discussing my appointment. Drementhol may be gone by the time we get there."

Kaladin's lip curled as he neared Gundrag's shoulder. "You're quite right. We'd best get a move on."

Gundrag rose, now that Kaladin was secured on his back. Arrax turned and walked out of the already open door. Marcello's smaller green dragon, Sarin was waiting for his rider and when he was mounted, the three dragons made their way to the exit. Sarin and Marcello led the way, Sarin spreading his wings, pushing off from the ground. As Gundrag rose into the air, Kaladin pulled his mask out from his pocket, sliding it down over his face. He was relieved to be in the air once more, even if it was for less than pleasure.

The hours of paperwork were among the most tedious tasks that he had to endure and any break from them where he could spend time with Gundrag were most welcome. They followed the lead of the green dragon, as he rose above the city lights, many of which were now fading from existence for the rest of the evening. The dozens of ballistae paid them no attention, not even swivelling towards them, seeing that they had come from within the city. Their return journey, however, would be more dangerous.

They soon left the city behind, and Kaladin turned to see it behind them. The Haven was among the largest cities he had ever seen and her crystallising lights on the horizon made her shine like a gemstone. Yet where Marcello was leading them was the opposite. Their destination became clear as the mountains rose up around them, and Sarin was already beginning his descent. Drementhol was not a small dragon and needed plenty of space to make himself comfortable. Finding him would present the same challenge as finding any other mountain in this mountain range.

Kaladin kept his eyes forward, expecting the great bronze dragon to rise out of the ground in front of him. Sarin crested another ridge, and as Gundrag followed him over it, Drementhol came into view. He was curled up in a ball, taking up the entirety of the valley, spread across it from one side to the other. If Kaladin had not been paired with Gundrag, he would have wanted to have been paired with the gargantuan beast that was known for his sheer power and size that rivalled any elder dragon. Since the Ashbourne rebellion, Anton had simply underutilised Drementhol.

The wyrmguard dragons flew ahead of Gundrag, and as they neared the ground, Drementhol raised his head. The enormity of his stature darkened the surrounding landscape more than the mountains did as he raised his head, blocking out what moonlight spilled into the valley from above. A thunder like rumble split across the sky, deafening Kaladin.

"Why are you here, Kaladin!"

In response, Gundrag spoke for Kaladin, issuing a roar at first as they came into land beside Drementhol. "We have come to speak to you, Drementhol."

"I can see that, do not treat me like your common dragon. What would you have to talk to me about?"

"It is not I that wishes to speak with you."

"Then bring the Overlord close so that I may hear his pathetic voice properly."

He is in a good mood, Kaladin. I wish you luck.

This is a good mood? Are you serious?

Of course not. Regardless, do not let his power intimidate you.

How could I not? You would not want to face him even at your size.

I merely respect those that came before me. Just because you have certain feelings towards his former rider does not mean you should not treat the dragon with no respect. He is in mourning. How do you think I would feel if I lost you?

You raise a fair point.

Gundrag moved closer to Drementhol and as he did, Drementhol rose from his prone position into a sit. The ground rumble underneath his feet as he moved and Kaladin was glad that he was not at that level, thankful for the safety and elevation that Gundrag provided. As Drementhol continued to rise past Gundrag's head, Kaladin still felt like the size of an ant compared to the giant creature.

"Speak now, Kaladin or forever hold your peace."

"Drementhol! Welcome back to the Haven. We thought you were long gone."

"I am in mourning, what else would you have me do! I needed to leave the Commonwealth for a period."

"We would expect nothing less having lost your rider. I can understand your pain. I would feel much the same way if I lost my rider." Gundrag spoke for Kaladin, and it would have been the exact words that Kaladin would have used if he had been the one to speak.

Drementhol sneered at Gundrag in response. He stood up to his full fight, now towering over Gundrag. Somehow if it was even possible, Kaladin felt smaller. "You know nothing of my pain! I feel as if there is a hole in my chest, my heart torn out and removed. Not even the pain I felt when I lost Vicus comes close to this."

Kaladin raised his hands trying to calm Drementhol. "We meant no offence, Drementhol. We are merely trying to assure you that we have no expectations of you and are just here to speak to you."

"Why have you come then, Overlord? I have only just returned to the Commonwealth and find that I am already over the antics of humans. They have cost me both my promised, and now my rider. I am better off flying to the north and becoming another buried relic in a world full of them!"

"No! We came because there is a great war is coming Drementhol. I can feel it in my bones."

"And I can feel the loss of Anton weighing heavily on my shoulders. What is feeling war coming in your bones supposed to do?"

"The man that caused the death of both your promised and your rider will be the man we are fighting the war against. Will you aid us in our fight against him?"

Drementhol swished his tail behind him as if he was swatting an insect away from his gargantuan body. He flicked his head and his wings unfolded from his back. Gundrag tilted his head away, wanting to protect Kaladin should he rear up and attack. Instead, the attack never came and Drementhol continued to huff.

"You ask me to aid you in your fight when it has already cost me everything? Do you understand what you are asking of me, Kaladin?"

"I do. I would hope that whoever became Overlord after my passing would ask the same of Gundrag should there be an opportunity to avenge me."

"Vengeance is a powerful driving force. I saw it consume many dragons and their riders during the Ashbourne rebellion, and you would ask me to do the same with no guarantee of claiming my revenge?"

"I promise you. If Dalton Ashbourne remains alive, you may have him to dispose of him as you please."

You can't do that, Kaladin. Don't make a dragon, especially Drementhol promises that you cannot keep.

I can keep it, as much as I would like to rip Dalton's head from his corpse.

Drementhol shifted his massive form, and a deep, resonant rumble echoed across the vast landscape, reverberating off distant hills. His eyes, sharp and penetrating, glared down at them with a disapproving intensity, his face marred by a frown that cast shadows over his rugged features, like storm clouds gathering in a darkened sky.

"Do not keep promises that you cannot keep, Overlord. I already do not view your race favourably because of your actions that were taken against Anton. Do not push me further."

Gundrag spoke for Kaladin. "Apologies, Drementhol. We did not mean to. Will you assist us in our fight or not?"

Drementhol turned his scaled head towards the night sky, bronze scales glinting under starlight as he shook his massive horned crown in disapproval. Even from his precarious perch atop Gundrag's ridge, Kaladin could feel the hurricane-force gust that swept from the dragon's cavernous nostrils and wing membranes, the displaced air carrying the unmistakable scent of brimstone and ancient magic that clung to the beast's enormous serpentine body.

"Since you have asked and since you have promised me, vengeance, yes Overlord. I will assist you against Dalton Ashbourne. Do not make me regret this decision."

SEVENTEEN

Elanor tapped her foot against the floor in annoyance as she sat over the edge of the bed. Having the ability to spend the night at the Haven without the stressors of any meant rest and it did not sit right with her, especially when Evor's life was hanging in the balance. Yet she was running out of time, and she did not want to leave here without Kaladin's permission. If he was in the mood, he'd probably chase her down and demand to know what she was doing. The Overlord of the Commonwealth was not exactly the person that she could disclose why she wanted to leave the Haven to.

She felt a hand caress the back of her neck and turned to face Ayr who was sitting behind her. He sat naked, embroiled in the bedsheets, an expression of concern written all over his face. With no words spoken between the two of them, Elanor readjusted herself and found herself pushing her back into him. Ayr scoffed, feeling her weight against him, but his arm that wrapped around her body, otherwise told her that he cared.

Elanor enjoyed his embrace and played into it. He ran his fingers over her breasts, teasing her nipples. Eleanor pulled his hand away, raising it to her mouth. Ayr shuddered as she placed kisses on his hand, feeling his veins underneath her lips.

"Are you alright, Elanor?"

"No, we've got too much to do and not enough time to do it in. I can't think straight, and it is all that is occupying my mind. Even if we do manage to get to Ashenfort before Evor begins to succumb to the scalebane again, how am I going to kill the Dragon Lords?"

"You're forgetting something. I can help you."

"Ayr, I'm not going to ask you to do that. This is my task."

Ayr's lips moved to the back of her neck and Elanor shuddered as he moved her hair to the side, leaving her exposed. By Chilijo that felt good as he breathed into her. Goosebumps erupted all along her skin, down her neck, her back and even down her arms. Ayr's other hand began to snake its way down her spine, sending the goosebumps running even further down her spine.

"You need to remember that my father does not care how the task is completed. If you need me to march in there and help you incinerate the Dragon Lords, I can do that."

"I don't think you understand just how powerful the Dragon Lords are. What if they're with their dragons?"

"Crassus was isolated from Baindussa when I infiltrated his chambers. We could manipulate the scenario with the Dragon Lords as well."

"Yes, but you didn't kill Crassus. Did you?"

Ayr froze behind her, his hand no longer wandering down her back. Instead, it remained in place, just below her shoulder blade, his lips mere inches from her skin. An uneasy silence passed between the two of them before Ayr spoke again.

"How long does Evor have left?"

"Days at the most. Any second we spend here is another second we waste. I need to be moving towards completing the task."

"Then why are you still here, Elanor?"

"Kaladin. You know that if I left, he would hunt me down."

Ayr resumed touching her, his fingers slowly running down towards her waist where they sat for another moment. "Why can't we make him think that we are returning to the Obelisk? You have not seen your mother since we were brought here, have you?"

Elanor shook her head. "No, of course not. It isn't like she could fly here on her own accord with how frail Draxion now is."

"Will Kaladin understand?"

Elanor shrugged. "I doubt it. That man has a hide as thick as dragon scales. The last time he knew heartbreak was when we split, and he has not stopped pining after me since. You've seen him."

Ayr's hand was now on her hip, and Elanor arced her back, raising her hand, caressing the back of his neck. They were close together, their bodies pressed against each other, just like how they had spent the last night together. It felt good to be wanted and not by someone who was simply trying to assert power over her to affirm his own position within the Commonwealth.

"And despite the Obelisk being integral to the safety and security of the Commonwealth, he has not spent time there since his ascension to Overlord."

Elanor was trying to maintain her focus on the conversation as Ayr kissed the back of her neck again. "It is not likely. He seems more focused on what he can do here."

"We need to change his thinking. That's the only way we'd be able to get to Ashenfort without arousing any suspicion."

"You're making this sound so simple."

Ayr chuckled, a warm breath on her back. "I try not to overcomplicate things when they don't need to be. Everything seems easier when I am with you."

"I would like to check one thing before we leave. The library here would be able to tell me if we were to make anymore enemies. If we somehow managed to pull this off I'd rather know if they have any hatchlings. I'd rather not have an entire bloodline hunt us down."

Ayr leaned back from her, and this allowed Elanor to turn. He was staring at her, his hands now once again still as her took hers in his. "You need to remember something, Elanor. I made a promise to you. I will do this for you, for Evor."

"I'm not asking you to. This also isn't for me, it's for Azura."

"It may well be, but without her, I am nothing."

Evor raised his head from the bed that he shared with Azura. Both dragons were mimicking what was happening on the human bed with Evor wrapped around Azura, his larger frame providing her with warmth and protection. It was uncanny for Ayr. Part of him wanted to protect and cradle Elanor, meanwhile the part of his mind that was with Azura wished for the opposite.

"If you manage to succeed, I will be forever in your debt, Ayr. But Elanor is correct. I do not have long. I can feel the poison pulling at me already. Whilst it has not taken hold, it is there."

Elanor could hear the softness in Evor's voice. "We're going to get you cured."

"As long as this is the last of it. I will not be enslaved by Dalton Ashbourne any longer."

"You won't be, Evor. If this is not the final task for him, I will speak to him myself."

Elanor pulled away from Ayr and spun around. "You know where he is?"

Ayr shook his head. "I may have done a few months ago when I left for the Seminary of Fire, but since then, no. Especially now that Dalton has access to Sinibad, he could be anywhere in the Commonwealth."

"We need to find him."

"As does Kaladin. What do you want to do?"

"We need to get dressed. I need to speak to Kaladin and try and find more information about the Dragon Lords."

Ayr scoffed and a smirk tugged at his lips. "Good luck. If you find anything be sure to let me know."

I do not know why, Elanor. Yet something tells me that he is going to do it. I can't help but feel like I can trust him.

I know exactly what you mean.

Watch out.

Ayr opted to wrap his arm around the back of her neck once again. Elanor wanted to get moving, but was drawn in, not wanting to miss an opportunity to say goodbye, despite the little time that they would be apart. Elanor went in at the same time as Ayr did, her eyes closing when she was inches away from his face. Their lips met in a slow and deep, yet longing kiss, their mouths moving around each other, jostling for position. The hairs on the back of her neck stood up again, and Elanor knew where this was going. She indulged in the kiss for a few more seconds before pulling away.

Ayr's eyes darted open just after hers and his hand loosened on her neck. "What was that for? We can keep going."

Elanor shook her head. "Time sensitive task. We need to go!"

You really need to stop doing that in front of me. How would you like it if I treated the little one the same anytime I was in her presence?

It's a little different.

Not to us it is not. You're lucky we just need more space.

Gross, Evor.

How is it gross? She will carry my hatchlings one day. We are promised, after all.

Not today, Evor.

Elanor rolled off the bed as she could feel Evor's passion beginning to rise. She could not look at Azura in the same light either. Shaking her head, Elanor stood up and moved away as Ayr's touch left her body. As per usual their clothes were at the base of the bed, but Elanor wanted a fresh set this morning. She crossed the room as the early morning sunlight filtered in through the large windows that Evor would no doubt soon open as he left to hunt, if he wanted to. He was not feeling hungry, but Elanor would never say no to a hot meal. As she opened the wardrobe, she saw Ayr climb off the bed out of the corner of her eye. He came up behind her, wrapping his arms around her torso.

"What are we doing?"

Elanor wanted to turn to face him to push him away, but she was halfway through pulling a jacket from the rack. "What do you mean, what are we doing?"

"This, us. What does it even mean?"

Now Elanor let go of the jacket and left it hanging on the rack. She turned to face him. It was clear that he wanted reassurance. "We're a pair of riders to promised dragons. What do you mean what are we doing? We're building a connection, Ayr. I rushed a previous relationship, and I don't want to do it again."

"I understand that, but what's the end game?"

"I don't even know what is supposed to be happening in five weeks, let alone five years, Ayr. I could tell you that we are supposed to live a long and happy life together, but I cannot guarantee that. Dalton could attack the Haven tomorrow and one or both of us could die. We just need to live in the moment."

"Live in the moment."

She could tell that it was not the answer that he wanted to hear, but it was the only answer she could give him now. The future was uncertain, and nothing was set in stone. The world had changed significantly in the past month, and she hated to think just how it would look in the next. Ayr let her go and Elanor took the opportunity to push him away, but this time it was gentle. She took advantage of the separation and found a jacket and pair of pants, thrusting them at Ayr.

"Here, wear these."

Ayr took the garments, beginning to throw them on over his underclothes that he had just found. Elanor set about dressing herself as well, and within moments she stood before Ayr, pulling her boots on as the last piece of clothing she needed before she was complete.

"Do you have anything you need to do today?"

"Yeah, I was thinking about being active today. Azura needs her armour refitted."

"Good, well if you go and do that today, I will investigate the library and Kaladin. Hopefully one of those two sources will gift me with an answer about what to do next."

Ayr's eyes narrowed. "I'm ready for whatever you decide."

"Good." Elanor brought him close cupping her hands on either side of his face. The kiss was brief; nothing more than a passing moment shared between the two of them. "I'll see you soon."

I am ready, Elanor.

Excellent. You know where we need to go.

Evor reared his head, pushing open the window with his head. As soon as the glass pane was open, a crisp breeze cut through the room, filling it with fresh morning air. Azura stood up underneath Evor's shadow, extending her body towards Ayr. Evor stepped over towards Elanor and got into position for her to be seated on his back.

Within moments they were in the air and soaring high above the Haven. Unlike the Obelisk, the Haven was more spread out, allowing space between amenities, each facility their own home with their own structure. The journey was quick, Evor angling down towards where the library was situated. As Elanor expected, the entrance was far too small for him to enter the building and just like their usual trips to the library in the Obelisk, Evor had to wait outside.

Elanor snorted at the thought of a fully grown dragon that could breathe fire inside a library. One accident would be all it took for decades and centuries of knowledge to go up in flames. As he settled down to the ground, Elanor patted Evor and thanked him for his service. Evor's gentle hiss filled her mind as she dismounted from his back. He retreated away from the library door and sat himself down as Elanor entered the structure.

It was much the same as the library found within the Obelisk, albeit much larger. The front desk was unoccupied and dozens, if not hundreds of dragon assistants flew overhead. She watched as they circled the high ceiling, all of them a different colour filling the library with different streaks of colour. Elanor made her way to the counter and placed her hand upon it, drumming her fingers into it, creating her own beat that she bopped her head to. With the size of this library there was no chance that she was going to scour through all these books herself.

As she waited for someone to assist her, a small black dragon dropped down from the ceiling and hovered in front of her. It reminded her of Chorru, but this dragon was just one of the many that was in service to the Commonwealth. Amber scales streaked across its back to give it a distinct unique tone.

Elanor, we have guests.

Are you serious?

Take care of what you say.

"Hello! My name is Kalliceus, how can I assist you!"

Elanor smiled at the small dragon and matched its polite tone. Clearly, things worked differently here as there was still no human within sight. "Hello, I'm Elanor. I was wondering if you had any information relating to the Dragon Lords and their dragons."

Kalliceus circled around her head, three times before it came to rest in front of her again. Each time it circled around her, Kalliceus emitted a hum from deep within its belly.

"No, I do not think we do, unfortunately. Only the Overlord can access such records."

"It's important. I need to know sooner rather than later."

Kalliceus barked out loud, something that sounded like a strangled bark. "Well, shittius happenus, Lady Sunfire, but I cannot give you that information. It is against my mandate. If you take issue with it, might I recommend you take it up with a record keeper."

"Are you not a record keeper?"

Kalliceus shook its head. "No, I am merely a servant. As I said that information is outside of my mandate. I wish you luck on your quest. Goodbye."

As Kalliceus rose back towards the ceiling, Elanor remained in her spot, stunned. "Are you fucking serious?"

"Yes, Lady Sunfire, the dragon assistants here are very serious."

Elanor groaned under her breath and turned to greet Kaladin who was stepping inside. His large frame was shrouded as per usual by a dark cloak, today's variant almost as black as night. He removed his mask from his face, tucking it into his vest and he took full measure of the library, nodding with satisfaction.

"What are you doing here, Kaladin?"

"Whilst as Overlord, I never have much, if any spare time, I am making efforts to research the Keeper and her pet dragon. If we ever rid of ourselves of Dalton and his pet, there is no doubt in my mind that we will have to face them."

"I see. And it just so coincides with when I happen to arrive here? Anyone might think you're watching me, Kaladin."

"I don't trust you."

"So, am I wrong?"

Kaladin shook his head. "No, you're not wrong."

"Okay, then I'd like to return to the Obelisk please."

Kaladin frowned, his eyebrows querying her. "The Obelisk? You have everything you need here, why would you want to go back?"

"You might have everything you need here, but I have family at the Obelisk. And business that I would like to finalise there before I throw my life away trying to kill Dalton's dragon."

"I see. And why are you asking me?"

"If I left without your permission, you would hunt me down."

Kaladin pulled back and put his blackened hand into one of his vest pockets. What was happening with it? Was the magic that had blackened it causing him pain, or was it now just a useless limb?

"Yes, however it is very unlike you to ask for permission to do anything."

"I'm a changed woman now. Having been forced together with a promised, I know what it is like to take responsibility of my actions."

"Really? I find this all very convenient."

Now it was Elanor's turn to be curious. "How?"

"If you are to return to the Obelisk, I think it would be wise to accompany you."

"You don't need to hold my hand everywhere I go."

Kaladin went to smile, but instead a pained grimace spread across his face. "I'm not going back there to hold your hand, Elanor. I have not been there for a few weeks and as someone that has a vested interest in its security and wellbeing, I think it would be smart to ensure everything is going as planned. Someone also needs to introduce Barrett as Lord Chairman."

Elanor raised an eyebrow, still suspicious of Kaladin's motives. "So, it serves a dual purpose?"

"I'm not trying to do everything to vex you, Elanor. But if you wish to return to the Obelisk, do so with myself. I will prepare, and we will leave tomorrow morning."

"Sounds good to me."

EIGHTEEN

You know, I wish I could get used to this overnight. It would make my life so much easier.

How is it, Azura? If it is uncomfortable we should have had it changed sooner.

It is much better now, thank you. Some of those pieces were just too small. It is a shame that we need to resort to such barbarian measures.

As long as it helps you stay alive, I think it is worth the sacrifice. I just wish that it would not cause you discomfort.

It was early the following morning, and they were assembled outside the Hall of the Dragon Lords. Ayr and Elanor were not alone, however. Not only were they joined by Kaladin, but once again they were joined by a whole contingent of wyrmguard. They were waiting for the last of the dozen to join them. Judging by both Kaladin and Gundrag's demeanour, they were growing impatient waiting. When the last of the wyrmguard dragons circled overhead, a silver and orange, Kaladin gave the command for them to take flight, throwing his hand up in the air. As one, the wyrmguard dragons rose into the sky, their wings shining in the early morning light.

Ayr was surprised yet happy about this turn of events, even if he knew what was coming. They would be able to move faster than what they had done on their way to the Haven, with Evor and Azura no longer enshrouded in the dragon's maw. It was clear that Kaladin was in a hurry to return to the Obelisk. Now all they had to do was force a stop at Ashenfort so that they could complete their task.

Azura could not tell him how far it would be until they had reached their destination. The time that she had spent in Anton's cage was discombobulating to say the least. However, unlike last time, she was free to fly the journey. Travelling to the tomb of Chilijo and the Frozen Wastelands had been long journeys, but Azura had proven that she could keep up, even if the wyrmguard were flying faster than usual.

As the leagues passed below them, Ayr grew comfortable in the saddle once again. It would have been his preference if they could have had more day's rest, but this was what he had been trained and conditioned for. At first the all too familiar cityscape of the Haven faded from view, giving way to farmland, and then finally the forests and breathtaking landscapes that Ayr enjoyed watching pass underneath him.

The day was calm, Azura's wingbeats the only sound that filled his ears outside the rushing of the wind on either side of his head. His mask and Azura's saddle protected him from the elements and Ayr sat back, ready to endure the flight that would take as long as Kaladin dictated. There was little to do, and Ayr had ensured that he had prepared as much as possible the night before. His bag was tied around the saddle, and he checked on it to ensure that it would not get torn away with the rising winds.

I am looking forward to going home, you know.

As am I, Ayr. I have not been away from the Obelisk in such a long time.

Well, if you and I are ever released from Kaladin's side, now that we are bonded dragon and rider, I'd hoped that we could see the rest of the world.

Careful, you ask for too much. If we serve the Commonwealth, we must abide by their mandates.

To Chilijo's tomb with their mandates. You and I will be a force to be reckoned with. Who is going to stop us?

Ayr smirked as he felt Azura shift underneath him. A jolt of power surged through her body. Nobody.

We need to grow stronger if that is to happen, Azura.

We do. We have time on our side.

There are graveyards full of men who thought they had time.

I am no man.

More time slipped by as Ayr fell back into the saddle. They were making good pace, already flying over what many considered the mid-point of the Commonwealth. Even though the Commonwealth was expansive, outside the major cities it was sparsely populated. Many chose not to live life in a state of constant danger, relying on only their wits and the land to provide for them.

Those that did often had little nearby neighbouring support, even if they were resource rich. All it would take would be for one family member to contract a virus and succumb to it and it would then pass to their whole family. The post Ashbourne rebellion world had shown this to Ayr firsthand. Throughout the day they had passed over as many as half a dozen similarly constructed homesteads. Ayr was willing to wager that they were all abandoned, the overgrowth threatening to claim them.

Dalton had once wanted their family to flee to the land to thrive without Commonwealth support. Dalton's power had meant that it was possible, making some of the more mundane tasks to be more manageable. However, the riders, particularly Anton had suspected that after the battle of Ashenfort his brother would attempt to live out his life in exile like the other hermits.

Upon hearing word that Anton was obliterating any hermit hovels that he had found and was instructing other riders to do the same, Dalton had opted for the family's safety, moving them back to the cities, never staying in one place for long. Despite the constant threat from riders discovering them as they went about their business, the cities were safer and allowed Dalton to begin rebuilding his empire in the shadows of another.

Evor and Elanor do not look comfortable.

Perhaps it is the scalebane. We're unsure of how much time Evor has before it takes over again.

Hmm. I just hope that Elanor can complete her task before it's too late.

I do not want to lose Evor.

Neither do I. What will happen if you fail to continue his bloodline?

That's exactly what will happen, Ayr. If Evor and I do not procreate then his lineage will be gone forever. How many other great black dragons do you see like him?

Not many. I wondered if that was just an issue isolated to the Obelisk.

Azura shook her head underneath him. *Certainly not.*

And what about you? You are the only white dragon that I have seen.

We do not exist anymore for the same reason. It is a miracle that I am compatible with Evor, let alone any other dragon. The stories say that Chilijo cursed us.

Why would one of your own curse you? I thought more white dragons in the sky would have been a good thing.

Not just white dragons, dragons. It is not talked about anymore. Perhaps when we get some time at the Obelisk, we could explore it.

The more I hear about this Chilijo the more I wonder why you view him as a god.

Without Chilijo, dragons would not exist.

I am so very confused right now.

Perhaps Otheria can provide us with some answers. I have been thinking about it ever since our interaction with her.

She's not trustworthy. She and her pet dragon almost incinerated us.

Dragons are far more reasonable than humans are, Ayr. Perhaps you and Kaladin need to sort your differences out before time goes much further.

He almost murdered me in Ashenfort. I'd rather cut off my hand than forge an alliance with him.

I'd hoped you'd say that.

What's your game, Azura?

The same as yours, rider. Wait, look at that. We could be in trouble here.

Ayr looked up at the skyline and saw that storm clouds were growing on the horizon to the south. A pit opened in his stomach as they were no doubt coming from somewhere around the Obelisk, and as the minutes ticked by it was clear they were moving to the north. It was almost impossible for Ayr to tell just how far away they were, but the lightning that was surging from the clouds, despite not able to hear the thunder that accompanied them was daunting.

Where is he going now?

Gundrag was angling himself towards the ground, preparing himself for a landing in the opening in the trees that was coming up ahead. The descent was fast, but it had to be to follow Gundrag. Azura circled around Gundrag several times as the wyrmguard dragons came into land. Gundrag turned his head to the sky and snapped at her, calling for her to land. Azura did as she was told and Arrax was moving to Gundrag's side.

Kaladin sat up out of the saddle, with his mask removed from his face. "I am telling you right now. We can push on through the storm! Our dragons can handle it!"

"It's not worth it, Kaladin! We'd be much better off resting at Ashenfort until it passes. Why would we risk getting shot out of the sky? There will be plenty of opportunity for that if or when we face Dalton Ashbourne in the field."

"Ashenfort, why Ashenfort?"

"Based off our location now, we're only a short distance away. It would take us no more than an hour to get there. You're being ridiculous, Kaladin!"

Gundrag was just as brash as Kaladin however, judging by the silence from the two of them they were deep in conversation with each other. The wyrmguard dared not say anything against Kaladin, even though Ayr full well knew that there was at least one that wanted to.

"I don't want any delays in our arrival to the Obelisk."

"Who's waiting for us, Kaladin? I'd prefer that we arrive in one piece. I do not want the Dragon Lords having to elect another Over-lord within weeks of the last one dying."

Kaladin's jaw clenched shut, the muscles in his face pulling against each other as he realised that Barrett had a point. He turned his head towards the sky once again, his mask resting in his hands. Kaladin twirled the fabric over with an increasingly annoyed expression on his face. The storm was getting closer, inching towards them like an ever-encroaching tide ready to swallow the beach. Lightning was be-ginning to crackle across the sky with increased frequency as Kaladin finally came to his decision.

"We fly for Ashenfort. If we can make it there by the time the storm hits, we will be better off. Get in the air!"

The wyrmguard dragons all roared as they launched skyward. Ayr patted Azura, and once the wingbeats of the wyrmguard had faded as they climbed into the blue abyss, Azura launched from the ground as well. She raced after the wyrmguard, all of whom could have gone faster, if they were not creating a protective barrier around Gundrag and Kaladin. Ayr snorted, finding it ironic that such a powerful figure needed protection, yet even when Anton had held the title, he had always kept wyrmguard near him as well.

Considering Ashenfort was not in sight yet, Ayr wondered if they would be able to make it there before the storm hit. If they did not make it there in time, Ayr did not want to spend time huddling underneath Azura in Kaladin's presence. The Catalyst had been one of the worst times in his life, and he was not willing to revisit that any time soon. Azura was not the fastest of the dragons in their entourage, but she kept pace with most of them.

The sky continued to ignite with a growling fury that soon was shaking with a roar that rivalled that of the dragons. Ayr kept his eyes to it, watching as the flashes of light rocketed down to the ground. Suddenly, he was back in the Catalyst, on top of that mountain, surrounded with the other recruits and their dragons. He remembered the ravenous look in their eyes as Gable had engaged him for the first time, hungry to right whatever wrong he thought the Ashbourne's had brought onto the Commonwealth. He remembered how their faces had changed to horror as Gable was swept off the Catalyst, falling to what Ayr thought was his death. How times had changed. They were no longer here, and yet he was the one that remained.

They kept cutting across the sky, and at long last, Ashenfort came into view. It was still distant, just within the horizon, the back of the city built into a nearby mountain. But as the storm raged in the background, Ayr just wanted to be in the city. Azura, feeling his anxiety about the storm, did what she could to calm him, but the memories of the Catalyst did little to soothe his thoughts.

Ashenfort was increasing in size, but the storm was engulfing everything on the horizon. Ayr could see the rain band now moving across the sky as the wind whipped up, almost knocking him out of his saddle. He leaned forward, as Azura dove towards the ground, picking up her pace, but it was also an attempt to protect him from the elements. The rain was coming down on a forty-five-degree angle and Ayr could almost not see underneath his mask. Azura lent her sight to him, and he could see them swooping over the city walls.

Ayr, even though he was already hanging on, gripped into the saddle with all his strength. He trusted Azura, but she was coming in far too quickly. A bolt of lightning ruptured through the air right beside them and Ayr almost fell sideways from his saddle. Another bolt shattered the sky just in front of them, scorching the earth in the city and causing Azura to pull up. She did so with millimetres to spare.

Can you stop them, Ayr?

The lightning? Are you serious?

We need to land!

Quickly before we're taken out of the sky!

Now it was Azura's turn to panic. They had flown over the walls of Ashenfort, but the city was much smaller than Ayr remembered and now Azura was trying to find a place where she could land. Ashenfort was a beautiful city, and courtyards littered its surroundings with plenty of open space. Yet with the lightning frequency, nowhere felt safe. Azura passed by three courtyards, before she saw one that fit her liking.

The wyrmguard dragons on the other hand were falling from the sky one by one as they found a resting place. Somehow all of them were evading the lightning that seemed closer to Azura than any other. Azura lined up her descent, but as she was ready to come into land, an enormous shadow cut across her path. Ayr turned his head, glaring at the dragon that had cut them off, pushing Azura out of the way. It was none other than Gundrag. Azura turned away from him, almost into another bolt. She maintained good control and was not phased, completing a full circle before coming around again to land in behind Gundrag. He turned his head as he lowered it to allow Kaladin to hurry off his back.

"It appears you are too slow, little one."

"I would have been fine if you could have just waited a few seconds."

"Hesitation is what kills dragons and their riders."

Ayr had no time to waste, and slid off Azura, her scales and the shape of her body acting like a water slide that helped him get down. More lightning struck around them and Ayr darted underneath Azura's wing for protection. They had landed near one of the entrances to the cliffs, however this entrance was only large enough to fit humans inside it. The arching gateway called to them, and as Kaladin made it underneath with the assistance of Gundrag, Ayr had a sudden need to get there as well.

Evor is safe.

Good. Let's join him then.

Ayr started forward, and Azura raised her wing over him in a protective blanket that ensured that he would not be struck by the lightning as he ran. They were underneath the cover of the archway after a quick sprint from Ayr saw him to safety. The lightning continued to fork into the ground as Kaladin stood side by side with Ayr. The two dragons huddled into the wall, trying to avoid the storm as best they could. Unsure of where the tunnel led, Kaladin stood back and folded his arms across his chest.

"I'm glad we made it."

Ayr did not warrant him with a response instead opting to turn away and watched as Azura made herself comfortable. The very few lightning strikes that came near her, now that he was safe, did not phase her. Unsure of what awaited them in Ashenfort, Ayr pulled his riding mask from his face and waited for the storm to pass.

NINETEEN

Elanor was on edge. The storm raged around them like a tempest unleashed. She peered out from underneath the shelter that Evor had delivered her to. She did not want to venture inside, not at least until she had some sort of backup that could come inside with her. Despite Ashenfort having been reclaimed since the rebellion, dangers still lurked in its nooks and crannies. The fact that Kaladin had brought the Dragon Lords here to hide was absurd. Evor stood over the door, protecting it with his body, but even with his enormous form cradled over the door, the wind was still ripping through the gaps he left. The rain was also becoming torrential and becoming a problem as it pooled in over him.

Evor, we need to find a better place to wait out the storm!

It is too dangerous to move, Elanor. This will have to do.

Elanor sighed. Evor spoke the truth, as the lightning was becoming even more frequent. If it was not for his body dulling some of the sounds from outside, the thunder that accompanied the lightning would have been deafening. Another lightning bolt shot down and cracked across Evor's back. He threw his head back, roaring into the sky.

Evor! You need to go!

I am fine. Lightning does not affect me.

Clearly that did. Seek shelter.

I do not want to leave you, Elanor.

I will be fine. Now go!

Evor obeyed her and rose to his feet, standing up as another lightning bolt broke across his body. He roared again, but lumbered upwards, searching for a shelter that would keep him protected. Elanor turned away from the opening and towards the shut door that would have been her protection from the elements. She could still sense Evor, he was not far away, only a few hundred meters by the time he settled down underneath a rocky outcrop. He felt anxious as the storm continued to rage around them. With her protection from Evor gone, the doorway was her only option. Elanor moved towards it and drew her sword as she pushed against the door.

Just like she expected, Ashenfort was not the fortress that it once was. Whilst there had been some effort to restore it to its former glory after Kaladin and Gundrag had gutted it, there was still much work to be done. As the lightning flashed around her, Elanor could see the scorch marks left by Gundrag on the walls and could only imagine the horrors that those that had occupied the city had experienced in the war.

She moved into the empty structure with caution her sword afloat in front of her. Elanor reached into the pits of Evor's strength grasping at what power he would let her have. Evor was accommodating and gave her what she needed, and a naked flame appeared in Elanor's palm. She held it out in front of her illuminating the room and she had stumbled into was what appeared to be a large kitchen.

There were large ovens stood side by side, with each of them all emptied, their glass shattered all over the floor. What were once benches lined the room and in the middle of it all stood a tall fireplace that stretched up to the ceiling. Elanor paced around it, holding the firelight towards it, inspecting it. It was like the fireplaces of the Obelisk, but due to the scorched surroundings of the kitchen, it held nothing but charred insides. As Elanor completed a full circle around the chimney, she heard a rustle that was not the thunderous roar from outside. She held her firelight up next to her face and peered out into the darkness.

We are not alone here, Elanor. Someone draws near.

Who?

I do not know. Stay alert.

The rustle interrupted her again and Elanor flung the flame over her head. She caught something flicker overhead, but this time the rustling was replaced by a beating of small wings. In the firelight something moved over the fireplace and Elanor through the fire towards it, only for a surge of fire to come back at her. The flames died as quickly as they had shot at her, a hissing coming from the direction of the fire.

"Lady Sunfire. I trust that your task that Dalton gave you is going well?"

Elanor snorted and shook her head. She conjured another flame with her magic, holding this one afloat and she found Chorru well out of her sword's reach. He clung to the wall like a four-legged spider, hanging down from above, staring at her.

"You know that it is not. If I had managed to kill the Dragon Lords by now, news would have spread across the Commonwealth."

Chorru slinked his way down the fireplace, making his presence even more known to her. He was camouflaged in the darkness, but his eyes glowed in Elanor's light.

"Do I need to remind you of our arrangement?"

"No. The arrangement is very straight forward."

"Good."

"As soon as I discover where the Dragon Lords are hiding. They're in this city, are they not? Ironic, considering the crimes that took place here many years ago."

"Dalton knows this. Why do you think he sent me here?"

"How did you know? There's no way you would have beaten us here."

Chorru's eyes twinkled, and the small dragon's tongue flicked in and out of his mouth. "Dalton has spies everywhere."

"Who? I told nobody!"

Chorru just smiled at her in return. "You told his son, didn't you?"

Fear jolted down Elanor's back like a lightning bolt had struck her. "How do you know that?"

Chorru's smile was still spread across his face. "I didn't. You two are the riders of promised dragons. It was an assumption that you've proven correct. Well done, Elanor. I can read you like a book."

"You need to fuck off before I put this sword in your brain."

Chorru remained unmoved, almost mocking her with the way his eyes darted around at her. He was manic, trying to take in every part of the visible room. "I trust that your preparations are going well then."

"Yes, they are. The task will be completed soon."

"Excellent." Chorru's voice became a hiss as his tongue once again flicked in and out of his head like a snake. "Dalton is watching with great interest."

"If Dalton wanted to come and speak to me himself, that would be much appreciated. I am sick of him hiding in the shadows behind a servant."

"And what makes you think I am hiding, Elanor?"

Another jolt of pure fear shot down Elanor's spine as she heard the voice from behind her. She had only heard it a handful of times prior, but with Dalton's smooth pronunciation of words, along with the way that he weighed them was unique. Elanor closed her eyes, praying that she was hearing things and that Chorru had learnt how to project and change his voice.

But with the soft orange light that she could see through her eyes filling the room she doubted that Chorru had the power to manipulate it. The hissing, scratching sounds that he made were far too removed to be anything but his voice. A dragon, even one as small as Chorru was extremely difficult to replicate or for them dragons themselves to change. Dalton was very much real.

Evor...

What would you like me to do, Elanor? If I act against him, he could end us.

Just be ready. I don't think he will do anything to me. He wants something from me. He could ask anyone to kill the Dragon Lords.

"Are you speaking to your dragon, Lady Sunfire? What does the mighty Evor want to do? Rip me limb from limb to protect you?"

"No, Dalton."

"Open your eyes so I can look into them as you lie to me. I had a dragon that would have done that for me once."

"Do you wish to do me harm?"

Something light touched her face, and Elanor recoiled, flashing her eyes open. Dalton had appeared in front of her, somehow not ushering a sound. Was this an illusion? The touch had been all too real. Dalton took a step forward, his hand still outstretched. Elanor tried to dart away, but he was too fast for her. Dalton caught her, grabbing her by the throat and Elanor froze in place. Her muscles refused to respond when all she wanted to do was kick and scream and fight back against the man that had executed her father.

Elanor!

"Stop."

There was no anger and no malice in his voice. Just control. Dalton stared at her, his gaze intense and powerful. For a moment, Elanor thought she was staring back at a reflection of Ayr, except this face had none of the boyish charm and youthful exuberance that Ayr carried. This was a face more rugged, a face that had experienced hardship and loss. Yet there was no denying that Ayr was Dalton's son.

"I came to give you a gift if your task was completed."

"You know it isn't."

"And I have no doubt that the Overlord wants to move you along as soon as the storm is over."

"You'd be correct, Dalton."

"Then I'd suggest you hurry. Your time here is limited."

Elanor stuck her chin out as Dalton continued to pace around her. "What do you want, Dalton. You would not have come all this way just to gloat. Did you bring Sinibad or one of your other servants?"

"The others, the boy that Ayr made fall off the Catalyst. He awaits my arrival just outside the city. And before you think about it, do not send Evor after him. I want to confirm something."

"What?"

Dalton did not speak, instead Elanor felt a jab at her neck, just underneath his hand. It was quick, the pain lasting no more than a second. Dalton withdrew at last, with a small red bubble held between his thumb and forefinger.

"What do you want from me, Dalton?"

"Control, Elanor."

"Control? You already own me!"

Dalton turned away from her like he could no longer hear her. Instead, he was engrossed staring at the small bubble of her blood that he had drawn. It sat floating between his fingers, his magic keeping it suspended in place. The spell that he had cast around it was unlike anything that Elanor had seen apart from control and power that Crassus had. That was only because of Baindussa. Dalton had no dragon bonded to him.

"I want to confirm your lineage."

"My lineage? Why would you need to do that? Weren't you the cowardly piece of shit that tore my father down during the night?"

Dalton stopped and looked back over his shoulder. A smirk washed over his mouth, and he licked his lips. "Like I would give anyone else the privilege of killing one of the men that stopped me at the peak of my powers. He took my betrothed from me."

This was beginning to get ridiculous. For the third time since their conversation had started, more fear crept down Elanor's spine. She took a moment's silence to consider what Dalton said.

"Your betrothed? You mean my mother?"

For the first time in the conversation, Dalton's expression changed to one of sorrow. "Yes, Grace."

"She's so old."

"You don't remember her before the rebellion, do you, Elanor? She was beautiful once. What she did to Draxion was inexcusable. All in the idea that they could use the magic to defeat me and the army of riders I had at my back. You should ask her about it. Crassus and Baindussa had no right extending their life as much as they did."

"She was his wife and Draxion was Baindussa's promised. What were they supposed to do? Let them die?"

Dalton's eyes darkened. "Yes. Dragons are not supposed to be in servitude to humans of the Commonwealth."

Elanor snorted. "Was your rebellion solely built on that lie? Or was it the pursuit of my mother? If it's the latter, you're sounding a lot like Kaladin."

"The new Overlord? The one that pines after you? Him and I are nothing alike."

"I think that you're mistaking the situation, Dalton. This is not the same as your first rebellion. You are lurking in the shadows."

"All in good time, Elanor. You are not prepared for what's next. Complete your task."

"And if I don't?"

Dalton turned on his heel once again and clicked his fingers. "I should not have to explain that to you. Chorru, come, we're done here."

Elanor remained stagnant on her heels, watching as Chorru leapt over her head and sailed down to Dalton's outstretched arm. Chorru landed on him like a parrot and then proceeded to crawl up his arm.

"You're running out of time, Elanor. Finish the job before I have to."

She stood transfixed, watching as Dalton disappeared, slinking around through the ajar door at the end of the room. It was as if he vanished into thin air, conjuring his magic around him once again. Elanor grit her teeth as she slid her sword back into her sheath.

We cannot trust him.

We need to kill the Dragon Lords. That is your task, is it not?

If their dragons are nearby, I do not know how we are going to achieve that feat. Whilst they are old, their magic is still powerful. I cannot kill them by myself.

We don't need to kill their dragons.

The storm will be our greatest ally in its ability to assist us with this task. Kaladin and the wyrmguard will be distracted.

But we don't know where they are!

Oh, Elanor. You seem to forget who you're bonded with. I was raised in this city for many years before I was transferred to the Obelisk. There are only a handful of places that the Dragon Lords could hide.

Take me there then.

It is not safe.

I don't care. This is for your benefit, Evor. I will walk underneath you.

Evor cut the communication between them and Elanor moved from the room, making her way outside. Part of her expected to see Dalton waiting for her, his arms held over his chest, smirking at her, with Chorru over his shoulder. Her fear was not realised as she stepped outside, but that did not mean that she could not feel his presence. He was in the air around her, as if he was part of the lightning and the thunder. She wished that she could cast a spell, wiping his scent free from her nostrils, but no such thing existed.

The ground shook as Evor was making his way towards her, and she could see the distain written all over his face. Lightning struck the ground around him, not phasing him as he stormed forward.

Where is Azura?

She is safe.

How do you know, Evor? Where are they? Can they help us?

She is speaking to me. They are with Kaladin right now, somewhere deeper within the city.

And where do you think the Dragon Lords are?

Nearby, close to them. If we are going to make this happen, we will need to be swift, however we will also need a distraction.

"Have you decided how you're going to complete your task, Elanor?"

Elanor almost jumped out of her skin. Dalton's voice came from behind her. She turned, trying to control her anger, not lashing out and stabbing at the bane of all her problems with her sword. She instead chose to lash out with her tongue instead.

"No, I haven't! Are you lingering to offer me assistance?"

Dalton's smile spread across his lips. It seemed warm and genuine despite the pouring rain that was encroaching upon their space. The rain continued to teem down but Dalton raised his hand toward the sky and a moment, the rain slowed.

"I don't know, am I?"

"You conjured the storm?"

Dalton's smile did not fade. "This was never going to be just a one-person job. They call me mad, not stupid. I did not almost topple the Commonwealth by sheer luck alone. The storm was my doing."

Elanor did what she could to keep her jaw from falling to the floor. How was Dalton so powerful that he could summon this tempest on his own? Sinibad had to be helping him, but something told her that he was alone with his magic. They would know if the giant elder dragon was nearby, his presence was impossible to miss through either the ground quaking or the sky shaking.

"So, what are you proposing, Dalton?"

"I will take to the air and give something for the Overlord to chase. You find my son and the Dragon Lords. Together you will rid them from this place."

"Are you going to kill the Overlord?"

Dalton chuckled with a rumble that rivalled the thunder. "If I did, that would leave nobody reputable to report my activities to the rest of the riders. If they will not join me, I want them afraid."

"You want riders to join you?"

"My goals are not simply to turn the dragons against their riders, Elanor. The entirety of the Commonwealth must see itself for what it is and for what they have done to thousands across it. Now go."

TWENTY

Ayr. Evor is trying to reach us with a message from Elanor.

Elanor? What does she say?

Dalton's here.

The two words sent a shiver down Ayr's spine, and he peered out from underneath his hiding place as if Dalton was the sun beaming down upon him. Kaladin was still nearby, however with his back to Ayr. He had his head tilted as if he was speaking to Gundrag as well. Ayr continued to watch Kaladin as he conversed with Azura.

Here, what do you mean he's here?

He just spoke with Elanor about her task.

And what did he say?

Evor wants to know where we are. We need to do it now. Can you get away from Kaladin?

Ayr flicked his eyes towards where Kaladin still stood. Kaladin looked back at him as well. He started stepping towards Ayr, his mind still clearly somewhere else until he neared Ayr.

"What are you doing, Ashbourne?"

"Nothing."

"Good, then I need you to stay here. I will return."

"Why, what's going on?"

"Nothing you need to be concerned about. Your father has been sighted."

"My father? What's he doing here?"

Kaladin's face twisted into an unpleasant grimace. "I don't care. Hopefully I can kill him, at last."

Ayr scoffed, laughing. "Good luck with that. The Commonwealth has been trying for years."

Gundrag's roar interrupted him, shaking the sky like the thunder that came from above. Kaladin pushed pass him and out into the rain. Gundrag's footsteps reverberated the air around them and he came into view. He lowered himself towards the ground and despite the lightning still striking the ground around them, Kaladin climbed onto his back, lowering his mask over his face as he climbed. If a lightning bolt struck him, he would be unprotected. Gundrag's eye passed over Ayr and he snarled, rising into the stormy sky.

Lightning continued to strike around Gundrag, Kaladin unmoving as he reached his saddle. Ayr watched them rise and with only a few giant wingbeats, Gundrag had vanished from view. No sooner than Gundrag had vanished from sight, Ayr reached out to Azura again.

Kaladin's gone. Where are you, Azura?

Coming, rider.

No sooner than the words had entered his head, Azura appeared, crashing down to the ground with all the urgency of a racehorse bolting from the start gate. Her wings were almost caught underneath her body as she scrambled to stand upright, her eyes wide with anticipation and perhaps fear.

Hurry!

Ayr sprinted towards her as she lowered herself to the ground. He scrambled up her leg and side like his life depended on it. She turned her head to watch him make his ascent, waiting until he was seated in the saddle, ready for take-off.

What's going on Azura?

Dalton is leading Kaladin and the wyrmguard away. We need to find the Dragon Lords.

Where are they?

Evor knows.

Azura kicked off from the ground, and as she did, Ayr turned his head, hearing another dragon behind them. He was ready to see Gundrag, already on the way back to them, but instead, saw Evor barrelling towards them. Gundrag was nowhere in sight, already swallowed by the stormy sky. Evor roared and then soared past them, sailing overhead. Azura turned her head and followed him as he tore around the side of the mountain that Ashenfort backed into.

They chased Evor, and Ayr had seen Ashenfort like he had never seen it before. He had spent months within the city's walls, when it had once been a bustling metropolis before Kaladin had come. If the Dragon Lords were not his main priority, Ayr would have turned Azura in the air, chasing after where Kaladin and Gundrag had gone. The storm would be the perfect cover in knocking them from the sky once and for all. As much as his heart desired it, only fuelled by Azura, they flew around Ashenfort. Evor picked out one of the darkened pockets on her side as his landing point.

He moved towards it, lightning missing him by mere inches once again as he neared the mountain. Against the scorched earth of the undercity, the summit of Ashenfort was stunning, showing what it could truly be if the Commonwealth decided to restore what had once been its crown jewel to its former glory. The bleached white mountaintop stood out from the surrounding darkness like a lightning bolt.

Evor shot into the mountain, folding his wings to ensure that he was small enough to enter it. Azura was only a few wingbeats behind him, not needing to do anything to her wings to slip inside. Evor pulled up, attaching himself to the opposite wall of the mountain, hanging over the void that descended into darkness. Azura followed him, landing on the wall beside him. Evor turned his head, his black scales making him almost vanish into the darkness. All Ayr could see were his eyes.

Evor spoke with a rare soft tone, one that barely sounded louder than a whisper on the wind. "The Dragon Lords are close. I do not know how much time Dalton will give us. We must move."

It was not enough information for Ayr. "What plan do you have, Evor? How are we going to kill them?"

"If we do not. I will become crippled. I have nothing to lose."

Ayr raised an eyebrow. "You're going to kill five other dragons?"

Evor shook his mighty head. "We are expecting assistance. They are old and this mountain is ready to come down at any moment, thanks to the Overlord. Come."

Evor opened his wings once again, and pushed off from the wall, falling down the chasm that was open beneath them. As they followed him, Ayr could still not see the bottom. It was only when Evor's wings started beating that Azura slowed down. Ayr had not spent much time inside the mountain, and he had no idea where they were. At this point they had to be beneath the city. The darkness was all enshrouding. Ayr and Azura trusted that Evor would not lead them astray and as they kept falling, Evor hit the ground. Azura adjusted her angle and landed beside them in a long corridor that had a dim glowing light along it.

"We're here. Follow me, little one."

Evor stood tall in the corridor, the height of it just taller than he was, the crest on top of his head scraping against the ceiling. Everything about this corridor reminded Ayr of the Obelisk all the way down to its colouring. As Evor scraped his head against the ceiling, pieces of it came loose, rubble dropping to the floor around them. Azura darted around the wreckage, doing what she could to protect from its fall.

A tall double door that appeared to be made of steel stood in their way, even if it was only just ajar. Evor pushed against it, and as he did, Ayr heard a sound from behind them. Loose rocks tumbled down the chasm. Ayr frowned. Even Evor had not made that many loose stones tumble. He heard a vacuum that sounded like a dragon was drawing in a breath. Then a flutter of wings like a pack of bats descended the chasm, and dozens of wyvern were swarming in the corridor.

Stay calm, Ayr. We can get through this.

The wyvern continued to swarm, out of reach of Evor and Azura's fiery breaths like they were waiting for something. Then from the pack, one wyvern emerged with a rider on its back. The wyvern cut through to the front of the pack and the faint outline of the rider raised their hand. Ayr could hear Evor snarling beside him, an orange glow coming from his closed jaws. As the wyvern drew nearer, Ayr could now make out the features of the rider on its back. He rolled his eyes, seeing Dalton emerge from the darkness as Evor's snarls subsided.

"What are you doing here?"

"Thought you could use the help."

"I thought Kaladin was chasing you across the sky."

Dalton's lopsided grin spread across his face. "A simple illusion. That troll wouldn't know proper magic if it bit him on the arse."

"Did you really need us if you were going to pull this trick?"

Dalton laughed. "The wyvern are basic beasts that are only going to convince Kaladin that it was me. I would not want the blame solely on you, now, would I?"

Elanor sat up in her saddle. "If you attack us..."

"The wyvern are under my control. Fear not, Elanor. You're far too valuable for that."

"Then why are we standing around here. Should we not complete this task?"

Dalton gestured with his raised hand. "Evor knows where he is going. Lead on."

I do not trust him, Ayr.

Neither do I. Something doesn't feel right.

If those wyverns get too close I will incinerate them.

With another rumble from his chest, Evor turned away from Dalton and continued down the corridor. Azura, scowled at the wyvern, and Ayr could feel her uncomfortable underneath him. Doing as she had instructed, Ayr turned in the saddle, keeping an eye on the wyvern that were behind them. Dalton kept his hand raised and the wyvern advanced behind him. Ayr shook his head, unable to believe him. Dalton was more powerful than he had ever let on.

Are you seeing this?

Do I want to?

No, probably not.

Of course I can see it, Ayr. I can see everything through your eyes. It is terrifying and something I would rather not think about. If your father willed it, he could have us shredded to pieces in a heartbeat.

I know. That's why I'm not willing to do anything against him at this point.

When does it end then?

When we make it end, Azura.

I look forward to the downfall of Dalton Ashbourne.

They followed Evor as he continued down the corridor. After what seemed like leagues, he started to slow down as more light filtered into the corridor. Up ahead, the corridor opened into a massive chamber, one that stretched as far as the eye could see with its edges the only reprieve from its expansiveness. Ayr stared around at the empty space that had clearly been constructed with dragons in mind. They were well and truly underneath the mountain now. Had this been one of the places that Dalton had vanished to when Ayr had been too young to understand what was going on around him?

Ayr saw Dalton's eyes light up in recognition, but otherwise he portrayed no emotion. There was an eerie silence behind him, considering the amount of wyvern that were moving out of the corridor behind them. Ayr turned away from Dalton at last, and continued to take in the chamber they were in. Straw lined the archways high above, with balconies jutting out over the lower floor. As they moved under the balconies, Ayr looked up and saw that this chamber was alive with dozens of smaller, mostly black dragons that he first mistook from wyvern.

Was this where the Commonwealth brought some of the library assistants and other small dragons from that remained unbonded? The small dragons shrunk away as the pack of wyvern passed underneath them, opting to flee to where they had a better vantage point, and with the relative safety of having something between them.

Before long, the chamber narrowed and amongst the straw clad balconies and dragons watching on a new platform appeared, rising out of the ground. Behind it stood two dragons, one a royal blue and the other an onyx that rivalled Evor that Ayr had only seen briefly outside of the hall of the Dragon Lords, and he knew they were in the right spot. Then the Dragon Lords rose from behind the platform one at a time.

First came the blue clad Alexandria. She looked frailer than she had done in their previous encounter, her flesh seeming almost ready to peel itself away from her body. Next came Roderick, and despite being broad chested looked much the same. No more than a step behind him came Adonis, who despite his age seemed to be the most alive of the three. Another woman stepped out from behind their shadows, yet she had not spoken during the trial and Ayr did not know who she was.

Each of them was old and powerful, yet despite their power, Ayr could feel something waning on them. Something was different compared to the last time that Ayr had seen them. It was almost as if their dragons were no longer providing them with all the power that they could, and their aura was depleted. Alexandria being at the forefront of the group was the first to speak.

"Ah, Elanor Sunfire, Ayr Ashbourne, I did not think that we would be seeing you here. Why have you come with a pack of wyvern?"

"We were told of your presence here and thought that it would be time to return you to the Haven."

A grimace spread over Alexandria's fading face. The mere movement of her lips seemed to exhaust her just that little bit more. She raised her hand, gesturing towards the lady that Ayr did not know. "Helda, you have the gift of foresight, read her mind."

Helda was dressed in an all-black veil that covered her from head to toe. There were few discerning features that Ayr could see apart from her eyes. Judging by her slow movements, she too was old, held together by only the deep purple dragon that emerged from the shadows. As it stepped closer, she raised her head, her eyes wide with fear.

"They seek to kill us!"

Alexandria scoffed with a laughter that filled the chamber. "Kill us? They have two dragons."

Ayr heard a movement from behind him and turned his head to see Dalton moving around from behind Azura. The wyvern was only half the size of Azura, and she would have blocked it from view. Yet how the Dragon Lords could not detect Dalton was beyond him. His power radiated from him like the sun penetrating through dark storm clouds on a rainy day.

"They may only have two dragons, but I thought it would be fun if I tagged along."

The mood in the room shifted on a dime. At first, the Dragon Lords appeared as if they did not recognise Dalton, but as he moved into the light, their demeanour became more certain. Each of the Dragon Lords turned their necks to get a better look, and then withdrew as if wishing they had not, like evil itself had thrown itself on their doorstep.

"Dalton Ashbourne. Overlord Kaladin brought us here to get away from you."

Dalton bowed, a smile curving over his lips. "Yet here I stand."

Alexandria could have spat venom at him with the dark tone in her voice. "Yet here you stand. What do you want?"

Dalton raised his hand and gestured back towards the wyvern that were behind him. "I would have thought that it was obvious. All four of you were instrumental in destroying my rebellion. I came here to send a message."

"And what message might that be?"

"Dearest Alexandria, I thought you were always the sharpest of the Dragon Lords. I thought it was obvious. I want your heads on a pike. The Commonwealth needs to know that nowhere is safe from me."

Roderick stepped forward and he raised his hand, wiping it in the air in front of his face. Ayr saw a shimmer of magic before it disappeared once more. "We hoped that you would see the irony of coming to this place."

"It's not lost on me, don't worry, Roderick. In fact, I find it rather fitting. Now come, it is time for a new generation to take their place at the head of the Commonwealth."

"You lie, Dalton. That's all you have done your entire life. That is what your rebellion was built on after all."

"Helda. You're smarter than that. Look into my mind and tell everyone here that I am lying. I'll give you full access, I don't give a shit anymore."

Helda turned her nose up at Dalton. "I can see you have at least brought two traitors with you."

The rest of the Dragon Lords chuckled in unison. Alexandria was the most confident of the Dragon Lords, despite their situation being dire. "And they will be dealt with in due process. It appears we made an error."

Roderick nodded beside her. "They should have been executed on the spot."

Dalton groaned, unwilling to play any games. "Again, Helda. I implore you. Look into my mind. Tell me my intentions."

Helda raised her hand towards Dalton, and Ayr could already feel the energy bubbling from within Dalton.it was like he was a conduct for everything around him from the wyvern to the other small dragons sitting up in the rafters. Helda took a step back, her eyes opening wide as she realised what Ayr had far too late.

"Defend yourselves!"

As one, the dragons behind the podium roared, their roars echoing off the enclosed walls. Ayr cringed as he covered his ears to protect his hearing as the wyvern roared back. They surged forward like a black tide, as one, all of them under Dalton's command. The Dragon Lords had their hands full, as dozens upon dozens of wyvern leapt into the air. Azura turned, as the large blue dragon reared its head back, fire spitting from its jaws. The first of the wyvern that had attacked were swallowed by the flames, howling as they were engulfed.

Evor surged forward, engaging the black dragon, Vorrax with Elanor firmly seated in her saddle. The chamber was large enough to accommodate both of them launching into the air. With Vorrax occupied the remaining wyvern swarmed the remaining three dragons. Alexandria's blue snapped at Azura who dodged the blow as she sailed past its head. However, she did not miss with her tail swipe. The blow was powerful, and even though Ayr had not been hit by it, he still felt the concussing effects of the strike.

Azura yelped in pain as she was struck, and she tumbled out of control, falling from the air. Ayr did everything he could to brace for the impact as the floor rushed up to greet them. Azura regained control of her flight, just before she made impact with the ground and spun on the tiles at her feet. Ayr jolted in the saddle but was otherwise unharmed. Azura snarled up at the larger dragon.

If we sever the bond, we can cripple them.

Right, get in the air.

But what are you going to do?

They're powerful, but between Dalton and I we can kill them. I just need you providing support. Keep their dragons away from us.

Ayr!

We knew what we signed up for when we said we'd help Elanor with this task. Do you trust me?

With all my heart.

Then take flight, Azura!

Ayr leapt from the saddle as dozens of wyvern all soared overhead, angling to attack Alexandria's blue dragon. Azura retreated, shrinking in size as some of their talons came close to her head. Ayr slid from Azura and onto the ground without so much as breaking a sweat. He drew his sword from its sheath, not that it would do him much good against the dragons that were fighting against the wyvern. All it would take would be one misstep from the creatures and he would be flatter than a pancake.

Dalton stood at the base of the platform that the Dragon Lords stood on. Each of them had their hands raised, with a shield around them. Dalton was working overtime, magic pouring from his fingers as he tried to puncture the shield that the Dragon Lords had conjured. Sweat was pooling on his brow. It was evident to Ayr that between the control of the wyvern, his illusion outside and whatever other countless spells that he was trying to maintain, that Dalton was overexerting himself. The Dragon Lords were winning the fight where their dragons were losing it.

The wyverns were all beginning to tear at the dragons, the chamber allowing them more manoeuvrability than their larger cousins. Fire ripped through the air, engulfing dozens of wyvern at any given time, but Dalton had amassed an army. Evor kept Vorrax busy, trading blows with him. Vorrax was no stranger to fang and claw combat, but he was losing. Evor was younger, faster and stronger and with his rider on his back, unstoppable.

Vorrax swooped in aiming for Evor's throat, their teeth gnashing against each other as they clashed. Evor darted away, leading Vorrax into an attack that led to nothing but open space. Except Evor over-reached. Vorrax hit him and with the hit something went sailing from Evor's back.

"Elanor!"

Azura! Fuel me so that we can end this!

It was like a damn had burst open somewhere in Ayr's mind. Time slowed down and Ayr dropped his sword, as she arced through the open void above Evor. She would have broken bones and shattered organs from the impact of Vorrax, but if she hit the ground falling from that height, there would be nothing left of her. As soon as he called it, he felt the power surging through his veins, unlike anything he had ever felt before. With Evor unable to catch her, Ayr slowed Elanor's fall, making it appear as if she was moving in slow motion.

Ayr flung his hand towards Vorrax who was now retreating from Evor. Something snapped inside Ayr's mind and forked blue-light lightning surged towards Vorrax. The dragon took the blow on the chest, except this was not any lightning. Vorrax groaned as the lightning engulfed his entire body, sustained by Ayr's force.

Roderick screamed in paint, echoing the Vorrax's and Roderick tried to lash out with magic of his own. The Dragon Lord's barrier broke, and Dalton pressed the advantage. Ayr flung his left hand up towards them, and more lighting erupted from it at his command. His power, combined with Dalton's was too much for the Dragon Lords to fight back against. Despite their casting, Ayr's lightning began to seep through the Dragon Lord's defences. Roderick was the first to fall, crumbling at the same time as Vorrax underneath the weight of Ayr's magic.

For the time being, the remaining Dragon Lord's kept their barrier strong, through the statue that was Adonis. Ayr directed his power towards him next, the lightning forking out away from the barrier and sneaking into the gaps that Roderick falling had left. Adonis could not keep Ayr back and the lightning began to overpower him. His dragon started to roar in pain, as it was not only being struck by Ayr's sustained lightning, but the wyverns had now made their mark.

With Adonis falling, his body crackling as Ayr's magic surged through him, the last of the Dragon Lords were easy pickings. Ayr directed all his power towards Helda and Alexandria. They resisted, but against the combined power of both Ayr and Dalton, their barriers were already crumbling. Their dragons were no different. Evor slammed into Helda's green dragon, but Ayr redirected his energy towards her. Much like Vorrax before her, Helda's dragon was overpowered, both by Ayr, Evor and the wyvern that swarmed her. Rider and dragon fell together, leaving only Alexandria.

Dalton raised his hand waving it towards Ayr. "Stop."

"Havar!" Alexandria called to her blue dragon that was fighting off the horde of wyvern. It was a sad situation, the smaller creatures beginning to get on top of him. He roared with vigour that was matched by Evor a moment later. Ayr lowered his hands and felt the lightning fade. It was good, he needed the reprieve, yet Azura kept pumping him full of magic. The task was not completed yet.

Dalton lowered himself to the ground, into a crouch, a smirk sliding over his lips. Sweat continued to drip from his brow as he reached out to touch Alexandria, but he was stopped short by her barrier that was almost invisible. "And then there was one, Alexandria."

"Exile was too good for you, Dalton. We should have had you incinerated by dragon fire!"

"It was always my intention to come back after you ruled to have me expelled from the Obelisk. I am most surprised that you and Helda both did not have that hindsight. You could have stopped everything from happening."

"Fate is a funny thing."

"Indeed, it is." Dalton gestured towards Ayr, beckoning him closer. Ayr responded, moving in and Dalton wrapped his arm around him. "Take my son, for instance. Without him, this would not have been possible."

"Did you train him?"

Dalton nodded. "Of course I did."

"It shows. You did a good job with him. I have never seen such power come from a magic user within the Commonwealth."

"Thank you, Alexandria. I'll take that as a compliment."

A wry smile came to Alexandria's lips. "The only one that I will ever give you."

"Well then. I think it is time that this farce comes to an end. Don't you?"

Alexandria nodded her response. "It is time."

"Rest then, Alexandria. The Commonwealth thanks you for your service."

A grimace came to Dalton's face as he glanced around at the room. Ayr tensed, wondering if he was going to be the executioner. Out of the corner of his eye, he saw Dalton give a firm nod as he squeezed his shoulder.

Ayr, what have you done?

"Do it."

Ayr coiled, feeling all of the power that Azura had given him surging through his veins. He raised both of his arms and with one final surge, sent out the largest fork of lightning yet. Rather than probing at the edges of Alexandria's barrier, the magic burst through it, blowing the barrier to pieces like glass being blown out of a window. It shattered in every direction, spraying Alexandria with magic as the lightning surged through the gaps.

She screamed as she was engulfed. The lightning surged towards Havar as well, and a pained bellow came from his belly. The wyvern were still relentless. Those that were not struck by Ayr's lightning continued to scratch and claw at Havar and the much larger blue dragon started to fade. Together, dragon and rider fell, one final time. As Havar hit the ground, the side of his head smashing into it, Ayr finally relented, lowering his hands and cutting off the lightning. Azura let out a sorrow moan as she flew overhead, now looking for a place to land.

Beside him, Dalton clicked his tongue, and it was as if he had spoken to the wyvern. The horde all turned and started for the exit, each of them as obedient as the next. All of them except for one that came towards Dalton like a dragon would come towards a rider. Ayr had done enough, and he let out a sigh, collapsing towards the ground, coming to a stop on one knee.

Elanor stood up from her prone position. She had seen the whole thing, her eyes wide open with fear. She surveyed the area, the wyvern now retreating like a tide at Dalton's command. No dragons remained standing except for Evor and Azura, the others all a crumpled pile, a mere shadow of what they had been moments ago. She raced over towards Ayr, and he could almost feel her heart beating out of her chest as she wrapped her arms around him.

"You killed the Dragon Lords and their dragons?"

Ayr raised his eyes, panting up at her. He could feel the sweat that covered his brow, making him feel like he had dunked in his head into a body of water. "I told you. I would do anything for you. This secures yours and Evor's futures."

Behind him, he heard Dalton scoff. "If you hadn't had done what you just did, I would be hard pressed to call you my son, Ayr. Either way, the task is completed."

"That's it?" Elanor held her sword afloat, pointing it towards Dalton. "Evor and I almost get killed and that's all the thanks you give us? Where is the scalebane elixir?"

Ayr heard a ping that sounded like a coin and saw a glint of light flash above his head, as it sailed towards Elanor. Elanor caught what had been flung at her and she held it up to the light. It was another vial of scalebane elixir. She snorted, turning on her heel, spinning away from Dalton and back towards Evor.

"Don't forget the second part to this task! You've done well but now is where the challenge starts. I look forward to seeing how you navigate this!"

Elanor shot daggers back over her shoulder at Dalton. "I will ensure that the Commonwealth has new leadership."

TWENTY-ONE

Elanor raced towards Evor, the precious vial of liquid clutched in her right hand. Her heartbeat with each step and she could feel it pounding, matching Evor's much larger heart, beat for beat. Whilst he was not affected by the scalebane, the sooner she gave him the elixir, hopefully the sooner it was flushed from his system forever. Dalton was leaving on his wyvern, at last taking off into the air. Now all they needed to do was leave this place before Kaladin and the wyrmguard returned.

Elanor reached Evor and placed her hand against the scales of his foot. He swooned at her presence and her touch. She felt his warmth embrace her entire body and wanted to administer the elixir sooner rather than later. Elanor drew back from his foot and opened the vial that Dalton had given her. If it had not worked in the past, Elanor would have doubted that the contents contained the cure to the scalebane. She poured it onto his scales and Evor let out a loud sigh of relief.

Thank you, Elanor.

You are so brave for what you did.

I did what I had to do to ensure my survival, but you know that they will brand us as a traitor to the Commonwealth if they find out.

I don't care. You and I can live out the rest of our days beyond their reach. We can run. Dalton is smart. He and the wyvern will take the blame for what happened here today. I don't see how the blame will come back onto us.

I marked them. Kaladin is not stupid, Elanor. He will be able to figure out that a dragon aided Dalton, even if Ashbourne is willing to take the blame for what we did here today.

There are thousands of dragons in the world, Evor. Many of them are not you.

Elanor, you cannot pretend that everything will be fine.

We will play the game. Nobody will know what really happened here today.

If you say so.

Evor closed his eyes and groaned again. The scalebane elixir was doing its job. Or so she hoped. If it was not, she would have more problems with Dalton. However, as it stood, right now they could not afford to wait for the elixir to do its work.

Can you fly?

Evor scoffed out loud at her, smoke exhaling from his nostrils. *Can I fly? Elanor, please.*

I didn't know if it was influencing you.

Whether it was or not was not, it does not matter. Climb onto my back, Elanor. Let us leave this place. It reeks of death and chaos.

Elanor cast a side eye at Ayr as she set about the monumental climb that awaited her. *I know. You know, I still can't bring myself to fully trust him.*

There are people just as close to you that you should not trust more. You know he did that for us. Regardless of his flaws, Ayr Ashbourne is true to his convictions and to date, he has kept his word.

That's what worries me.

How so, Elanor? If he is honest, he is no threat to us. I am willing to destroy Azura's rider if he wishes us ill.

It's not his honesty that concerns me. Who is the one person he would have sworn allegiance to before he even met us?

Ah. Dalton.

Don't let your feelings for Azura get in the way of your rationality, Evor.

Much like you need to not let your feelings get in the way, Elanor.

Evor's words struck a whip, punching into her gut like a fist. Elanor lifted her mask over her face and readied herself in the saddle. Ayr was on Azura's back and he gave her a nod. Evor stepped forward, spreading his wings, even though he could not fly properly in this chamber. Instead, he started to run, sprinting towards the chamber entrance where Dalton and the wyvern had disappeared to only moments ago. The wyvern were swift and there was no evidence of them left as Evor followed the way that they had come in, pushing up through the mountain until they were outside once more.

Unlike when they had entered, sunlight now shone down on Ashenfort and the surrounding landscape. Elanor frowned, wondering where the storm had gone to, and it was as if it had disappeared into thin air, like Dalton practicing one of his spells. He had said that he had summoned it. With control of that many wyvern and considering the relationship with the largest elder dragon that she had ever seen, Elanor believed that the stories regarding his magical prowess were true.

But Ayr. Ayr had been something else entirely. She had fallen from Evor's back, and something had caught her. Not only if he had caught her, but he had also struck down every single one of the Dragon Lords and their dragons with nothing more than lightning. She had felt the power as he had been casting it, and it terrified her. Was he going to be more powerful than Dalton?

She could not afford to think about it yet. The gravity of what they had just done together was still sinking in. For the most part, they had just completely obliterated the entire power structure within the Commonwealth in one foul swoop. Yes, the positions would be filled by riders who wanted vengeance against Dalton, but that would be four riders that would be taken off the frontlines. Elanor paused again. Dalton wanted her to become a Dragon Lord.

Evor swooped down the Ashenfort mountainside and the sun was coming through stronger than ever. Elanor checked over her shoulder and saw Ayr and Azura trailing not far behind. She made Evor descend straight towards the ground. He made his way down towards the courtyards that awaited them and landed smoothly in the tall grass. Elanor checked over her shoulder and saw Azura

"We cannot speak of that to anybody."

"Obviously. You only attacked a dragon. I murdered the entirety of the Dragon Lords. I also did it with Dalton. What do you think they'll do to me?"

"Nobody will hear it from me. We need to get further away from here. Do you remember where you were when Kaladin left?"

"Not here that's for sure. I think I was somewhere further in the city. It looks different without the torrential rain."

"Well, it's too late now."

Elanor pointed towards the sun and Ayr raised his hand to his face. A few more than half a dozen dragons were making their way towards Ashenfort. For the moment they were nothing more than black dots against the sun, until they lowered themselves towards the city. Gundrag led the way, followed by the other familiar dragons of the wyrmguard. They banked hard towards Ashenfort and angled towards them. When he landed, Gundrag looked furious and Kaladin's body language mirrored him.

"Kaladin! You went out in a storm. Are you insane?"

"Did you not hear the call? It was Dalton fucking Ashbourne on dragon back near the city!"

"Well did you catch him? Unless it was Sinibad, surely Gundrag would out speed most others."

Kaladin ripped his mask off his face. He was a bright shade of crimson. "Not in a fucking storm. Besides that, it was an illusion! We were catching up to him and then he vanished into thin air! He is a trickster."

"So was my father here or not?"

Kaladin narrowed his eyes and scowled at Ayr to her side. "No. He was not." He spat at the ground. "We were so close and had him dead to rights! If it wasn't for the fucking storm! We lost two good men! And dragons!"

Barrett came into land beside Gundrag on Arrax. "Overlord. The storm dissipated the moment that Dalton did. He is as slippery as an eel. We did well to get so close to him."

"It makes me think he wanted us to chase him. Especially if he cast himself as an illusion."

"Do you think..."

"No! The Dragon Lords! Everyone with me!"

Gundrag's head turned towards the sky, and he launched himself into the air. The rest of the wyrmguard rose with him and Elanor gave Evor the same direction once they were above them. She knew exactly where they were going and could have closed her eyes as they ascended the mountain. The only difference to their journey was the fact that they did not stop where Evor had stopped before descending into the depths below. Kaladin must have been pushing Gundrag to break all known speed records. He flew up the side of the mountain and down into the hole where the Dragon Lords had been hiding. The wyrmguard dragons flew in before Evor with Azura bringing up the rear.

Do you think he will suspect our hand in this?

Stay quiet and do not bring attention to yourself, Elanor. His rage will guide him through his next acts.

The dragons roared as they came into the chamber, the bodies of the dragons evident against the floor of the chamber, their fallen corpses rising up to stand over the platform. Gundrag and the other wyrmguard dragons all let out a mournful roar and Elanor nudged Evor to follow suit. One by one, the wyrmguard dismounted from their dragons, and crossed the room to where the Dragon Lords had all perished on the raised platform. Kaladin was the last to remove himself from Gundrag, with Elanor and Ayr following his lead, not wanting to give away their true intentions.

Whilst the dragons were mournful, the helmeted faces of the wyrmguard were unreadable. They stepped up to the platform, and some of them knelt to inspect the Dragon Lords bodies while others drew their swords, staring around at the ceiling. Kaladin marched up onto the platform and hissed at them.

"Put your swords away. What are you going to do?"

Barrett was not convinced otherwise. "Sir. If the Dragon Lords are dead, there is a clear and imminent threat to your life as well."

"There's only one person who could have done it. The only person powerful enough to walk in here on his own without the assistance of any other riders and eviscerate the Dragon Lords. He's not here anymore. Fucking Ashbourne."

Barrett stood up from the crumpled bodies of the Dragon Lords and puffed out his lips. "He roasted them alive; can you feel that magic in the air?"

Kaladin nodded and closed his eyes. "I should have kept them at the Haven. They would have been safer there. Hiding them here was stupid."

"How did he know? You only told a handful of men within the wyrmguard."

"Then that tells me that we have a spy in our midst."

"You don't think he could have seen you bring them here? He has had over a month to prepare for this event."

"We only moved the Dragon Lords at night. We can't have been followed. I just refuse to believe it. Someone would have told him!"

"Then we need to work out who the spy is, sir."

If Elanor felt anything towards Kaladin, she would have felt guilty, but it had been Chorru who had probed her. All she had done was confirm his and Dalton's suspicions about the whereabouts of the Dragon Lords. They had already known and there was only so many places that the Dragon Lords could have been realistically hidden inside the Commonwealth. Now that they were gone, a power vacuum would open. Kaladin as Overlord also had complete control. Had this been an intention move on his behalf? The Overlord was the only person that could confirm Dragon Lords and raise them to their position, and likewise, they were the only people who had the power to appoint an Overlord. One could not exist without the other.

Kaladin kicked at the ground beside Alexandria's withered body in frustration. "We chase this man across the Commonwealth for decades. He hides and then when he reemerges again, we cannot catch him. How are you supposed to keep a man like that from striking out against your valuable assets?"

"We can't sir. If anything, we need to bunker down and wait for him to come to us."

"We did that once upon a time. If you remember something about that, is that it did not work, Commander. When did the tide turn in the war?"

Barrett looked down at the ground. "When you burned the soul out of this city."

Kaladin rounded on him with more anger. "This city never had a soul once it sold itself to Dalton Ashbourne. I did what had to be done."

Elanor flicked her eyes towards Ayr, and she thought that she could see a faint trace of lightning circling around his fist once again. It circled his hand once before fading away into nothing. She wanted to reach out and grab his hand, but Kaladin was once again circling. He moved past every member of the Dragon Lord shaking his head at each of them.

"It appears that once we return to the Haven from the Obelisk, we will need to have an election. There is nothing more that we can do here for them."

"What of the bodies?"

"There's nothing we can do for them now. We will send someone from the Obelisk to take them to the Haven. The sooner we get to the Obelisk and get you installed as the Lord Chairman, the better."

Barrett nodded, still trying to understand the gravity of the situation that had unfolded around him. "If this does not set everyone on edge, I don't know what will."

"First Anton, now this? What's next for Dalton?"

TWENTY-TWO

The Obelisk was just on the horizon and Ayr was finally feeling relieved. The weeks that they had been away had only been for the most part, terrible. Whilst he had been able to spend all of it with Elanor, the time away from Azura had not been worth it. If Dalton could have kept his nose out of Ayr's business, he would have also appreciated that as well. With Kaladin believing that Dalton had been the sole perpetrator behind the deaths of the Dragon Lords, he could breathe a sigh of relief.

For the first time since they had ventured to the underbelly of Ashenfort to murder the Dragon Lords, there was a sense of excitement coming from Azura. This was her home, and she was most eager to return to it, even though they had no idea what was in store for them. From the outside, the Obelisk appeared normal but considering it had been some time since he had last seen it, Ayr doubted that it remained the same inside.

Ayr sat back in the saddle, knowing what Azura was pondering. She thought about his power, mulling it over in her mind. Yet it was her assistance that had also helped him surge when he had needed it the most. It felt good being that powerful and he wondered if that was how Dalton had felt during the peak of his powers. However, it had come to him in a moment of rage, not only because of Elanor's fall, but he felt like he had been urged on by Dalton. Was this now the accumulation of years of grooming that he had been subjected to? What was Dalton's end game.

You did it for me.

Ayr snapped back to reality as Azura entered his thoughts. *I don't want you to be without your promised. That's no way to live your life.*

I am aligned to your goals. I will not go against you as I can see your true intentions.

I just wish we knew what was next.

I want to ask about your power, but I also do not want to know.

I am still wondering about it myself, Azura.

That's why I'm giving you the time if you are not ready to tell me yet, Ayr. I may figure it out before you.

You are incredibly gifted, Azura.

As are you.

Ayr went silent, as he focused on what remained of their journey. Azura was filled with joy, and he opted to be present for that, revelling in the emotions with her. As they approached the Obelisk, Gundrag and the rest of the wyrmguard circled it once, before Gundrag was the first dragon that turned towards the roof. It seemed that Kaladin was going against the protocols that Crassus had set in place. If one man in the Commonwealth was going to go against the grain, it would be him.

As they swooped overhead, Ayr felt a pang of guilt in his gut. Spread across the tall spires and pillars of the Obelisk lay a dragon that Ayr had not seen in weeks. His mind flashed back to the Colosseum. Baindussa stood above him, smoke curling around his mouth as he glared down at both Ayr and Elanor as they stood at his mercy. Dalton's entrance had been a most welcome distraction.

Do not be afraid of him, Ayr. Now that it is clear that Dalton was behind Crassus' murder, Baindussa will not harm you.

I still don't trust him.

You will have to.

Baindussa reared his head as the wyrmguard dragons came to land in his courtyard. Even though Crassus had passed on, Baindussa was still amongst the regalest of dragons that Ayr had seen. As the wyrmguard landed, Baindussa stood up on the roof of the Obelisk, stretching his long neck out towards Gundrag.

"Gundrag, do you have my permission to be here?"

"The chairman is dead, Baindussa. There is no such protocol in place. Considering the Overlord is the one upon my back, I can land where I choose. You did not question Drementhol, did you?"

A loud hiss came from deep from within Baindussa's chest. His head arced towards Gundrag, but due to his blindness, he was too slow to follow it. "You still do not have permission to be here. I will rip you from the sky."

"You can sense the dragons that I am with, Baindussa. I do not think it would be wise to resist. Now stand down."

With another hiss, Baindussa recoiled, retreating to where he had been laying in between the spires. Gundrag roared again as he circled the ceiling once more before coming into land. Azura flew in behind the rest of the wyrmguard and as she touched down, Ayr was just glad to be back on solid, familiar territory again, even under the gaze of Baindussa. He looked around at the rest of the wyrmguard who were dismounting. Each of them kept an eye on Baindussa as they did so, and it seemed that nobody trusted the enormous green dragon.

"You may have the numbers for now, Gundrag, but just know that if it was the two of us here alone, I would tear you limb from limb."

Gundrag snorted, as he glared up at Baindussa. "You're an old, blind dragon, Baindussa. You'd be hard pressed defeating the Ashbourne boy."

Azura snorted in Ayr's ear. *Pfft. Little do they know.*

Ayr contained a smirk as he removed his mask from his face, now feeling the fresh breeze in its full glory once more. He shook out his hair and looked to Evor where Elanor was doing the same thing, albeit with more majesty. Her auburn hair caught the light shining down from above, and all Ayr wished to do was to cuddle her from behind so that he could indulge in her scent.

Soon, Ayr.

I wish you wouldn't do that sometimes.

What you see is what I see.

Right, sorry.

Ayr slid down Azura's neck and touched down on the ground. His legs were stiff but that was to be expected. Spending days on end in the saddle, regardless of how comfortable it was, was still enough to cause some discomfort. Maybe one day he could ride her for days at a time and not be bothered, but for that he needed more time in the air with her. As he moved away from Azura, Kaladin and the wyrmguard were congregating underneath Gundrag's enormous shadow.

"Call an assembly. Our priority is to inform every one of the new Lord Chairman. Then I have some other matters to attend to. The untimely death of the Dragon Lords has left a hole in our command structure."

Barrett nodded and went to comply and then frowned. "Sir, I am the new Lord Chairman."

Kaladin smiled at him, clicking his fingers at one of the still helmet clad wyrmguard. "Precisely, Barrett. Someone else will need to be given the role of commander. Gunther, off you go."

One of the tallest men nodded and turned on his heel, making his way towards the platform that connected Baindussa's courtyard with the rest of the Obelisk.

Barrett still looked confused. "And what should I do, sir? I was not exactly made for the role of Lord Chairman. Nor do I know precisely what my duties are."

"I would say that we need to dress you appropriately, but I am sure that you are more comfortable in your armour are you not? These are pressing times after all. I'm sure that we can forgo tradition just this once. Come. I will introduce you. Walk with me."

With the exception of Barrett and Gunther who was now out of view, the wyrmguard formed up around Kaladin in a protective circle. Kaladin glanced back over his shoulder at Ayr and Elanor who were waiting for their instructions, and he clicked his fingers.

"You two, with me. I do not want you out of my sight."

A chill ran down Ayr's spine. The last time he had been out of Kaladin's presence, he had killed the Dragon Lords. He remained neutral, daring not to give anything away. He entered the circle that the wyrmguard had formed and Kaladin clicked his fingers again. As one, the wyrmguard started to move, an armoured and now impenetrable wall around them. whilst he was moving away from Azura, Ayr still felt comforted by Elanor's presence. Her fingertips were only inches away from his, and they brushed against each other as they walked. They could exchange glances, but with Kaladin looming their opportunity to speak was nullified.

They moved into the heart of the Obelisk, taking the platform down into the lower levels. The dragons had not remained on the ceiling, Azura's vision filling his own as she flew down beside the Obelisk, making her way back towards their chambers. She was filled with a sense of safety and security, a feeling that he had not felt from her since they had first left the Obelisk.

I'm glad you're happy to be home.

So am I, Ayr.

We'll do what we need to do here. Hopefully Kaladin doesn't keep us too long.

I will rest in the meantime. Who knows when I will need my strength again.

Hopefully not anytime soon.

As they moved into the corridors of the Obelisk, they were already beginning to draw attention of the other riders. Gunther was ahead of them, spreading word, advising everyone to make their way towards the main hall. Some riders he could tell were not pleased with the announcement, however others looked somewhat relieved. The Obelisk was in a different state than to how he had left it all those weeks ago, and it did not seem for the better.

The riders that were being rounded up by Gunther and then further ushered on by the wyrmguard, all looked like they'd rather be anywhere else. Yet as they made their way into the hall, Ayr found it to be mostly full, with dozens, upon dozens of riders. Some sat at tables, their dragons standing overhead, but every eye turned towards them. Now that they were in the hall, the wyrmguard split, allowing both Kaladin and Barrett to pass through. More riders were filtering in through the open doors, and Ayr received a shove in his back from one of the wyrmguard that remained behind him.

Kaladin and Barrett made themselves visible at the end of the hall and waited with their hands hanging by their side while they waited for more riders to gather. Each remained stoic until the hall was full enough to a point where Kaladin was happy. He swept his cloak over his arm so that it covered his ruined hand and started to yell across the room.

"Thank you for all attending at such short notice. This is an important update, one that I hope will bring stability and direction to the Obelisk. This is well overdue, but I bring to you, your new Lord Chairman Barrett Wyatt."

Kaladin gestured towards Barrett who took a commanding step forward, taking centre stage. He cleared his throat as a small round of applause broke out. He nodded his head towards several of the riders in attendance before he began speaking.

"Riders, let me be frank. As you should be aware of by now is that Dalton Ashbourne has reemerged. Not only did he murder the Lord Chairman, but he has now murdered the Overlord. We need to prepare the Obelisk and every rider and their dragon for all-out war."

Murmured conversation began to fill the hall as riders looked to each other for answers that they did not have. Barrett and Kaladin both let the conversation continue for a few moments before the former raised his hand quelling the conversations coming from the riders. Kaladin stepped forward again.

"The Obelisk is not at all equipped to deal with a full-on attack from Dalton Ashbourne at this stage. He has access to an elder dragon unlike we have never seen before. Whilst the Obelisk has the greatest number of dragons anywhere in the Commonwealth aside from the Haven, we need to ensure that it is defended. Our future generations will rely on it. I will remain here for the time being as both the Lord Chairman and Obelisk are prepared for the future."

A rider at the front of the hall stood up. "Sir, when do we begin? Do you need volunteers to scout out where Dalton Ashbourne may be hiding?"

"No, not yet. We will prepare our defences first. We begin today. This is the biggest priority for everyone here."

As one, those riders that had been seated rose to their feet, some more hurried than others. Judging from the conversations that broke out around them, it was clear that the riders were concerned. Kaladin cut an imposing figure as he charged towards them. He raised a finger, pointing at both of them, calling them to him. They fought against the tide of outgoing riders and when they drew level with them, Kaladin puffed out his chest.

"You two are going to be the exception to the rule."

"What rule? That we're not going to help?"

"Correct. With all the dragons and their riders that are situated here, there are more than enough bodies to get the Obelisk shaped to my liking. If either of you two are somehow working for Dalton, I do not want our defences to be comprised by either of you."

Elanor raised an eyebrow. "So, what would you have us do, Kaladin? Are you going to lock us in a void cell once again?"

"No, not yet. You will have a guard on your door each night, and you will report to me each day."

"To do what, exactly?"

"The Overlord is a busy position, Elanor. I will decide when I need things to be done. For now, go with the wyrmguard to your chambers. Remain there for the evening and I will see both of you at dawn."

TWENTY-THREE

Kaladin gestured to the wyrmguard that were stationed by the door. Half of them split off from the rest, making their way towards Ayr and Elanor. As the foremost guard approached, he reached up and removed his helmet, revealing the familiar face of Marcello, his youthful exuberance shining through his bright eyes and a wide grin that seemed to promise adventure and mischief. "Sir?"

"Escort these two back to their quarters. They are to remain under your guard until I deem otherwise. Feed them should they ask for it, and let them out in the morning, only to bring them to me."

Marcello gave Kaladin a curt nod. "Sir! Come on, you two."

Ayr glanced at Elanor who shrugged at him. "It could be worse you know."

"What do you mean?"

"More time alone with our dragons, only having to answer to Kaladin. Sounds easy to me."

Ayr frowned, still feeling uncertain about the situation. "We don't know what he wants yet."

"Don't worry about Kaladin. I can handle him."

"Are you sure? I can help."

Elanor turned her head and a smirk spread to her lips. "I know. I wouldn't mind seeing you do that to him."

Ayr shook his head, urging Elanor to not say anything further. Here in the presence of the wyrmguard was more risk than he needed to take on. "I can't. You know that."

Elanor caught onto his body language and looked away from him, staring into the back of Marcello's blond head. Ayr also focused on it, watching where they were being led. Nothing seemed untoward and he was beginning to come familiar with the towering hallways of the Obelisk that were more than perfect for ferrying both riders and dragons through it. Marcello led their group to their chambers, where he stopped outside, switching the hand he carried his helmet in.

"Well, here we are."

Elanor looked up and down at the closed door. "Here we are indeed."

"Now, you heard the Overlord. We'll send food here and water here but that's it. You're only to come out tomorrow and then you'll be escorted by us."

"Kaladin really needs to let us go at some point. This can't be sustainable."

"He will continue to do this for as long as he does not trust you."

Elanor just rolled her eyes. "I know. He needs to grow up at some point."

Marcello scoffed as did one of the other wyrmguard that still had his helmet on. "We'll be just outside here for anything you need Lady Sunfire."

"Wait, are you not going to take me to my own chambers?"

Marcello shook his head. "What would be the point in that? We would have to double the guard. For now, both of you will be in this one room, please."

"For now? As much as I like Ayr, I'd like to have my own space."

"I'm sorry, we can't provide that. Enjoy your night."

Elanor raised her hand and pushed on the door. "Don't worry, we will."

The doors opened as Elanor pushed against them, and at last, Ayr took a deep breath as relief washed over him. This place was the first place he had felt like had been a permanent home in as long as he could remember. When Anton and the first wave of wyrmguard had ripped him from it, he'd felt like he was back with Dalton, on the move again. Now that he was back, the feeling brought a sense of overwhelming relief. Both Evor and Azura were already waiting inside for them, both dragons bowing their heads as they wrapped themselves around each other in the hay bed that had once only housed Evor.

Good to see you again, Azura.

It is good to see you too, Ayr.

Was your flight down okay? Has anything new happened since we've been apart?

My flight was fine. I must inform you though that if we want to go anywhere, there are wyrmguard dragons outside keeping watch.

Great, so he's cut us off from the outside world again.

It would appear so. As a positive, this is only temporary. Is it not?

I would hope so.

Use this time to recover. Who knows when you'll need your strength to pull off another unforgettable feat.

I want to forget it.

Do you feel guilty? You did what had to be done.

That doesn't mean I don't feel any less guilty about it, Azura.

You humans are strange. I do not think that I will fully understand you, Ayr. I will take the pain of your memory from you. Enjoy your time with Elanor today.

Ayr cut off the communication and turned his attention to Elanor. She was already striding across the room, removing her riding jacket and stripping off down to her undergarments. He half expected her to continue, now that they were in the room and they had the space all to themselves except for their dragons. Yet Evor would have seen her in her most vulnerable states thousands of times and would have just turned a blind eye to it. He was an extension of her, just as Azura was an extension of Ayr.

Elanor flopped forwards onto the bed and let out a loud groan that echoed Evor's for its volume, even though she was face first in the sheets. Ayr followed behind her, looking forward to the comfort of the bed. Ayr made his way across the room to the bed and sat down beside her. Elanor flipped over onto her back and stretched her arms towards the ceiling.

"I'm so glad to be back."

Ayr sighed as he agreed with her. "Me too. We've been away for far too long."

"Indeed, we have. I did not think that I would be living in a world where the last remaining piece of my father would be Baindussa. I thought that they would crawl into a ditch somewhere and die together of old age."

"I'm sorry that it happened the way it did."

Elanor sat up and wriggled towards him. Ayr remained unmoving as Elanor took his hand in hers and turned it over so that she could see his palm. "Don't be sorry. It's not your fault. Dalton wanted Crassus dead even before the rebellion started. My father became too complacent in his victory."

"He thought he had won. Anyone would sit on their laurels."

Elanor frowned as she continued to trace her fingertip down Ayr's forearm. She paused for a moment and then raised her eyes to his. "I need you to tell me something, Ayr. Did you kill the Dragon Lords by yourself or did your father help you? That was an incredible display of power."

Ayr swallowed as he stared back into her deep green eyes. They were searching for an answer in his.

Tell the truth. She knows why you did it.

But I don't want to lie to her.

Tell the truth, Ayr.

"You know why I did it."

"I do, but I don't know how you got to be so powerful."

Ayr sighed. "It's hard to explain. When you were flung from Evor, something came over me. You're right, it was unlike anything I've ever done before. Even more wild than the aftershock."

"So where did it come from then?"

"I don't know exactly, but as my connection deepens with Azura and the more we grow connected, the more she can feed me."

"That wasn't just magical energy from Azura being sent to you. There was intent there and I think you did most of it yourself. Azura at her maturity surely isn't capable enough to direct such magic."

Azura raised her head over Elanor's shoulder, her blue eyes staring straight into Ayr's soul. *Do not lie.*

Ayr puffed out his lips and reverted his gaze to Elanor. She was searching through his eyes, looking for an answer.

"I did. Azura can fuel me, but without Dalton there, there was no way I was pulling that off myself. I'm not that powerful yet."

"Yet?"

"I grow stronger every day. Dalton theorises that one day I will be as powerful as he is. He wants his sons to continue his legacy. I just do not have more decades of spellcasting underneath my belt."

"So, when I showed you how to use magic for the first time in the cave all those months ago..."

"You didn't need to. Everything is just there, bubbling underneath the surface. Dalton trained me for years before sending me to the Seminary."

Ayr glanced down at his forearm that until that moment, Elanor had been tracing her fingertips over. His hairs stood on end because of her touch, but it was not what he was looking for. Instead, he was focused on the heat rising from his arm. It started just beneath Elanor's fingers and then started to shoot out in every direction, warming him.

"Can you feel that?"

"By Chilijo! What the fuck, Ayr!"

Elanor retracted her hand, snatching it away as if she had been scolded. Ayr let the same magic cool away, sapping most of the heat from the spot in an instance.

"I can do this and more without Azura. I can theorise the reason why the aftershock had such a profound effect on me was because of the magic I already had existing in my body. Azura was the key to unlocking it all. As are my emotions, apparently."

"So, what more can you do?"

Ayr paused, the magic still pulsing through his veins. It was unlike when he had murdered the Dragon Lords, with nothing but a quiet calmness in his mind. What was there, however, was Azura. He saw Elanor through her eyes, but he did not need her encouragement to help him formulate his next move more than he already had. Elanor's pupils were dilating as she started back at him, and Ayr leaned forward. He was eager and raised his hand, pushing against her chest.

Elanor fell back, but only because she wanted to. Ayr followed her a smile spread across his lips as he pushed himself onto hers. Elanor landed flat on the mattress mid kiss and responded in kind, holding in a laugh as Ayr also tried to contain one. Was it Azura in his mind and Evor in hers? The result was the same as they fell into a heap. Elanor was fighting against him, half trying to regain control of the situation, half egging him on, wanting him to do more.

Ayr embraced her challenge, his tongue joining hers in a wild, yet slow and lustful exploration. With her hands wrapped around his neck, Ayr had nowhere to go except closer to her. He pulled away from her lips, and began to kiss at her neck, feeling the softness of her skin yield to his lips. Elanor's moans started to fill the room as her hands continued to tug at his hair. Her hips bucked against his in a protest, that begged to ask why they were still clothed. Within moments, Elanor's hands were tearing at Ayr's tunic, meanwhile his hands began to remove what was left of her undergarments.

He could not keep track of where every body part was, or what was happening to his clothes, but within moments, Ayr was naked and had his head already between Elanor's thighs. Her relentless pushing down of his head and the grabbing of him with her legs told him all that he needed to know. With how wet she already was for him, it was almost as if she had been thinking about this moment for hours or days before hand. Ayr grabbed her hips and pulled her close to him, a movement that Elanor let out a short squeal for as she was manoeuvred to where Ayr wanted her.

His tongue was a whirlwind, licking her in every direction. Ayr listened to Elanor's verbal queues, or where she was pulling him, and the bucking of her hips as she ground herself against his face only urged him on. Her moans grew louder and louder as his pace increased. He still held onto her thighs, digging his fingers into her warm flesh. If he was worried that he was going to bruise her, it was well past the point. She would be lucky if she did not pop his head between her thighs with the amount she was clenching around him.

"Fuck!"

Ayr recoiled as he felt Elanor shake, and watched her body convulse for a moment as her moans reached a crescendo. Her hand was over her face, but one of them remained in his hair. She had taken enough and was now wanting to pull him up.

"You taste so fucking good."

"Fuck me, Ashbourne."

Ayr raised his head from between her thighs, an animalistic grunt escaping his throat. He grinned up at her as he moved away from where his head had been only moments ago. This was what he had been waiting for. A smile spread across his lips as he moved back towards her.

"No need to tell me twice."

Ayr with the grace of striking dragon, slid up onto his knees and pulled Elanor's legs so that she was over his hips. He was already more than ready for her, the sounds of her arousal doing enough to get him to where he needed to be for her. Ayr jostled for position and Elanor was grabbing for him again, begging for him to be closer to her. He complied, sliding into her, as he watched her face change. Elanor's eyes began to slide back in her head, and her mouth parted as he entered her.

Ayr's first thrust was slow and purposeful, ensuring that she felt him the entire way in. When he was all the way in, Ayr paused to look down at her and Elanor adjusted her grip on him, moving to his shoulder. There was no doubt she could feel him inside her, and as she opened her eyes, a wicked grin spread across her face.

"Come on, you can give me more than that."

Ayr growled and decided to give her what she asked for, plunging into her with a hunger that surprised even him. Elanor's nails dug into his shoulders, but instead of complaining, she arched her back, urging him on. He obliged, driving into her with abandon, their hips slapping together with the ferocity of a summer storm.

The room filled with their muffled moans, the headboard banging against the wall in time with their frantic rhythm. Elanor's breasts bounced with each forceful thrust, and Ayr found himself mesmerized by the sight. He grabbed them, his fingers squeezing the sensitive flesh, eliciting a loud moan from her lips. Ayr continued to massage her breasts as he drove into her, the pressure building in his core with every demanding movement.

Within a few moments they were both drenched in sweat, their bodies locked together in a primal dance as old as time itself. Elanor's walls clenched around him, her inner muscles tensing in the most delicious way, and he knew she was close.

"Ayr! I'm... I'm..."

That was all it took. Ayr's restraint shattered, and he let go, burying himself as deep inside her as he could, growling out his release as they both tumbled over the edge together. The world dissolved into the white-hot pleasure that coursed through their veins as they collapsed together. Elanor still pulsed around him, as her head fell back against the sheets, a sigh escaping her lips. Ayr stared down at her, and she pulled his head closer to hers. Their lips met once again in a passionate kiss, one final time.

She pulled away after a while of their interaction, a deep look of lust in her eyes. "Well, that was different."

Ayr pulled away and glanced over at the two dragons that were resting nearby, their massive, scaled bodies curled into crescent moons against each other. Neither had their heads raised or even their eyes open, the thin membranes of their eyelids pulsed with dreams. Evor's nostrils flared with each exhale, releasing wisps of smoke that dissipated into the air, while a rumbling vibration like distant thunder emanated from deep within his throat, a sound remarkably like human snoring, though far more primal.

"Was that either of you two?"

Azura responded but did not bother to open an eye. "No."

Elanor laughed beside him, trying to pull him back down into the covers. "Not everything is magical, Ayr."

"But you said it was different."

"Stop overthinking everything. Just come and lay with me."

Ayr flopped down on the bed beside her, his muscled frame sinking into the feather mattress with a soft creak of wood. She grinned at him, her eyes glinting with mischief in the amber light as they traced a deliberate path from his tousled hair down to the lean contours of his chest.

"Hmm. We should go again later. I'd like to relax for the rest of the day if I can. Who knows what our Overlord will have in store for us come the morning."

"Who indeed?"

Elanor rolled over onto her stomach; her fingers splayed across the silken sheets high above her head. She stretched out to her full height, the curve of her spine creating a perfect arch that accentuated the delicate contours of her shoulder blades. Her auburn hair cascaded across the pillow as she exhaled, her muscles unwinding one by one until she sank into the plush mattress, leaving only the gentle rise and fall of her breathing to disturb the stillness.

She turned her back to Ayr, and he curled his body around her warm form, one arm sliding beneath her neck while the other draped across her waist, his knees tucking perfectly behind hers. Their bodies fit together like puzzle pieces, his chest rising and falling against her spine in a gentle rhythm that mirrored how Evor would coil his massive, scaled body around Azura.

Time seemed to slip through Ayr's fingers like grains of sand as he drifted in and out of a restless slumber. His consciousness wavered, caught in the delicate balance between dreams and wakefulness. Sleeping beside Elanor was peaceful and he enjoyed each moment he woke up, staring into the back of her head, wondering how he had gotten so lucky. As darkness fell, Ayr heard a knock at the door.

He wanted to wake Elanor, but judging from the way her limbs were spread in every direction and the light snoring that came from her parted lips, she was out cold. He would need to face whoever this was himself. Evor was out, much like Elanor. The only other being that stirred in the room was Azura. The room was darker than what it had been before, and it was clear to Ayr that they had lost track of the time. Who was knocking on their door at this late hour.

What is it?

Someone is at the door.

Open it. If they are hostile, I will incinerate them.

Surely it is just the wyrmguard.

Do not be surprised if it is your father. After Ashenfort I would not put anything past him.

You don't trust the man, do you, Azura?

I have no reason to. He lives in the shadows, using lies and deception to bend the world around him to his will.

Yet none of the wyrmguard dragons outside have roared. Their riders must be okay.

Just be careful.

Ayr climbed out of bed and grabbed a hold of his trousers before he made his way towards the door. He wore a frown on his face, and he went to open it, pushing against it with a gentle touch so that he did not wake Elanor. The door slid open and standing on the other side was none other than Marcello.

"Can I help you?"

"Your father is not wrong."

Ayr blinked, unable to confirm what he had just heard. "I'm sorry?"

Marcello repeated what he had just said. "Your father is not wrong. I told you that some of us were not satisfied with how the Commonwealth was running things."

"Have you gone mad? You're a wyrmguard. Why are you voicing this in front of one of your comrades?"

Marcello's face softened into a laugh. "Oh, don't worry. Malachi here feels much the same way."

The second wyrmguard nodded, his gauntleted fingers rising to the clasps at his neck. The helmet came free with a soft hiss of released pressure, revealing a face so much like Marcello's that Ayr blinked twice to ensure his eyes were not deceiving him. The same sharp jawline, the identical scar bisecting the left eyebrow. It was as though someone had cast Marcello from a mould and produced this uncanny duplicate, with perhaps only the more pronounced cheekbones to distinguish them.

"Twins?"

Marcello shook his head. "Brothers, but we're as close as we can be. Neither of us want to see the Commonwealth continue down its current trajectory. We've seen too much."

"What did you see?"

"We were there. At Ashenfort."

A chill ran down Ayr's spine as he thought back to the memory of Ashenfort. Kaladin had not been the only rider present as Gundrag's fire reigned down upon the innocents that had called Ashenfort their home. There had been too much for just one dragon to be present. Ayr tried to remember the events of that day, and everything he had seen, yet all that came to mind was the enormous purple dragon that had reigned supreme.

Marcello continued. "Don't worry, I know what you're thinking. We weren't there to destroy the city. We were in it, the same as you."

Malachi lowered his helmet and cradled it in his arm. "We're what remains of the Marshadow family."

"You can't be. You all died in the fires!"

Malachi chuckled under his breath. "That's what we wanted everyone else to think. Our parents whisked us away just before the attack and sent us straight to the Seminary of Fire. They might have died, but we endured."

"And now you stand in the Overlord's personal bodyguard. You hate Kaladin as much as I do."

Marcello winked at him. "You didn't hear it from us."

"So why are you telling me this?"

"To let you know that you're not alone here. Whatever you've been sent to do, we can help you."

Ayr was still sceptical. "I don't trust either of you."

Marcello shrugged his shoulders and shot Ayr an unconvincing look. "You might not trust us, but it's the truth. We wanted to let you know that whilst the other wyrmguard were rotating."

"And did you expect for anything to come out of this conversation?"

Malachi shook his head. "No, just the fact that you know. We will build trust over the coming days and weeks, Ayr. We're here to support you."

"Do you follow any words from my father?"

"No, we have not seen him in the flesh since Ashenfort. Yet it is better that way. Nobody suspects a thing."

Marcello's twisted grin came to his lips again. "Not yet at least anyway."

Ayr's ears picked up the sound of booted footsteps coming towards them, and the two wyrmguard heard it as well. Malachi turned his head and nodded his understanding of the situation to Marcello.

"It's time. It was a pleasure speaking to you Ayr."

"Likewise. I will not tell a soul."

"We most certainly hope not. I would hate for our trust to be fractured so easily."

"It will not be. Goodnight." Ayr grabbed at the door and began to pull it shut.

"Goodnight, Lord Ashbourne."

Azura was inside Ayr's thoughts within a split second. *Lord?*

I want no title, Azura. That is something that was thrust upon my family during the rebellion.

You'd best do what you can to ensure it stays that way. I do not know how I would feel addressing you as Lord.

TWENTY-FOUR

Ayr did not sleep. He was still restless, but Elanor awoke, which kept him occupied. They tousled and frolicked amongst the bedsheets as the night dragged on, falling in and out of sleep at will when they were done with each other. He did not mention their visitors to her, but instead, indulged himself in everything that she had to offer. Azura and Evor slept through the entire night, allowing their riders to have peace and a few quiet moments alone together, which in truth was something they had deserved.

As the first rays of the morning sun broke through the windows above their heads, Ayr was already awake. He had not been keeping track of the time as he had been otherwise occupied, and due to the frantic activity had chosen not to fall back to sleep, instead thinking they had more time than they did. Instead, the rude and untimely reminder of the day that awaited them made Ayr groan. He heard a shuffle on the sheets beside him as Elanor stirred. Her arm smacked against his elbow, and she jolted upright.

"Ayr!"

He laughed as he comforted her. "We're fine. Good morning."

"Oh."

Hearing the commotion was enough to force both Azura and Evor out of their coiled states around each other. They both raised their heads, Azura giving him a look of concern.

Are you okay, Ayr?

Yes, it was only Elanor.

He almost heard her roll her eyes in his head. *Why am I not surprised?*

You would do the same if you and Evor had more room, would you not?

There is no need to hurl such accusations around. It is a beautiful morning after all.

You can see outside now, can you?

No, but I can feel the warmth in the sun and can envision the breeze outside. If Kaladin allows us to fly it will be a glorious day.

Let's hope that he does then.

"You all good, Ayr?"

Ayr retreated away from Azura as Elanor grounded him back in the real world. "Yeah, just speaking to Azura."

"You've really got to get faster at that."

"I didn't know we had a time limit on how long conversations with our dragons could take."

Elanor winked at him. "We don't. I'm just trying to teach you best practice."

"Now there's a first time for everything."

Elanor scoffed and picked up the nearest pillow, throwing it at his head. Ayr was far too close to avoid the blow and took it in the face. He feigned falling back into the sheets like he had been struck by a heavy blow, but his laughter slipped out. Elanor joined him in laughter and for a moment, Ayr forgot the world's problems. He pulled her towards him, bringing her in for a kiss. Their lips met and for another moment the world stood still. Elanor pulled away and patted his chest.

"I think we need to get a move on."

"Yes, the Overlord awaits us."

Ayr rolled out of bed and his feet touched the floor. His clothes were where he had left them from the previous evening. Considering the state that they were in, he did not want to put them on again. He heard a knock on the door and ignored it as he crossed the room to the shower. He turned it on as another knock came from the door, which was drowned out by the sound of the tumbling water.

Elanor stepped under the water with him. "Are we going to bother with that?"

"Not until we're done here."

The water was warm as if it had been breathed from a dragon's mouth, but it was not so warm that it scorched their skin. The knocking at the door continued to grow louder and louder and more prevalent until Azura had enough. She stood up, groaning and moved towards it before pushing it open with her snout. The wyrmguard that was standing on the other side of the door, stepped back, not expecting a dragon to answer the door.

I've got this, Ayr.

"Can I help you?"

The wyrmguard spluttered. "The Overlord requests the presence of riders."

Azura turned her head to look at them and blinked. "They are preoccupied."

"The Overlord requests their presence. He will not be denied."

"If the Overlord wishes for them to join him, he can come and collect them. Otherwise, he can wait until they are ready."

"I speak his will. If you will not come, then we will make you."

Azura stood up to her full height, in an attempt to intimidate the man. "Will you? Do you think that you would be able to defeat both Evor and I in such an enclosed environment?"

The wyrmguard backed away from the door. The Overlord will not be pleased."

"Thank you."

Azura stomped away from the door and swatted at it with her tail as she went. She smiled at Ayr and Elanor as they still stood under the running water of the shower. Ayr could not believe what he had just witnessed from her. Azura looked pleased with herself as she swished her head around.

"Told you that I had it."

Ayr felt a warmth fill his heart. "I never doubted you, Azura."

"You should hurry though. Kaladin will not take kindly to this delay."

"Are you done then, Ayr?"

Ayr nodded at Elanor and as he stepped out from underneath the shower, the water was shut off. He began to drip dry, but Elanor threw a towel at him that landed on his shoulder. Ayr swung it around his body and wiped off as he made his way towards the wardrobe. He flung it open as Elanor stepped up, reaching over him, grabbing one set of the few remaining undergarments and uniform that matched her size.

They dressed in silence, the only sounds that filled the room were that of Evor and Azura breathing as they readied themselves for the day ahead. There was a fresh meat slab that had been delivered to their room, and Azura was now taking her time, picking at pieces of the meat that she wanted. Evor loomed over her, awaiting his turn to pick at or devour the rest of the carcass.

Ayr and Elanor finished dressing as the dragons finished their meal, leaving the scraps and smaller parts of the carcass for their riders. Azura held part of the deer's thigh over Ayr, and he reached up to grab it. He smiled at her as he bit into it.

Thank you.

You're most welcome.

Elanor came up behind him as he took a second bite into the deer thigh. "Are you ready to go?"

"Yeah, what are you going to do?"

"We will need to see what the Overlord has in store for us before we will know if it is safe for the dragons to leave the room."

Azura drew back her head. "I can outmanoeuvre the wyrmguard dragons in flight, but with how much open space is around the Obelisk, they would catch me eventually."

Elanor smiled up at her as she stretched out towards Evor. "Which is exactly why we must uncover what Kaladin's intentions are first. Stay here and wait for our word."

Evor bowed his head. "As you command, Elanor."

Elanor turned away from Evor, gesturing for Ayr to follow her and walked towards the door. She pushed it open, only for the wyrmguard waiting on the other side to jump. These were new guards, but as Ayr looked down the corridor behind them, he saw Marcello striding towards them. He was side by side with Malachi, both in deep discussion with the other. They spotted Ayr and Elanor and Marcello hailed them.

"Ah, Lady Sunfire! Lord Ashbourne! We did not think that you would be joining the Overlord today."

Elanor laughed. "We were getting ready for the day, Marcello. Who told you that we weren't coming?"

Marcello nodded to the existing guards. "Thanks for taking the night watch. Did they play up all night?"

One of the helmeted wyrmguard shook his head. "Nothing outside this morning."

"Good. Let's go. We'll lead from here."

The other wyrmguard nodded and let Ayr and Elanor pass them before they fell into line. Marcello and Malachi turned and took the lead. Ayr felt like he was boxed in again, as the two wyrmguard closed in behind him, but at least he had free passage to his left. With Elanor to his right, he felt secure, but was already sick of moving to the wyrmguard tune. Marcello and Malachi led them through the corridors towards the elevator that would take them to Crassus' old lodgings.

Marcello raised his arm over his chest, completing the motion that granted them access to the highest point of the Obelisk. As they waited for the platform to emerge, two riders and their dragons were walking down the corridor towards them. Ayr frowned as he turned to examine them. Both riders were young men, both dressed in their black rider's uniform. The one that had drawn Ayr's attention had his own small black dragon in tow, while the other walked in front of a red. They both eyed him, both new recruits to the Obelisk, who must have just finished in the Seminary of Fire.

Ayr continued to frown at the rider in front of the black dragon, thinking that he looked familiar. As the door to the platform opened, he pulled away, slipping from the grasp of the wyrmguard. Ayr charged towards the rider with the black dragon, and he was able to confirm his suspicions. Bryne Ashbourne had made his arrival to the Obelisk and had been successful in the Seminary of Fire.

He was older, but only by a few months, however the boyish exterior he had carried before was gone. In the past few months, he had gained lean muscle mass, and was very much a spitting image of Ayr, despite his new hair colour. His dragon, despite being small, was still close to the size of Azura despite being months behind in its development. It would be a threat, but he could handle it with confidence. Bryne realised that Ayr was coming towards him, and his hand went to the sword that was on his hip, but it was too late. Ayr, using all his power collided with him, knocking him to the ground.

Bryne let out a grunt as he hit the ground and his dragon snarled above him. The snarl was cut off as quickly as it had started, and with his elbow on Bryne's throat, Ayr wondered if he had already called it off. He pressed down with anger.

"What the fuck are you doing here, Bryne?"

"Bryne, who's Bryne? The name is Shia."

"Shia? Just because you've changed your hair and have got a dragon by your side doesn't mean you are not my brother, Bryne."

Bryne's eyes narrowed as Ayr pressed down more on his throat. It was not out of anger or frustration, but more so curiosity.

"Are you who I think you are? Ayr Ashbourne?"

"You know exactly who the fuck I am. Stop pretending."

"Ashbourne! Ashbourne!"

Bryne's eyes flicked towards where the wyrmguard were coming from. Ayr was not done yet and continued to press against him.

"How did you sneak into the Seminary?"

Bryne flashed a smile at him. "Same as you. The job isn't finished yet."

"What are you talking about?"

In the next moment, Ayr felt rough hands seize his shoulders and biceps, yanking him backward with such force that his boots skidded across the stone floor. The wyrmguard swarmed him, their faces contorted with rage, spittle flying from their mouths as they screamed orders that blurred together into a cacophony of meaningless sound. Their armour plates clattered against each other, drowning out individual words. Through the forest of arms restraining him, Ayr's gaze remained locked on Bryne's face as a smirk spread across it.

"You're just like your fucking father! An uncaged animal, ready to rip and tear at anything that you don't like the look of!"

At last, Ayr was clear of Bryne, despite his efforts trying to pull himself back towards his younger and more insolent brother. The wyrmguard were too strong and right now was not the time to lose his cool and unleash his magic. Azura flooded his mind.

Are you okay, Ayr? Who is that rider?

You know who that is. That's my brother.

Your brother? Why is he here?

I don't know. That's why I am concerned.

Hmm. We can only investigate it. What's to say he is not here for a legitimate reason? To be a rider.

Because I wasn't sent here to just be a rider. Now, was I?

He heard Azura hesitate, measuring her next words. There was no need for her to hesitate, but Ayr could still feel her formulating her thoughts. Instead of waiting for her to be finished, he was distracted as the wyrmguard pulled him to his feet once again. They were not gentle in their handling of him as the helmeted wyrmguard checked on Bryne. Ayr had not taken his eyes off him. Bryne was still throwing verbal jabs.

Ignore him, Ayr.

"Unbelievable that four of you can't control him! What good are the wyrmguard if you can't protect anything?"

Marcello glared at Bryne with anger. "Our job is to serve the Overlord. Nothing else."

Bryne spat at the ground as he passed them, his black dragon with its angry red eyes trailing right behind him. "If the new Lord Chairman wasn't one of you, we'd be having words."

Marcello failed to hide a smile and laughed. "Whatever you say, recruit. Just think yourself lucky that we were there to stop anything else from happening to you."

Bryne's expression could have cut glass. His friend was consoling him, shaking his head as he glanced back in anger. Now the helmeted wyrmguard stepped in front of Ayr.

"There needs to be some sort of punishment here, Marcello. We can't have Ashbourne continually walking around the Commonwealth taking his anger out on other riders, especially at this time."

"We will let the Overlord decide his fate."

The wyrmguard groaned underneath his helmet. "Great, so nothing will happen to him, as always."

Marcello rounded on the man. "You've seen his power when he opened the door to the Keeper's cavern. What would you do? Punish him so he turns against us? We've had one Ashbourne that's done that in the past few decades. I don't want another one."

The wyrmguard shrunk back and shook his head. "Careful, Marshadow. Not everyone here has forgotten which side of the rebellion your family took when push came to shove."

"My family has nothing to do with the choices that I make."

"I'll believe that when I see it. Keep your head screwed on properly, otherwise I'll report you to the Overlord."

"That'll be your funeral, Anders. Let's move."

Marcello turned on his heel and proceeded towards the closed door. He raised his hand and made the all too familiar motion across his chest. The door opened and Marcello gestured for them to enter the platform. The six bodies cramped into the tiny room and rode it to the top. As the door slid open revealing Baindussa's courtyard, the golden morning light spread across everything that was in sight. Baindussa, as per usual raised his massive green head, staring down at Ayr and his escort as he approached.

Gundrag lay near Baindussa, stretching out in the sun as well. His purple scales caught the light, and he appeared brighter than usual. He was slower on the uptake, only rolling around as Baindussa rose.

"Ah, wyrmguard. I see that you have brought Ashbourne and Sunfire behind schedule."

Anders groaned behind Ayr. "See, I told you that he wouldn't be pleased."

Gundrag let out a low hiss, the edges of his mouth curving. "No, he is not. The Overlord is a busy man and has no time for impotence. You'd best hurry."

"Thank you for the advice, Gundrag."

"You're most welcome, wyrmguard."

TWENTY-FIVE

yr felt uncomfortable passing underneath the purple dragon, wishing that Azura was with him. She reached out to him, sensing his discomfort and Ayr stared up at Gundrag's underbelly. He stepped down from the roof, and moved over them, his shadow blocking out the sun. Even though he had slain dragons as big and as powerful as him, Ayr still felt weak. Those other dragons had not held malice towards him until it was too late. But this dragon radiated hatred towards him from his rider. It was not time to act yet.

Ayr quickened his pace, not wanting to fall far behind Marcello and Malachi, being stepped on by Anders and his unfamiliar friend. He cast a glance at Elanor who had otherwise remained stoic. If only he had a connection with her like he did Azura. There was something there, but by no means was it telepathically an option right now. Perhaps he could find a way with magic when he had time to sit down and study it. It was not like he did not have access to her.

They entered the chambers of the Lord Chairman, and its familiarity came crashing back to Ayr like a wave had washed over him. He wondered where the poisoned book was. Was it perhaps about to be picked up by Barrett? The man was driven by combat, much like Kaladin. He would have considered books beneath him.

As they walked down the long corridor, towards where Crassus' desk had sat, Ayr was not surprised to see that he had been correct in his assumption. Where Crassus had spent hours upon hours mulling over texts and the paperwork that had stood on his desk like white towers, Barett was occupied. He stood still dressed in his wyrmguard armour, with his sword raised as he waited for Kaladin to strike. Both men darted around the other, circling like sharks, waiting for the opportune moment.

Kaladin was faster, and was the aggressor in the situation, taking a long stride forward, thrusting his blade towards Barrett's ribs. For as quick as he was, Barrett was just as fast, stepping backwards, dragging his blade down across his body. It met Kaladin's with a loud crash and the two fighters sprung apart no sooner than they had come together. Barrett struck back, with a blow that looked heavy, yet with the quickness of his feet, made it appear as if his sword was made from nothing but leaves.

They continued, back and forward, trading blows, locking their swords only to back away a second later. Kaladin nodded with approval as he parried a hip height strike from Barrett. In his next movement, Kaladin spun, turning it into a back fist, aimed at Barrett's head. He dodged underneath the strike, lashing out with a kick that connected with Kaladin's knee. Kaladin grunted out in pain and stumbled, raising his sword to protect himself as a two-handed killing blow from Barrett looked to crash down upon his head. It connected, buckling Kaladin's arm underneath the force of the strike and he looked up at Barrett with a smirk.

"Stop."

"Sir!"

He turned his attention towards the corridor and stood up as he saw Ayr and the entourage approaching. Kaladin stood up straight and he waved Barrett's sword away. They both stood stoic as they were approached with Barrett thrusting his sword over his shoulder, an expectant expression upon his face.

Marcello bowed before them. "Lord Chairman. Overlord. Ashbourne and Sunfire as you requested, sir!"

Kaladin sheathed his sword, sneering at them. Barrett mimicked his movements. "What about first light do you not understand?"

Ayr spoke up for them. "We were otherwise occupied."

"Make yourselves less occupied in the future. We have important business to attend to today."

"We do? What could you want from us, Kaladin?"

Kaladin turned and smirked at Barrett. "Lord Chairman, don't you have some operations to be attending to?"

Barrett bowed his head and stepped away. "Sir."

As Barrett's footsteps started to fade from earshot, Kaladin's smirk remained upon his face. "What have I got for you today? Administration, mostly. I'm sure that a man and woman of your talents wouldn't mind at all."

Ayr heard Elanor groan from beside him. "Are you serious? We could have just done this in our chambers."

Kaladin placed his hands on his hips and laughed, gesturing towards the desk that had a mountain of paperwork collected on it. "I'm not sure that you could have. These tasks are things that I would generally consider beneath myself and Barrett, yet they need to be done. You both know how to read and write considering your backgrounds. You can fulfill basic requisition orders for supplies."

Elanor folded her arms across her chest. "And if we refuse?"

A rare glint found its way to Kaladin's eyes. "I can make life even more unpleasant for you."

"What could you do to me that you haven't done already?"

Ayr felt a strange sensation knot in his stomach. He glared at Kaladin but did not let his true intentions be known. If only he could somehow communicate with her. Yet knowing that Kaladin had done things to her in the past, was not something that Ayr could overlook, especially not when Kaladin alluded to it on a regular basis. This work would be uncomfortable.

"You should not ask questions that you do not want the answer to, Elanor. Now that your tardiness has been explained, as poorly as it may have been, you have work to do."

Ayr rolled his eyes, and Kaladin caught the movement.

"If you have nothing better to do, Ashbourne, perhaps I should throw you from the side of the Obelisk? Your dragon will not catch you."

Realising his expression had given him away, Ayr stiffened his spine. "No, Overlord."

Another smirk crept over Kaladin's face, and he gestured towards the desk behind him. "Good. Then if you don't mind, let us begin. Marcello, Anders, remain here. Malachi, Travis, allow your rotation to take over."

The wyrmguard nodded as they were given their orders. The two that were dismissed turned and made their way back down the long corridor, moving back towards wherever they were currently being lodged. At least they still had one ally watching over them. Ayr glanced at Elanor who nodded, before she made her way towards the desk that had once been her father's. She swallowed as she stepped around behind it and Ayr joined her.

The chairs that Kaladin had provided were neither supportive nor were they comfortable. They were little more than black, round stools that barely allowed Ayr to view over the edge of the table. It would have been better if he was standing, but something in Kaladin's glare told him that he was not allowed to. With a heavy sigh, Ayr sat and immediately felt dwarfed by the papers that towered over him. Kaladin moved in between both him and Elanor without a word. Kaladin's seat appeared to at least be comfortable, with a reasonable back on it, the very same chair that Crassus had once sat in.

Yawning and feeling hunger beginning to develop in his belly, Ayr grabbed the first stack of papers that he could reach. What he had eaten before they had left the room clearly was not enough. The sooner this day was over and done with, the better. Surely, this was not all that Kaladin had in store for them all day. This would soon get repetitive and boring. It would be even worse if he had to sit beside Kaladin for the entire day.

"Everything here has already been vetted. You can sign it on my authority, and it will be acceptable."

Ayr just shook his head at Kaladin, unable to believe what he was hearing. Azura entered his mind to calm him.

Just do as he says, Ayr. I know you want to kill him but now is not the time. Not when the record would state that you have been in his presence.

If not now? When? The four of us could run away together and leave the Commonwealth entirely.

Do you want to be hunted like Dalton was for decades? That's no way to live your life. Think about Elanor and Evor.

I have a funny feeling that as long as she was with Evor it would not bother her.

If that's true, then ask her.

The day dragged on, each new piece of paper seeming like an impossible, and never-ending task that was still growing by the moment. Whenever Ayr scribbled at the bottom of one requisition request, another two seemed to take its place. It was no illusion; the papers were being replaced. As his hand grew sorer from all the signing that he was doing, he looked up at the ceiling. Small dragons were going about their business, flying in and out of the chambers, carrying letters to and from the desk. It was clear that in this time of great need that their talents were more useful than hiding away in the libraries all day.

Ayr put his head back down, continuing to sign his life away on Kaladin's behalf. On occasion he tried to steal glances at Elanor to see how she was coping with the task. She would have been the only other person in the room other than him that hated this more. Not only was she sitting beside Kaladin, but there was no sword fighting, magic or flying involved. Unfortunately for him, he could not steal a glance at Elanor as Kaladin was sandwiched in between them. Or rather they were sandwiched around his broad frame.

Azura continued to sing and hum to Ayr, filling his head with a gentle, soothing noise, so that with every scratch of his quill that Kaladin made, Ayr did not want to stand up and throttle him. It took every fibre in his being not to turn and glare every time that Kaladin coughed or grunted under his breath, otherwise interrupting the serene silence that surrounded them. Azura's song continued to play until the sun was nearing its highest peak and Ayr's hunger was threatening to consume him.

Ayr!

What? The suddenness of Azura's shout almost made him jump up off his stool.

I've just heard from the wyrmguard dragons that are guarding us. There are some new arrivals that just touched down on the Obelisk.

Okay? Ayr was confused as to why this was vital information. It had not been anything as large as Drementhol, otherwise Ayr would have heard it.

It would appear that Kaladin has recalled some old friends.

Old friends?

You'll see. Keep signing. They will be with you in a moment.

Curiosity was going to kill Ayr. Who were they? No doubt through his decades of service Kaladin had plenty of friends, even if how he treated Elanor was anything to go by. The Commonwealth respected strength above all else, and Kaladin for the most part was the embodiment of that strength despite all his flaws. When Ayr next glanced up from his work when he heard three separate sets of boots approaching them.

At the end of the hallway, he saw three riders approaching them, each had clearly left their dragons outside with Gundrag and Baindussa in the courtyard. Each of them, looked less impressed than the next, two males and one female. As Azura saw them through him, she shuddered in response.

Oh no.

Who are they, Azura?

Threats. I have a feeling that you might know their names.

Who are they?

That eldest man is Baldur Cole.

Fear shot down Ayr's spine. The name was very familiar to him, and he had heard the stories from none other than Dalton. Baldur Cole was in the same league as Anton Ashbourne, his name spoken with equal parts fear and admiration around them. He stood in a similar stature to Kaladin, tall with broad shoulders and narrow hips that came with decades of combat experience. Baldur wore his grey hair slicked back, which then flowed smoothly into his thick beard that matched it. His narrow eyes were solely focused on Ayr.

The other two riders were much the same in their approaches, both looking as grizzled as the other. Ayr assessed the second male, who appeared to be half the age of Baldur, equally as broad and just as powerful. Instead of greying hair, this man had none, bald to the skin on the top of his head, with a thick black goatee.

That is Romulus Khan.

I know who he is, Azura. That woman is Leyla Argoss. These are all riders that played their part in the war. I've seen them before.

Ayr stared at them. These men and this woman were not future Dragon Lords, they were targets. Each of them had played a hand in the fall of Dalton Ashbourne, each of them in some cases were all as pivotal as Kaladin himself had been. Yet unlike the previous Dragon Lords, these riders were not coming towards the end of their existence. Except for Baldur, they were all very much be in their prime. Despite Baldur being older, he was still in tremendous shape and looked as sharp as any other rider that Ayr had seen to date.

I'm going to have a harder time with them than the last lot.

Just because they played their part in your father's downfall does not immediately make them a threat.

I somehow feel like Dalton's influence has reached through into the politics of the Commonwealth once again.

Your father's rebellion built the Commonwealth into what it is today. Everything by proxy is due to his influence.

I am envious.

Careful, Ayr. That is not a positive trait to have.

I just want to build my own legacy.

I know, but there is no time for that. Go and be polite if they are happy to reciprocate. They cannot suspect anything is untoward.

TWENTY-SIX

Ayr rose off his stool, conflicted. There was no possible way that he could shake hands with this group. Baldur, having been the most vicious and vindictive both during the Ashbourne rebellion and afterwards. He and his dragon Rotang had slain thousands on the mere suspicion that a town had an inkling of a connection to the rebellion. There had been more than one time that Ayr had seen him reprimanded by Kaladin and others for being too hard on the people of the Commonwealth.

Leyla whilst not being on the same level as Baldur in terms of her destruction, was more beautiful, rivalling that of Elanor. Yet there was something about her that set her apart, making her more ragged with a deep hatred behind her brown eyes. Her equally as dark hair sat around her head like Elanor's running over her shoulders with ease. The sneer that she sent in Ayr's direction told him all that he needed to know about her as she approached him.

Romulus on the other hand was the most reserved of the three riders and had the smallest resume. Yet he had still burned villages throughout the Commonwealth to ensure that law and order was followed. He would also be very much a threat, skilled with both a blade and magic.

"You didn't tell me that you were keeping Ashbourne as a scribe, Kaladin! Is this how you lower yourself to Dalton's standards?"

"If keeping his son close to me is a downfall, I don't know what you want from me Leyla. Considering Dalton Ashbourne has already made his presence felt multiple times throughout the Commonwealth, we need to be utilising any asset that we can."

"Is he as powerful as you say he is?"

Kaladin stood up and nodded. He pushed his chair back, and moved around beside Elanor, running his hand over her shoulder. She shuddered at his touch, and the way that Kaladin turned his eyes towards him, told him everything that he needed to know. Ayr wanted to step towards him and throttle him for the action, but the situation demanded that he stay put. Kaladin's smirk spread across his face once more as he rounded the desk, greeting the three riders.

Kaladin extended his hand. First Romulus shook it, followed by Leyla and then finally Baldur clasped his hand around Kaladin's wrist and nodded.

"So, I doubt you called us here for no reason, Kaladin."

Kaladin smiled at Baldur. "You're always in alignment with what is going on in the world, Baldur. You are of course, correct."

"What was so pressing?"

"The Dragon Lords are dead, just as I suspected. Dalton Ashbourne showed his hand and had them killed."

Baldur and the others all drew in a deep breath, with Baldur turning his gaze towards Ayr. It hardened as he shook his head. "You need to kill him."

"And spark the wrath of Dalton more so than we already have?"

"We're surprised that it's taken you this long to send a taskforce out in pursuit of him. You could have killed him weeks ago if you were serious about this situation."

"If I could have caught him, I could have. He has an elder dragon, Baldur."

Baldur's tone was flat. "We've heard. That's no excuse, Kaladin."

"No, it's not, but as we both know, Dalton Ashbourne is dangerous. I have done my best to start protecting the people of the Commonwealth within what cities we have left. I do not need him showing
up on my watch and torching another city without being a thorn in
his side."

"Yet you refuse to murder his son. Why?"

Kaladin's eyes flicked towards Elanor and back to Baldur. "He has
value to me."

Romulus licked his lips and then spoke with a slow, deliberate
tone. "This is unlike you, Kaladin. Has the title of Overlord already
made you soft?"

Kaladin scowled at him. "You know that I am still the same man
that I was in the war. I called you all here today because I need to
appoint new Dragon Lords. You are the riders that best suit what we
need going forward into this new age."

All three of them, even Baldur took a step back. "You cannot be
serious, Kaladin."

Kaladin nodded and raised his eyebrows, breathing out through
his nose. "Desperate times call for desperate measures. I know that
none of you want that position thrust upon you."

"It's a lifetime of servitude. I do not think that Rotang and I can
be bottled up within the Haven until the day that we die. I would be
better served out there, hunting down Dalton."

"But your experience and calm head are needed at the Haven.
What if the people begin to gravitate towards Dalton?"

A darkness filled Baldur's eyes. "Then Rotang and I will deal with
them."

"I had no doubt in my mind that it would be any different. That is
why I want you as a Dragon Lord. The people will see your strength,
power and Rotang and will bow to you. Especially if you command
the title that I want to bestow upon you."

"You speak of all of these promises of power and glory, Kaladin, yet despite this, it relies on us taking more action than you have to date."

"These things take time."

"Hunting down Dalton Ashbourne should have been your first priority."

Kaladin grumbled and scowled at Baldur. "Do you have anything else to say? We should be working on this problem together. Dragging me across the coals will not help this cause."

"You were appointed as the Overlord due to your ability to act, were you not? Prove it before you decide to name us as the Dragon Lords."

Kaladin puffed his lips out and moved back towards the desk. Ayr narrowed his eyes wondering what his next move was. Instead of coming back around behind it, Kaladin raised his hand to one of the papers at the top of the pile in front of him. He grabbed and raised it towards Baldur.

"Do you see this? Do you see everything here before you? I am acting, Baldur. If Dalton Ashbourne rises out of the ground with an army at his back, we need to be prepared."

"We have thousands of riders ready to face him."

"And what happens when he has hundreds at his back like he did last time? Our advantage goes out the window."

"All we are hearing is excuses, Kaladin." Leyla had her arms folded over her chest as she glared up at him. "I personally will accept your offer to become a Dragon Lord. I want the title, and the responsibility that comes with it. The Commonwealth is my responsibility as a rider to look after."

Kaladin turned on her and extended his hand. "Thank you, Leyla. We will make history together."

Romulus' weathered face creased with doubt, his thick eyebrows drawing together like storm clouds over pale eyes. Still, he extended his calloused hand, the sleeve of his worn leather jacket sliding back to reveal an old scar burnt across his wrist. He mulled over the thought, teeth worrying his bottom lip until it reddened, shoulders hunched forward as he waited with patience as he waited for Kaladin to acknowledge his presence.

"I too, will become a Dragon Lord. The Commonwealth will not stand on its own without them at their helm. The servitude is something that will not deter me from achieving my goals. In fact, it is something that I have craved for many years."

Kaladin clasped Romulus's calloused palm, nodding once before pivoting toward Baldur. His right eyebrow arched high on his weathered forehead, a silent challenge hanging in the air between them. Baldur's face darkened like storm clouds gathering over mountains, his jaw working beneath his salt-and-pepper beard before he finally thrust forward his massive hand, his fingers thick as sausages, scarred knuckles white, accompanied by a guttural grunt that seemed to rise from the depths of his barrel chest.

"I'll accept your offer to become a Dragon Lord then, Kaladin. It appears you are not willing to take no for an answer."

The corner of Kaladin's mouth curled. "No, I am not."

"Yet there is only three of us. Outside of the Overlord, there were four Dragon Lords was there not?"

"I have not found a suitable replacement for the fourth yet. Three will suffice for now."

Elanor shifted in her seat beside Ayr. There was an opening for her, she just had to take the opportunity but now was not the time to capitalise upon it. Ayr had no doubt in his mind that she would be able to work her ways, opening Kaladin up to the idea of making her a Dragon Lord. She had the lineage, the dragon and the strength to do it.

Baldur nodded, satisfied with the response from Kaladin. "Then we will discuss the future of the Commonwealth and what your plans are in the coming days. I assume you will want us to travel to the Haven when you find the fourth?"

"Yes, despite these being trying times, we should keep to tradition. I will find the fourth in the coming days and we shall proceed to the Haven."

"And what is Dalton doing in that time? Preparing."

Kaladin spun to glare at Romulus. "And so are we. Do not think for a moment that I have been sitting here idle. As you will soon find out, it takes a lot to keep this place operational. We have dozens of new riders entering the fold, their dragons ready to take to the sky against Dalton."

"New riders will not win the coming war."

Kaladin raised an eyebrow. "Like they didn't win the last one, Baldur?"

Baldur finally turned and took a step away. "Summon us to the Haven when you have decided on the fourth Dragon Lord. I'll be waiting. Good day, Kaladin."

Romulus and Leyla also bowed to Kaladin before they turned on their heel, following Baldur down the corridor without another word. Kaladin stood stationary like a statue and watched them leave, not calling out, or so much as conveying a single emotion until they were well and truly gone. Once they had vanished from sight, he turned with a coiled fist.

"Ungrateful fucks."

Ayr caught Elanor's eye, noting how the corners of her mouth curled upward in that familiar way that made her eyes dance with mischief. The smirk spread across her face like wildfire, dimpling her right cheek. But as Kaladin pivoted back toward them, her expression transformed in an instant. The playful light extinguished, her jaw setting firm, shoulders squaring beneath her fitted tunic. She matched Kaladin's granite-like demeanour, not a flicker of emotion betraying her previous amusement. Kaladin lowered himself into the ornate chair behind the desk, his movements deliberate and measured, his gaze never once drifting toward Elanor as his calloused hands came to rest on the polished wood surface.

"Sit Ashbourne. We're not finished yet."

Ayr did as he was told and stared at the stacks of paper in front of him. In the time that Kaladin had been speaking with the new Dragon Lords, the assistant dragons had not stopped bringing more paperwork in for them to sign. Without needing further encouragement from Kaladin, Ayr went back to work, burying his head in the papers. The day continued to drag on, as Azura's song filled his head once more, keeping him focused on the work ahead of him. The shadows were beginning to grow longer in the room when Kaladin looked up from his work.

"Elanor, you can go."

Elanor turned her head, staring at the papers still in front of Ayr and Kaladin, perplexed. They were still just as high as they had been before they'd begun. "But we're not finished yet?"

"You're finished. Now leave us."

Elanor shot Ayr a look of confusion but rose from her stool regardless. Kaladin nodded, confirming his wishes. Elanor left her quill on the desk before she stepped away from it. She said nothing, her footsteps heavy, filling the void of silence that surrounded them. Heat rose at the base of Ayr's neck. Why had Kaladin sent her away when they still had so much left to do?

Stay calm.

Is now the time?

No.

Ayr felt like he was back in the cage with Bersos lurking just outside it. Even though Kaladin was barely paying any attention to him, he felt like he was being watched. The dragons continued to soar overhead, dropping more letters into their piles, and Ayr continued to sign away with his quill. Hunger consumed him, and he wanted nothing more than to put the quill down. Having sat at this stool for hours, slouched over and scribbling a hasty signature on hundreds of documents was finally getting to him. Darkness was starting to creep into Kaladin's office when he finally put his quill down.

"You can leave now Ashbourne."

Ayr glanced at him with a side eye. "Are you sure?"

"Yes. Go."

Not wanting to wait for another moment so that Kaladin could change his mind and give him another task, Ayr pushed the stool out from underneath him and stood. His eyes locked on the door that seemed so far away. He had only taken a few steps when he heard Kaladin's voice once again.

"So, your brother has come to the Obelisk, has he, Ashbourne?"

Ayr's head snapped back around, not believing he had heard what Kaladin had said properly. Kaladin still had his quill resting against his palm with a casual demeanour. "What did you say?"

"Your brother, Bryne Ashbourne. You believe he resides within the Obelisk now?"

Ayr straightened his back. "I do. I have seen him in the flesh."

Kaladin's hand fell to the stack of paper that was still beside him. It was a lot smaller than it had been at the start of the day, but the growing hunger in Ayr's stomach made him want to treat the papers as food. If only Kaladin was not in the room, he would have devoured them. Kaladin stared up at him, as if chewing on his next thought.

"And what does your brother want to do here?"

Ayr frowned. "I'm not sure."

"You're not sure? You're his brother, aren't you?"

"That does not mean that our goals and values align. I do not know my father's plans, nor am I privy to them. If I was, I'd assume that it would be more meaningful than spending my days rotting away in your office completing paperwork for you."

Kaladin leaned back in his chair and frowned, his eyes running over Ayr's face, up and down like he was a doctor examining him for any flaws. Yet Kaladin's gaze ran deeper than that, his cold, calculating stare telling Ayr that he was searching for more. Ayr's jaw tightened, not wanting to give Kaladin any expression that he could assume about.

"You're a strange creature, Ashbourne. No wonder why the white dragon chose you. It's a shame that she did. She had so much potential."

Ayr grit his teeth in frustration, now no longer able to look past Kaladin's slight. "She chose well. The potential is still there. I will do whatever I can to serve the Commonwealth."

Kaladin snorted. "The last time an Ashbourne said that an uprising started not long after. I don't believe you."

"For your sake, you'd best start. Is there anything else, Overlord?"

Kaladin waved his hand with a dismissive gesture. "No, I'm sick of wasting time on you. Retreat to your chambers and the lovely Lady Sunfire."

Ayr stuck his chin out. "Thank you for the wonderful suggestion, Overlord."

Be careful. Now is not the time. Not after what we've just done.

Hmm, it is not. He needs to be dealt with sooner rather than later. We can't keep living like this under his thumb.

I know, but your brother is here, is he not?

He is. I don't trust it.

Perhaps we should trust it. Perhaps Dalton is readying his next phase. He did take his time with you, did he not?

But that took months before I was ready to do something for him.

Yet he trained you your entire life for this did he not? Have patience and be wary.

I don't like waiting for something to happen to me.

I know, Ayr. That's why I'm here. Enjoy the time with Elanor, Evor and I. Once the powder keg is ignited, who knows when life will go back to normal?

Ayr could feel the warmth radiating from Azura's words like sunlight through stained glass, each syllable glowing with affection as she spoke to him. His lips curled into a smile, the tension in his shoulders melting away. As Azura's melodic voice guided his thoughts away from Kaladin and the stern-faced new Dragon Lords, his mind drifted instead to the silk-draped bed he would share with Elanor once he returned to their chambers.

TWENTY-SEVEN

I have serious doubts about Ayr, Elanor.

I know you do. My opinion of him has not changed, however. You need to know that.

He destroyed the Dragon Lords with ease. How can we continue to entertain him? I can feel that he is corrupting Azura.

I can fix him. He did it for us.

And what if he kills Kaladin right now?

How many times have I wanted to kill someone, yet who was there to step in on my behalf? If Azura deems it as not wise, will she?

Not if she is compromised.

She's your promised, is she not?

Evor rolled his eyes at her as he settled down in the bed. Elanor on the other hand smiled to herself as she laid back down on her bed. She could sense Evor's discomfort, as he wrapped himself around Azura again. Azura had said nothing to her since she had returned, but she could tell that she was in conversation with Ayr. Her silent demeanour was otherwise echoed by Evor's as he now settled into rest.

The braziers that hung around the room were lit, providing the room with an ample amount of light as darkness fell upon what had been an interesting day. If Kaladin had another potential future Dragon Lord in mind, he had not betrayed any sign to knowing who it would be. If he had only found the three candidates who could lead the Commonwealth forward, Elanor believed him. Kaladin was many things, but a liar was not one of them. Could she leverage her way into his mind and into making him pick her? This was not an ordinary position. Perhaps, she could sell it as a way that he could maintain his closeness to her.

She mulled her thoughts over in her mind, Evor sometimes agreeing, but otherwise sighing in disagreement. Elanor could feel his disappointment at some of the questions she posed to herself, but he remained quiet and unjudgmental. As she lay in the bed, Elanor stared up at the ceiling. The two wyrmguard, Marcello and Malachi had met her in the courtyard, refreshed and reinvigorated after their shift, escorting her back to the chambers. She kept finding her mind drifting towards Ayr. Why had Kaladin let her off early when there had been so much to do. Azura had not yet been alarmed, so she doubted that anything had happened to him, but with Kaladin, anything was possible.

The minutes continued to tick by, and at long last, the doors to the chambers creaked open. Elanor shot up, hoping to see Ayr, and as the gap widened, she was rewarded. Ayr stepped into the room, looking like he had just run a marathon. His face was tight, even as Azura raised her head with glee.

"Kaladin suspects something."

"We've given him nothing to be concerned about."

Ayr shrugged and sighed with a sound so loud that it sounded like it had come from Azura. He crossed the room towards where Elanor laid on their bed. She sat up to greet him and swung her legs around so that they dangled off the edge of the bed. "We can't be certain."

"It's his hatred for you. Ever since you took me from him."

"Ever since I took you from him?" Ayr raised an eyebrow, confused. "How long before we became bonded together were you still seeing him?"

Elanor puffed out her lips. "Only a couple of months, if that. Things had turned sour when I knew he would not be the one for me. I left him, but we kept seeing each other discreetly. He did everything he could to try and win me back, but I led him on."

"Why would you do that?"

Elanor's lips curled as she sniggered. "I enjoyed the chase. I could have laid with a dozen other riders here, if not more. As you know age isn't a real defining factor here amongst riders. Yet there was something about him and his status that I enjoyed."

"So, you toyed with him?"

Elanor shrugged, even though she did not need to explain herself to Ayr. "I did, but he wanted to be toyed with. He kept chasing me, despite having burned the house down around him on the way out."

"Who broke it off with who?"

Elanor found herself staring into Ayr's eyes. "I did. But that will not happen with you. You made a promise to me. Our dragons are promised to each other, and nothing will be able to break that bond. The only way we could make it more permanent is if we magically bonded ourselves together."

"I can make that happen."

Elanor laughed and her smile continued to spread. "I know you can, but there's no need. I'd have an easier time cutting off my own arm. I'm drawn to you, and there's a warmth with you that I don't get with anyone else."

"All of this sweet talk is lovely, Elanor, but how was the rest of the day?"

Elanor blew out her lips again. "My day? What about yours? What did Kaladin want you to remain behind for?"

"Nothing out of the ordinary. I signed more papers, more orders and when I left, he asked about my brother."

"How did he know about that?"

Ayr frowned, the creases in his forehead becoming more prevalent. "I'm not sure. Nobody spoke to him whilst we were there. No wyrmguard or anything. It was just a day of signing documents."

"Are you suggesting he knows something that we don't?"

"I am."

"What interest would he have in your brother?"

Ayr chewed on his bottom lip. "Outside of Dalton, the only swordsman that could beat me regularly was Bryne. A point that he made whenever he got the chance."

"Has Dalton sent Bryne here to kill you then?"

Ayr rubbed the side of his face. "I don't know! I wish I knew. But you know as well as I do, that Dalton never reveals his full plan to anyone. It's only the pieces that he wants to tell you. I can't make any guesses as to why Bryne is here. Is it because I haven't done my part yet?"

"What was your part?"

"I had to bond with a dragon and become a rider. That was it. He told me nothing more."

"Did he tell you nothing or is that all that you're telling me?"

"I made a promise to you, Elanor. I'm not going to lie to you now."

"And your magic?"

"Something that I didn't know that I had. That's the truth of it."

"Hmm." Elanor frowned and turned away from him.

Based off what Azura has told me in confidence, I do not think he is lying, Elanor.

But you have your doubts.

About him. Not her.

They are one. You need to cast your doubts aside before they rub off on me.

"It was something that Dalton was not impressed about either. He expected me to have more. The fact that I could do what I do to the Dragon Lords is very much a surprise to me as well."

"I should have pushed you further when I was training you."

Ayr shook his head in response. "There was no need. My father often told me that if I didn't have magic from his training that it would come when it was ready."

Elanor raised her eyebrow, sceptical. "And that just so happened to be when the Dragon Lords were in danger?"

Ayr's dead gaze met her eyes. "It just so happened to be when you were in danger."

"I don't know what you want me to say. Do you want me to be impressed?"

"It's the truth. That's what happened. I'm never going to lie to you."

Elanor flicked her eyes towards Evor and Azura. Azura's head was still above her paws, and she nodded. It was clear that she thought that Ayr was telling the truth. If it was good enough for her then it was good enough for Elanor. Evor grunted his agreement and settled back into a tight circle around Azura. He was unbothered, not wanting to argue with Elanor any longer. It was a rare moment, but one that she was welcome for as silence filled her head.

Ayr moved into her space with deliberate steps, his tall frame casting a shadow that enveloped her. Underneath this protective darkness, Elanor loosened her shoulders as she took in a deep breath. The tension melted from her face like ice under sun. He wrapped his strong arms around her, one hand cradling the small of her back while the other pressed between her shoulder blades. Elanor collapsed into him, her forehead finding the hollow of his collarbone, her fingers clutching at the fabric of his shirt as though he were the only solid thing in a world gone liquid.

"What are we doing, Ayr?"

He pulled away from her with a sudden motion. Elanor looked up at him as she looked down at him. A moment of stillness passed between them. "What do you mean?"

"I've never felt this way about anyone before. How can I be sure that you won't betray me should it be convenient to you? I thought Kaladin was a secure option, but even he turned his back on me. What's to say that you won't do the same to me?"

"You know I won't."

Elanor's breath caught in her throat. "I've heard it all before. I know you made me a promise, but how can I trust you, Ayr? You're still enslaved by your father. Ashenfort showed that. He could have killed the Dragon Lords himself, even though he entrusted me with the task."

Ayr's eyes darkened. "Did you really want me to take that risk when you were in danger?"

"No."

"Then we will continue to play this game with Dalton, until the Commonwealth can work out how to stop him, or until he lets us go."

"Is he likely to do that?"

She already knew the answer to that question. She could read it in the tightening of Ayr's jaw and the cold dread settling like a stone in her stomach. If Dalton wanted to keep his hold on them, he would do as much as his fingers would continue to weave those invisible threads of control around their necks. She brought Ayr closer to her, fingers trembling against the warmth of his skin, and he sunk towards the bed with her, the mattress sighing beneath their combined weight as shadows from the window bars stretched across them like prison gates.

Ayr shuffled his weight and came to rest in beside her, and within moments they resembled Evor and Azura, curled up against each other. Even though there was almost none of their skin touching, it was still intimate. Ayr wrapped his hands around hers, snaking his fingers in between hers, holding her hand. She could feel his breath against the back of her neck, and she felt like Evor was warming her. She shuddered and felt the hairs on the back of her neck stand up, and Ayr chuckled.

Elanor felt at ease in his grasp, allowing herself to relax. She allowed herself to slip into the familiar rhythm that they had become accustomed to. Ayr was not only just comfortable, but he had also shown that he could be reliable. Yet as she laid there, enjoying his presence, one pressing question was at the front of her mind.

"What do you want to do about the new proposed Dragon Lords?"

"Well, that's what I was going to ask you. Are you going to put your name forward to become one?"

Elanor frowned even though it would have been unseen by Ayr. "I was considering it. Is it what Dalton wants though?"

She felt Ayr shrug behind her. "I don't know. He is hard to read. Even when I was under his care full time, I could not discern his next movements. Dalton does what Dalton wants to do with no reason or rhyme."

"But he has a plan, doesn't he?"

"I don't want to guess as to what it is. He's killing everyone that played a part in ruining his rebellion, and he's taking his time doing it. I don't like it."

"And your brother?"

"We will need to investigate further."

"Can I trust you with that? I don't need to be following you around again after another instance of you trying to rip someone else's head off."

She felt Ayr's breath on her neck as he breathed into her. "Yes, Elanor. I can manage that."

Elanor groaned and flexed her hands. "Good, now do you have something else you can show me that you can handle?"

Ayr gathered the cascade of her hair in his calloused fingers, sweeping it aside to expose the vulnerable curve where her neck met her shoulder. His lips pressed against that tender hollow, slow at first and then with mounting hunger that left her skin flushed and tingling. The heat of his mouth sent electric currents racing down her spine, pooling like molten gold in her lower belly. Elanor arched against him with a half-suppressed sigh, her body shifting restlessly beneath the sheets as Ayr repositioned himself behind her, the solid warmth of his chest against her back promising pleasures yet to come.

TWENTY-EIGHT

"I'm bored, Elanor."

"Well, what do you want me to do? Kaladin has insisted on keeping us couped up here. If I go against him, he'll just punish us even more than he already is."

"He's kept us locked in here for days. All we've done is sleep, eat, fuck and repeat."

Elanor sighed as she rolled over to look at him, her auburn hair spilling across the rumpled sheets like liquid fire. She reached out, her slender fingers cupping his stubbled chin, feeling the warmth of his skin against her palm as she guided his face towards her own. Her eyes, heavy-lidded with desire, locked onto his lips before she brought them to hers for another lingering kiss.

As he pulled away from her, Elanor laughed. "Some people would not complain about that."

"I'm not. I would just rather be out there flying or training, doing something that will make a difference."

"You're incredible."

Ayr raised an eyebrow. "How?"

"Because even after all that you've achieved in such a short amount of time, you still want to go out there and find something else to do. Relax."

"I can't. Especially now that Bryne is here. Kaladin has kept us busy in his office for days. That is the only reprieve that we get from this place."

"Then I will speak to him today. Tell him that someone he's supposed to be keeping a close eye on is bored of his mediocre tasks and company."

Ayr grunted as he sat up. "No. We're riders, Elanor. We have our dragons; I am sick of being at the beck and call of Kaladin."

"You know what, you're right. What's the worst he can do?"

Evor raised his head at last. "Kill us."

Elanor rolled her eyes and let out a soft laugh as she followed Ayr's ascension. "What's new? I think I'm hearing what you're saying though. We should just do something."

"That's what I was thinking. What did you have in mind?"

"We should go for a ride."

Evor shook his magnificent obsidian head, sending ripples down his serpentine neck. The razor-edged spikes along his spine rose like a forest of daggers, catching the light as they flared outward with a soft scraping sound. He rolled his muscular shoulders beneath the leathery folds of his wings, which rustled like ancient parchment as they shifted against his gleaming scales.

"I do not think that is wise. The wyrmguard dragons are still just outside."

Azura laughed as she stood up. "You don't think that we both can't out speed them? I thought you were bolder than that, Evor."

A snort erupted from Evor's snout and smoke filled the room around his head. "I am little one, but if you want a race worthy of Chilijo himself, then I will give it to you."

"I think we can manage that, don't you, Ayr?"

A smile came to his lips. "I've got nothing better to do today."

"Then we ride."

Elanor leapt up out of bed and crossed towards the mantle above the fireplace. She reached for their masks which had sat there for the past few days. They had done nothing except gather dust as they waited for clearance from Kaladin to be able to fly again. With both masks in her hand, Elanor crossed back towards the bed with a cheeky grin on her face. She threw Ayr's mask at him, and he caught it in one hand.

Ayr stood up off the bed, the cool stone floor sending a shiver through his bare feet as he crossed to where Elanor stood. She was retrieving a fresh uniform from the wardrobe; it's crisp black fabric with silver threading that caught the morning light filtering through the curtains. As she slipped the fitted jacket over her shoulders, Ayr reached past her, his arm brushing against hers, and withdrew his own uniform hanging beside hers. Like her he dressed in haste, and within moments they were both ready.

Ayr shot a side eye at Elanor. "Are you ready to do this?"

She responded with a mischievous grin that crinkled the corners of her eyes, followed by a slow, deliberate wink that promised adventure. Elanor's auburn hair cascaded around her shoulders as she flicked it outward, her slender fingers working through the silken strands to untangle any knots. With practiced precision, she gathered the wild mane into a tight, severe bunch at the nape of her neck, ensuring not a single rebellious strand would escape once she slipped the obsidian mask over her head.

"Evor!"

"Yes, Elanor. I will draw the wyrmguard away from little one."

Evor reared his head and careened his neck so that his head ended up beside Elanor, making it easier for her to climb aboard. Whilst Ayr did not have as much of a climb to make his way onto Azura's head, she kept it lowered for him to make his journey easier. He climbed with his mask in one hand, and as he made his ascent, he could feel Azura growing more excited underneath him. Whilst she was not rebellious, he was feeling a new energy coming from her.

Are you okay, Azura?

I get to fly with my rider and my promised, something that we have not done in days.

Even if we are racing against the wyrmguard dragons?

Azura turned her head, just so that Ayr could see her dazzling blue eye. He swore that he could have seen her smirk, and the tone of her voice inside his head, told him that she was. Evor stretched out and pushed against the window that was their barrier to the outside world as Elanor tried to find her seating on him in her saddle.

Ayr found no problems as he climbed up Azura, using the armour that was still embedded in her scales as a new leverage point. Azura did not complain about him moving up her body, nor did she complain about the armour that he knew was causing her discomfort. She was as hardy as ever; the armour having not bothered her for many days. Ayr was glad that it was no longer causing her any discomfort, nor was her saddle. He climbed into it, feeling relieved that they were doing something once again.

There's no going back now, Ayr.

Evor started forward, surging forward with the raw power that only he could muster with his enormous frame. He leapt from the window, issuing an enormous roar, that let the outside world know that he was coming. Evor burst through the open window in a flash and with one beat of his wings he had vanished from sight. With Evor out of the way, Azura surged forward, following in his footsteps. With the wind in his face, Ayr felt alive once again. Azura was revelling in delight underneath him. Evor came back into view, but he was not alone.

The two wyrmguard dragons, one red and one blue that had been guarding the window were chasing after Evor in hot pursuit, with their riders on their backs. Azura made her presence known, issuing a roar of her own as she shot out into the sky. The first of the wyrmguard dragons turned its head, and saw them, and then broke away from the pursuit from Evor. Azura dove, underneath the dragon's gaping maw, avoiding its claws as its massive body soared overhead.

Well done, Azura! Keep going!

Azura streamlined her wings and shot towards the ground, further evading the wyrmguard dragon above. Ayr threw his head back to see it turning in the sky, underneath the protection that the Obelisk provided, but it was already far too late for it to catch Azura. Ayr leaned forward in the saddle, a smirk on his lips underneath his mask as Azura shot off after Evor. The first wyrmguard dragon was still chasing him, but Evor was pulling ahead.

With her newfound burst of speed, Azura shot past the first wyrmguard dragon, its red scales flashing like angry pennies in the sun as its yellow eyes widened in surprise. The beast's massive head swivelled to follow her, its forked tongue tasting the wind where she had been. The distraction allowed Evor to pull further ahead, his dark wings cutting through the clouds like blades. He roared again, a sound like thunder cracking stone, as Azura moved in underneath his shadow. Ayr could already feel the cool darkness of Evor washing over both of them.

Azura kept her head straight ahead, and focused, whilst Ayr made sure that the wyrmguard dragons were not catching them. As Azura's wingbeats struck down around his ears, Ayr noticed that the wyrmguard were beginning to fall behind, until they reached the point that they had given up the chase. There was no point in trying to track Evor when his powerful wings made him almost uncatchable except to the largest of dragons. For the first time since the pursuit had begun, Ayr spotted Elanor in her saddle as Azura rose around Evor.

She circled around Evor, and judging from the reaction that came from Evor, he was happy about their progress. They continued to fly away from the Obelisk, and the city below gave way to the all too familiar landscape that surrounded it. There was a sense of freedom coursing through Ayr's body that he had not felt in days, if not weeks, since they had first been taken to the Haven. Now that the wyrmguard had fallen off their trail, Azura felt more at ease underneath him.

Azura followed Evor as he made his descent towards the forest that awaited them below. Evor circled over the forest as he searched for a place to land. Azura hovered above, her wings beating down on either side of Ayr as Evor brought himself to the ground. Trees fell where they stood underneath his massive weight and silence fell over the area as he settled in the clearing that he had made.

Azura needed no direction and made her way down to land beside Evor. He watched her descent, refusing to take his eyes off her. Ayr felt Azura melting underneath his gaze, enamoured by the attention that he was giving her.

"You glow under the sunlight, little one. If only the rest of the world was as radiant as you."

"I only glow because of you, Evor."

Ayr smiled underneath his mask, feeling electric with their connection bubbling away. All Azura wanted to do was cuddle into Evor, and indulge in his presence, even though it was already what she had been doing for days as they had rotted away inside the Obelisk. As Azura touched down onto the ground, Ayr felt a sense of freedom and fullness he had not experienced in weeks. Being outside in nature, with the sun fully upon his body, was not a sensation he had become accustomed to. It filled him with as much warmth as Azura did, and he realised he had missed it.

The earthy perfume of pine needles and damp moss filled Ayr's nostrils, while the unmistakable sulfuric tang that always clung to Azura and Evor, like struck matches and hot springs woven through it. The combination swirled in his senses, heady and forbidden as strong wine. Ayr continued to smile, happy to be outside the restrictions of the Obelisk and enjoying time with Azura. He went to dismount from Azura, swinging his legs out of the saddle and slid down her neck, landing feet first on the ground.

His boots sunk into the soft terrain, under his feet, and he revelled in the forest that grew up around him. Being on the ground gave him a different view of the world, once again being the smallest thing within the vicinity, outside of the fallen trees that Evor had crushed under his weight. He moved around, flattening more underfoot, making more room for Azura to move around.

Elanor whipped her mask off her head and flicked her hair out behind her. "Thank Chilijo for that. It's about time we had some space to ourselves."

"We had the room."

Evor snorted down from above Ayr. "You know that's not what she meant. I am grateful for the opportunity to fly once again, Elanor, even if it is only brief."

"Our next flight will be longer."

A grumble came from deep within Evor's chest as he turned towards the sky once again. "I do not think so, Elanor. We have company."

"For Chilijo's sake!"

Elanor's fingers brushed against the worn leather belt at her waist, seeking the familiar cold steel of a sword that was not there. Her eyes darted skyward, pupils contracting against the harsh sunlight, and Ayr followed her gaze with a sharp turn of his head. He exhaled, his breath catching as Azura's massive, scaled body tensed before unleashing a thunderous roar that shook the very air around them. Above them, half a dozen dark silhouettes were approaching in a hurry. Each dragon was another member of the wyrmguard.

"That didn't take long."

Ayr raised an eyebrow towards Elanor. "Did we really expect anything else?"

"Not really."

Ayr braced himself for the arrival of the wyrmguard, watching as they descended like dark shadows hanging over the surrounding landscape. He could feel Azura's heart beating beside his, her anticipation rising with his own. If the wyrmguard wanted to fight, they would be outmatched physically, but Ayr could already feel his power beginning to course through his veins as Azura started to feed him.

Not yet, Ayr.

But they're coming.

Do you want the entire wrath of the Commonwealth brought down on our heads? Kaladin believes that you are valuable. If they attack, then we know.

Ayr tightened his fist until his knuckles blanched white against sun-browned skin, the tendons in his forearm standing out like cords as they waited beneath the canopy of ancient oaks. A bead of sweat traced the line of his jaw. It was all that he could do unless he wanted to go against Azura's guidance. Her words still echoed in his mind, her voice carrying that familiar iron certainty that brooked no argument. She was right, for now, though the admission tasted bitter on his tongue. Elanor's voice broke through the silence of the forest.

"I'll handle this, Ayr."

"Are you sure?"

"We've seen what happens when you are pressed. We don't want that getting out of hand again, now do we?"

Ayr shook his head and smirked, unable to argue with her. The wyrmguard continued to surge towards them, and within moments, were touching down in the forest around them. Their dragons, all a similar size to Evor crushed trees underneath their weight, as they surrounded them. Ayr still felt Azura pushing magical energy into his system, but it swirled around his body like a halo. If they attacked, he and Azura would be untouchable. The first wyrmguard that had touched down leaned forward in his saddle.

"Lady Sunfire, Ayr Ashbourne, what the fuck do you think you're doing?"

Elanor stepped forward, bravado and cockiness written across her features as she grinned up at the wyrmguard. "You need to relax.

"You broke out of your containment and left the Obelisk without the expressed permission of the Overlord."

"He was keeping us and our dragons imprisoned for days at a time. I thought it would be wise to let them get a flight in for once."

"The Overlord will hear of this insubordination, Lady Sunfire!"

"Good, tell him. If he wants us to return, he can come and get us himself."

The wyrmguard turned his nose up underneath his mask. "You will not like where this goes."

"Maybe not, but Kaladin needs some flexibility. We cannot perform to our high standards if he is insistent on this course of action."

The wyrmguard glanced around at his peers, a silent communication passing between them. Ayr wondered if Marcello and Malachi were under any of the masks. Their dragons did not seem to be present in the group that surrounded them. He wanted to lash out, but Azura kept prodding into his mind, wanting him to stop thinking his violent thoughts.

"You will do as the Overlord and the Commonwealth command!"

"You don't want this fight. If Kaladin wishes to speak to us, bring him here. I'm enjoying our time in the sun."

The wyrmguard turned away, his dragon turning back towards the Obelisk. "Enjoy your time then Lady Sunfire and pray you haven't flown too close to the sun. The rest of you remain here. I will fetch the Overlord."

The lead wyrmguard left, leaving the others behind. They kept their enclosure around them, and all that Ayr and Elanor could do was stand underneath the enormous shadow of Evor. Even with his size standing between the riders and the wyrmguard, Evor could not assist them to be free of their gaze. The wyrmguard and their dragons were like hungry jackals, however frozen in place, all of them waiting for the arrival of Kaladin.

In hindsight, I do not think we should have done this, Ayr.

We had to break the chain, Azura. If this comes down on us hard, so be it.

You humans are reckless.

I'm with Elanor, we've had enough. Kaladin can't keep doing this to us.

Kaladin is the Overlord of the Commonwealth, Ayr. You swore an oath to serve the Commonwealth, and you have gone against his wishes.

Spare me the lecture, Azura. You know what's coming, as well as I do.

I do, but that did not mean that we had to be so brash.

It's done. We will work through it like we always do.

The purple figure of Gundrag emerged on the horizon and he was not alone. Ayr kept his eyes on them as they approached, wanting to discern what Kaladin was thinking before he got there. If Kaladin had been furious with them, he had not shown it in his body language. He and Gundrag had arrived with a fresh entourage of wyrmguard.

Gundrag and the dragons that landed were graceful, not in a rush, instead taking their time ensuring that they did not skewer themselves on any trees. Malachi and Marcello were the only two not to come into land, the brothers remaining in the air just above the heads of Evor and the other tall dragons.

Kaladin swung down from Gundrag as the mighty purple dragon lowered his head, and he touched down on the ground with as much grace as a man half his size. He strode across the fractured ground towards where Ayr and Elanor waited for him. Elanor was the first to approach him, stepping out from underneath Evor's shadow and Ayr followed her, only steps behind.

As he approached them, Kaladin tore off his silver-etched mask with a violent jerk, revealing a face contorted with rage. Deep lines carved valleys between his brows and his jaw clenched so firm, a muscle twitched beneath the stubbled skin of his cheek. When he finally spoke, his voice carried the same cold, cutting edge as the wyrmguard's with clipped syllables that fell like stones into still water.

"Do you have a death wish? I could have you executed for this!"

Elanor's outburst was immediate. "For this? What? Going on a ride with our dragons? Are you serious, Kaladin? Pull your head in! They need exercise and stimulation as much as we do, regardless of what you think. Just because you are happy for Gundrag to laze around the Obelisk all day does not mean we are all like that."

Kaladin's scowl was growing deeper, by the second as he stepped closer to them. When he stopped only paces away, he folded his arms over his chest and puffed out his chest. "You were supposed to be helping me! I don't trust either of you and now you've eroded what little trust I had!"

"I asked you time and time again to let us out, yet you refused. I saw it justified to take matters into my own hands."

"Did he put the idea in your head?"

Kaladin's finger shot out, pointing at Ayr's face, only inches away. Ayr took a step back and recoiled, out of disgust. The magic and the adrenaline that Azura had been feeding him was still flowing through his blood. All Ayr had to do was turn his hand over and will the energy from his body for Kaladin to be engulfed. "Careful of who you're accusing, Kaladin."

"Or what, you'll call your father on me?"

"You have no idea what I'm capable of."

Kaladin's expression held nothing except distain for him. "You've both turned your back on the Commonwealth. I am going to finish this once and for all. I will deal with your father, Lord Ashbourne and show him your head upon a spike."

"Kaladin, stop this. This can be fixed."

Kaladin's eyes flicked to Elanor's once again. There was nothing but anger behind them. "No. Bring Evor. Follow me back to the Obelisk. I would have a word with you in private, Elanor."

Ayr spoke up. "And me?"

"The wyrmguard will escort you back to your chambers where you will await my judgement once more. Leave this time, and we'll have your head."

TWENTY-NINE

Elanor's throat constricted like a vice, the muscles seizing beneath her skin though Kaladin had merely gestured with those long, calloused fingers of his. She scrambled up Evor's scales, each one warm and slick beneath her palms as she climbed. The dragon's neck pulsed with power beneath her thighs. Her stomach plummeted as if she'd swallowed a stone, the weight of dread spreading outward until it consumed her from navel to spine, from ribs to hips. Evor did his best to comfort her as she climbed up him and made her way to the saddle.

What is done is done, Elanor. We must accept our fate.

Kaladin won't do the right thing.

We cannot control him. Do what he wishes of you if you wish to see another dawn.

It can't be that serious, can it?

You know him as well as I do, Elanor. If he made an appearance, especially with how chaotic his role is now, then you know it's affected him.

What does he want, Evor?

I dread to think.

Then fly and see us to our fate.

Elanor locked her legs into the saddle as Gundrag took off in front of them. His enormous form shot up into the sky and beckoned with his tail for Evor to follow. There was no compulsion or magic that made them follow them, only Kaladin's threat and the looming presence of the wyrmguard that remained on the ground. Whilst slower, Ayr had mounted Azura, and they were also looking to take to the sky. There was nothing she could do for them now. The only sound that filled Elanor's ears was the sound of Evor's wings as they ascended back towards the Obelisk.

Elanor continued to mull the same questions over in her mind as Evor hummed to her, in an attempt to calm her nerves. With the shadow of Gundrag and Kaladin looming in front of her, there was nothing she could do. Evor followed Gundrag all the way to the rooftop of the Obelisk, where Baindussa reared his head staring towards them with his cold, dead, empty eyes. Since the death of Crassus, the great green dragon had only grown more absent, his old age and the loss of Crassus catching up to him.

"Gundrag, Evor. Why are you here again?"

"Official Overlord business, Baindussa. Let us pass."

Baindussa's head tracked Gundrag's movements as he came to land in the courtyard. Smoke pilfered out of Baindussa's nostrils as he recoiled upon hearing the landing of Gundrag and Evor was making his landing right behind him. Baindussa looped around one of the spires, his head transfixed towards Gundrag.

"No! I have had enough of you desecrating my home!"

Gundrag's snarl matched Baindussa's in ferocity. He stood up tall, reaching his neck towards the rooftop. "Leave us, Baindussa!"

"This is my home, Gundrag. I have nowhere else to go."

Gundrag's eyes narrowed akin to Kaladin's as he stared a hole through Baindussa. "You have a promised still, do you not? Call her to you and take a flight elsewhere otherwise, we will need to have a further conversation."

A rumble escaped Baindussa's chest as he stared back down at Gundrag. "You are lucky you are the Overlord's pet, Gundrag. I would not tolerate such disrespect from any other dragon."

"Yet you still tolerate it."

Baindussa shook out his neck, hissing with his tongue and refused to respond. He unfurled his wings and stood up, staring at the sun for a moment. The warm light glowed against his scales, and then without warning, Baindussa shot up into the sky. His long body wrapped and coiled over itself before he then dropped from sight, disappearing over the edge of the Obelisk.

Gundrag turned his head to glare at Evor. "We will wait here. The riders will go inside."

"What will we do?"

"Wait."

I don't like it, Evor.

Neither do I, Elanor. But we must endure. Leave me. If he attacks, I will be able to hold my own.

I worry about you.

The feeling is mutual. This is where we part ways, Elanor.

So, it would seem. Stay safe for me.

I have lived through worse than Gundrag. I will not die today.

Elanor licked her lips and shifted out of the saddle. Evor lowered himself to the ground, mirroring Gundrag's movements. She watched as Kaladin began his descent, and then mirrored his movements, sighing as she left Evor behind. His voice continued to fill her mind, in an attempt to calm her, but seeing how erratic Kaladin was, there was something in the back of her mind that told her that his intentions were not pure. She had angered him, and she was willing to accept the consequences.

She touched the ground and before she had time to regain her breath, Kaladin was already beckoning to her, wanting her to follow him. With her fate sealed, Elanor's feet carried her forward into the chambers that had once been her father's home. With Baindussa no longer watching over the courtyard, it felt empty and unfulfilled like it was missing a piece of its soul. She followed Kaladin inside, his shoulders seeming to broaden as he crossed the threshold of the open corridor.

He was moving with purpose, striding down the corridor, almost not paying any attention to Elanor at all. If she retreated and went outside, she would have to deal with Gundrag and considering the steam that was rising off Kaladin's body, she did not want to risk more of his anger. Kaladin swept into Crassus' old office and waited for Elanor to walk past the door. He went to close it, but Elanor stepped towards him and caught his hand.

"We don't need to close that. There's nobody else here."

Kaladin clenched his fist, and Elanor felt his veins underneath her hand. "No, you're right!"

There were two loud roars from outside, and Elanor's focus was taken off Kaladin for a moment. Evor was struck by a mighty blow by the back of the head that sent him spiralling forward. But much like Elanor, Evor was fast on his feet and through his eyes, Elanor saw him turn to face his attacker. Gundrag. The purple dragon had the advantage, and was already on top of Evor, his jaw clamping down on the top of his neck.

Evor!

He will not cage me. If he wanted me dead, I would be. Deal with Kaladin!

"You don't understand it, do you Elanor?"

"Understand what?"

Kaladin's voice waivered as he continued. "Ever since we split, it's been torture to me. Having you so close to me, each day. You walk around the Obelisk, simply reminding you of your existence. You were so close, yet so far. So distant, so cold. When Ashbourne arrived here and Azura picked him, I was almost relieved. At first, I thought I could move on, but now it is evident that I cannot. That is something that I cannot do."

Elanor reached up towards his face, her fingers grazing against his tight jawline. His grip was still tight against her wrist. "You don't have to. Make me a Dragon Lord and we can remain close."

She'd overstepped her mark. Kaladin's eyes narrowed as he stared down at her, the grip tightening. "This warmth is not something you've shown towards me since he arrived here."

Elanor spoke with a soft hush, bringing her finger towards Kaladin's lips. Her eyes followed her fingers, dropping to his lips before flicking back to his eyes. This was her best chance of navigating this situation. "Yet it is genuine. I've missed it."

Kaladin's face continued to contort, his jaw clenching tight enough to make the tendons in his neck stand out like cords. His eyes, usually the colour of burnished steel, darkened to storm-cloud grey as anger and confusion warred across his features. He shook his head, jerking back from Elanor's outstretched fingers as if they might burn him. Though he recoiled, his grip on her upper arm only tightened, his knuckles whitening against her pale skin. Elanor stiffened beneath his hold, her breath catching in her throat as she sensed the dangerous shift in him, like watching distant lightning before the thunder strikes.

"No. No you haven't. Don't lie to me, Elanor. I can see through your deception now. Everything makes sense to me."

"I'm not trying to deceive you, Kaladin. There have been no lies within my actions."

Kaladin's fire began to burn and only intensified. "You've been lying to everyone here since the day that Azura chose Ashbourne as her rider."

"That was not my intention."

"Yet it was the result that you created as a lack of action, Elanor!"

"What would you have me do, Kaladin? What is this? Do you want me to take you back?"

Kaladin snorted in her face and leaned in closer. "It's far too late for that now. You have betrayed me for the final time."

"Betrayed you? I haven't done anything!"

"Stop lying! You think I don't know what you did for Dalton Ashbourne? There was a reason why Ayr Ashbourne was sent to us. It was by Dalton, Elanor. Use your brain!"

"Yes, he was sent here to become a rider!"

"A rider that just so happened to bond with your dragon's promised. I don't think that was a mistake, do you?"

"That's not something that we can help! The dragon chooses the rider."

"It was no coincidence that Azura chose him with the magical power that he possesses, Elanor. Everything started to occur here when he arrived. I don't think I need any other justification for ending his life."

"You wouldn't do such a thing."

Kaladin sighed, his calloused fingers relaxing just enough for a sliver of air to pass through Elanor's constricted windpipe. In the past she had welcomed him choking her, but this was different. She gasped as the cool rush of oxygen shot down her burning raw throat before his grip tightened once more, his knuckles whitening against her skin. His steel-grey eyes, rimmed with sleepless shadows, bored into hers with such intensity that the amber flecks in his irises seemed to smoulder like dying embers. Elanor's heart hammered against her ribs as she withered beneath his gaze, feeling as insignificant as a sparrow beside Evor's mountainous form, her very existence diminished by the weight of Kaladin's silent judgment.

"The only reason that I've kept you alive since the Colosseum was as a courtesy. As respect for what we once had. Now that you've done this, I have no choice but to end your life. The only person who will mourn your passing will be your mother. I should have known that I couldn't have trusted you, Elanor! I knew that Ashbourne had corrupted you!"

Every word was a struggle as Elanor tried to speak. "Ayr didn't corrupt me. That was his father's doing. I did it to save Evor!"

Kaladin almost spat at her. "Evor? Please. The time for excuses has passed, Elanor. You won't become a Dragon Lord now. You'll join your father, where you belong."

"Not if I have anything to say about it, you won't!"

Kaladin struck before she could. His fist flew and before Elanor could raise any part of her body to combat him, he struck. The massive blow connected with the side of her head, making her crumble under the force of the blow. Evor cried out in her mind, unable to break into the building, trapped underneath Gundrag's insurmountable presence. She could not feel Gundrag physically on top of her, but she could feel Evor's panic as for one of the first times in his life, he felt small and insignificant.

Evor!

Fight back, Elanor!

I can't leave you!

Fight him!

Elanor snapped back to reality as her spine collided with the oak door, the iron hinges rattling against the frame. The room spun, a complete reversal from where she'd stood mere heartbeats ago. Kaladin's fingers dug into her shoulders like talons, his knuckles bleached white with effort. She clawed at his wrists, nails scraping against skin, but his arms might as well have been forged from Gundrag's scales. His breath, hot and sharp with anger, grazed her cheek as he leaned in, forcing her head back until her skull thudded against the weathered wood, sending splinters of pain down her neck.

"You will give me everything that I once had! You will give me everything that he took from me!"

"He took nothing from you!"

Kaladin's eyes were darkening as he enshrouded her. "He took everything from me, Elanor! He took you! So now I will have you!"

"No!"

Elanor tried to scream, but here at the summit of the Obelisk, the only other beings that would hear her screams were fighting outside. Their thunderous footsteps echoed down the corridor as they slammed against the Obelisk. Elanor was split between both herself and Evor, and neither of them was winning. They were stronger together, but not whilst they fought two separate battles.

Pull away, Elanor!

Evor pushed Elanor out of his mind, and she snapped back fully focused on Kaladin as they continued to struggle. Her grip was slipping against his forearms, even though he was closer than ever to her. Kaladin's hand tightened once again around her throat and the world was turning black. Elanor just wanted to make contact with something, anything that would give her a reprieve. With Evor fully preoccupied, her magic was stifled, as she tried to claw Kaladin with her fingers.

Elanor brought her knee up as Kaladin took another step closer to her. The protective leather of his rider's uniform only offered so much protection from direct impact, and her knee found its mark. For the first time since they had become physical, Kaladin's hand slipped from her throat and Elanor pushed forward, forcing him off her as he keeled over.

The reprieve was not for long, Kaladin standing back up to his full height once again. Elanor lashed out at him with a fist, the only weapon she had available to her now, but she was stopped in her tracks. Kaladin's hand met hers before impact, and he pulled her towards him.

His right fist came clubbing down and Elanor screamed as she felt her chest shatter underneath his blow. She fell backwards and Kaladin capitalised on her stumble.

He followed her to the ground but used his height to retain control over her. His hand found her hair, and Elanor tried to lash out, but Kaladin's control of her head, brought it to his knee. Elanor's head snapped back, as pain radiated throughout her entire body, and she felt a trickle of blood leaking from her nose. She was stunned, unable to fight back as Kaladin picked her up again. Elanor's arms were on autopilot, Evor unable to help her. She could still feel Gundrag's claws and fangs raking down her back.

Another blow from Kaladin tore her mind away from Evor and she crumbled once again. Evor's roar filled her ears as Kaladin stood over her again, picking her up. Elanor tried to defend herself, but he hit her again, this time the back of her neck the target. She buckled and Kaladin was moving her towards the desk. Kaladin swiped at the stack of papers that had been neatly piled up by the dragon assistants.

Elanor threw out her arms as Kaladin slammed her forward head-first onto the table. Her attempt to block the motion was futile, only serving to compound the damage that had already been done to the rest of her face. She groaned as her eyes rolled back in her head and she felt Evor reaching out, trying to keep her conscious. She tried to stand, but Kaladin pushed into her, keeping her pinned against the desk.

His voice was little more than a whisper. "Scream for me. Nobody can hear you, Elanor."

Kaladin's calloused fingers dug into her hips, bruising the tender flesh as he wrenched her pants down with such force that the seams split with an audible tear. Elanor's palms slapped against the polished desk, fingernails scraping desperate half-moons into the wood grain as she attempted to scramble forward. Her blood was warm, viscous, and startlingly crimson as it splattered onto the burnished oak in perfect droplets that spread like dark stars across the whorls and knots of the wooden surface.

"Kaladin! Stop! Kaladin! Please!"

She heard him grunt, a guttural sound that drowned out her desperate whispers. Her words bounced off him like raindrops on stone as he shuffled behind her, his boots scraping across the floor. Kaladin pressed his weight against her. He was a wall of muscle and heat that crushed the air from her lungs. Her fingers scrabbled at the desk edge as she continued to struggle with her legs pinned beneath her. She wanted to kick at him, to drive her heel into his shin or groin, but her body was trapped at an impossible angle, offering no leverage for her to launch an attack.

"You are mine!"

This was not like the last time they had been together. What had once been passionate love making, had now been replaced with anger and passion. Tears formed in Elanor's eyes as she felt the pain that Evor was experiencing, and as she felt Kaladin spreading her legs apart. She had no fight left. He'd beaten it out of her, and this was what he wanted. As he forced his way inside her, she heard Evor cry out one final time in anguish.

THIRTY

The wyrmguard had escorted them back to their chambers, even though Ayr knew that if he had willed it, there would be nothing that they could do to contain him and Azura. He went willingly, and in silence, speaking to nobody, not even Azura. They flew in silence, back in through their window, and Ayr turned his head to see the wyrmguard and their dragons setting up outside. Despite them thinking they were in control, it was only because of Elanor's proximity to Kaladin that was keeping him in check.

Ayr dismounted from Azura the moment her massive talons scraped against the stone floor of their chambers. He ripped his mask from his face and threw it onto the ground at her feet. She bent her serpentine neck to his unspoken request, lowering her white-scaled head until it nearly touched the ground. He slid off her shoulder, his boots landing with a hollow thud that echoed through the chamber. His hands trembled at his sides, fingers curling into white-knuckled fists as a primal urge to destroy something, anything, coursed through his veins. Ayr stormed away from Azura, each footfall heavy with purpose, while her smouldering blue eyes tracked his retreat and wisps of smoke curled from her nostrils. Rage clouded his vision like a gathering storm, anger filing through his mind with the precision of a blade being sharpened against stone.

You need to remain calm, Ayr!

Remain calm? Kaladin has taken her, and he's doing Chilijo knows what to her!

Calm down!

Azura's voice crashed through Ayr's skull like a thunderbolt splitting an ancient oak. Like her scales she was white-hot, searing, and impossible to ignore. Her thoughts obliterated everything else in his consciousness, leaving only her commanding presence in its wake. Ayr winced and pressed his palm against his temple, feeling the rhythmic pulsation of Azura's will hammering against the walls of his mind, each mental blow reverberating down his spine and making the fine hairs on his arms stand rigid with primal recognition of her power. He fought back against her.

We don't know what he's doing!

Evor has not alerted me to any suspicious activity, Ayr. Elanor is safe for now.

She's alone with him!

Do nothing!

No, I need to go. This is the last time that I'll accept Kaladin interfering in our lives.

Ayr! Get back here!

Are you going to take me to Kaladin?

No, you heard him. We would also have to get past the wyrmguard and their dragons undetected. I think that is impossible right now, don't you?

So, you won't take me?

It is not wise. We cannot risk it right now, Ayr.

Fine, I'll do it myself.

Ayr!

Ayr waved his hand over his head, summoning a blocking spell that would reflect some of Azura's cries. No sooner than he had removed his hand, she sounded muted and far away as if trapped in a bubble. Azura continued to keep yelling at him. Ayr stormed across the room, not paying Azura any attention even as she tried to scold him. He extended his hand and pushed the door open and before Azura could stop him, he burst outside.

Two wyrmguard greeted him on the other side of the door. They turned to face Ayr, but he raised his hands and both men fell to the ground, sinking at the knees like their legs had been pulled out from underneath them. When they woke, they would question how they had found themselves on the floor but would likely not remember seeing him storm past them. Ayr's jaw tightened, his only concern for Elanor now that she was in Kaladin's grasp alone.

He stormed down the empty corridors of the Obelisk, half expecting to see dozens of riders along the way. Instead, he met nobody, as he marched towards where he could take the elevator that would see him to the roof of the Obelisk. If Azura had decided to help him he could have already been there, but he was forced to make the journey on foot. It was better this way. Nobody was chasing him. He moved with purpose, allowing his magic to form up around his body, using some of it as a shield to hide his presence.

Ayr turned down the next corridor to his right and did not see a soul. He frowned, wondering why the Obelisk was so sparsely populated. It was a glorious day outside, yet when they had made their escape from their chambers, the skies had also not been populated. Ayr continued down the corridor and reached the end, turning right again. He was getting closer. His heartbeat fastened as more magic surged through his veins.

An unknown dragon roared far in the distance. At last, there were signs of life within the Obelisk. Ayr quickened his pace, heading down the corridor, feeling a foreboding sense of dread. He stepped around the next corner and on the ground in front of him, was a rider, face down against the tiles. From the back of his head, Ayr did not know

who the man was, or what his purpose was, but as he looked up, he saw
a familiar retreating figure turning down the corridor to the right. The
hair was different, but he'd already seen the man before. It was Bryne.
As Ayr neared the rider on the ground, he could see that it was not
a recruit, but instead, despite his lack of helmet, Ayr recognised him,
only by his face. It was a wyrmguard. What was Bryne doing?

This had been no accident. Bryne had been trained, the same as
Ayr. Ayr took off after him despite having no weapon at his side.
He stormed down the corridor, keeping his footsteps light so that
there was a limited chance of being heard. Ayr's magic was reaching
a fever point, as Azura was still attempting to contact him. She had
not stopped since he had left their chambers. He removed the blocking
spell and Azura filled his mind in an instant.

Ayr! Ayr! Ayr!

Azura!

Ayr! Where are you going?

*To stop my brother from causing anymore destruction around the
Obelisk. He's just killed a wyrmguard.*

Azura probed his mind, seeing the most recent memory that had
just entered his head. He could feel her shudder, upon seeing the blood
spilling from the wyrmguard's head across the empty, cold tiles. As
Azura hesitated, he sensed that it was not just because of the wyrmguard murder.

*Wait! There is something more pressing. I can sense Evor. He is in
danger.*

How?

Gundrag. In the courtyard. You were right.

I'm coming back! I need you, Azura.

Quickly.

All thought of Bryne was gone from Ayr's mind. Even if he had
killed a wyrmguard, it paled in comparison to the threat that Gundrag

posed to Evor. And if Evor was in danger, so was Elanor. His legs carried him faster than they ever had as he sprinted back past the wyrmguard's body, leaping over it like it was nothing more than a log on the floor. Whilst he had been closing in on the courtyard, doubling back to retrieve Azura would be quicker.

He rounded the next corridor and saw the two wyrmguard that he had knocked out only moments ago. They still had not moved, and if Ayr had his way, they would not move for a while. He pushed open the door like he had done when he had left only moments ago and saw Azura waiting on the other side. However, she was not in a position that would allow Ayr to easily climb aboard her.

"Come on Azura, let's go!"

"Ayr, we can't go!"

"I just knocked out two wyrmguard and tried to get to the court-yard on my own! We must go!"

"No! No! No!"

"Ayr! You cannot go! Kaladin has forbidden it!"

"You said that Evor is in danger!"

"He is! Gundrag can kill him!"

"Then we fly! Get over here!"

Azura resisted, her scales bristling in the half-light, and something in Ayr snapped. More rage flooded his veins with liquid fire. He lashed out, fingers splayed and trembling, as tendrils of midnight-blue magic spiralled from his palms. The energy coalesced into a shimmering lasso that wrapped itself around her serpentine neck, tightening with each pulse of his will. Azura's thunderous roar split the air as she thrashed against the binding, her massive wings beating, creating whirlwinds that bent the nearby saplings. Despite her formidable strength, Ayr's magic held true. He dragged her down with gritted teeth and sweat beading on his brow, forcing her to yield beneath his unrelenting grip, even though he did not want to hurt her.

"Azura! We need to go now! To save Evor! To save Elanor!"

"Ayr…"

"Listen to me!"

Ayr's voice echoed around the chamber like a dragon's roar and Azura shrunk in size, her wings moving closer to her face as if to protect herself from his rage. She coiled up, and Ayr could feel her not wanting to agree with him, nor did she want to disagree. Panic seeped into her mind and Ayr pressed her. He crossed the room to where she stood, only taking a brief pause in his step as he threw his arm out, which called his mask to him from the floor. He pulled it back on over his head.

"We need to go now!"

"Yes, Ayr."

With reluctance, Azura lowered her head, and allowed Ayr to climb aboard. He was barely seated in the saddle before she made her way towards the window and pushed it open. The wyrmguard dragons outside heard the motion and turned their heads, but by then it was already too late. Azura had dropped out of the window and was already underneath them. The wyrmguard dragons roared and they dropped from their perch.

Faster, Azura!

Azura roared as she beat her wings faster, changing her angle of flight so that she could ascend on the outside of the Obelisk. The wyrmguard dragons were slower, having been surprised with Azura's sudden appearance. Ayr urged Azura on, infusing her body with his magic, allowing her to speed up. The difference was noticeable, but he needed to keep most of it for Gundrag and Kaladin.

As they rose up the side of the Obelisk, new sounds reached Ayr's ears. There was no roar like he would have usually expected, but instead, it was a whimper. Azura rose over the edge of the Obelisk, and now they could both see the courtyard below them. Azura let loose with a wild scream that split the sky.

Evor was inside the jaws of Gundrag, pining, crying for release. He kept trying to spin himself loose from Gundrag, but the purple dragon kept him underneath his legs. Gundrag was too focused on Evor to even notice Azura as she flew closer, overhead. She reared her back and unleashed a torrent of fire at Gundrag. The effect was immediate. Gundrag turned his head, even though Azura's fire did nothing to scathe him from this distance. Evor used the momentary distraction to turn underneath Gundrag and pushed up from underneath him.

Evor tells me that Elanor needs you! We will take care of Gundrag. Can you catch yourself if you fall?

I can.

Go!

Azura's voice ripped through his mind, and he felt compelled to obey her. Azura had not slowed down as she turned in the air, shifting her angle of attack for another pass over Gundrag and Evor. Ayr unhooked himself from the saddle and stood up as Azura descended towards the courtyard once again. The wyrmguard dragons that had been pursuing them had now summited the Obelisk. They saw Azura and locked onto her as Ayr leapt from the saddle.

He shot towards the Obelisk, in free fall, but the fall was not that far. With a wave of his hand, and the power of his magic guiding him, Ayr found the Obelisk moments later, landing as if he had just run down a flight of stairs. He passed underneath Evor and Gundrag as they continued to battle on ground level, Azura unleashed another fiery breath in Gundrag's direction. The battle roared on behind him, but Ayr ran forward wondering what he was going to discover inside.

The dragons were moving away, and Ayr was able to follow the battle in his mind, seeing it through Azura's point of view. She led the wyrmguard dragons away as Evor tried to lead Gundrag in the opposite direction. The sounds from outside were becoming duller, but it did not stop Ayr's heart from beating faster. He rounded the corner and was now staring down the corridor that revealed Kaladin's desk. He saw the man, standing in front of his desk, but something was not right. Kaladin was moving, his pants down around his ankles.

Ayr squinted trying to see what was going on, and it was only then that he saw another set of naked legs pressing against Kaladin's. There could only be one person here, Elanor. Panic set in as Ayr continued to race down the corridor towards them, but that's when a new sound reached his ears. It was faint at first and he thought he was mishearing things but as he grew closer, it all but confirmed the sound that tore at the deepest pit in his stomach.

Elanor's screaming and grunting was high and desperate, filling Ayr's ears like molten metal poured into a mould. It was a sound worse than Azura being in pain; it was the sound of innocence shattering as Kaladin forced his way inside her. Ayr had no sword, no weapon in his hand, but a nudge from Azura, warm and electric against his consciousness, reminded him that he was the weapon. Energy surged through his veins like liquid fire, burning away his hesitation, and he picked up his pace, boots barely touching the ground as he sprinted forward.

The space around him crackled with ozone. He wanted to unleash a surge of energy towards Kaladin, but the bastard was too good for that, even if he was forcing himself inside Elanor. Instead, as Ayr ran, the energy he had summoned around him coalesced, crystallizing from formless power into something tangible. A jagged dagger of pure light that hummed with deadly intent in his palm. Ayr's lungs burned as he closed the distance, wishing with every step that Elanor's terror would end.

Every whimper from Elanor's lips drove him forward, a sound that he never wanted to hear again. Kaladin was pressing himself against her, faster, his grunts filling Ayr's ears as well. Ayr no longer cared that he'd be heard. He was glad that Kaladin's massive frame blocked Elanor from sight for the most part, and he was far too distracted. Only when Ayr was three steps away, close enough to see the sweat beading on Kaladin's neck, did he realise that something was wrong. But by then, the blade was already arcing toward his throat.

"Fuck you!"

Kaladin was turning as Ayr screamed at him, the knife coming down from above. Before Kaladin had even finished turning his head, Ayr struck, the blade he had formed shimmering as it pierced Kaladin's shoulder. Kaladin reared his head back, unleashing a cry that drowned out Elanor. At last, he pulled away, but with his pants around his ankles, he stumbled. Kaladin swiped at Ayr, but with the dagger in his shoulder, could only turn halfway.

Ayr caught the blow, trapping Kaladin's arm underneath his own, and he twisted, pulling Kaladin away from Elanor. He used the dagger to direct where he wanted Kaladin's body to go. He saw Elanor scramble onto the desk behind Kaladin, as he twisted, swinging his arm forward, bringing it up into Kaladin's nose. Ayr felt a crack as Kaladin's nose shattered, another grunt coming from the Overlord.

Kaladin took another half step, trying to bring himself square to Ayr so that he could attack, and blood was already beginning to spill from his nose. He swung wildly again, and the blow connected with the side of Ayr's head. Ayr groaned and stumbled but dragged Kaladin with the knife. Kaladin raised a knee into Ayr's chest, and he lurched forward, the force of the strike feeling like it shattered his sternum. Ayr coughed and wrenched down on the dagger, pulling Kaladin with it.

An elbow followed as Ayr tried to bring Kaladin down to his size. He almost collapsed, but the strength of the elbow was less than the knee had been. Kaladin was tiring. Kaladin unleashed a roar that sounded like it had come from the bowels of Gundrag, even though from Azura's presence still in Ayr's mind, he knew they were not close to the Obelisk anymore.

He pulled down on the dagger again, and the blade passed through more of Kaladin's muscle as he stepped to the side. Ayr shoved his left hand forward, magic surging from his fingertips and he pushed Kaladin back. Kaladin stumbled again, his boots catching in his pants once again. If it was not for the dagger still imbedded in his shoulder, he would have landed flat on his back beside Elanor. With momentum on his side, Ayr removed the dagger before sending it forward again. Kaladin keeled over as the dagger entered just under his solar plexus. The fury was still twisting on his face as he tried to fight back, grabbing Ayr's hands, having just missed the knife.

Ayr could feel Kaladin's magic trying to push back against his own as Elanor shuffled beside them. Ayr had not taken his eyes off Kaladin's as he drove the dagger deeper, not only with his arm strength but his magic as well. From the look in Kaladin's eyes, Ayr could tell that he knew he was fighting a losing battle. With one final shout, Kaladin tried to force Ayr off him, but Ayr held fast, his magic an impervious barrier as he glared Kaladin down.

With each passing second, the light slipped from behind Kaladin's storm-grey eyes as Ayr twisted the dagger deeper into his abdomen, the blade scraping against bone. A look of pure hatred flashed between them, Kaladin's gaze burning with betrayal while Ayr's mouth curled in a cold smile. Blood bubbled between Kaladin's cracked lips as his calloused fingers finally fell loose from their desperate grip around Ayr's wrists, leaving crimson smears across his pale skin. Kaladin's knees buckled first, then his shoulders sagged as he sunk, the front of his dark coat now soaked through with spreading scarlet.

Breathing hard through his flared nostrils, Ayr withdrew the dagger with a wet, sucking sound as Kaladin's body went slack. Blood as dark as midnight spilled over his trembling fingers and was beginning to pool on the stone floor beneath them. A heady surge of satisfaction bloomed in Ayr's chest, spreading outward to his fingertips as he watched Kaladin pass into the void. The eyes that had once burned with such hatred for him now stared at nothing. Kaladin would not be rising again. Elanor was safe, and that singular thought eclipsed all else in Ayr's mind. She turned towards him, a state of confusion spread across her face as she realised what was unfolding in front of her.

THIRTY-ONE

"What have you done?"

Ayr stood over her, and Kaladin, his legs apart, a strange dagger in hand. Ayr's chest rose and fell as he breathed. There was little light behind his eyes, even though his smile curled on his lips. Elanor felt exposed and vulnerable as he stared at her, Kaladin having torn her uniform to shreds. Fresh blood marks-stained Ayr's uniform and the knife that he wielded. He glanced down at it, before it dissolved into nothing a moment later. Elanor ogled at the empty space where the knife had just occupied. Ayr caught her eye as he looked up, and she felt an unnatural sensation pulse through her body. He'd saved her again.

A dragon's roar ripped overhead breaking the silence that had come between the two of them. The sound was haunting, echoing through the halls as if it had come from far away. The dragon was in pain. Ayr turned his head towards the ceiling and then peered down at Elanor when he could not figure out which dragon had roared.

"Was that Evor?"

Elanor shook her head. The pursuit had stopped, and there was now separation between Evor and Gundrag. "That was Gundrag. He knows Kaladin is dead."

"Then we need to end this."

"You can't keep getting away with this. You've killed the Overlord."

"He forced himself upon you, Elanor. What else did you want me to do?"

Elanor's gaze traced the outline of Kaladin's body sprawled across the cold floor; his once-imposing frame now crumpled like discarded parchment. The blood pooled beneath him, dark and viscous, seeping into the cracks between the tiles. Her heart remained unmoved, a fortress of ice where warmth had once resided. Memories flickered inside her, the memory of his rough hands on her skin and his quiet whispers in the dark. That's all they were. Memories, yet they stirred nothing within her now, even though he had just been inside her.

Elanor. Now that she had a moment of calm, Evor reemerged in her mind. She reached out towards him, rekindling the connection. *I can kill him. He is distracted, wounded. Did you kill Kaladin?*

Yes. Is he running?

Yes.

Hunt him down. He can't speak of what happened here. If he escapes, the wrath of the Commonwealth will come down upon us.

Yes, Elanor. I understand. I will end his life.

Evor was the one to cut the connection between them this time, and Elanor felt him surging away from the Obelisk in pursuit of Gundrag. She wished that she was there with him, fuelling him with the energy that he required to chase the fleeing dragon. Evor had given her the strength to stand tall, but her legs were very much still shaking. She cast another glance down at Kaladin's body, and shuddered, still able to feel him inside her. If only she knew a spell that could remove the sensation. Perhaps Evor bringing back Gundrag's head to her would suffice.

Elanor used the table behind her as a crutch, leaning some of her weight against it. Ayr was once again staring at Kaladin's half naked dead body. There was no pity or remorse in his eyes for what he had done. What stood in his place was a stone-cold killer. His eyes shifted after a moment, and they softened as they landed upon her. He stepped closer to her and moved to embrace her.

"Are you okay, Elanor?"

She nodded, the only motion her body could manage as the numbness closed in. Rage, guilt, and gratitude twisted inside her chest. Elanor collapsed into Ayr's blood-slick embrace, uncaring that Kaladin's lifeblood soaked her clothes. The chill from the corridor's breeze slipped over her torn pants, biting into her exposed skin, but against him, she felt untouchable. His arms were trembling, iron-strong yet desperate, and she clung to him tighter. The world smelled of copper and smoke. Her mind threatened to fracture, but in his hold, for a heartbeat, she let herself believe she was safe. Ayr held her tight against his body, Elanor focusing on Evor as he continued to chase Gundrag. The purple dragon had a head start, but she willed Evor on to catch him.

She slipped out of Evor's mind again as Ayr caressed her face. He leaned in and she felt his lips press against her forehead. She felt warmer than she had done moments ago and looked down at her legs. Had Ayr just magically repaired them? She could not ask him as Evor drew her back into his mind.

Evor let loose with a roar, getting closer to Gundrag with each wingbeat. As he neared, and Elanor could see Gundrag's tail flashing just in front of Evor's eyes, something rocked her physically. She slipped back out of Evor's mind and into the present where Ayr was staring up at the ceiling once again. He lowered his eyes towards her.

"Did you feel that?"

"I think we all did."

"What the fuck is going on? Where's Evor?"

"Evor isn't big enough to make that kind of noise, especially here."

"Then what was it?"

From the look in Ayr's eyes, he was perplexed as much as she was, but the sinking feeling that was within her gut told a different story. "Azura can't see anything. Everything here is normal. She's coming back now."

Evor!

Yes Elanor?

You need to come back here immediately. Something is not right at the Obelisk.

But you gave me the command to chase Gundrag.

Yes, but I need you.

I am coming, Elanor.

Another explosion rocked the Obelisk, and this time Elanor had cut off the connection from Evor just in time to experience the full force of the blow. She was steadfast, but she still rocked by it.

"No, there's something not right here. Was it you?"

Ayr shook his head. "I just saved you from Kaladin! Don't accuse me. I've done nothing to warrant this!"

"There's nobody else that powerful left here that could do something like that with magic! Who else would it be?"

As Ayr's lips parted to speak, a dragon's roar that sounded like tearing metal ripped through the air erupted that vibrated the floor beneath their feet and sent dust cascading from the ceiling beams. The ancient walls that usually dulled dragon noises from outside might as well have been made from parchment. The beast's cry pierced through them with such clarity that Elanor felt its hot breath against her neck, each scale-rattling note reverberating inside her skull until her teeth ached. As the dragon quietened, her eyes locked with Ayr, both of them understanding in the moment, what terror was outside.

"Shit!"

"He can't be here."

"He is!"

A third explosion rocked the Obelisk, this one shattering the air with a thunderous crack that made the previous two sound like distant thunder. The floor beneath Elanor's feet buckled and heaved like a living thing, sending hairline fractures racing across its polished surface. The vibration shot through her bones, rattling her teeth and blurring her vision before violently pitching her sideways. Her shoulder slammed against the floor as the world tilted, the metallic taste of fear and blood flooding her mouth as she sprawled across the ground.

Then the world came crashing down around her. Ayr was on his feet, and he threw his hands up over himself. The rubble that descended from the shattered frame slowed to a halt, skimming past her as if he had commanded it to part around them. There was movement from beside her, and Elanor rolled her head to see what had caused the roof to collapse. No sooner than it had come down, it was already moving again, and it was something that Elanor had not hoped to see. The massive golden talon that had been beside her was moving again, rising from beside her as Sinibad made his presence felt.

Ayr was yelling down at her. "We can't stay here!"

He thrust his hands out towards her, and Elanor shot to her feet, commanded by Ayr's magic. Rubble was still crumbling around them as Sinibad's back foot came into view. He brought it down further away from them, but there was no denying now that with the thunderous, quaking sounds that he was on top of the Obelisk. Whilst Elanor could only see part of his foot, she wondered how the golden dragon would linger on the Obelisk, despite its size being one of the few structures in the Commonwealth that could hold him.

Ayr was turning away, but he did not retreat down the crumbling corridor. Instead, the air above them split with a thunderous crack as Azura shot through the jagged remains of what had once been the ceiling. She landed with such force that dust and fragments of stone cascaded around them, her talons gouging deep furrows in the floor.

Her sides heaved with laboured breath, wings half-folded and twitching with urgency, blue eyes fixed on them both, waiting, demanding they mount her before more of the structure around them collapsed.

"Hurry! He's attacking the Obelisk!"

Elanor needed no further explanation, and thanks to Ayr, she was already on her feet, able to run towards Azura. Ayr vaulted up Azura with no difficulty and when he was half in the saddle he turned and offered his hand to her. He lifted her up with ease, and she stood just behind him.

"I'll do what I can to protect you, just hold on."

Elanor nodded as Azura's wings opened on either side of her. Without waiting for Elanor, Azura shot upwards and out of the now ruined building. Evor was still closing in on them, Elanor could see the Obelisk through his eyes and the sight that was just below her in real time as well. Sinibad was crawling along the Obelisk and reared his head back as more dragons were flying up out of the Obelisk approaching him.

Azura flew away from the hotspot, angling towards Evor. Elanor could see him coming now, racing towards them as if her life depended upon it. Elanor's heart hammered against her ribs as she spotted him, a blur of obsidian cutting through the clouds, racing toward them with desperate speed. Clutching Azura's spine ridge, Elanor twisted to look back. The sight made her blood run cold. She saw Sinibad, terrible and magnificent, batting away the approaching dragons with casual brutality, their bodies tumbling from the sky like broken toys.

He is inconceivable. Why attack now?

What does Dalton want? Does he know that Kaladin is dead?

I just chased Gundrag away.

There was guilt in Evor's voice. How could Dalton have known what was going on within the Obelisk. The only other person that had been there was Ayr. Elanor lowered her eyes towards him, and she felt

Evor shift with a sense of unease. Had it been him the entire time? Was Ayr Ashbourne just his father's vessel. If that had been the case, why in Chilijo's name would he have saved her from Kaladin's wrath?

Would it end now if she scooped Ayr up out of the saddle and threw him from Azura's back? She imagined his body tumbling through the cold air, arms flailing against the rushing wind, his scream fading as he plummeted toward the ground below. Or would she simply be forced to confront Azura's flame-hot rage and an infuriated Ayr once she retrieved him bruised and bloodied, eyes burning with betrayal from the unforgiving ground where he'd fallen?

No, it was not the answer. He was far too powerful to fall for some basic trick. If he had killed the Dragon Lords almost on his own, he would be one of the best assets they had in the fight that was unfolding on the Obelisk. Where was Azura taking them? Evor changed his angle of flight, even though he would be one of the most qualified dragons to assist in taking down Sinibad. However, as the moments went by, it seemed less likely that the riders would win.

"Turn around, little one!"

Evor sliced through the air like a black scythe, cutting directly across Azura's flight path. His obsidian wing as glossy as volcanic glass and rippling with corded muscle beneath it missed Elanor's head by inches. It was close enough that the downdraft tore at her hair and the leathery membrane's passing made a sound like thunder cracking. Azura reared back mid-flight, her sinuous neck arching as she hissed.

Evor!

Apologies, Elanor. I had to make a point. Why is Azura running?

I'm not in control here.

Get control. He is your promised as much as she is mine. If you do not, I will.

Moving around on Evor was something Elanor was more comfortable with. Azura on the other hand, being a smaller dragon and not her own, was a different story. She wanted to let go of the ridge that she clung onto, but as Azura was still moving through the air with speed, it would make it hard to get close to him.

There was no time to waste. Elanor let go of Azura, even as she started to turn. Whilst Azura was smaller, there was still plenty of room for Elanor to walk as she stepped down towards Ayr. Her hand hooked around the back of the saddle, as one of the few stable places on Azura's body. Ayr felt her hand behind his head, and he snapped around to yell at her.

"What are you doing!"

"Where are we going? The Obelisk is under attack!"

"What exactly do you think Azura is going to do?"

"Your magic! That's our home! Aren't you going to defend it?"

"Against that? Are you serious? Now is not the time to fight it!"

Sinibad's massive form towered over the Obelisk, his scaled body casting a shadow that swallowed the entire structure. His golden scales caught the sunlight like armour plating, and when he unfurled his wings, they seemed to stretch as wide as the Obelisk. Elanor's throat tightened as she caught the sulphurous scent of his breath. She grunted and said nothing further to Ayr. What could stand against a creature whose smallest talon was longer than Evor was? Even as Evor's sleek obsidian form darted back toward the crumbling Obelisk, his impressive wingspan now seeming delicate by comparison, Elanor knew the situation was spiralling beyond anyone's control as he swatted more dragons from the sky.

We can't win this fight, Evor.

We can Elanor.

No! Look at it. We do not have the power to match him.

Elanor...

Evor, I know, but do you want to stand up to that?

The number of dragons hovering around Sinibad, launching fire balls, trying to strike at him with their claws was dwindling. He swiped at another passing dragon, and it crumbled, despite trying to avoid the massive talon that swung towards him. The dragon's rider was sent flying from the saddle, sent in an arc, their body no longer part of this world. Sinibad turned, not paying them any further attention. Both the dragon and rider, with years of training and experience were snuffed out in an instant.

Elanor strained her eyes, looking behind Sinibad. Something was coming towards him, something almost as large as he was. Another roar split the sky, and between the gaps in Sinibad's legs, Elanor saw an all too familiar brown behemoth heading towards the Obelisk. Drementhol had arrived and was challenging Sinibad. She saw Ayr turn to look at her out of the corner of his eye as they watched the two monsters draw closer together.

"Maybe Kaladin knew what he was doing after all."

"Now you're giving him too much credit."

She heard Ayr snort, a sharp exhale of disbelief. Sinibad launched himself from the Obelisk. The ancient structure, its obsidian walls gleaming like wet ink in the sunlight began to buckle. Hairline fractures spiderwebbed across the surface, each crack releasing puffs of centuries-old dust. The foundation stones groaned like dying beasts. How had those massive pillars sustained Sinibad's mountainous bulk for so long, not to mention the weight of every other dragon inside, only to fail now? As the golden beast left the Obelisk behind, the entire structure convulsed. Stone shrieked against stone.

"Ayr! What the fuck is happening?"

There was no stopping it. Ayr thrust his hands out in front of his body; fingers splayed wide like a drowning man reaching for shore. Elanor saw a flicker of magic at his fingertips, pale blue sparks that guttered and died before they could coalesce. Sweat beaded on his forehead as his shoulders trembled with effort, but either he was too weak from the battle with Kaladin, or they were simply too far away for his powers to reach the Obelisk. He threw his hands down in defeat a moment later, the tendons in his wrists standing out like cords, and they were forced to watch as the Obelisk started to crumble toward the earth in a cascade of dust and stone as the gold and bronze titans drew closer together above it.

Elanor's breath tightened as Drementhol loosened another roar, only a few wingbeats away from engaging Sinibad. Sinibad responded in kind and as his roar faded, a torrent of fire erupted around him, as Drementhol struck first. The flames wrapped around Sinibad, and he burst through them, unleashing a torrent of his own as the two dragons came together, over the top of the Obelisk as it continued to fall to pieces.

Dragons were fleeing in their dozens, each of them, the size of pigeons compared to the behemoths that battled over the crumbling Obelisk. Dust was still rising and now the dragons were beginning to vanish into the smokescreen that it was creating. Those same dragons dared not to approach Sinibad and Drementhol as they exchanged blows, opting to flee from their falling home.

The two enormous dragons continued to circle each other as the Obelisk continued to shatter. Whilst it was crumbling it was not a total capitulation, almost like the structure itself was hanging onto some kind of life with a stoic stubbornness that refused to die. Above the dust, Drementhol struck at Sinibad, but missed, and Sinibad capitalised. He used his bigger frame to surge forward and struck out, diving down. Drementhol was slower and could not avoid the blow.

"No!"

Drementhol screamed as Sinibad bit down into his neck, the sound echoing over the Obelisk as it continued to crumble away. The two dragons were high above all others as more painful screams erupted from Drementhol's mouth. He twisted and turned in the air, but there was no getting away from the indomitable jaws of Sinibad as they closed around him again. Drementhol tried to break free, with one final whimper escaping from his chest. Then as Sinibad bit down for a third time, the giant bronze behemoth's head was severed from the rest of his body.

Sinibad was still in flight and using Drementhol's body as a shield, drove it down into the Obelisk. Another earth-shattering boom shook the surrounding area to its core. With the impact of the two behemoths crashing down into it, the Obelisk gave way at last. It was a ripple effect, the base of the Obelisk giving out first. As the base gave way, the Obelisk started to topple, splintering apart as larger cracks continued to form along it. It fell to the south, away from where Elanor watched on Azura's neck as Evor entered her head once again.

It cannot be.

It is. There's nothing we can do Evor. The Obelisk has fallen.

We need to take the fight to him.

If Drementhol just failed, what chance do we have against him?

Drementhol did not care for this place. I have more fight than he did. I will come and get you. If these are to be our final moments together, then I would have you on my back.

Evor, it's too dangerous!

Do as you are told! Jump!

THIRTY-TWO

*N*o! Ayr could feel Elanor's hand near the back of his head as he remained locked in the saddle, unable to believe what he had just witnessed. Azura was screaming in his mind, distraught at the loss of her home, and there was nothing that Ayr could do except listen to her cries. He turned his head to glance back at Elanor, but they both had their masks on, both unable to see each other's faces. As the Obelisk tilted over, Sinibad rode the wave down, unmoving as he stood in the wreckage. He threw back his head and unleashed the largest torrent of flame that Ayr had ever seen, turning the sky red.

The dragons that remained above Sinibad were scorched and half a dozen of them fell out of the sky, their wings set ablaze by the elder dragon that roared in the remains of their home. Evor had turned back towards them, despite being seemingly intent on chasing down Sinibad only moments ago. Ayr felt Elanor's hand leave the saddle behind him. He tried to reach out, but she was gone, slipping from view as Azura's wings covered where she had just been.

What is Elanor doing?

Evor seems to think that he can fight Sinibad.

That's suicide!

I am aware, Ayr.

You need to change his mind. Now isn't the time for that. We can't beat him.

When I'm not conversing with you, what do you think I am trying to do? Evor is incensed.

You can't lose him. Wait. Look!

A flash of burnished gold caught Ayr's eye. It was another dragon, smaller than Sinibad but with the same distinctive scale pattern that shimmered like liquid metal in the sunlight. It streaked northward towards them, its sinuous body undulating against clouds that were stained orange by Sinibad's continuing inferno. The dragon's wings beat with desperate urgency, each powerful downstroke leaving ripples in the smoke-filled sky. Atop its back were two silhouettes clinging to the saddle. One of them stood, broad-shouldered and commanding, the other slight and hunched forward. It was Onoss with Dalton and Gable, fleeing the destruction. Beneath Ayr, Azura's muscles tensed like coiled springs. Her head whipped toward the escaping pair, neck scales bristling into jagged points. A guttural snarl vibrated through her body and into Ayr's legs underneath the saddle as she bared her teeth like polished daggers, her pupils narrowing to vengeful slits.

It's him, that's Onoss! I'm going to kill him!

Azura! Don't!

It was too late to stop her and if Ayr pulled on her, it could send her spiralling out of control towards the ground. Ayr prepared what magic he could, bringing it to the forefront of his mind. Azura was hellbent on her course, and given the situation, he could only support her in her endeavour. Azura let loose a roar, and Onoss turned his head towards her, acknowledging her for the first time.

He deviated from his course, his red eyes flashing as he now made his way for Azura. Ayr could make Dalton out clearly as he sat behind Gable, almost as if he was floating on air on Onoss' back. He wore no mask, despite Gable wearing one, and yet was unaffected by the winds. Ayr knew that Dalton was powerful, but not needing to worry about the basic elements was something else. Had Dalton limited his power whilst Ayr had been training under him?

Onoss streaked towards Azura like a golden comet, scales glinting in the harsh sunlight. His massive jaws unhinged with a sickening crack, revealing rows of obsidian teeth before molten fire erupted from deep within his throat. The inferno billowed forth with orange and crimson flames laced with blue-white heat. Ayr felt Azura's pupils narrow to slits as she detected the approaching wall of death. With a powerful thrust of her wings, she banked hard to starboard, her sinuous body twisting into a desperate corkscrew that carried her just above the scorching torrent. The manoeuvre sent Ayr's body lurching sideways, his stomach dropping as the centrifugal force threatened to tear him from the saddle.

Strike him down!

Ayr had not been expecting Azura to turn so suddenly, and still had his hands locked into the saddle. They passed over Onoss, in a flash, but to Ayr's surprise no magic came back at them. Whether Dalton had missed or had not fired at all, was of no concern as Azura levelled out, now higher and behind Onoss as she turned again. The chase was on, and using her new height advantage, Azura was faster.

Onoss was racing towards the mountains as if his tail was on fire. Azura's muscles tensed beneath Ayr, her throat glowing with the heat of restrained flame, but the distance between them remained too great for her fire to be effective, even as her powerful wings closed the gap yard by yard. Dalton twisted, his face a cold mask beneath his windswept hair, eyes meeting theirs for one calculating moment before turning forward again. With a sudden tilt of his wings, Onoss angled downward toward the mountains, his form growing smaller against the vast landscape. Ayr urged Azura to follow their quarry into the treacherous terrain below. There was no turning back now.

Onoss swooped in and landed on the ground, his wings scattering in each direction as he tried to steady himself. Azura soared overhead, scorching the ground with flames. As she passed, Ayr swung his head around, seeing that both Dalton and Gable were unscathed. Ayr clicked his tongue with frustration as he saw both men dismount from Onoss. Azura made one more pass, lowering herself to the ground, landing with more grace than Onoss just had.

I can take him, but you cannot handle both your father and that rider.

Azura snarled at Onoss, responded with a thunderous roar that shook the mountain air, his massive jaws snapping with enough force to shatter bone. Dalton stepped forward, his weather-worn face grim as he raised his hands, palms out, fingers catching the faded sunlight. Onoss lowered his horned head, though defiance still burned in his angry eyes. The golden dragon's spiked tail lashed behind him, carving furrows in the rocky ground, each swing releasing a sound like leather cracking against stone.

"Ayr! What do you think you're doing?"

"Stopping you. How dare you destroy the Obelisk!"

Dalton folded his arms across his chest, the embroidered gold threads of his jacket catching the fading sunlight as he scoffed, a sound like gravel underfoot. He beckoned for Gable with two fingers, impatience tightening around the corners of his mouth. Gable lingered just long enough to pat Onoss on the snout one final time. He stepped forward with a smirk that did not quite reach his ice-blue eyes, his calloused hand falling to the hilt of the curved sword that hung from the tooled leather belt at his waist.

"Yes, Dalton?"

"Bring him to me."

I can handle this, Azura.

Are you sure?

Dalton doesn't want either of us dead.

Gable strode forward with a predatory grace, his boots crunching against the mountain gravel as he unsheathed his sword. The metal sang as it left its scabbard, a high, thin note that promised blood. Ayr's hands hung empty at his sides, his fingers flexing uselessly; he had nothing, but Azura's presence and his own magic. He dove into his own toolkit, drawing a longer blade than what he had used against Kaladin out of nothing but the air in front of him.

Dalton perked up and his eyes widened with surprise. "A magic blade, Ayr? Good, so my teachings weren't wasted on you. Will it hold up to real steel?"

"Shut up."

"Gable, do it!"

Gable lurched forward again, now wary that Ayr had a blade in hand. If he knew about Ayr's magic, Gable did not show it, instead focusing more on the sword that he now carried. Ayr took a step forward to match him and then Gable started into a run. Ayr smirked, realising that he had not learnt from their first encounter. Gable's face contorted into rage as he charged forward. Ayr shook his head; he had no time to waste. Magic whirled around his hand, and Dalton's eyes shifted, but he was too late to stop him.

Ayr struck, lashing out with his magic, creating a writhing sphere of crimson and gold that crackled as it tore through the air between them. There was a heartbeat's pause as Gable flung his own hands up, palms outward, his eyes widening in recognition of what was coming. The fireball collided with his chest and exploded outward, engulfing him in dancing flames that licked up his torso and across his face. His sword clattered against the ground as his fingers spasmed open. His screams were raw and animal, echoing off the mountainside. Dalton observed the carnage from three paces away. The only movement he offered towards his burning companion was the curl of his lips at one corner. Satisfaction glinted in his eyes as Gable collapsed to his knees, his skin blackening, still shrieking as he clawed at the relentless fire consuming him.

Onoss raised his head towards the sky and loosened a roar that made the ground tremble underneath Ayr's feet. The gold dragon stepped forward snarling, smoke rising from his nostrils.

Get behind me, Ayr.

Dalton raised his hand again and Onoss paused. "Stop."

Ayr paused, confused. "You can control other dragons that aren't yours?"

Dalton nodded and lowered his hand. Onoss began growling again, but this time it was softer than it had been. He retreated, taking steps away from Dalton that were too deliberate to be anything but directional. Ayr waited for Onoss to leap forward, but Dalton was smiling, his mischievous grin spreading across his face.

"You really don't remember anything I told you throughout the years, do you, boy?

Ayr threw the magical blade forward and it vanished into the abyss the moment it had left contact with his skin. "No, I don't. I've slain your solider. What happens now?"

Dalton snorted and cast a glance at where Gable's scorched body lay. "I don't need soldiers, Ayr. I don't need to raise an army. I have a weapon, and I can bring the Commonwealth to its knees by myself. I did it once with no dragon. Imagine what I can do now with Sinibad by my side."

"Is your plan coming to fruition, father? First Crassus, then Anton, followed by the Dragon Lords and the Obelisk? That was Azura's home! Why did you do it?"

"The sooner you figure out that I do not care for your dragon, or your promised, the easier this will be on you, Ayr. The Obelisk represents the Commonwealth's power. Now that it has fallen, the riders are weakened."

"Who remains then? What's left for you to take control of?"

"I will take the Commonwealth, Ayr, piece by piece. The dragon riders have proven themselves not to be trusted with the running of things. Dragons deserve to be free and not sworn to some demonic blood oath that was placed upon them by a misguided charlatan. They are better than that."

"Then what of the existing riders? What if they swore an oath to their dragon and they choose to join you?"

"Their dragons will be released from their bond."

"So, you'd kill us? Me included?"

"I am Dalton Ashbourne. I am not insane, Ayr. No, you would be permitted to keep Azura by your side if she chose it, but I would break the chain, ending the endless cycle of slavery."

"Father, Azura is my life. I cannot allow you to break what we have."

Dalton exhaled and the corners of his mouth curled. "Then if you are not willing to give her up, I will tear her from your soul. Humans and dragons are not meant to be bonded together, Ayr. It is unnatural. When you go beyond the walls of the Commonwealth you will see that it is a rare part of the world."

"So then why do both of your sons have the one thing that you can no longer possess? Is that the reason why you're so hellbent on taking the dragons away?"

"I see the errors of my ways now. I should have sent Bryne first. It is clear to me that you were not ready to do what was necessary. I should have known a distraction would have crossed your path."

"Elanor isn't a distraction."

Dalton's eyes narrowed. "Really? Then why is it that you went against my mandate? Your teacher was not supposed to be your love interest, boy. Let alone the daughter of Crassus fucking Sunfire! You've overcomplicated everything."

Ayr lowered his eyes. "Father, my allegiance is still to you and what you want to accomplish. That hasn't changed."

"Do not lie to me, Ayr!"

"I'm not!"

"Whilst I'm here, why don't we try an experiment? Sinibad will rip Evor from the sky and we will see if you beg for him to be released."

Ayr stiffened his back, glaring at Dalton as he flared his nostrils. "I won't."

A sinister smirk spread across Dalton's lips. "We'll see if you are lacking in your convictions."

Dalton closed his eyes and looked as if he was conversing with a dragon. A roar came from Sinibad a moment later, and Ayr saw him leap into the sky, his eyes locked onto none other than Evor as he flew towards him. Somewhere Elanor was on his back, riding into the storm headfirst with her sword raised. Sinibad's explosive power was on full display as he launched himself at Evor. The latter did not have a chance to defend himself.

Sinibad ripped Evor from the sky, placing his talons around Evor's neck and body, locking him into place. Evor roared in alarm, a sound that carried across the open expanse, but in the collision, Ayr saw something topple from Evor. Elanor! There was no chance that Evor would escape from Sinibad's grasp and be able to save her. Ayr thrust his hands out, desperate, wanting to catch her, but Elanor kept falling, despite his magic. She was nothing more than a dark speck against the sky, but there was nothing he could do.

I'll get her!

Azura leapt into the air, but within a single wingbeat, she froze, terror overcoming her. Dalton raised a hand towards her and shook his head as he kept her locked in place. Azura roared, trying to break free, but his grip was iron.

Ayr! Save her!

The magic was radiating from Dalton, pulsing from him like the explosions that had rocked the Obelisk, pure and powerful. Azura continued to fight against Dalton as Ayr shot a wave of magic towards Elanor that would catch her, but as soon as the spell had left his fingertips, he felt it jolt as if it had been cut off. Dalton took another step forward, his face tight with concentration, a vein on his forehead appearing as the only sign of strain.

"You are powerless, boy! Everything is as I will it!"

Ayr tried to throw another spell, just something that would stop Elanor from falling for just a few seconds longer. Dalton cut it off again, a snarl escaping his lips as Onoss launched himself into the air. Onoss shot towards Elanor like a dart, but as she continued to fall, Ayr knew that he would not be able to catch her. Until she stopped, frozen in flight, her body in an arc, her legs and arms hanging below her torso.

Ayr turned to face Dalton properly. "How are you that strong?"

"The Obelisk didn't fall on its own, boy."

Sinibad was approaching the mountainside, with Evor in his grasp. As Ayr kept his eyes locked onto Elanor's rag dolled form, he saw a single solitary black dragon heading towards them as well. It stood out alone amongst the chaos as the rest of the dragons, fled to the south away from Sinibad. As the smaller dragon grew closer, he could make out something that it clutched in its talons. It looked like a thin rope hanging out, but it was clear to Ayr that it was a dragon's tail.

He was still fighting to free Azura from Dalton's grasp and could otherwise only watch as the other dragons approached them. Sinibad crashed into the mountain, slamming Evor against it, keeping him pinned with one giant clawed foot. A rumble that moved the earth and almost knocked Ayr to the ground erupted around them. Sinibad's neck shot down towards them, as long as the mountain was tall, his yellow eyes taking in every detail before him.

"You commanded me to bring him to you, Dalton. Do you want me to end his life?"

"Not yet. We will wait for them to arrive."

Sinibad nodded as he retracted back up the mountain, casting his gaze out over where the Obelisk had once stood proud and strong. A smirk came to his lips as his eyes narrowed.

"Is this it? Is this the fall of the riders?"

"Yes Sinibad. Brought about by your will and power."

"Good. I have prayed for this day."

"As have I, but this is only the first step."

Ayr grunted as he struggled against Dalton's magic. "What are we waiting for then, father? Get this over and done with. I'm sick of fighting. Let Evor, Elanor and Azura go."

Dalton's eyes flicked to Ayr once again. "I can't do that boy. I still need to have my revenge. Don't get any funny ideas or your dragon will die."

THIRTY-THREE

Let it go, Ayr. He's too powerful.

I need to free you!

And have me be swallowed by Sinibad? Is that something you want? Stop trying to fight him. It won't end well for us!

Ayr grunted in frustration, his teeth grinding together as sweat beaded across his brow. He could feel Dalton's spell gripping tighter around Azura like a hangman's noose, the invisible tendrils of magic constricting with each passing heartbeat. Her blue eyes, usually bright with fire, had dulled to a resigned glaze. Ayr faced Dalton across the mountain clearing, the taste of copper filling his mouth as his own magic flickered and died within his veins like candles snuffed by a cold wind.

"What more do you need to do, father! You've destroyed everything!"

"I need everything, boy."

Let it go, Ayr. Your brother comes.

As the smaller black dragon approached, Ayr recognised it from their brief interaction earlier in the Obelisk. It was Bryne's mount. Though similar in size to Azura, perhaps a hand's width taller at the shoulder, its build was more serpentine, its neck longer and more sinuous. The dragon banked towards the mountain, then descended in tight spirals, talons extending forward like curved daggers. The beast's talons uncurled to reveal Draxion and Grace Sunfire. Draxion was covered with dried blood, and Grace's once-pristine robes were now tattered and singed at the edges, both bearing the hollow-eyed look of those who had witnessed horrors beyond telling as they looked up at their new surroundings.

Grace was no doubt seeing through Draxion's eyes and she crawled back on her hands and knees towards Bryne's dragon. It sneered down at her and Draxion, smoke pilfering from its nostrils. A snap of its jaws startled Draxion, sending her scurrying forward. She assessed the landscape, her eyes lingering on Ayr and Dalton before flicking to the mountain overhead, where Evor remained pinned by Sinibad. The larger obsidian dragon had not moved since Sinibad had landed upon him and had grown increasingly quiet. As Draxion's eyes locked onto Dalton again, Grace started to quiver.

"No! You can't be here!"

Dalton's face was carved from stone. There was a flicker of emotion crossing his chiselled features as he advanced toward her with measured steps. His boots crunched against the rocky ground; each step deliberate and menacing. Despite Dalton's attention being divided, the invisible chains of his spell still gripped Azura like a vice, suspending her form in midair where her wings remained splayed against the wind. Draxion, too, stood motionless nearby, her scales dulled and wings drooping, her slender neck and limbs looking as brittle as Grace's bones.

"I am, Grace. You know, I thought I would have felt something, seeing you again after all this time. But frankly, I am disappointed."

"Disappointed? Dalton, you haven't changed in years."

Dalton squatted down in front of Grace who visibly recoiled even though he had moved no closer to her. "The years have not been kind to you, Grace. It's written all over your face. Was it worth it?"

"Yes, yes it was."

Dalton rocked back on his heels with a scoff. "You can't say that. You were invested in me and what we were going to build together."

Grace parted her cracked lips, but before she could utter a word, Onoss' deafening roar shattered the air above them. The golden dragon's wings cast rippling shadows across the mountain stone as he descended, his scales gleaming like burnished coins in the sunlight. He settled with a ground-shaking thud beside Bryne's obsidian beast, talons scraping against rock as he unfurled his claws. Elanor tumbled from his grasp; her auburn hair matted with sweat and dirt as she hit the ground with a painful grunt. Wincing, she pushed herself to her knees, her torn sleeve revealing a fresh crimson gash. Her eyes, wide and alert despite her exhaustion, darted across the jagged terrain before locking onto the tense figures of Grace and Dalton mere yards away.

"Mother! Why are you here?"

"I willed her here, Lady Sunfire."

"Why? She did nothing to you!"

Dalton moved his arms to the side of his body like he was drawing a weapon. Ayr saw the flash of a blade, much like what he had just discarded in Dalton's left hand as he drew nearer to Grace. Elanor stepped forward, but Dalton raised his right hand, stopping her in her tracks, much like Azura remains suspended over them, all still under the watchful gaze of Sinibad as he breathed down the mountain at them.

"Grace is the reason why all of this started, Elanor."

"Started what, your rebellion? You were the one that wanted to break the chains of the dragons!"

"I still do. They do not deserve their fate."

Grace raised her head. "That's not what you told me."

"You should not have lied to me, Grace. You betrayed me when you told the Dragon Lords what I intended to do."

"I didn't mean it; it was experimental at best! I just wanted what was best for us. What was best for the Commonwealth!"

"The best for the Commonwealth? My dearest Grace, together, you, Crassus and my brother led it into an age of stagnation. You knew what they were doing to the dragons, yet you continued the practice!"

"Who was I to go against a thousand years of tradition? It was written in our texts, and I could see it in my visions!"

Dalton snarled and rounded on her. "Draxion was corrupted by Baindussa's magic, and you know it as well as I do, Grace."

"He did that to save her!"

Dalton raised his hand to his temple, rubbing it as pain spread across his face. "No! She did not have to do anything. I could have saved her, you know that!"

"You would have killed her. Your magic was dangerous then and I'm not sure that it has changed. I saw what you did in the war, and my visions have told me what you have done recently. There is nothing left between us."

"I know. You refused to let me break the bond. If you wanted to be with me, you would have let me break it."

Grace bowed her head. "I wanted to be with you. That was all I wanted. You showed me that we couldn't."

Dalton was close enough to Grace to be able to touch her. He lowered his voice, but Ayr could still hear what he was saying. "We were not meant to be together, Grace. It's a shame what happened to you. We could have been something more, but the years and Crassus destroyed you. Now it is my turn."

"Dalton! Don't!"

Dalton turned his head towards Elanor, his scowl still prevalent on his face. It turned into a smirk as he leant in towards Grace, for the first time now touching her. Ayr saw Grace recoil again, but if she moved back further, she would bump into Bryne's dragon. Dalton had her cornered and she looked even smaller and frail than before.

"Don't? What are you going to do Elanor? Your dragon's head is inches away from Sinibad's mouth. Your pleading will earn your mother no mercy."

"Please! You've already killed one of my parents, take mercy on the other. She's all I have left."

The knife tightened in Dalton's grip as he chuckled. "All you have left? Elanor, you have Evor do you not? You failed your tasks if it was not for Ayr. Evor lives because I allowed it!"

A lone tear streamed down Elanor's face. "Just let him and her go! Take me instead!"

"Elanor..."

For the first time since he had been slammed into the mountainside, Evor spoke. To Ayr it still looked like he had not moved, still pinned by Sinibad's foot. Sinibad lowered his mouth closer to Evor's neck, ready to rip it to shreds just like he had done to Drementhol, his eyes on Dalton, just waiting for a command to strike.

"I will lay down my life for you."

Dalton sighed again and rolled his eyes. Elanor's fists bunched beside her at her waist, her frustration growing more. Ayr could tell that she wanted to strike against him, but with Evor near the jaws of Sinibad, she would not win their exchange, even if she managed to kill Dalton. "Then set us free, Dalton. We've done enough for you!"

"It is never enough, Elanor! The Commonwealth needs to fall!"

"What's it going to take to stop you, Dalton?"

"I will stop at nothing until it all burns down. You know, I had less qualm with Crassus. This is nothing more than a formality, Grace. You chose poorly when you chose to abandon me all those years ago."

Grace was defiant. "Crassus was a good man! More than I can say for you."

"Your words lost their meaning years ago. I only ask you do one last thing. Plead for your life, so I can hear you say my name one final time."

"I won't bow to you."

Dalton paused, the knife quivering an inch from Grace's neck. Even his hands were not still in this moment. His face flickered as he suppressed a grunt, forcing the knife to remain still. He pressed it with a quiet confidence into Grace's throat, just enough to pinch the skin, but not enough to draw blood yet.

"Say my name."

"No."

"Acknowledge me, Grace."

Grace lifted her chin, remaining silent as her empty eyes stared into the space in front of her face. She was still seeing Dalton through Draxion's eyes. Dalton's shoulders sunk as he took another deep breath, staring at the woman that he had once loved.

"I'm glad I took your blood, Elanor. You're not my daughter. I don't need to cause you anymore pain than I already have."

"Good."

Dalton shifted his weight forward, striking out and Elanor screamed. The blade flashed through the air, sharp and direct into Grace's jugular. Blood sputtered from the wound onto Dalton and the blade as he rammed it deeper into her throat. Draxion howled, darting forward, trying to knock Dalton over, but before she had even taken a step, Bryne's dragon had snatched her by the tail. Draxion, now concerned for her own safety screamed as she was flung into the air. Before Draxion could regain her sense of direction, Bryne's dragon extended his neck upwards and snatched her from the sky.

Another scream tore across the mountains from Draxion as she was torn to shreds by the larger dragon. Ayr stood transfixed as blood sprayed all over the ground in front of him, covering Bryne, Elanor,

Grace and Dalton. Elanor was mortified and wanted to move, but the threat of Sinibad still loomed over both her and Evor. She took half a step and then stopped. There was nothing she could do. A smirk spread to Dalton's lips as Onoss bowed his head in approval like a proud parent.

"Well done, Zaurien. Was that your first kill?"

Zaurien's voice was raspy and hollow as he licked his lips. "No, I tasted blood in the Seminary of Fire. It brings back fond memories."

Onoss continued to nod in agreement. "As we all did."

The dragons fell to silence, as Elanor continued to weep on her knees in front of them, the only sound that filled the space beside the rustling of the wind through the trees nearby. Grace's blood stained her robes and continued to pool at the neck seam. As Dalton stood up, he let her body go and it fell to the left in front of Elanor. Tears filled Elanor's eyes, as she was unable to do anything. Dalton was impervious to her cries. He stood transfixed, the dagger by his side as he stared down at her withered body.

"Goodbye, Grace. That was a better ending than you deserved."

Elanor's scream came from deep within her chest, sounding as if Evor had roared alongside her. "I hate you!"

Dalton shifted his gaze towards her, and his expression softened. "People have hated me for less in the past, Lady Sunfire. Holding onto a grudge against me won't help you. Sinibad.

"Just a wound, Dalton?"

Dalton nodded and Sinibad bowed his head. The giant golden dragon stretched out, digging his front most claw into Evor's chest. Evor let out a howl that echoed around the mountains, striking into Ayr's soul as Azura reacted to the pain of her promised. Sinibad's strike was direct and the damage was immediate. As he removed his talon from Evor's chest, Ayr saw the dark red blood that covered it all the way up to the knuckle. Evor continued to howl, only growing quieter as Sinibad withdrew.

Elanor continued to sob. "No!"

Dalton flicked his hand in her direction and Elanor's mouth slammed shut. Her eyes widened in terror, and she raised her hands to her mouth, clawing at it, trying to part her lips. Dalton moved towards her, much like he had done to Grace, except this time, rather than summoning a dagger, he discarded it, throwing it to the side. Much like Ayr's, Dalton's blade vanished into thin air as it left him. Dalton stooped down in front of Elanor, his eyes level with hers.

"You'll listen when I tell you what comes next, won't you?"

Ayr's hairs on the back of his neck stood on end as Elanor nodded her compliance at Dalton. She stopped shaking, even though Evor was still pining on the mountain above them.

"You will go forth, back into the Commonwealth and become a Dragon Lord. Even better if you can claim the Overlord's seat at the table. You will then begin weeding out the riders who will not serve me and begin breaking their links with their dragons. Particularly those that will still pose a threat to Sinibad. I do not wish to rule a kingdom of ash, and this will make the upcoming war bloodless. You will disarm the Haven and present it to me. Can you do this for me?"

Elanor nodded in silence, the tears beginning to dry on her face. Satisfied, Dalton nodded back at her and stood, holding out his hand. Elanor questioned him with her eyes but then took it and Dalton helped her to her feet. At the same time above them, Sinibad released pressure on Evor and backed away. Evor groaned and coughed as he tried to rise. Dalton was not finished and turned back to face Ayr for the first time since Grace had landed.

"You'll come with me, boy. Your dragon can be stronger."

"I thought you didn't want me."

Dalton snorted as he walked towards Onoss. The golden dragon was lowering his head towards Dalton and Ayr saw the saddle on his back.

"You're far too valuable. The riders are weak, and you do not possess the political power to venture into those waters alone. You will be my sword, once she is stronger. Azura, come here and collect your rider."

Azura lurched forward in the air as she was unfrozen. She caught herself and breathed again and then turned towards the mountain. She was slow, making sure each wingbeat was calculated as Sinibad raised his head once more before launching himself into the clouds.

Dalton controls me.

Can you fight him?

No. It would not be wise.

Dalton went to step up onto Onoss and turned back towards Elanor, who was still standing where he had left her. Her eyes remained locked on him, unable to tear them away even as Evor rose. Ayr could only imagine the conversation that was going on between the two of them. Dalton waved his hand, almost in a mocking manner as he grinned at her.

"Best of luck with your endeavours, Lady Sunfire. Chorru will be keeping tabs on you if you need any advice. Ayr, get a move on. We have many preparations to make."

"Where are we going? Home?"

"No. There is somewhere new that I need to take you. Somewhere that will unlock your potential."

Azura came into land as Elanor showed signs of life. She turned towards him, her eyes wide with fear and the tears that had still not dissolved. Azura's wing lifted over Ayr's head as he stared at Elanor for a moment, unable to find the words that would bring her comfort. Dalton was now on Onoss' back and Bryne leaned forward in his saddle on Zaurien. He could feel the heat rising from their bodies, as they stared at him.

Part of Ayr wanted to remain on the ground, to tell Azura to turn around and fight them both off. Sinibad was far enough away now, his enormous form shrinking to the east. With Evor closer, they stood a chance. If they could fight and win, then they could run away together.

Ayr...

We can't leave her.

Elanor and Evor now have their own path to follow.

We need to become stronger. We should be able to fight him.

Whatever is coming is just beginning, Ayr. You and I are already extremely powerful.

We need to be able to stand against him alone. When we come to blows, he will use you against me.

Then we will train with him and in doing so learn how to defeat him. Do you trust me, Ayr?

With all my heart, Azura.

Then we will go with him. Let it play out. Everything burns, Ayr. Even your father will in time. He is not immortal.

No, but we will be.

Climb aboard, rider. We'll see it done.

TO BE CONTINUED...

Acknowledgements

Wow would you look at that, it's already the end of 2025 if you are reading this right after release. Crazy how time flies when you're having fun, right? It's been a rough year and I'm glad it's over with! I feel like it was only yesterday that I released Shadows of the Dragon. I had a lot more fun with this one than the first two when I was not in a funk. This will serve as a springboard for the rest of the series. Three books to go?

This is the part of the book that everyone wants to see their name in! Firstly, to my readers. If you're still loving the Ashbourne Saga at this point, thank you so much. We're still in for more of a wild ride. Ayr and Elanor still have plenty of tricks up their sleeves, but what happens now? Dalton? Oh, just you wait. Thank you for sticking with me as I pump this series out. If you're reading this when the whole series is published, congratulations! Get onto the next book and enjoy the ride.

Now my circle is small, and this is almost a one-man operation when it comes to production, but there are some other people I would like to thank. Secondly, I'll thank my parents, Mr. and Mrs. Mememaro senior. They've been a massive help this year. I hit rock bottom earlier on, and I don't know how I'd have gotten back on my feet without them. Hopefully one day I can pay them back because my books have shot to the moon.

Thirdly, there's Ajay. If you're on my socials, you'll know her. A random author friend that is now the book bestie and sometimes (most of the time) who I'm going to for life advice and support. She doesn't have to do it, and I don't know why she does, I'm just a random dude, but I swear she solves more of my problems than her own. Sometimes I don't follow the advice and tell her things she doesn't want to hear, but we've all got that one friend that is there for us regardless. Then there's everything else she does as a number one fan. When she's not working on her own stuff, chances are she's doing something for me. If I listed out everything that she does, there'd be a whole new novel about it. Maybe I should do that? Who am I kidding, I don't need more novel ideas already. Either way, if you're having a hard time and are struggling, just having that one consistent person who shows up for you time and time again can be all the difference to helping you get back on track. Reach out to someone if you are not in a good place.

That will do for this book! I've taken up too much of your time with real life words, rather than something that's in a fantasy fictional world. So, with that being said, if your name isn't in here, I would love for it to be next time. Just reach out. I am always open to new ideas and plot points as well. If the Ashbourne Saga is also the first series of mine you have read, I highly recommend checking out my other dozen plus books too. They're a good read! Until the next one, stay safe and enjoy your life! Live in the moment and find something good to cherish every day.

Everything burns, even the Ashbourne family.

About the Author

Matt Mememaro is an Australian author that exists somewhere in the void in Australia, as he battles with the unsettling fact that he is no longer a true spring chicken and is experiencing grey hair growth all over his head. He constantly stresses about his books and whether or not the meaning of life is in fact fourty-two.

In his spare time when he is not at his day job that he wishes to retire from, he is probably writing, playing paintball or working out. Matt wishes to one day soon become a full time author, but he cannot do that without your help.

If you enjoyed Desolation of the Dragon, please consider leaving a kind review and or checking out Matt's other works and social medias in the QR code below. Matt would also very much appreciate it if you subscribed to his newsletter in the link below so you can keep up with his new releases.